THE
FIRES
OF
FU
MANCHU

Also by Cay Van Ash:

TEN YEARS BEYOND BAKER STREET
*(Sherlock Holmes matches
wits with Dr. Fu Manchu)*

By Cay Van Ash and
Elizabeth Sax Rohmer:

MASTER OF VILLAINY
*(A biography of Sax Rohmer,
creator of Dr. Fu Manchu)*

THE
FIRES
OF
FU
MANCHU

CAY VAN ASH

1817

Harper & Row, Publishers, New York
Cambridge, Philadelphia, San Francisco, Washington
London, Mexico City, São Paulo, Singapore, Sydney

FIRST EDITION

Copy editor: Marjorie Horvitz
Designer: Erich Hobbing

Library of Congress Cataloging-in-Publication Data

Van Ash, Cay.
  The fires of Fu Manchu.

  I. Title.
PR6072.A55F5   1987   823'.914   87-45083
ISBN 0-06-015819-0

87 88 89 90 91 HC 10 9 8 7 6 5 4 3 2 1

In Loving Memory
of Sax and Elizabeth

CONTENTS

FOREWORD

Much has been written concerning the sinister career of Dr. Fu Manchu, but there are gaps in the record and questions which remain unanswered.

Who was he? In modern parlance, he was a terrorist, produced by the collapse of the Manchu Dynasty, which had dominated China for nearly three centuries—a fanatic devoted to a lost cause, armed with the forgotten weapons of the ancient East and the fiendish technology of the twenty-first century.

On the eve of the Great War—so called because we did not then dream that we were going to have another—Fu Manchu withdrew his forces from England, where he had been conducting a series of outrages, on and off, for the past four years. The ship which carried them was wrecked, and we hear no more of him till 1928, when the nefarious business of his murder society, the Si Fan, was resumed.

What had happened to him in the meantime? From later records, we learn only that, about 1917, he had been in Egypt. What did he do there, and what were the circumstances in which he concealed the secrets of the Si Fan in the Tomb of the Black Ape?

If anyone knew, it would surely have been Dr. Petrie, who chronicled the earlier episodes—and who had also been in Egypt at that time, having at long last wrested the beautiful Egyptian slavegirl, Kâramanèh, from the cruel hands of Fu Manchu, married her, and transferred his suburban practice in South London to Cairo.

I am happy to report that my inquiries into the matter have been rendered eminently successful by the kind co-operation of Mrs. Fiona Jefferson, of Palm Springs—Dr. Petrie's granddaughter, and the custodian of his papers.

Dr. Petrie had, in fact, left a file of detailed notes covering the period from September to November 1917, disclosing a bizarre sequence of events which might well be considered incredible, had more recent developments in history not taught us otherwise, and from which the present account has been compiled. The reason why he did not choose to write them up in the form of a narrative and did not wish them to be published during his lifetime will be at once apparent to the reader who takes the trouble to pursue this tale to its astonishing conclusion.

C.V.A.

1

ONE NIGHT IN ZAMALEK

The long blades of the ceiling fan turned lazily, casting a shadow pattern and dispensing a warm, moist current of air faintly scented with jasmine. In Cairo, after dark, the parched atmosphere of the surrounding desert gives way to a stifling humidity.

Half an hour had passed since I had left the small laboratory next door to my surgery and sat down at the desk to write up notes of my latest (unsuccessful) experiment. It should have been a simple task. Yet, time and again, I found myself staring into space and listening—for what, I had no idea.

The house was silent and from outside came no sound but the buzzing of nocturnal insects agitating their wings against the fine gauze screen which covered the open window behind me.

Putting down my pen, I glanced at the yellow stain on the sleeve of my white overall, which would not have disfigured it when Kâramanèh had been there to terrorise the laundryman. I missed her—not only for such reasons, but as I had always missed her whenever we were apart. But Nayland Smith's orders had been explicit.

I stretched out my hand for his cablegram, then remembered that I had left it upstairs in my study. It did not matter. I recalled every word.

GET KARA OUT OF EGYPT IMMEDIATELY. EXPLAIN LATER. SMITH.

What did it mean? I thought I knew and dreaded to learn my suspicions were justified. Rather than believe, I sought refuge in some alternative, however unlikely.

Could Smith, far off in Burma, have learned of some desperate scheme of the German High Command to offset the stalemate in Europe by an offensive against Egypt? Egypt had never been in danger, though the second battle of Gaza had shown the Turks to

be tougher fighters than we anticipated and cost Murray his job.
But—

My thoughts were cut short by the ringing of a distant bell. I
started slightly. I was expecting no one and had few friends likely
to call on me without notice. A patient, then? Not unless the case
was urgent. While I waited for old Hassan to come blundering
across the hall and announce the visitor, I reflected that I had little
time to change if I meant to go out for dinner.

Sa'îd, who was supposed to look after the cooking, had taken
French leave and failed to put in an appearance since breakfast time.
I shook my head, sorrowfully admitting that a suburban practice in
South London had furnished me with little experience in handling
Arab servants. In the absence of my wife, I was domestically help-
less.

The bell rang a second time—longer and more stridently.

"Why the devil doesn't he answer it?" I muttered.

Was it possible that the caller was Nayland Smith? Hardly. The
cablegram, headed "Rangoon" and dated "9th September 1917,"
had been despatched only a fortnight previously. Yet in these days
of advanced railway networks—even aeroplanes—it could be
done. . . .

I leapt impatiently to my feet and strode out into the *mandarah*—a
lofty apartment, rising the full height of the house, where the
prosaic appointments of my surgery gave place to an *Arabian Nights*
fantasy. Behind me, two narrow staircases led up to a sort of min-
strels' gallery covered by a finely latticed screen. In the centre of a
sunken, elaborately tiled floor, a small fountain splashed cooling
streams into a marble basin. The house had been built midway
through the past century by some wealthy pasha of Khedive Ismail's
despotic régime and, with the cushioned divans on either side, this
part of it made an excellent waiting room.

A short corridor at the far end gave access to an arched door
opening upon a small, square courtyard. I paused en route to peer
into a cupboardlike recess, dimly lighted by an oil lamp. It was
barely deep enough to contain more than a single chair, and in this
sat—or, rather, sprawled—Hassan, the *bowwab,** attired in a
pyjama-striped robe, his feet thrust out and the toes of his pointed
slippers turned ceilingwards. Head thrown back and mouth wide

---

*Dr. Petrie, like Lawrence, uses no consistent system of transcribing Arabic words,
since the colloquial is not a written language. [Ed.]

open, he was snoring regularly, with a repulsive, gargling sound. As a gatekeeper, this ancient monument of unrighteousness was less than useless, but he had lived there longer than I, and I hadn't the heart to discharge him. I called to him angrily and shook him by the shoulder, but without response. On the stone ledge at his side stood an earthenware *kullah,* half filled—ostensibly, with water. I picked it up and sniffed at the contents.

One sniff was enough. Hassan, whose venerable beard was his only pretension to saintliness, transgressed the laws of the Prophet. I knew now for certain that the diminishing level of the whisky in the cut-glass bottle on my sideboard was not due solely to evaporation.

The old-fashioned doorbell fixed to the wall above my head bounced on its coiled spring and jangled frantically. Hassan grunted and resumed snoring.

Clearly, if the summons was to be answered, it must be done by myself. Leaving the gatekeeper to his unlawful dreams of Paradise, I took the few remaining steps along the passage, dragged back the wooden bolts of the heavy, iron-studded door, and threw it open.

Somewhat to my surprise, my visitor was a woman, slim, tall, and dressed in some kind of loose gown reaching to her ankles. She carried a large snakeskin handbag. In the faint light percolating from the hall, I could see little else about her, but I gained the impression that she was young.

"I was beginning to fear that nobody was at home," she said.

"I'm sorry," I answered, "but, to tell you the plain truth, my servant is drunk."

"So? Then you should beat him."

Waiting for no invitation, she turned sideways, slipped past me, and walked confidently through the *mandarah,* leaving me no choice but to close the door and follow. In some strange fashion, since I felt certain that she had never been there before, she seemed to know the way. Gliding across the tiled floor of the *durka'ah* with a smooth, phantomesque tread, she paused to kick off tiny golden sandals ere stepping upon the carpet, and entered my surgery— guided, perhaps, by the journals scattered about the divans and the light flowing out from the doorway.

I hurried in behind her, switching on the ceiling fittings, since, hitherto, only my desk lamp had been in operation. I saw now that she wore what I took to be an evening gown of a shimmering, pale green hue, cut on the lines of an Ancient Greek chiton, sleeveless, and clasped at one shoulder by a large lapis lazuli scarab.

"Madam," I said, a trifle uncertainly, "I take it that you wish to consult me, but I do not see patients in the evening—unless, of course, it's an emergency."

"It is an emergency—in the sense that I can visit you at no other time."

Her voice, high-pitched and clear, had a strangely icy quality, and suddenly I understood why the Chinese use wind bells to relieve the heat of summer. She spoke with a slight accent, but I was totally at a loss to guess her origin. Certainly, it was not European. Her face, framed by jet-black hair cut straight across the forehead and falling vertically to her shoulders, set me thinking of Egypt under the pharaohs. So also did her eyes, which, though covered by tinted spectacles, so that I could not discern their colour, were long and almond-shaped, like those of a goddess on a wall painting.

With a chill which I could not explain, I thought suddenly of Nephthys, the consort of Set, Lord of Evil. . . .

"What seems to be your problem?" I asked.

"Over the past few months, I have felt a general sense of debility. I fall asleep without warning. Sometimes my arms and legs give way and I just collapse."

I nodded, unwilling to accept her as a patient but, despite my unwillingness, interested as a doctor. Cataplexy . . . narcolepsy . . . or something more serious—a brain lesion . . .

"On such occasions, have you actually lost consciousness?"

"Once or twice." She smiled. "I am afraid, Dr. Petrie, that I am very poor at describing my symptoms. You will have to examine me."

"In that case," I said, "you had better come back to-morrow, when a nurse will be present."

"It is unnecessary. You are a man of honour, and I am not modest."

She dropped her handbag upon a chair, reached up to the scarab clasp, unclipped it, and the robe fell in a silken heap about her feet, revealing to my astonished eyes that she wore nothing beneath.

"You see," she said, "I came prepared."

She stood quite still, inviting my appraisal in a manner neither tempting nor provocative, but more like that of a princess demanding homage to her regal beauty. Beauty, of a somewhat unusual kind, she indeed possessed. Her skin was the colour of old ivory and her figure more typical of Asia than of Europe, with slender hips and a small, perfectly formed bust. I judged her to be no more than twenty.

I hesitated an instant too long, and she laughed softly—a cadence of silver bells.

"Why, Doctor, you are surely not embarrassed, are you?"

Muttering something, I turned aside and sat down at my desk in a belated endeavour to regularise a situation which threatened to become compromising—though there might, after all, be a charitable explanation of her seemingly wanton behaviour. If she was the property—wife or child—of some zealous old Wahhabi, how else could she consult me than in secret? She would not otherwise be allowed even to speak to me—far less submit to a physical examination.

"There are certain formalities to be gone through," I said. "You are not on my register."

My visitor shrugged gracefully, picked up her handbag, and seated herself, facing me. Opening the bag, she took out a flat, enamelled case, fitted a cigarette to a long jade holder, and ignited it from the glowing red tip of a lighter like none I had ever seen.

"First of all," I continued, fumbling with papers, "I must have your name and address. Particulars of any illnesses from which you have suffered in the past . . ."

I broke off, conscious that my well-meant efforts lay in the wrong direction. With the cigarette holder clamped between her teeth and the incongruous sun glasses, which she had not yet removed, the spell of divinity was shattered. My would-be patient was transformed into a woman—desirable and accessible, sitting with her legs crossed and one arm hooked over the back of the chair. She, too, was aware, perhaps, for she leaned forward, crushed out her cigarette, almost unsmoked, in an ashtray on my desk, and stood up quickly.

"I have no patience with such details," she said scornfully. "First, tell me if I need treatment."

I nodded and picked up my stethoscope. I still felt an uneasy suspicion that I was being subjected to the sort of attack to which a doctor is peculiarly vulnerable, but I had placed myself in an impossible position by letting her inside the house.

Who was this woman, with the face and figure of a young girl and the demeanour of royalty? Where had she come from? Zamalek was a fashionable quarter of consulates and the properties of rich officials—the Palace Hotel and the Sporting Club only a short distance from my doorstep. She could be the daughter of a diplomat, or the favourite of some wartime profiteer. . . .

When I touched her, I found her skin satin smooth and, despite the heat of the evening, incredibly cool—almost reptilian.

"Do you feel cold?" I inquired.

"I am always cold. Do you think it means something?"

"Possibly."

Thus far, she had behaved with perfect decorum, responding so little to my touch that I began to suspect a loss of muscle tone, just as she had indicated. Now, however, she swayed suddenly on her feet, leaned against me, and clutched at my coat, so that I was forced to throw my arms about her to keep her from falling. For an instant, we were locked in a close embrace.

"Forgive me," she whispered. "It is difficult for me to remain standing in one position very long. Could I not lie down?"

Releasing her grasp upon my coat lapels, she attempted to straighten up and move away from me.

"Yes, of course," I said quickly. "Let me help you."

I guided her to the long, black leather couch and assisted her to recline at full length upon it. It was designed for such a purpose and, in more ordinary circumstances, I might sooner have suggested it. But now, in order to complete my examination, I must bend over her and assume an attitude of intimacy which, as a physician, had never previously occurred to me. As I did so, I became aware of a subtle perfume emanating from her hair, faint but pervasive.

Still nothing untoward transpired. She neither moved nor spoke, but lay supine like an embalmed figure stretched upon a catafalque. I tested the reflexes of one slender arm from wrist to shoulder, then the other, and, though I could detect no abnormality, felt ashamed of my suspicions.

"Permit me to see your eyes," I said.

She raised one hand obediently and pushed the dark glasses up to her forehead. The almond-shaped eyes—slightly oblique and shielded by long lashes—which I had thought to find soft and brown, were lustrous and green: feral, like those of some jungle beast. They were no longer expressionless, but mocking and contemptuous. My gaze locked with hers and I was conscious of a battle of wills—as when one's eyes chance to meet those of a stranger and both hesitate to give way.

Where had I seen such eyes? I knew—yet I could not remember! I felt, yet was powerless to resist, the deadly fascination of staring into an abyss. Her lips did not move, but the silvery voice echoed in my mind.

"If you are a healer, heal me. . . . I am so cold. . . . Take me in your arms, and warm me to life with your youth and your strength. . . ."

Closer I bent, and closer, unaware of what I was doing. My lips brushed lightly against hers, evoking fairy-tale memories of the Snow Queen—whose kiss freezes the blood.

"Your will is mine . . . you have no will but mine . . ."

A harsh, metallic sound tore through the veil—discordant and agonising. I resisted it—then sprang upright, vision returning as though a shutter had been lifted from a window. My strange visitor lay motionless upon the couch, hands at her sides, eyes closed.

"Excuse me," I faltered, scarcely knowing what I said. "Someone is at the door."

I stumbled across the *mandarah* and down the corridor, feeling as though I had been aroused from an alcoholic stupour. With each passing second, my mind became clearer—yet, at the same time, I found it more difficult to recall the immediately preceding events, like one awakening from a dream. Knowing only that the dream had been a nightmare—that I was thankful for any interruption—I reached the door and drew the bolts, careless as to who this second caller might be.

A tall, gaunt man stood upon the threshold. He wore the uniform of a British Army officer, and I failed to identify him till he stepped forward and the light of the perforated brass lantern in the passage fell fully upon his bronzed, square-cut features.

"Smith!" I exclaimed. "Thank God!"

2

THE BIRD OF ILL-OMEN

Laughing at my expression, which must have been comic, Nayland Smith entered the hallway. His laugh was a trifle grim—as it usually was—but good to hear.

"You didn't expect me?"

"Indeed, I did!" I replied, closing the door, but not troubling to secure the cumbersome bolts. "I knew you would come. But I never dreamed it could be before next week."

"Three days by train from Calcutta and a fast boat from Bombay."

I seized his hand warmly.

"You were never more welcome!"

Smith laughed again. "Even though you suspect me to be a bird of ill-omen?"

"No matter," I said firmly. "If there is danger to be faced, we will face it together, as we have always done." I broke off, staring at his uniform. "But what is this? Are you in the Army now? Or"—I hesitated—"is it just a disguise?"

"A part of both, perhaps. I am temporarily attached to British Army Intelligence, with the honorary rank of colonel." He smiled whimsically. "Well, at least I know now what a Burmese police commissioner is worth!"

Crossing the tiled floor, he sat down on the carpeted verge to unlace his shoes, and looked about him while I looked at him—the same, ageless face which had never been young, windswept and burned to a coffee-coloured complexion deeper than that of many native Egyptians. The lines above his steely grey eyes were etched a shade more deeply, the set of his jaw was a shade more stern, but the short, crisp hair remained dark, sun-bleached at the temples.

"God!" he said softly. "It's been three years—three years since we parted here with the clouds of war gathering on the horizon. But I see that you've changed nothing."

"Not out here," I said. "I've made short work of the mirrors and the fake Louis Quinze furniture in the other rooms. Come up to the study—"

I ceased speaking abruptly, as memory returned.

"Good heavens!" I exclaimed. "I had completely forgotten that I have a visitor! I must get rid of her. . . ."

Leaving my friend where he sat, I hastened towards the surgery. In the excitement of our meeting, all thought of her had passed from my mind, and still I found it curiously difficult to recall just how the interview had ended.

I pulled up short in the doorway with a cry of astonishment.

A large brown beetle buzzed about my desk lamp. The screen door into the garden stood wide open—and my mysterious "patient" had vanished. Smith, startled by my cry, burst in behind me.

"What is it?"

"She has bolted!" I said, pointing to the open window. "When I left, she was lying on that couch."

"H'm!" he muttered. "Distinctly odd!" He approached the couch and bent close to it, sniffing suspiciously. "Was your visitor, by any chance, a native of South-East Asia?"

"I don't know what she was," I said. "But certainly not English. Why do you ask?"

"She has left behind her a distinct odour of *ylang-ylang*—a perfume popular in Malaya."

I shrugged, closed the screen over the open window, and glanced at the desk lamp, where a second beetle had joined the first.

"I'll deal with those fellows later," I said. "Let's go upstairs and make ourselves comfortable."

I led the way out and up the nearer staircase to the gallery from which veiled ladies of the *harêm* had once peered down, discreetly unseen, at the festivities taking place below. The narrow space was faintly scented with aromatic woods—camphor, cedar, and sandalwood. At the back, it opened out into an apartment similar to the *mandarah*, with cushioned divans along the walls, which we used as a sitting-room.

My study was less exotically furnished, with armchairs and a desk. Here nothing hinted of Egypt save the gauze-covered window and the scent of jasmine from outside.

Smith picked up a framed portrait of Kâramanèh, executed by a Bruton Street photographer. With her hair dressed stylishly and her face exquisitely made up, she looked completely European.

"Still the same old Petrie!" he observed. "Even though you oc-cupy the same house, you keep her picture by you!" He put the frame back in its place on my desk. "She has gone?"

"Directly after I received your message. Even at the risk of an Austrian U-boat, I couldn't doubt its urgency, and, by a stroke of luck, I was able to get passage for her on a hospital ship taking some convalescents to San Michele."

"She asked for no explanation?"

"I had none to give her."

"Good."

Smith threw himself down into one of the armchairs while I bu-sied myself with mixing drinks.

"Barton has a house on Capri," I went on, "where he was doing some excavating on the Villa Iovis when the war broke out. Since then, he's had an Italian family looking after the place. She'll be safe enough there—if there is any safety in this world gone mad."

He nodded gravely. "Mad is the word for it, old man! Well, at least I'm thankful to see that you've so far escaped—though, know-ing you, I was half afraid you'd volunteer."

"I'm in no hurry," I said grimly. "I'm ready to lay down my life for my country, if need be—you know that—but I don't fancy having it thrown away by the kind of mentality that inspired the Gallipoli landings."

"No . . ." Nayland Smith nodded again and laughed shortly. "The truth is, we're both too independent to make good soldiers."

I agreed, but as I looked at him seated there with the glass in his hand and his long legs extended to the empty fireplace, I could not help feeling that the army uniform suited him. It occurred to me then that I had never seen him in his police uniform—that I did not even know what it was like.

"You will stay here, of course?" I asked. "There's a room ready for you—"

"I was counting on that!" He grinned boyishly. "My new superi-ors have reserved accommodation for me at Shepheard's—but I had no intentions of availing myself of it."

"But where is your luggage?"

"On its way through the canal, I hope! I jumped ship at Suez and took the train—six hours in a dusty compartment infested with half the flies in Lower Egypt. I was anxious to avoid any reception which might have been planned for me at Port Said. I put on my uniform, partly because I had no civilian travel pass for the Canal Zone, and because I hadn't worn it aboard. With most of the men here in khaki, I thought it might make me harder to spot. . . ."

I glanced at him sobrely. The question trembled on my tongue, but I hesitated to ask it—just as one who fears himself the victim of a dread disease hesitates to seek confirmation.

"All in good time," said Smith, as though reading my thoughts—which, at that moment, should not have been difficult. "I'll tell you what I know—though it's little enough. But first let's—" He halted in mid-sentence. "What was that?"

"What was what?"

"I thought I heard a door closing."

I shook my head. Personally, I had heard nothing.

"Unlikely," I said. "Wait . . ."

It was possible that Sa'îd had come in. I went out into the gallery and looked down through the intricate tracery of the latticed screen. No sound came from below but the gentle splashing of the fountain. I could see across the *mandarah* and down the short passage at the far end, but no one was present.

"Nobody," I reported, coming back to rejoin Smith. "You must have been mistaken. Sa'îd is God knows where—I haven't seen him since this morning—and Hassan, the *bowwab*, has drunk himself unconscious. Greba has a key, of course, but—"

"Ah, yes! Greba . . . Eltham's daughter," he murmured. "How is the arrangement working out?"

"Well enough," I answered. "She has nursing experience and your idea that she might like to come out here as my receptionist was a good one. When you see her, you may not recognize her. Her father's death hit her pretty hard, but she's grown up a lot since Redmoat."

Smith gave me a quick look of approval and a nod. "It was the least we could do. Neither of us knew her all that well, but Eltham was a friend—even though I never approved of his missionary activities in China."

I smiled reminiscently. "As I recall, you once accused him of starting the Boxer Rebellion!"

"Well, I didn't mean single-handed! But he certainly did his share."

Standing up impatiently, Nayland Smith crossed to the window and stood looking out into the garden. He turned.

"Is Greba living here?" he asked.

"Yes—normally," I said. "She has a room across the hall. But, for

the time being, she's staying with the Patersons—some people I
know at the club. They have a houseboat over on the Embâbeh side.
Obviously, with Kâramanèh out of the house, I couldn't keep her
here—"

"So, for the sake of her reputation, you send her off to live on a
houseboat and be eaten alive by the mosquitoes! Poor girl!"

Giving me a sardonic look, Smith rummaged in a pocket of his
tunic, drew out the well-worn briar which I had seen him smoking
in London, or its twin, and charged it from the familiar oilskin
pouch. Then, with the pipe fuming to his satisfaction, he began to
pace the room restlessly—and I knew that the moment was at hand.

"Do you know General Fernshawe?" he inquired.

"Sir Edgar Fernshawe—Army Intelligence?"

"Yes."

"I know him by sight, but I have never spoken to him."

"My orders are to report to him direct. But I am not expected till
to-morrow at the earliest." Smith shook his head and scowled. "In
the meantime, I prefer to act before my duties are clearly defined.
I don't like it, Petrie! I am no longer working for Scotland Yard, and
I'm very much afraid that I'll have less of a free hand than I always
had in the old days."

He drew back his left cuff and consulted his watch.

"It's a bit late," he muttered, "but I propose to go across to the
Kasr en-Nil Barracks. Will you come with me?"

"Of course—if you wish it."

"I do. There is a man there whom I want you to see. No one will
yet know the precise extent of my authority—I don't myself—and
I think I can get you in."

I waited, knowing that there was more to come, but again Smith
was silent. Taking the pipe from his mouth, he tapped it out carefully into an ashtray. Then:

"Did you hear," he demanded, "about the fire at the Hotel Iskander, a week before I sent you that cable?"

"No," I said, feeling a trifle puzzled. "I don't think so."

"Probably you wouldn't have. It wasn't a big affair. The Hotel
Iskander is a second or third-rate place in the Shâria' Elfi Bey, and
though the top floor was burnt out, there were only three casualties."

He turned and resumed his pacing, at the same time raising his
right hand, clenching and unclenching it as he talked, as if to under-
line each phrase.

"One man is missing. Another, who had come there with him and occupied the adjoining room, was burned to death. It was in his room that the fire started—they say that he had been smoking in bed. But there is some mystery about that, since it seems to be definitely known that he did not smoke. The third man . . ."

He stopped, meeting my eyes across the room.

"The third man," he said quietly, "is he whom we are going to see at the Kasr en-Nil. You will find the case interesting, I'm sure. He is in a state of deep amnesia. He has lost not only his identity but his language! Since the night of the fire, he has spoken only two words—two words which have brought me post-haste across India: *Fu Manchu!*"

3

THE FLAMES OF HELL

"The classic case of amnesia," said Major Lindsay, "is a state of hysteria in which the victim is denied access to certain areas of memory. But, though he may cease to know who he is, he usually retains the store of general knowledge acquired during his lifetime."

With the white coat thrown over his uniform, Jack Lindsay looked what he was—more the doctor than the soldier. I knew him slightly and remembered that, before entering the R.A.M.C., he had been working in the Anglo-American Hospital, situated not far from my premises. He had gained some notice in the field of neurology, and that, I supposed, was why he was here now.

"But this case is different?" said Smith.

"Notably."

The room in which we stood was sparsely appointed, like a bedroom in a hospital, with whitewashed walls and an iron-framed cot, beside which the man we had come to see sat in a wheel-chair, wearing pyjamas and a dressing gown. Lindsay gestured towards him and went on talking to Smith, paying me the compliment of assuming that I needed no explanations.

"He cannot walk and he cannot speak—because he has forgotten how! He is in full possession of his senses—by which I mean perceptions—but his mind is a blank slate, like that of a newborn child."

Left to my own devices, I ventured to make a closer inspection of the patient—if such he might be called. He was a thickset man, swarthy, and apparently about forty-five years of age. His fingers, which he kept clasped upon the arms of the chair, were short and powerful. Apart from the certainty that he was a Caucasian, his nationality was unguessable. I peered into his deep-set eyes and read in them curiosity, rage, and frustration.

"Emotion is also present," said Major Lindsay, glancing in my direction. "Go ahead, Doctor! Examine him. I shall be glad of your opinion."

Watching, I found something peculiarly horrible in the rapid, birdlike motions of the man's head as he followed the movements of my companions about the room. I passed my hand slowly before his eyes and his head turned—the eyes fixed, like those of a wax image.

"My God!" I cried. "He cannot move his eyes!"

Lindsay nodded imperturbably. "Except for the paralysis of the motor oculi, there are no other physical aberrations."

"But how did this come about?" asked Smith.

"That is what we are anxious to learn. As yet, we understand little of the means by which memory is achieved. But we know roughly where it is stored. Pavlov's experiments with animals have shown that the excision of sections of the brain—"

"You mean that this was done surgically?"

"Not surgically, but chemically." The major sat down on the edge of the bed. "There was evidence of an injection made at the base of the skull. Bruises on the arms suggest that he was forcibly restrained while it was done, and blood samples showed traces of a substance which we have been unable to identify."

A silence ensued. I moved to the narrow window and stared out at the lights reflected on the water. Iron bars across the panes put me in mind of a prison or a mental institution, rather than a hospital. I wondered at the purpose served by this room in the sprawling complex of military buildings bordering the east bank of the Nile, and doubted that it was a part of their medical facilities.

Who was the man in the wheel-chair?

"What were the circumstances?" pursued Smith impatiently. "He was rescued from the fire at the Hotel Iskander, wasn't he?"

Major Lindsay smiled apologetically. "As to that, I know only what my officers have told me. I gather it was he who gave the alarm. Soon after retiring, he came staggering down the stairs—"

"And it was then that he uttered the words 'Fu Manchu'?"

"Yes—several times. He tried to say more, but could not be understood. His speech was already affected, and by the time that help arrived, he could neither speak nor walk."

"It has been impossible to discover who he is?"

"Quite. He was fully dressed, excepting for his shoes, but his pockets contained no clue to his identity. Any papers which he may have had in his room were destroyed. He had signed the hotel book in the name of François Duhamel, with an address in the Rue de Rastignac, Paris—both evidently false, since later inquiries revealed that there is no such street!"

"H'm!" said Smith thoughtfully. "Therefore, whoever he may have been, he was there for no good purpose!"

Major Lindsay smiled. "There are many people in Cairo who are here for no good purpose."

"True. There always were."

Taking the dilapidated briar from his pocket, Nayland Smith glanced inquiringly at our host and, meeting with no objection, lighted it. The man in the wheel-chair turned his head, watching.

"You see?" said Lindsay, pointing. "He wonders what you are doing. He has never, to his knowledge, seen anyone smoke—yet he had cigarettes and matches on him."

"He has reverted to infancy," I commented, "except that, unlike an infant, he does not try to use his limbs or voice. But could he not be taught?"

"Yes, he could, and if, as I believe, his memory is not merely inhibited but erased, he will have to be. But he will still be unable to tell us anything."

"What is the connection between this man and the other two victims?" inquired Smith. "The man who disappeared, and the man in whose room the fire broke out?"

Lindsay looked at him in some surprise.

"I don't know that there is any connection," he said slowly. "They were occupying rooms on the same floor but, so far as we know, had never met him."

"You suggest, then, that the fire was just a coincidence—that it was not started deliberately by Dr. Fu Manchu?"

"There's no evidence that it was." Major Lindsay hesitated and frowned. "But, according to witnesses, there was something odd in the way it erupted and the speed with which it spread. In a matter of seconds, the room in which it started was a raging inferno—as if the flames of Hell had been let loose in it. . . ."

Smith glanced at me significantly.

"Then I have only one more question," he said. "This man is presumably a civilian. Why, then, and on what authority, is he being kept here in a military establishment?"

"I have no idea," replied Major Lindsay, a little uncomfortably. "You will have to ask General Fernshawe about that."

We had gained less from our visit than we had hoped. However, as neither of us had eaten since breakfast, we gladly accepted the offer of a meal in the officers' mess, where we were hospitably entertained, and spent the rest of that evening talking of mutual acquaintances, the current popularity of Oriental fantasies among the theatregoing public—*Chu Chin Chow* in London, and *Kismet* in New York—of anything, in fact, but the war. It was late when we rose, finally, to make our way back to Gezirah Island, but we did not bother to summon an *'arabîyeh*. Both of us felt restless and looked forward to a pleasant stroll up the long, tree-bordered road to Zamalek as an aid to sleep.

As we crossed the bridge, with the lights of the city shining softly at our backs, our thoughts turned, naturally, to Major Lindsay's strange patient.

"He knew who had done this thing to him," mused Smith. "How, I wonder? It was the last thought in his mind before all vestige of memory slipped away. . . . And what does it all mean? There must be more to it than this. The mere mention of Fu Manchu's name could not have been enough to have me transferred to Intelligence and brought all the way from Rangoon. . . ."

We traversed the square and turned up into the avenue. Through the canopy of palm branches, the velvet darkness sparkled with a million tiny points of light.

"Where has Fu Manchu been these past three years?" I asked. "Neither you nor I ever really believed him dead. But I thought he was in China."

My friend shook his head. "No. I don't think he has been back there. I don't think he *can* go back! China is faltering on the brink of anarchy, and Fu Manchu is in exile. Till now, he has lain low. Now something—what, I don't know—has brought him out again." He turned towards me. "Petrie, I have no right to ask it, but will you see this through with me?"

I felt a warm glow of pride. In the past, Nayland Smith had gladly accepted my help when it was offered, but never before had he asked for it.

"You have every right," I said. "You know I will."

He nodded and, in his impulsive fashion, clapped me hard on the shoulder.

"Good man! I sent Kâramanèh away because I knew that if Fu Manchu was active again, he might strike at you through her—as he has done before. But for selfish reasons, I would have counselled you to go too. I didn't because I need you."

It was midnight. The chant of a *mueddin* calling the Faithful to prayer echoed faintly in the stillness of the night from a mosque across the river.

"*Prayer is better than sleep! There is no god but God!*"

"Your help will be invaluable," continued Smith. "Egypt was my first post, but that was years ago. You have been here since the war started. Not only that, but you know as much of Fu Manchu as I do. You can identify agents of the Si Fan whom I have never seen—"

His words triggered a memory, and I pulled up short.

"My God!" I exclaimed. "It was *she!* Of course it was! The woman who came to visit me to-night . . . the woman I once saw on a train . . . who was at the meeting of the Seven . . . whom you believe to be Fu Manchu's daughter!"

"What! Are you sure?"

Smith halted beside me, staring into my face.

"I am now," I said slowly. "Perhaps I suspected it all along, but, somehow, I couldn't consciously believe it. After all, it was three years ago. Her hair was done differently then, and a dull gold colour. To-night it was black—very straight, and cut in a sort of Ancient Egyptian style."

"The colour of a woman's hair is not much to go by!" snapped Smith. "And the style which reminded you of Ancient Egypt is also typically Chinese. . . ."

We were already in sight of my house, but as I made to go on, he grasped my arm, holding me back.

"Wait!" he ordered. "Before we go in there, I want to hear all about this curious interview—every detail. Unless"—he added dryly—"you consider it a breach of professional etiquette."

"Hardly," I answered, smiling. "I had never formally accepted her as my patient."

While we stood there under the stars, with a soft breeze from the Nile fanning the leaves above our heads, I told him everything that had occurred, as clearly as I could remember—though not, I confess, without a trace of embarrassment—and when I had done, he laughed.

"So it seems, then, that you've been privileged to behold the unveiled goddess of the Si Fan and still to live—and not a bad disguise, since you had never seen her with nothing on! But her object was simply to hold your attention and give her a chance of hypnotising you."

"And she almost succeeded!" I said, shuddering. "If you hadn't rung the bell when you did . . ."

"Fortunately, she is not yet as good at it as her father—if he is her father." Smith turned back towards the house. "I was a fool to think I might escape them so easily. They saw me leave the ship at Suez—and where else should I go but to you?"

We passed through the small, square courtyard, pausing for a moment before the door while I took the primitive key from its hiding place and fitted it into the old-fashioned wooden lock—a simple but ingenious device, secured by five iron pins which dropped into holes in the bolt. Similar pins on the key pushed them up, enabling it to be withdrawn.

"You should get a decent lock," growled Smith, watching me. "Any burglar's apprentice could pick that!"

"Does it matter?" I retorted. "I have yet to see a lock that an Arab thief cannot pick! That's why we have a gatekeeper."

"Who, at the moment, is drunk!" Nayland Smith entered behind me. "Let us take a look at him."

In the shadowy cave adjacent to the passage, old Hassan, asprawl in his chair, still slumbered noisily. Smith bent over him, rolled up one eyelid between finger and thumb, and peered closely.

"As I expected," he said curtly. "Not just drunk—drugged!" He picked up the baked-clay *kullah* and sniffed at it, as I had done. "H'm! The odour of the whisky is too strong for me to tell what else is in it. But I'll warrant there's something."

"How could they have—"

"Easily!" Smith pointed to the little *mushrabîyeh* recess in the fretworked window projecting upon the court. "That's where it stood, isn't it? It was no big problem to insert a thin tube through the lattice and squirt the stuff in." He put down the *kullah*. "Sa'îd, your other domestic, who's been absent all day, was got rid of in some way too—I hope they haven't murdered him! Your charming visitor wanted a clear field in which to operate."

"But to do what? Why did she come here?"

"Isn't that obvious? To set a snare for me!"

I nodded sombrely.

"You may well be right," I said. "Thank Heaven you arrived sooner than she expected! So, having failed in her purpose—"

Smith glanced at me, his clear grey eyes hard and steely.

"*Did* she fail? I think not. She opened the window to make you think she had fled via the garden—then came out after you and went upstairs while you were heading for the door!"

Leaving me at a loss for a reply, he strode briskly across the *durka'ah* and, halting to discard his shoes, stabbed with one stockinged foot at the pair of golden sandals lying beside them.

"You see? She came out this way while we were talking in the study, but abandoned her shoes so that we should continue to think she had gone earlier by the window. We are dealing now with an artist—not just one of Fu Manchu's thugs!"

"The audacity of the woman!" I said indignantly. "She must have snatched up her dress and, without even stopping to put it on, run up the stairs behind my back—or you would have seen her."

We ascended the staircase in silence.

"You have only two spare bedrooms," remarked Smith, as we reached the top. "Greba has one, and, I assume, most of her things are still in it, so the other—which I am to occupy—could be identified with no difficulty. Show me which it is, Petrie!"

"For Heaven's sake, be careful!" I muttered. "If your suspicions are correct, God knows what she has left in there. . . ."

"We will soon see."

He opened the door to which I had directed him and we hesitated on the threshold, looking around. Nothing appeared visibly amiss. The room contained not much furniture—a single bed placed in the middle of the floor, a small table beside it to support a reading lamp, and a chest of drawers. The floor-length window, leading to a stone balcony, was open like all the others in the house, but the mosquito screen remained closed.

"What did she carry with her?"

"Just a handbag—but rather a large one."

"Large enough, no doubt, to hold something deadly."

Treading warily, as though he suspected even the carpet, Smith crossed to the bed, took the thin coverlet by the top corners, and peeled it down with a quick, decisive movement. Nothing was revealed beneath but the white sheet stretched over the mattress. For a long moment, he stood frowning and tugging absently at the lobe of his left ear—the old ruminative habit, which he had never lost in all the years I had known him. Then:

"Have you a hot-water bottle?" he demanded.

I stared at him in astonishment.

"Yes," I said. "But, surely, on a night like this . . ."

"I should still find it comforting."

"Very well." I moved to the door. "And you wish me to fill it with hot water?"

"Of course!" he murmured roguishly. "Isn't that what a hot-water bottle is for?"

Mystified, but knowing better than to ask further questions, I went downstairs and sought for what he asked—an item superfluous in Cairo but sometimes effective in the treatment of stomach chills. I found it—not without some trouble, as it was months since I had last used it—then carried it into the kitchen and set a kettle on the stove. Waiting impatiently for the water to boil, I thought all the while of Nayland Smith in the room upstairs, feeling loath to leave him there alone, till at last steam poured from the spout. I filled the flat rubber flask carefully, screwed the metal stopper securely into place, and took it up to the bedroom.

"Here," I said. "Mind how you handle it, or you may scald your fingers. We'd better find something to wrap it in—"

"Unnecessary," he said shortly. Taking the bottle by the neck, he laid it down on the bed, moved back a few paces, and put his hand on my sleeve. "Now we wait!"

We waited—though for what I could not imagine. Ten, twenty, thirty seconds passed and nothing happened. Smith watched, frowning, his gaze fixed on the bed. I felt slightly foolish.

"What on earth—" I began, and got no farther.

A gust of air hit me suddenly in the face like the hot breath of *khamsîn* blowing in from the desert, and the entire surface of the bed burst into flame, blazing furiously, as though the mattress had been soaked with petrol. The flames were not of this world but of the Pit! Blue, green, and yellow, they leapt up nearly to the ceiling, filling the room with a thick, suffocating smoke, the heat driving us back as though a furnace door had been flung open in our faces.

In the midst of the conflagration, the hot-water bottle burst with a dull explosion, and the contents hissed up in a cloud of steam.

"Quick!" shouted Smith. "We shall have the house on fire! Open the window!"

Nearer to it than he, I clawed feverishly at the net screen, in my haste breaking the flimsy wooden frame, and wrenched it aside. Then, bent double, and shielding ourselves as best we could, we seized the bed by its legs—luckily, they were iron—and, half dragging, half carrying it, with the flames scorching our cheeks, we got it out upon the balcony and tipped it over the parapet till the mattress tumbled down into the garden. It fell clear of the house, and we left it there to burn itself out.

"Sorry, old man!" said Smith, with a wry smile. "I hadn't anticipated so violent a reaction, or I wouldn't have risked damaging your property. She sprayed the bed with some fantastic substance so wickedly inflammable that it would catch fire simply from the added warmth of the sleeper's body."* He raised his right hand to his lips and licked ruefully at a small burn. "It was what we heard to-night, and the recollection of a similar incident in Hongkong, six months ago, which gave me the clue."

"So Fu Manchu has a new weapon!" I said grimly. "And, in the past three years, since we last saw him, who knows what others he may have found!"

---

*No longer so fantastic. There are chemical compounds used to-day in the manufacture of plastics which will explode spontaneously at temperatures above 20°C. [Ed.]

4

SEALED ORDERS

Despite the alarms and excursions of the night, we slept well and it was after nine o'clock when we came down to the kitchen to think about breakfast—a matter about which we knew little. I put a frying pan on the stove, and we were discussing whether it required three eggs or six to make an omelette when Greba Eltham came in.

"Why, Mr. Smith!" she exclaimed. "You're here sooner than we expected!"

"Greba!" answered Smith, turning quickly. "Good Lord! Petrie was right. I don't think I'd have known you."

Clad in a fashionably short dress which did ample justice to her delightfully bronzed limbs and clear complexion, Greba was the picture of a healthy English girl on a summer's day—the hint of the young Diana we had seen in Norfolk bewitchingly fulfilled. She met his gaze frankly, laughed, and snatched the bowl of eggs from my hand.

"Here—let me do that! You'll only make a mess of it!" She cracked two eggs expertly into the pan. "Where's Sa'îd?"

"I wish I knew!" I said sadly.

I tried to speak lightly, but I was worried about Sa'îd. He was a good cook—a native of Algiers, speaking bad French and a weird brand of Maghrabi Arabic—and I should be sorry to lose him.

"How do you like Egypt, Greba?" asked Smith hastily.

"Oh, I love it! It's wonderful to see the sun again, and best of all to be among friends. Kara treats me like a sister."

"And Dr. Petrie likewise, I trust?"

Smith gave me an arch look and I glared at him.

"Oh, he's a perfect monk!" Greba, stooping to put a plate in front of me, squeezed my arm affectionately. "But an adorable one!"

She appeared easy and relaxed, but her blue-grey eyes were unusually grave, and presently:

"It's Fu Manchu, isn't it?" she challenged. "Whenever *you* come on the scene, Dr. Fu Manchu is never far behind." Smith made no reply, and she added: "They all said he was dead or a fugitive. But I shall never believe that my father's death was an accident."

Smith met her eyes, hesitated, and nodded. "Yes. Fu Manchu is here. But don't be alarmed. He has no reason to harm you."

"I'm not afraid! I've faced him before, and I can do it again!" She was silent for a moment, and, when she next spoke, there was a hint of tears in her eyes. "It wasn't till Father died that I knew how few friends we really had. All the people he tried so hard to help . . . they were just laughing at him."*

"Greba," I said quickly, "don't admit any new patients this morning, and see if Dr. Grayson can take care of my regulars from now on."

"All right, Doctor."

She nodded and went out. Smith frowned after her.

"Petrie," he said darkly, "you will have trouble with that girl. She is in love with you."

Ere I could think of an answer, the door opened once more, to admit old Hassan, leaning heavily on the formidable *nebbut* with which he was supposed to chase off stray dogs and urchins.

"*Hakkîm,*" he groaned, "my head is filled with *afârît* beating on anvils! In the name of Allah, the Compassionate, give me something to make them stop!"

I took him through into the surgery and gave him some aspirins, but, for the good of his soul, refrained from telling him that his headache was due to anything but his own indulgence.

I felt no sympathy for Hassan, but, to my profound relief, Sa'îd, whom I had feared dead, turned up soon afterwards—unharmed, but bristling with indignation. I gathered that he had been arrested as a pickpocket, while elbowing his way through the crowded street market to buy fresh green peppers for lunch. He had spent the night in a police station, where no one would listen to his outrageous Arabic, and gained his release only when it was found that his accuser had given a fictitious name and address.

The rest of the morning passed in routine fashion. I had only three patients to see and had just disposed of the last when Nayland Smith reappeared, sat down on the black leather couch, and com-

*In his fervour to help others, the Rev. J. D. Eltham forgot his daughter, who, after his death, was left almost destitute. [P.]

menced to load his pipe. I asked him if he chose to remain under
my roof or whether, in view of last night's events, he thought it more
prudent to take up his quarters elsewhere, and he shrugged.

"No. Wherever I go, Fu Manchu will find me. But I don't think
we are in any further danger for the time being." He smiled, rather
wearily. "In all the years that we've played this murderous game,
something like a pattern seems to have been established—though
I won't say rules! As soon as I enter the field, he attempts to elimi-
nate me, but the next move is mine."

I agreed—though later developments, of which we then had no
suspicion, were to prove us wrong. . . .

"I have spoken to General Fernshawe on the telephone," he went
on, "and he wishes to see me at once—but not at his office. He
prefers that we meet outside. But who, other than an Englishman,
would make an appointment for midday on the Gizeh Plateau?" He
glanced at his wristwatch. "We have scarcely the time to get there.
Can you leave now?"

"I am to accompany you? I doubt if he will like that."

"Then he must put up with it!"

I ventured no further argument, but I had seen General Fernshawe, and I did not like the look of him.

Scorning taxicabs—which past experience had led us to distrust—
we made our way to the rendezvous by the simple expedient of a
No. 14 tramcar, which, following the west bank of the Nile past the
Zoological Garden, presently turned off and rattled across fields
interlaced with canals, to deposit us, some thirty minutes later,
outside Mena House Hotel. Here we secured a couple of mangy
beasts from the donkey stand and clattered up the steep slope to the
high ground above. We were a little late, but Fernshawe was later.
Smith stood silent, hands thrust in his pockets, while I stared around
curiously.

There is nothing anywhere quite like the Pyramids. Brown and
rugged as the sandy surface on which they stand, not only their
colossal proportions but the sheer simplicity of their outline commands attention, and the world still comes to gaze in wonder, if not
always with respect. To-day the foreground swarmed with newcom-
ers—no longer the elegantly dressed, well-to-do sightseers of pre-
war days, but men in uniform: small, ferret-faced Cockneys, and big,
loose-limbed Anzacs wearing grotesque slouch hats with the brim
pinned up on one side. Among the khaki-clad throng, dark-skinned
hawkers in colourful rags weaved busily in and out, weighed down

with trinkets and with a hundred necklaces strung about their necks, doing a desperate trade where now they must deal in pennies instead of pounds.

"This must be him!" announced Smith ungrammatically.

I turned quickly, in time to see an army staff car bumping to a standstill. An orderly climbed down from the driving seat, opened the rear door, and stood stiffly to attention while General Fernshawe stepped out—a stocky, unmistakable figure, with the florid face of a port drinker and a moustache to rival Kitchener's. We walked across and Smith greeted him with a neat military salute. They exchanged a few words, but did not shake hands. My introduction, which followed, was acknowledged with a poor grace.

"Didn't expect you to bring somebody!" growled Fernshawe.

"Dr. Petrie was my partner in London," replied Smith, "and his integrity is beyond question."

"But, damn it, he's a civilian!"

"Does that make any difference?"

"Hr'mph!" grunted the general. "Deuced awkward. Have to see if some official position can't be found for him. . . ."

But I am thankful to say that he never did.

"We'll take a walk!" said Fernshawe, and strode off towards the Second Pyramid, expecting us to follow.

The orderly remained standing by the car, leaving the doors open and raising the bonnet to cool the engine.

We passed by a group of gaily caparisoned camels, seated with their spindly legs folded under them, like cows chewing the cud. Two were on their feet, with two private soldiers precariously balanced on the high saddles to be photographed with their own cameras.

"Bloody fools!" snorted General Fernshawe. "Donkey rides on Margate Sands!" He plodded relentlessly on, hands clasped behind his back. "Don't trust my house. Don't trust my office. Bloody walls full of ears in this damn' country."

Leaving the Valley of the Sphinx on our left, we were heading out into open desert—a limitless prospect of sandhills extending to the horizon. Our boots crunched deeply into the soft surface and the sun was hot on our shoulders—not unpleasantly, but rather with the dry, therapeutic warmth of a radiation treatment.

"Hear you went to the Kasr en-Nil last night," said Fernshawe suddenly, "though you had no orders to."

"I had no orders not to!"

General Fernshawe responded with something half incoherent. He had a mumbling way of speaking, as if through a mouthful of marbles, the words obscured by the hirsute hedge which concealed his upper lip. He brushed it up with one fingertip and achieved coherency.

"Wasting your time. Man's lost his bloody mind. Don't know who he is, and can't find out. Doesn't matter."

"Then why are you holding him prisoner?"

"Can't take any chances. Might be the Kaiser, for all we know!" Fernshawe forced a laugh, which rang false. "Point is, he put us onto this mad Chinaman who set fire to the place. It's the other two who matter—Crawford, and Brooker."

He broke off, as if unwilling to continue.

"Well?" prompted Smith.

"Can't really tell you much more than you know already," grumbled the general. "They were in the employ of our government—carrying a dispatch case which contained vitally sensitive material."

"So they were couriers?"

Fernshawe muttered what I took to be an assent.

"Why were they staying at the Hotel Iskander?"

"Nobody knows! They were supposed to be at Shepheard's. Didn't go there."

"Why not?"

Fernshawe laughed gruffly. "*You* didn't go there!"

"True," said Smith thoughtfully. "Perhaps they had the same motive. They may have felt themselves safer at some less pretentious establishment. Were these men well acquainted with Cairo?"

"No, they weren't."

Nayland Smith shrugged. "Well, Shepheard's is on the corner of the Shâria' Kamel and the Shâria' Elfi Bey. They probably took a taxi from the station, walked down the side street, and went into the first hotel they came to."

"Much good it did them! Fu Manchu found 'em—burnt Crawford to a crisp, kidnapped Brooker, and took the dispatch case."

"You are sure that it was not lost in the fire?"

"Couldn't have been. It was steel-lined."

Walking two paces to the rear, and patently ignored by the general, I had said nothing so far. But now an idea occurred.

"The man at the Kasr en-Nil . . ." I said. "He may have been just a chance witness, and Fu Manchu chose this bizarre means of silencing him rather than kill him."

"Right!" approved Smith. "You hit the nail on the head, Petrie. Ruthless as he is, Fu Manchu has a peculiar reluctance to murder innocent bystanders."

General Fernshawe glowered at me, resenting my intrusion, but nodded as though in relief.

"If so," he conceded, "that takes care of him! Adrian Crawford doesn't count either. He's dead. But Richard Brooker, who's in the hands of the Si Fan, along with the stuff he was carrying, is another kettle of fish." Taking a big, flat notebook from a side pocket of his tunic, he extracted a glossy quarter-plate snapshot and handed it to Smith. "Photograph. Keep it."

Smith glanced at it briefly, then, to the plain displeasure of the general, passed it to me. It was a half-length portrait of an elderly, somewhat scholarly-looking man, standing at the massive stone portico of a seemingly large building. My first impression was that this was not the kind of individual whom I would expect to be entrusted with the conveyance of secret documents, but, on second thoughts, I reflected that, for the same reason, he might be the least likely to be suspected.

"Apart from the fact that he is missing," commented Smith, "is there any evidence that he has been kidnapped by the Si Fan?"

"None," confessed Fernshawe. "But it's a safe bet. Man hasn't been seen since the night of the fire which Fu Manchu started. And what about his dispatch case?"

"But, if Fu Manchu wished merely to steal that, why should he kidnap the man who carried it?"

"Had to. It was chained to his wrist."

Nayland Smith shook his head perplexedly.

"If it was as simple as that," he muttered, "Fu Manchu would either have released him or killed him afterwards. All this occurred three weeks ago. So what do you expect of me now?"

"Find Brooker, if he's still alive. Find Fu Manchu, and get our property back!"

"A tall order, General!" Smith laughed more grimly than usual. "On the particulars you have given me? I shall need more help than that."

"British Army Intelligence will furnish you with any information which may provide a lead to the whereabouts of Fu Manchu or his agents, and you may make your own arrangements with the Egyptian police. If there is an emergency, you may also obtain the assistance of army units, subject to the approval of the local commanding officer."

It was an unusually long and lucid speech for General Fernshawe, signifying all that he intended to say. He turned about, leading us back towards Gizeh.

"I must at least know what I am looking for," insisted Smith, catching up with him. "What is this stolen material?"

"Can't tell you. Not authorised to tell anybody."

"But why does Fu Manchu want it?"

"How should I know?" Fernshawe laughed gruffly. "Point is, he's got it."

"H'm!" said Smith, frowning, and hesitated. "Well, if you can really say no more on the subject, I must accept that. But, surely, you can give me some details concerning the missing man? Where had he come from?"

"Doesn't matter. We know where he came from. Want to know where he went!"

Smith breathed hard and I saw that his temper, which was never of the most patient, hovered on the breaking point.

"I call that answer not only rude but stupid!" he rapped. "How can you possibly know what matters and what does not? It is for me to decide that after I have heard the evidence."

"Can't be helped," said Fernshawe stolidly. "Matter of policy. We never let our agents know any more than necessary. What if they get caught? And tortured?"

"Cold comfort for the agent," retorted Smith, "who is liable to be tortured to death for nothing! I tell you quite frankly, General, that I am most unwilling to take on an assignment of this sort without the complete confidence and co-operation of my superiors."

Fernshawe halted, scowling at him.

"You're not taking on an assignment," he snarled. "Let me remind you, Mr. Smith, that you are acting under Army orders."

"Very well," said my friend curtly. "If that is your attitude, I have no more to say—other than to remind you that, for the present, it is *Colonel* Smith!"

This was a sally which Fernshawe could appreciate, and, to my surprise, he chuckled.

"Very proper of you!" he replied. "Well, Colonel, the fact is we're all acting under orders, and it's not up to us to question 'em!"

5

SPIDER FIRE

"My orders came from Whitehall," said Nayland Smith, sitting down at my desk, which I had given over to him for the duration of our campaign. "Fernshawe does not want me, and I can't say that I blame him. I have no special genius that enables me to seek out Fu Manchu, and he fears that my blundersome efforts may uncover the very secrets he is so anxious to protect. . . ."

The brief Egyptian twilight was drawing to a close, and, once again, we were seated in my study. Five days had passed since our meeting with the general, and so far we had no concrete evidence that Dr. Fu Manchu, in person, was even in Egypt. As to the woman whom we thought to be his daughter, the Egyptian police believed that she had stayed, under four different names, at most of the principal hotels in Cairo. There she had often been seen in the company of British Army officers, two of whom we managed to identify.

Smith had questioned them both, but only with the foreseen result that they hotly denied they had ever met her, and, since the night of her visit to my surgery, she had vanished completely.

"A drink before dinner?" I said.

Downstairs, I could hear Sa'îd banging about with pots and pans in the kitchen.

Smith, no longer in his colonel's uniform, which he hated, but comfortably clad in drill trousers and a short-sleeved bush shirt with a convenient number of pockets, grunted an acceptance. I filled two glasses with sherry and put one down on the desk, noticing at the same time that the photograph of the missing man which Fernshawe had given us lay beside the blotter. Picking it up, I examined it curiously and frowned.

"Strange!" I murmured.

"What is?" My friend looked up at me quickly. "Do you think you know this man?"

"No . . ." I said. "But I have an odd feeling that I have seen this picture somewhere before. . . ."

"Possibly in a newspaper?" he suggested. "It's obviously not just a family snapshot. Well, try not to think about it for a while and it may come back to you."

Disregarding Fernshawe's advice, we had gone behind his back and visited the scene of the crime—only to confirm his assertion that nothing could be gained by it. A great deal of hammering was going on at the Hotel Iskander, where the top floor was under reconstruction, but the place was still open for business. We learned only that Richard Brooker and his companion had arrived at some time during the evening. Nothing more was remembered of them—save that the elder of the two had kept his dispatch case chained to his left wrist throughout dinner and eaten with the fork in his right hand, like an American.

"An oddly inept pair of couriers!" observed Smith. "They choose an inexpensive hotel, so as to be less conspicuous, and then proclaim that they have something valuable by carrying it about with them on a chain!"

"And if they were to deliver it to some Government office," I said, "why did they not do it immediately, instead of going to a hotel?"

Smith laughed shortly. "They couldn't. It was a Sunday, and the place was closed!"

Eager for action though we were, we had no idea where to begin. Often, in the dark days of the past, we had suffered a like frustration while Scotland Yard searched feverishly for some hint of Si Fan activity reflected in the suspicious behaviour of Orientals. But here, where the entire population was Oriental—and much of it suspicious—it was, as Smith said, less like looking for a needle in a haystack than for one particular straw.

A copy of the *Gazette* lay, still folded, on a side table. Taking it up, I glanced at the headlines and threw it down impatiently, for they told only an idiot's tale of a war like none in history. In Europe, the horror of Ypres dragged senselessly on. With a bleak sense of guilt, I thought of my countrymen who lived and died in ditches under shellfire, while I sat safe in the sheltered luxury of Gezirah Island, surrounded by my books and tended by my servants, and did nothing.

Nayland Smith, sharing my unspoken feelings, shifted uncomfortably in his chair.

"Eight years ago, in Burma," he said quietly, "it was chance alone which alerted me to the existence of Dr. Fu Manchu, and my first brush with him was very nearly my last." He looked down at the star-shaped scar on his left forearm—fainter, now, than when I had first seen it, but a lifetime reminder. "Since then, it seems to have become the custom to send for me whenever his name is heard. Yet I can do no more to find him than any other, unless he shows his hand by committing some new outrage."

"It may be an outrage against you!" I said grimly.

"Upon my soul," he replied, "I almost wish that it might!"

They were words ill-spoken, since he forgot to cross his fingers while speaking them.

I smiled sadly, carried my glass to the window, and stared out. In the half light of the afterglow, my property appeared a great deal more extensive than it was, the bushes at the far end concealing the road which separated it from the spacious premises of the Gezirah Sporting Club. I raised my hand to draw the curtains, then stiffened suddenly and turned.

"Smith," I said, "come here a moment!"

Lifting an eyebrow at the tone in which I spoke, he laid his pipe in an ashtray and walked across.

"Out there—" I added. "What do you make of that?"

"God knows!" he muttered.

Among the trees on the other side of the unseen road, a bluish light glowed faintly, like a gaslamp shining through mist.

"It has an evil appearance," I said uneasily.

For all that it might be harmless—some odd trick of Nature—that eerie effulgence in the gathering dusk made me think of nights disturbed in childhood by a macabre old Scottish folk song, telling of the spectral flame which appears outside a house of the dying, to wait, patient and unquenched, till at last it is joined by a second. . . .

"In the Far East, they call it spider fire," answered Smith, echoing my thoughts. "But I hardly expect such nonsense from you." He shrugged. "Well, whatever it is, we are not going out to look!"

Life under the shadow of Fu Manchu had taught us to be wary of all that hinted at wizardry. We watched in silence while the mysterious light, seemingly on a level with the treetops, hung motionless for a time, then drifted slowly downwards and vanished.

"It's gone—" I began, and stopped, with a chill of alarm, as I saw that it had *not* gone.

Screened by the bushes, it had crossed the road and shone now through the upper branches of the acacias at the foot of my garden. It emerged, growing brighter, and taking on the form of a nebulous sphere, scintillating like a cloud of fireflies. Having no fixed outline, it changed constantly in size, shimmering and shifting from some ten to fifteen inches—a microcosm of tiny stars, pulsating and spinning about an axis.

"Good heavens!" I exclaimed. "If Sa'îd or Hassan sees *that*, I shall have no servants to-morrow!"

Like a balloon floating on the wind, the alien visitant had descended almost to the path leading up from the gate, and was moving now in and out of the bushes. The sapphire nimbus which surrounded it glowed faintly on the white petals of a flowering shrub. It bounced to one corner of a rustic seat, settled fleetingly on the pointed tip of the sundial, and passed on, drawing ever closer to the house and moving from side to side in a horribly lifelike manner, as if searching . . . searching for a way in.

"Get ready for trouble!" said Smith tersely. "Here is the action you were yearning for!"

Watching the elfin dance of the thing in the garden, I knew, with a thrill of fear, that he was right. This was no phantom will-o'-the-wisp, but a deadly adversary of unknown power, directed by the fiendish genius of Dr. Fu Manchu.

"A bullet may stop it!" Smith took the pistol from his pocket. "Damn! It's disappeared under the balcony—"

He reached up to the catch which secured the insect screen. But, even as he did so, the uncanny object soared up above the parapet, hovered a scant six feet away, then bounded straight at our faces, and we leapt back instinctively. It touched the gauze, passed through without hindrance, and was in the room with us!

Instantly, I was conscious of a strong smell of ozone. My scalp prickled and every hair on my head rose erect like that of a golliwog. From downstairs came a sound like gunshots, as the fuses blew and every light went out.

In the semi-darkness, we stumbled towards the door—the room now lighted only by the flickering radiance cast off from the ball of viridescent fire hanging above my desk. But, as if endowed with intelligence, the awful thing darted sideways, cutting off our retreat. I saw Smith raise his pistol, and struck up his arm.

"Don't shoot!" I cried. "If you disrupt the field—"

My warning was left unfinished. The coruscating sphere flamed suddenly to a white-hot incandescence that hurt the eyes—and burst with a detonation like a thunderclap.

A stab of pain went through my ears, and I dropped to the floor as though felled by a blow to the skull.

6

THE CHINESE INQUISITOR

"Petrie! Petrie! Are you awake?"

Nayland Smith's voice came to me oddly muffled. I was half sitting, half lying, on a hard stone floor, and the wall at my back was not that of my study but rough and uneven. My ears were ringing and my head ached as though it would split, the darkness about me so profound that it seemed like a tangible part of the heavy atmosphere, suffused with an indescribable smell of years counted in centuries.

I tried to answer but achieved only a groan.

"Petrie! Are you all right?"

I felt Smith's fingers close on my arm.

"I—I don't know," I said thickly. "I'm half deaf and I can see nothing. Oh, my God! Am I blind?"

"No, no! Hold your hand in front of you. Look at your watch. Do you see it?"

Every movement was leaden, but I raised my arm, holding my wristwatch close to my face—and a greenish circle of luminous figures glowed out of the darkness.

"Yes!" I answered eagerly. "I see it. But I think it has stopped."

"So has mine." Smith's voice was stronger—less anxious, but grim. "They must have been magnetised by that damnable thing that knocked us out."

"It was electrical . . . a man-made thunderbolt."

"And made by whom, we have no need to ask! We don't know where we are, but we know in whose hands!"

I groaned again. Though we were unbound, I could not doubt that we were prisoners. I attempted to stand, but my legs buckled and I sank down upon the floor, shocked by my own weakness.

"How—how long have we been here?"

"Hours, or days—who knows? The concussion alone could not have robbed us of our senses for very long. We have been drugged with something."

A glimmer of light appeared, distant and dim.

"Someone is coming!" hissed Smith. "Pretend to be still unconscious."

I let my head fall forward upon my breast, keeping my eyelids fractionally raised.

The light brightened and revealed itself as a lantern held in the left hand of a villainous-looking man clothed in beggarly rags, with a filthy scrap of cloth wound about his forehead. In his right hand, he carried a crescent-shaped knife. Approaching us cautiously, he placed his lantern on the floor and stooped—grabbed me by the hair, and tilted my head back. I closed my eyes tightly, felt a fist thrust under my chin, heard the sharp crack of a thin glass ampoule, and further dissimulation became impossible. I started up, drawing in long, rasping breaths, with the pungent fumes of amyl nitrite burning in my throat and my heart beating like a trip-hammer.

Twisting my shirtfront in his lean fingers, the man hauled me to my feet and propped me against the wall. Smith scrambled up hastily before the same methods should be applied to him. By the faint light, I saw that we stood in a cavelike cell, only a few yards square, and apparently hollowed out of the living rock. Our gaoler snatched up his lantern and gestured fiercely with his knife.

"*Yallah!*" he snarled. "*Imshou!*"

I essayed a step forward and almost fell. I could scarcely stand, let alone walk, but a sharp prod with the point of the knife urged me to the effort. Smith clutched my arm, and, half supporting each other, we stumbled out into a dark passage.

"*Shemalkum!*"

We turned obediently to the left.

The nearer end of the passage, or tunnel, ended in a square opening with massive stone lintels but without a door, giving upon a long, narrow apartment, half constructed, half ruined, and furnished in a temporary fashion with canvas folding chairs and a rough wooden table, at which a man was seated. A globular lamp before him provided the only illumination, lighting the centre of the room brilliantly with an eerie flickering like that of firelight, and leaving the rest in deep shadow. The floor beneath our feet was as uneven as that of the dungeon in which we had awakened, but the wall behind the table was patchworked with small blue tiles which gleamed, here and there, where the fitful rays of the lamp struck upon them. Two hawk-faced men, wearing the loose robes and headcloths of desert Arabs, met us at the entrance.

"Senussi!" said Smith tensely.

I nodded, but had eyes only for the man who sat at the table—for, as we had half expected, it was Dr. Fu Manchu.

Grasping us by the arms, the two tribesmen conducted us to the chairs which faced him, shoved us down, and stood beside us, each with a hand on the hilt of a brass-sheathed dagger.

Fu Manchu gave no greeting but sat watching us, one elbow on the boards and his pointed chin resting on the upturned heel of his right hand. He no longer wore Chinese clothes, but was dressed in a black, monkish habit with the cowl thrown back upon his gaunt shoulders. The bizarre lamp, mounted on a small iron tripod, resembled a witchbowl, within which tongues of flame leapt and danced, and the light, cast upwards, produced the effect of a disembodied countenance floating in the shadows—a death mask of Satan, the cavernous eye sockets set with emeralds.

I noted that the tiled pattern of the wall at his back was interrupted by three large panels, inset, and graven with the image of a god or a pharaoh, surrounded by hieroglyphics. This, then, was some chamber of Ancient Egyptian origin—but where? Between the panels were small, windowlike apertures, but they admitted no light.

Nayland Smith was the first to break the silence.

"So you escaped from the wreck of the *Chanak Kampo*," he said quietly. "I always thought as much."

"Fortunately, I was not aboard," replied Dr. Fu Manchu. "I had planned to join the ship later at a little-known harbour in Sardinia. But there were also a few survivors—some of whom you know—who took to the boats before the yacht struck upon the Pinion Rocks, and reached the coast of France, bringing with them the most valuable items of the Si Fan's property."

Listening to that unforgettable voice, alternately sibilant and guttural, which I had hoped never to hear again, I tried vainly to concentrate. My head swam, so that the words ebbed and flowed in waves of sound. I slumped limply in my chair, and the man at my side dragged me roughly upright.

Fu Manchu switched his long green eyes towards me.

"My electrostatic vortex is a harmless toy which does little more than make a loud noise, but I see that you experience some ill effects. This must be remedied."

Among the few items set out upon the table was a Chinese box, lacquered and inlaid with mother-of-pearl, and constructed in tiers. Removing the uppermost tier, Fu Manchu drew a strip of lint from the lower, folded it lengthwise, and moistened it with the contents of a glass-stoppered phial, then beckoned to the ragged savage who had ushered us from our cell. The man took it from him, holding it outstretched between his hands, and approached me. By his tattered apparel, I guessed him to be a religious mendicant, and, by his untidy black turban, a dervish of the Rifaiyeh sect.

I was aware of a strong chemical odour as he laid the damp band across my forehead, keeping it firmly in place with fingers and thumbs, and muttering an incantation to add to its efficacy. Whether by reason of this or due solely to Fu Manchu's genius, my headache eased immediately and, in less than a minute, was gone.

The dervish grunted and withdrew into the shadows, where he remained leaning against the wall, mumbling, and picking at his gapped teeth with the point of his knife. He appeared to be half mad.

Fu Manchu turned back to Smith.

"We meet in troubled times. You see in me to-day but a homeless wanderer in this war-torn wilderness which you have made, and in which I would gladly leave you to mutual annihilation. My current state of health is maintained solely by the use of certain powerful alkaloids which will shorten my life—unless I may first find the means to prolong it, which I have sought fruitlessly for so many years, and to which end alone I had wished to devote myself."

"Nevertheless," retorted my friend truculently, "you have found time enough to create new horrors, such as the diabolical stuff which you used to set fire to the Hotel Iskander, and with which you attempted my life on the night of my arrival."

Fu Manchu nodded repeatedly, the movement of that great, bulbous head on the hunched shoulders reminding me grotesquely of the Nodding Mandarin figurines once popular on English suburban mantelpieces.

"I have conducted some interesting experiments on those lines," he confessed. "Though the art of making fire has been known for millennia, the processes of combustion are as yet but imperfectly understood. I have flame which will burn invisibly through steel, and flame which burns without heat."

Leaning across the table, he took two small bottles from the ornate coffer, poured a drop from one into the palm of his hand, and added a drop from the other. Instantly, an orange tongue of fire leapt up. Dr. Fu Manchu extended his hand towards us and, while the flame yet burned upon it, went on speaking.

"Your Western scientists are but children playing with fire. China had gunpowder centuries before it was known in Europe, but, because we did not use it to hurl iron shards into the bodies of our enemies, you call us ignorant and backward."

The flame died down and vanished. Fu Manchu raised his hand, palm upwards, to show the yellow, parchmentlike skin unmarked.

Impressive as this demonstration undoubtedly was, it proved altogether too much for the dervish.

"*Kutb en-Nâr!*" he screamed, and fell upon his knees, swaying backwards, forwards, and from side to side, in a weird, spinning-top motion, crying, "*Allah! Allah! Allah!*" and slashing at his limbs with the blade of his knife, as though intent upon suicide.

"*Uskut!*" commanded Fu Manchu.

But the Rifai, heedless in his frenzy of adoration, continued to call upon God with ever-increasing fervour until the nearer of the two hook-nosed Senussi kicked him in the stomach and rolled him over into the darkened part of the room. The man's knife, red with his own blood, rang loudly upon the floor and dropped almost at my feet.

"It seems," said Smith evenly, "that you have added dervishes to your corps of thugs and dacoits."

"There is a welcome under my banner," answered Fu Manchu, "for all who would resist your ambitions to turn East into West, but the Si Fan no longer functions as an organisation. Three of the Seven are dead. In the circumstances, I have assumed the presidency, but the symbols and artifacts which made the Si Fan mine lie buried deep beneath the sands of the desert and I have none to assist me but allies who owe me no allegiance—who may disobey or betray me at their will." His eyes blazed with a malevolence such as I had rarely seen in them. "For much of this, *you* are responsible. Yet I would not have raised my hand against you, had you not sought me out. Now I have questions to ask."

Beside the tiered cabinet lay a roll of coarse, bluish material—the only other item on the table. Fu Manchu turned it laterally towards him and began to unfasten the tapes which secured it.

"You will, of course, resist. Hypnotism induced with the aid of drugs is unreliable as a means of interrogation, since the subject often becomes unable to distinguish truth from falsehood, and I have no present access to the more subtle devices which I once possessed—which penetrate every nerve, every organ of the body, yet leave no scar. I must, therefore, resort to the crude but effective implements of a less enlightened age. . . ."

With a quick, febrile movement, he unrolled the cloth and heaped upon the table an array of nameless objects, the very aspect of which caused me to feel faint—viselike contrivances with serrated jaws, saw-toothed bands of copper, wooden spikes, and something resembling a pair of iron spoons, jointed like scissors.

"It distresses me to adopt barbarous procedures once reserved for the punishment of criminals," continued Dr. Fu Manchu, "but I cannot allow my purpose to be hindered."

From the lowest compartment of the lacquered box, he took out a pair of surgical gloves and put them on, smoothing them down over his talonlike hands. The stark horror engendered by that simple act, and the manner in which he performed it, was such that I felt near to fainting. Dimly visible in the shadowed area beyond the table, the dervish sat upon crossed legs, gibbering and moaning. The lambent flames imprisoned in the crystal globe gleamed on the things scattered beneath it, the obscene instruments of a madman's surgery—things such as only the hooded fanatics of the Inquisition had dared to employ, believing that they served the will of God.

I knew that at that moment I was closer to death or mutilation than I had ever been. We had no secrets to betray! My gaze fell upon the Rifai's knife still lying where it had fallen, unnoticed, less than a yard from my right foot, prompting a desperate response. If I could snatch it up . . . hurl myself upon Fu Manchu . . . I straightened in my chair, flexing my fingers and tensing my muscles.

The Senussi who stood beside me bent suddenly, picked up the knife, and thrust it under his belt.

Dr. Fu Manchu rose to his feet, his shadow leaping high on the wall and hovering above him like the wings of a giant bat.

"Your reluctance to co-operate is commendable but is ill-considered. The secret of the Midnight Sun will be better entrusted to me than to one who renounces his ancestors."

The course of the conversation—hitherto unpleasantly plain—had taken a curious turn. I glanced at Smith and saw that he was as puzzled as I.

"You speak in riddles!" he said. "We have no information to give you, and I know of no Midnight Sun but the one which shines over the North Pole. Are you, by any chance, referring to the papers which you stole from Richard Brooker, the man whom you kidnapped?"

For the first time that I could recall, it seemed to me that Fu Manchu hesitated. I saw the weird green film come down over his eyes, veiling their lucent depths—the well-remembered phenomenon which gave him an added touch of something other than human—and wondered what had aroused his emotions. At length:

"Mr. Commissioner Nayland Smith," he said slowly, "will you swear to the truth of that?"

"Swear? To what?"

"That you hold me responsible for his disappearance."

Smith exchanged glances with me and shrugged.

"Why should I not? Do you deny that you robbed one man of his mind, burned another in his bed, abducted a British Government agent, and stole his property?"

Dr. Fu Manchu reseated himself and drew a long, sibilant breath, curiously like a sigh. The veil lifted from his eyes.

"You are misinformed," he said softly. "I ordered the assault on the Hotel Iskander. But, because I am served by fools, Kurt Lehmann received the Blessing of Nepenthe, which I had intended for Adrian Crawford, who died in his stead. Dietrich Bruecker—whom you call Richard Brooker—escaped, taking his secrets with him, and I have no knowledge of his whereabouts. You were brought here because I believed that *you* knew!"

Smith and I stared at each other, at a loss for any reply. The entire foundation of our campaign, as laid down by General Fernshawe, had been struck from under us at a word—but, characteristically, neither of us could doubt that Fu Manchu spoke the truth. With a feeling of unspeakable relief, I heard the harsh, tearing sound of the rubber gloves being stripped from his fingers.

"You have saved yourselves from torture," he resumed, "but our long struggle is over. How shall we end it? It offends me to take the life of an enemy whom I hold helpless in my hands. Therefore, I will offer you an alternative."

Searching among his stock of phials and bottles, he selected one curiously shaped like a gourd, and raised it to the light. The contents pulsed and glowed as if with a life of its own.

"I will, if you choose, grant you the ultimate redemption—rebirth without death—which you witnessed in the case of Kurt Lehmann.

The effects of the drug are swift and painless, but they are not reversible. Do you accept?"

"No!" returned Smith. "I fail to see what difference there can be between death and a reincarnation devoid of memory."

Fu Manchu's thin lips curled in the travesty of a smile.

"That is dependent upon whether you regard life as synonymous with identity, or with *being* as distinct from *non-being*. My Tibetan associates would be happy to debate it with you." He restored the phial to the box. "You leave me, then, but one other choice. In the West, you consider my people cruel because we carry the unwanted offspring of our household pets to some deserted spot and there abandon them. But, rather than take the irrevocable step of ending their lives, as you do, we leave the decision to the guiding principles of the universe—or, as you would say, Fate. I will do the same. When we leave here, you shall remain behind and, after a suitable interval, be at liberty to make your way to safety—if you can."

I stared at him blankly, unable to determine whether we had been condemned or reprieved. Nevertheless, it was with a profound thankfulness that I saw him gather together the hideous devices upon the table and roll them up in their cloth wrapper. This done, he charged a large hypodermic syringe from a rubber-capped flask, and stood up with the syringe in one hand and a scalpel in the other.

A harsh word of command—and I started back in my chair, as the dagger of my Senussi guardian was laid edgewise across my throat.

"Do not move," warned Dr. Fu Manchu, "or he will sever the carotid artery before I can delay him."

Stooping over me, he used the scalpel to open two small slits in the material above both knees, and made an injection through each, so skilfully that I did not even feel the prick of the needle. But my flesh crawled at the touch of those evil, clawlike fingers, and, regardless of the threatening blade at my throat, it was all that I could do to prevent myself from flinching.

"This is a local anaesthetic," he explained, "based on formic acid, obtained from the African red ant. It will keep you from walking for approximately an hour, after which it will wear off and you may do as you please."

The action of the stuff was rapid beyond belief. Even while I watched Nayland Smith subjected to a like treatment, I felt the numbness creeping up from my ankles. Inch by inch, it spread upwards to the level of my hips, leaving my lower limbs useless.

Fu Manchu turned back to the table, disassembled the syringe, and began packing his impedimenta into the multi-tiered cabinet. "Since you cannot assist me with my inquiries," he said, "I must hasten to pursue them elsewhere." He turned his eyes briefly towards the dervish. *"Ya Mahmoud! Gibliyya el-fanous!"*

Mahmoud—such being, evidently, his name—got to his feet, picked up the lantern, which he had extinguished after our entry, and carried it to him.

"Light it!" ordered Fu Manchu.

The dervish stared back at him foolishly. *"Kutb en-Nâr!"* he whispered hoarsely. "Lord whom the fires obey! Do you but breathe upon it, and surely it will light itself!"

Fu Manchu's lips twitched and, had he been capable of laughter, I think that he might have laughed.

"What? Shall I use my magic for such lowly purposes?" he asked sternly. "Light it with matches, O Mahmoud." He addressed us once more. "It is not my intention to hinder you, so I will leave you this. You may find it inadequate, but all that you see here was built with the aid of less."

He closed and secured the lacquered box, and spoke a few words to the Senussi tribesmen, one of whom took it up, while the other burdened himself with the sinister roll of cloth. Fu Manchu picked up the strange, globe-shaped lamp, holding it in both hands, in a way which showed it to be heavy.

"This I must carry in person," he remarked, with the ghost of a smile on his lips. "These poor creatures, who are all I have now at my command, are afraid to touch it."

Preceded by his three servants, he made towards a second opening situated in the same tiled wall which faced us, but on the opposite side of the three recessed panels behind the table. Hitherto in shadow, it was now revealed by the movement of the light to be a square-cut doorway, furnished with a heavy stone frame, partially in ruins. Fu Manchu paused on the threshold. With his stooping shoulders, he looked, at that moment, like some anthropomorphic deity of Ancient Egypt—a vulture with the face of a demon.

He raised the lamp high, so that the captive flames played on the wall.

"Dr. Petrie, I commend your attention to the blue tiles."

He went out, and the light faded, leaving us in a semi-darkness relieved only by the feeble rays of the lantern on the table.

7

THE KINGDOM OF
THE DEAD

"The blue tiles?" queried Smith. "What did he mean?"

"God only knows!"

I answered indifferently, grateful only that I had no longer to sustain the baleful presence of Dr. Fu Manchu. In three years, I had almost ceased to believe in the reality of the Satanic aura which hovered about him, branding him as an avatar of evil, to whom evil was good. To stand face to face with him was not merely to fear for one's life but to feel in peril of one's immortal soul.

But now that he had left, the sombre aspect of that subterranean chapel of death and false gods came into its own—a place of shadows, lighted only by the dim glow of the lantern. It was a cheap affair such as may be had for a few piastres in the bazaars, constructed of waxed paper stretched over an iron frame, and filled with an inferior grade of oil which caused it to gutter like a candle.

By its uncertain light, rising and falling, the figures etched in bas-relief on the wall behind appeared to be in movement. Each portrayed a pharaoh who wore the tall, pointed crown of the South—twice depicted in a running or dancing posture, the third and farthest from us damaged and lacking a head.

All about us reigned a silence which beat upon the eardrums in soundless waves, like the vibrant notes of some great organ pitched too deep for hearing. Though there was no draught—no breath of air to hint at a connection with the world above—the wick in the oil lamp alternately flared and, sometimes, burned so low that I feared it might be altogether extinguished.

Nayland Smith gave vent to a sigh and looked at me with an acid smile on his lips.

"Well," he remarked, "we have had our interview with Dr. Fu Manchu—not in just the way we would have liked, and only to discover that he knows more about our business than we do! He knows the name of the man at the Kasr en-Nil. Kurt Lehmann—in other words, a German! Not only that, but he claims that the real name of our missing man is Dietrich Bruecker—implying that he, too, is a German!"

His calm, matter-of-fact speech awakened a latent memory and I started upright in my chair so violently that I all but pitched out of it.

"No!" I exclaimed excitedly. "Don't you remember what else he called him? 'One who renounces his ancestors.' Brooker was born and bred in England, but his father was German, and when the war broke out he changed his name as a gesture of loyalty. . . ."

"Just as the King himself did,"* murmured Smith, and stared at me sharply. "Are you speaking of facts, or a theory?"

"Facts! Fernshawe has deceived us, damn him! Richard Brooker is no mere carrier of official papers. I saw that photograph of him in a scientific journal more than two years ago, when he received the medal of the Royal Society."

"He is a scientist, then? In what field?"

"I'm sorry," I said slowly, "but I don't remember that. I only know that it isn't medicine, and so I took no particular notice at the time. It was the change of name that recalled it to me now."

"Good God!"

"What can it all mean?" I persisted. "Why did General Fernshawe deliberately mislead us? If Brooker is not in the hands of the Si Fan, where is he? And why, having escaped from them, did he not immediately go to the police or to the military?"

"Fu Manchu clearly thought that he had!" mused Smith. "As to why he did not—well, I don't know, but I have an unpleasant idea. . . ." He was silent for a moment. "Upon my soul, this is more than I can bear!" he declared savagely. "All that we have accomplished is to inform Dr. Fu Manchu that his quarry is on the run, and now we must sit here half mummified while that yellow fiend goes in pursuit!"

*It was only then that King George V, grandson of Prince Albert of Saxe-Coburg-Gotha, adopted the family name of Windsor. [Ed.]

Writhing his lean shoulders in a paroxysm of helplessness, he beat viciously at his thighs in an unavailing attempt to restore the circulation.

"Be patient," I said. "We will think about action when it is feasible. For the present, let us just be thankful that we are no longer in danger."

"Aren't we? We are not out of the wood yet." Smith laughed harshly. "Out of the wood? I wish to Heaven we were in one! Where are we? Are we in a tomb?"

"Possibly, and, if so, it should not be hard to get out. Such places are usually connected to the surface by a long, sloping passage—"

"True!" snapped my friend. "But what then? We may find ourselves miles out in the desert, with no means of knowing whether we are on the east bank of the river or the west!"

He was right, of course. In such circumstances, our chances of making our way back safely to Cairo would be slim. I made no reply, but sat looking at him with a crestfallen expression on my face, and, after a moment, he smiled apologetically.

"Forgive my ill temper. We will meet our troubles as they come." He shrugged and searched in his pockets. "Damn! I left my pipe on your desk. Ah, well—I suppose that even I could scarcely smoke it in this atmosphere."

Such thoughts as passed through my head while we sat waiting for the loosening of the invisible chains which bound us, I prefer to forget. We had no way of counting the minutes as they dragged by, while the oil lamp flickered and the weird forms graven on the wall performed their endless shadow dance. Almost I came to doubt the inviolable word of Dr. Fu Manchu—to believe ourselves condemned to sit there helpless till madness and starvation put an end to our sufferings. Such hope as I could cling to had reached its lowest ebb when, after an eternity, I felt the commonplace pins-and-needles sensation in my right foot.

Smith felt it at nearly the same moment and we sat up, massaging our limbs vigorously, and stamping our feet when movement became possible. Soon we were able to stand up, taking clumsy paces this way and that before our legs would properly support us. Smith staggered to the table, snatched up the lantern, and shook it.

"Be careful!" I warned. "It may go out."

"I can re-light it," he answered. "The question is whether there's enough oil to get us out. But nothing's been taken from us, so I have plenty of matches."

I blessed his habit of carrying at least three boxes.

"I have some too," I said.

"Good. Then they may see us through."

Ere leaving, we made a quick inspection of the chamber we were in, learning only that it extended some distance, in a ruinous state, to the right of the opening through which Fu Manchu had departed.

"Obviously, it was never finished," I commented. "The pharaoh for whom it was intended must have died too soon." I pointed to the hieroglyphics finely executed in relief. "Those are certainly the names and titles of a king. It might help to know which one, if only I could read them, but, unfortunately, I cannot."

"Nor I. I never dreamed that it might be advantageous to learn." Smith raised the lantern close to the decorated wall. "These are the tiles to which Dr. Fu Manchu directed your notice. Do they suggest anything to you?"

I bent under his upraised arm to study them. They were small and oblong, with a slightly curving surface of blue glaze, set in neat rows, as though upon the wall of a modern bathroom. How the work could have been done with such precision, in such conditions, I could not imagine. But, after a brief examination, I shook my head.

"No," I admitted. "I have seen nothing like this in an Egyptian tomb. If it was meant to be a clue, I fear it is lost on me."

"A riddle of the Sphinx!" grunted Smith. "A typical piece of Oriental cruelty, where the victim is invited to stake his life on the solution of an enigma!" He swept a final glance around the room. "Well, there are two entrances, but it seems logical to go by the same route as the others."

He stepped through the doorway. We looked for no ready escape—yet little did we anticipate the circumstances in which we were soon to find ourselves.

We came at once into a crudely hewn tunnel, just high enough for us to stand upright, but too narrow for us to walk abreast. The floor was as rough and uneven as the walls and roof, littered with heaps of stone and pieces chipped from the rock at the time of construction.

Smith led, holding the lantern outstretched and groping his way forward by its uncertain light, barely sufficient to warn us of the obstructions in our path. We could see nothing of what lay ahead. But we had taken no more than a few cautious steps when he halted.

"There is another opening here," he announced. "But let us keep straight on and see where this passage leads. Check the other side in case there are any more openings, and, if so, note them."

We resumed our course, proceeding at a snail's pace, a half step at a time, and wary of pitfalls. We were ill-shod for such a venture, in the heelless carpet slippers which we had worn in my study. The soles were too thin to give adequate protection against the sharp fragments over which we trod, and they came off continually. After another thirty yards or so, we halted again, where the passage turned to the right, tore strips from our clothing, and used them to bind our inconvenient footgear to our ankles.

The hoped-for shaft sloping upwards to the surface failed to materialise. No faint ray of light beckoned to us from a distant opening, and the air was deathly still. No sound came to our ears but our own laboured breathing and the dry scuffling of our movements as we stumbled onwards over the dust and detritus of the ages. Here and there, the rock walls sparked with microscopic grains of some crystalline substance which I took to be salt.

"There are no bats here!" observed my companion suddenly.

"I can dispense with them!" I said. "To have bats flying into one's face in a hole like this—"

"May not be pleasant—no. But the fact that there are none plainly indicates the lack of any easy way in and out."

Some sixty feet from the corner, my questing hand slipped into space, revealing a further opening to the left. But we ignored it and continued on. The corridor which we were following seemed to go on interminably, dark, silent, and empty.

I felt, and fancied I could hear, the drumbeats of my heart pounding as I sought vainly to subdue a primordial fear of the infinite which lies beyond Man's capacity to conceive. I can find no words adequate to describe the unique sense of terror which invested that dreadful kingdom of the dead—a sense of being lost in the dead afterworld of a dead civilisation, where even the gods had died. The atmosphere was untainted, but dry and lifeless with the indefinable quality of air sealed up for a thousand years.

Abruptly, the passage turned again, into a labyrinth of cross-corridors—four to the right, and another to the left. In its insane twists and turns, the place resembled a cave system—but here no sound of dripping moisture broke through the heavy silence; no scrap of moss clung to the barren grey walls.

Six paces beyond the mouth of the fourth tunnel, Smith stopped so precipitately that I blundered into him.

"Damnation!" he cried, in a tone oddly compounded of anger and despair. "We have come to a dead end!"

A close scrutiny of the wall which blocked our path showed this to be literally the case. The passage was not, as I had half expected, closed by a stone portcullis such as is commonly found at the entrance to a burial chamber, but simply ended where the workmen, for no apparent reason, had laid down their tools.

"This is less like a tomb than a Chinese puzzle," grumbled Smith. "What on earth could the purpose of such a construction be?"

Panic threatened, and I forced myself to get a grip on my nerves. With the meagre light at our disposal and the confused state of the floor, it had been impossible to detect footprints.

"We must go back," I said. "Fu Manchu must have turned off along one of the side passages."

Smith nodded. "Yes, that's obvious—and we have seven to choose from! Try striking a match."

I did so, holding it aloft while the flame burned down steadily to my fingers, betraying no telltale current of air in any direction, and the sulphurous smell of it lingered about our faces. For a moment following its extinction, neither of us said anything. Then:

"Come on!" urged Smith, and led the way back to the nearest of the tunnels.

I followed, reflecting gloomily that, wherever the tunnels went, we could not well be more lost than we were already. To our dismay, however, none of the four which we first explored went anywhere, each terminating in a blank wall. Again we paused, baffled.

"God in Heaven!" I said helplessly. "We don't know that there *is* a way out! Fu Manchu may have left by some secret exit known only to himself and closed it behind him."

"No," said Smith quietly. "His peculiar ideas of fair play would forbid him to do that. He has left the way open, as he promised— because he is confident that we cannot find it!"

I took a deep breath, feeling half stifled in that strangely dead air which seemed incapable of supporting life. A fifth passage had yet to be explored, but we entered it unhopefully, blundering grimly on through the Cimmerian shadows cast by our flickering lantern and fearing at every pace that it would end like the others. Surprisingly, it did not, but continued for a considerable distance and widened so that we could at last walk side by side.

"This looks as if it leads somewhere!" conceded Smith, with a cautious note of optimism in his voice. "But," he added darkly, "we are still getting no closer to the surface. All these damnable tunnels are on the same level!"

I concurred silently. By this time, it was clear that we were in no ordinary tomb, but wandering in an intricate maze of blind alleys and tunnels linked at right angles, designed to confuse intruders and guard the sepulchre from violation.

It was nevertheless evident that these ingenious devices had been in vain.

The passage floor was strewn now not only with chippings from the walls but with square slabs of diorite and the shattered remains of a great number of alabaster vessels. Picking up a piece, I examined it curiously.

"This must be a part of the funerary treasure of the pharaoh who was buried here," I said, "pillaged and destroyed by tomb robbers. Despite all that was done to prevent them, they got in."

"Good!" answered Smith. "Then we should be equally able to get out!"

I prayed that it might be soon. The soft leather of our slippers was already in rags, and the desiccated atmosphere parched throat and lips, so that even talking was difficult.

We could not see where the tunnel ended, but, all at once, we were out of it and again in some sort of chamber. Reaching out in every direction, we found neither walls nor ceiling, while a subtle change in the air suggested an expanse of space. But we had advanced only a few steps when further progress was baulked by an enormous heap of broken masonry, extending beyond the feeble rays of the lantern and piled up to a height above our heads. Feeling about with our hands, we could find no limit to it.

"I should say," hazarded Smith, "that we are in a cellar, but the roof has fallen in. If only we had a better light . . . Ah! Maybe I have something that will serve. Hold the lantern, Petrie."

He thrust the iron ring from which it depended into my fingers. Then, searching in his pockets, he produced a notebook and, from the inner side of the front cover, tore out a celluloid envelope intended for the storage of an identity card or other such personal documents.

"This stuff will burn fiercely for a few seconds. While it does so, let us see as much as we may."

Holding the panel of transparent material by one corner, he struck a match and applied the flame. It blazed up instantly, smoking and hissing, and he raised it above his head to the full extent of his arm. By contrast with the oil lamp, the white, spirituous glare of it seemed almost brilliant, revealing an extraordinary scene.

We stood at the base of a pit more than twenty feet square, the smooth walls rising up into an impenetrable darkness. Most of the floor space was taken up by a rectangular structure of pink granite, of which only the top part was visible, the lower half buried under jumbled blocks of stone. Staring up at the nearer wall, high above the tunnel from which we had emerged, I saw a ragged gap yawning like the mouth of a cavern, wide and too lofty for me to assess its height.

For an instant I was utterly bewildered. Then recognition came, suddenly and horribly, and a hoarse cry broke from my lips.

"God help us!" I burst out. "We are trapped beneath the Step Pyramid of Saqqara!"

8

THE TOMB OF ZOSER

The brief flare of the celluloid died down, leaving us once more in a semi-darkness of shifting shadows.

"The Step Pyramid?" echoed Smith. "Are you sure?"

"Yes," I said grimly. "The blue tiles! They are found only here, at Saqqara. That is what Fu Manchu challenged me to remember. Lepsius removed some and took them back to the Berlin Museum." I pointed to the boxlike construction rising above the heap of rubble. "That is Zoser's burial chamber. We are at the bottom of a vertical shaft nearly a hundred feet deep."

"Good Lord! We can never climb up that!"

"Useless if we could," I answered, with a sad smile. "They built the pyramid on top of it!"

"Let us rest for a few minutes and try to work out some plan of campaign."

Smith sat down on the piled-up blocks of masonry, disposing his long limbs as comfortably as possible, and I sat beside him.

"So we are only a few miles from Cairo after all," he muttered. "What do you know about this hellish place, Petrie?"

"Not much, I'm afraid," I confessed. "This is the oldest of all the pyramids—Third Dynasty—and the most complex. In the later ones, the corridors and chambers are inside. Here they are deep underneath—and they have never been fully explored."

"But there must be *some* way out!" Smith pointed upwards to the yawning gap in the wall, the lower part still dimly visible. "Is it up there? That looks like a pretty substantial tunnel."

"It was," I said. "The workmen used it when they were excavating. But, like the mouth of the shaft, the other end is covered now by the base of the pyramid."

"Madness!" he groaned. "But, in that case, there had to be another. How else could they have brought down the coffin?"

"There were several ways—and some made since by tomb robbers. But Heaven alone knows which we may reach or use now. Once they had served their purpose, the original passages were not intended to be used again, so they were filled in and sealed."

I fell silent for a time, trying desperately to visualise the plans drawn by Vyse and Perring, Lepsius, and other pioneers, which I had once studied with youthful eagerness, and ever since neglected.

"It's ironical," I said, sighing. "I've had nightmares about this place ever since I first saw it, and now that we are here, I failed to recognize it. . . ."

My companion glanced at me sharply, the glimmer of the lantern at our feet reflecting a steely glint in his eyes.

"What?" he demanded. "Do you mean that you have actually been down here before?"

"Yes. But only once, and a long time ago."

"But surely you have some idea how you came in?"

"All I remember is an impression of long, winding passages and a great many steps," I said bitterly. "Smith, I was only sixteen! I came down with a party of Egyptologists, when I still had some ideas of becoming one myself. I have a vague idea that there are four systems of passages like the one we have been in, and some of them are inter-connected. We could blunder about in them for hours, till the lantern goes out."*

Smith moved uncomfortably and swore.

"What *is* all this rubbish we're sitting on?" he inquired irritably. "It looks as if a house had collapsed."

"It's what's left of the packing with which this shaft was once filled. The Saîtes of the Twenty-sixth Dynasty cleared it."

"If the tomb had already been robbed, why did they bother?"

Momentarily forgetful of our dreadful circumstances, I managed a weak laugh.

"For the same reasons as ourselves," I said. "They wanted to re-discover the lost skills of the Old Kingdom. Six hundred years before Christ, the Step Pyramid was as ancient to the Saîtes as they are to us now. By that time, Egypt had been conquered and occupied by the Hyksos, the Nubians, and the Assyrians—"

My scholarly discourse was dramatically interrupted.

From a point well above our heads, a powerful beam of light cut

---

*Luckily for his peace of mind, Dr. Petrie was unaware that there are no less than *eleven* additional shafts at a lower level! [Ed.]

down through the gloom, shining upon our upturned faces as we leapt to our feet. A voice shouted, echoing from wall to wall.

"Petrie! Smith! Are you there?"

"Yes! Yes!" I shouted back breathlessly. "We're here!"

"Stay there! I'm coming down to you."

The light vanished.

I caught at Smith's arm, overcome by a surge of emotion that was almost hysterical.

"We are saved! God knows how, but we are saved!"

We waited in a fever of impatience while the minutes passed—five, perhaps ten, but seeming to us an eternity, till at last the bright light reappeared low down at the left-hand corner of the well. We hurried towards it, scrambling over the tumbled stones to a low, square-cut opening. A small, lean man stood within it, a large electric torch in his hand, and the light, reflected upwards, revealed a lined face which I knew—Rex Engelbach, of the Cairo Museum.*

"Thought you'd make for the main shaft," he said tersely, "so I tried here first, before we started searching the galleries. Either of you hurt?"

"No. We're both all right," I said.

"So you should be. Nothing much to hurt you down here—just a lot of dusty old tunnels." He turned to the three *fellahîn* workmen crowded into the passage behind him, each of whom likewise carried a torch. "*Yallah! Nerouh!* Let's get out of this."

He led us into a narrow corridor.

"Doesn't this go to another of those T-shaped tunnel systems?" I asked curiously.

"Yes, but there's a turning off which leads to the surface."

Thirty yards along, we reached a kind of crossroads. Rex Engelbach paused, gesturing with his torch, like a tour guide.

"West Gallery straight on, South Gallery to your left. We go *this* way."

He turned to the right and we followed. Soon we came to rough steps cut in the rock floor, leading upwards. The *fellahîn* brought up the rear, grinning, and talking volubly in their own language, from which I gathered that they took us for stupid foreigners who had somehow stumbled into Zoser's tomb and lost themselves. Neither Smith nor I troubled to disillusion them.

---

*Not named in Dr. Petrie's notes. But, from his description, I think it must have been Engelbach. [Ed.]

The crude staircase, becoming more uneven and precipitous, turned a corner and continued in a longer flight of steps. Engelbach bounded up in his agile, simian fashion, pausing at intervals to shine back his torch. Lithe and dark-skinned as any of his men, he was typical of the Egyptologist—not the popular misconception of a frail, ascetic figure, but a virile adventurer, sinewy and as tough as leather. I envied both his nerve and his tireless energy.

"Without you, we'd have been done for," I said fervently. "But how did you know where we were?"

"Your nurse girl—Miss Eltham—told me."

"Greba? But how did *she* know?"

The steps ended in a doorway framed by a heavy surround, from which we turned into an upward-sloping passage.

"None too sure about that," said Engelbach. "Seems somebody told *her*. I was just going to bed when she called me, but she was in such a state that I said I'd round up a few of my best workers and take a look. You can ask her about it when we get up top."

"You mean, she's here?"

"Of course she is! Wouldn't be left behind. I had hell's own job to keep her from coming down with us."

The passage turned yet again, giving access to a long, sinuous tunnel and curving off to the right. I had long since lost all sense of direction. I thought of the ancient builders, chipping patiently at the hard rock with copper-tipped tools, working solely by the light of primitive, baked-clay oil lamps. How, lacking the aid of modern surveying instruments, had they hewn out these tortuous corridors and contrived to arrive precisely at their destination, a hundred feet belowground?

"From here on," announced our guide, "it's just a straight walk out."

"What is the time?" put in Smith suddenly.

"Getting on for two o'clock, I imagine. It was nearly midnight when I left Cairo."

In that awful place there was neither day nor night, and, though all danger was past, I could not repress a shudder.

"You mean midnight Friday?" asked Smith. "Unbelievable that we have been down here only a few hours!"

A dark opening appeared in the wall to our right.

"Goes nowhere," said Engelbach, and we walked on.

The air became notably fresher. I counted forty paces; then the passage ended in a pit roofed only by the Egyptian night, bright with stars. The feeling of relief prompted by that simple sight defies my powers of description. We climbed out of the pit by means of ladders. Another of Engelbach's workmen waited at the top to assist us.

I glanced swiftly around, and saw the pyramid of Neterkhet-Zoser towering up behind us in five slope-sided steps, like cross-sections of five separate pyramids, two hundred feet above the desert—a familiar sight, but one which I knew that I should never again behold without a thrill of horror. A white dress fluttered, dovelike, against the dark background, and Greba Eltham came running up to us.

"Thank God you're safe!" she whispered. "Oh, thank God!"

She threw her arms about my neck, kissing me desperately, as one kisses a lost child, then turned towards my companion. "And you too, Mr. Smith!" she added quickly.

But I noted with some embarrassment that she did not offer him the same greeting.

"Let's go home," said Engelbach shortly. "The night's half gone, and I've got a long day to-morrow."

We trudged across an expanse of loose sand to an embanked highway, Greba walking beside me and clinging to my hand. A glare of electric headlights revealed a large, canvas-covered truck, resembling an army vehicle. A fifth Arab workman waited beside it— Engelbach, with the shrewdness of an old campaigner, had posted a rearguard—and a smaller vehicle stood parked behind. I recognized the hired Peugeot which I used when my professional duties summoned me to more distant parts of the city. Achmed Da'ud, who owned and operated the hire service, sat in the front seat, asleep.

Greba, who had had the foresight to bring a large thermos flask filled with water and ice cubes, brought it out and we drank thirstily, giving some also to Engelbach.

"I still don't know how you got down there," grunted our rescuer, "and I'm not sure that I shouldn't charge both of you with trespassing on property protected by the Service des Antiquités!"

"Do so by all means," retorted Smith, "if you can get Dr. Fu Manchu into court on the same charge!"

"That's all very well, but somebody's got to pay my men's wages, and the museum's not going to—"

"Debit it to Army Intelligence. Petrie can have lunch with you to-morrow, or the next day, and give you the full story."

Smith and I climbed into the back of the car, leaving Greba— somewhat to her displeasure—to sit with the driver. She elbowed

Achmed in the ribs, and we started back for Cairo.

The car bumped and rolled. Leaving the village of Mitrahîneh to our left, we passed through the scattered vestiges of ancient Memphis—the glorious capital of the Old Kingdom, of which nothing now remained but two fallen colossi of Rameses II and an alabaster sphinx. An extensive palm grove supervened, conducting us towards Bedrasheyn.

Nayland Smith, alert as ever, addressed Greba.

"It seems that we owe you our lives," he said, "but I am anxious to learn just how. What happened?"

"Well," she replied, with a shaky little laugh hinting at overtaxed nerves, "for some time after the bomb went off, nothing happened!" She hesitated. "I mean, it was a bomb, wasn't it? Hassan and Sa'îd just rushed outside and stayed there, arguing about what to do. Neither of them would go in again, so, in the end, they came across to the houseboat and got me to go back with them. By that time, all the neighbours were around and they'd called the police and the fire brigade. . . ."

"Was there much damage?" I inquired drowsily.

"No, not really—just a lot of glass broken, and things thrown about. All the fuses had blown, and everything made of metal seemed to be magnetised—as if the house had been struck by lightning. The police weren't very useful, and it was past ten before I could get rid of them. Then, while I was sweeping up all the broken glass and trying to tidy up the study, the telephone bell rang, and I thought it might be you. But it was a woman. She had the strangest, coldest voice that I've ever heard—and frightening. It was like—oh, somehow, like icicles!"

I sat up with a start.

"H'm!" said Smith thoughtfully. "I think we know who *that* was." Greba looked around quickly with a question in her eyes, but he shook his head. "Later. Finish your story first. And then?"

"She—she asked my name, and then she said, very slowly and distinctly, 'Listen to me carefully, for I shall not say it again. Nayland Smith and Dr. Petrie are lost in the passages below the Step Pyramid of Saqqara.' And then she hung up!"

"Motive obscure," murmured Smith, "unless . . ."

He glanced at me with a sly grin, and I scowled at him without deigning to reply.

"I knew it wasn't just a joke," went on Greba, "because nobody could have known you were missing, if they hadn't had a hand in it.

I wondered if I should call the police again, or maybe the military, but then I realised that they'd have to get outside help anyway, and I could do that quicker myself. So I looked up the number in your address book and phoned Mr. Engelbach. He said he had one foot in his pyjamas, and I practically had to throw a fit of hysterics before I could make him listen. But I won in the end, so here we are!"

Much remained to be explained, but, for the time being, my curiosity was satisfied. I slumped back into my corner and took no further part in the conversation. The soles of my feet burned and throbbed from a score of cuts and bruises, as if I had been subjected to the bastinado. Smith and Greba were still talking, but the words no longer made sense. My eyes closed and I dozed.

I knew no more of our journey till I awakened to find that we were running alongside the Nile, with Roda Island close on my right. I breathed a sigh of relief, ending in a yawn, and made an effort to straighten up. We were nearly home, and I looked forward to a hot bath, a stiff glass of whisky, and my bed.

But, as we crossed the Pont des Anglais, Smith bent over and spoke to Achmed.

"Drive on," he directed, "and make for Kasr el-'Aini. General Fernshawe has a house in the Garden City. . . ."

"What?" I faltered, aghast. "You are going to call on him at this hour—in the middle of the night? He will be furious!"

"He can be no more furious than I am," flashed back my friend. "We have been shamelessly tricked by our own side, Petrie. I am going to have this out with him, here and now!"

9

A STORM BEFORE DAWN

Gone were my hopes of rest and recuperation! Such is the price that one pays for the friendship of such a man as Nayland Smith.

Greba—a willing slave—said nothing. Achmed, for whom every extra hour of employment meant extra piastres, said nothing either. Only I wondered unhappily if I might be equal to a confrontation with Fu Manchu and General Fernshawe in the same night.

Crossing the Kasr en-Nil bridge, and leaving the domed building of the museum away to our left, we turned right-handed into the Shâria' Kasr el-'Aini. Cairo slept as we passed through neat squares occupied by the darkened premises of Government ministries and schools. Not even a dog barked.

"Be reasonable!" I said weakly. "We are neither of us in any state for visiting—social or otherwise."

Smith answered me only with a look which would have silenced Hindenburg. Under his terse directions, we turned off from the Ministry of Education and entered the quiet quarter of large houses known as the Garden City, simply because they had gardens.

"Stop," he ordered. "This is it."

We drew up before iron railings. Through surrounding trees, I could dimly make out a sizeable mansion, built in an ugly Baroque style, with a surfeit of pillars and cup-shaped balconies. Nayland Smith threw open the door on his side of the car.

"Wait for me," he directed. "I may be some time, but wait, anyway."

"Smith!" I protested. "It must be three o'clock!"

"You may come with me," he ground out, "or stay in the car."

He strode off towards the ornate portico and I, perforce, followed. Catching up with him, I snatched at his sleeve.

"Have a care," I said urgently. "You will find yourself in the glasshouse!"*

Smith shook off my restraining hand and pressed the electric bell push repeatedly, at the same time beating on the panels with his fist until, presently, we heard footsteps, and a voice cried:

"Shut up! Shut up! You'll wake the bloody 'ouse!"

The door was opened by a man ridiculously clad in slippers and an army trench coat, carrying an oil lamp. As he lifted it to shine on our faces, he oddly reminded me of the gatekeeper in *Macbeth*.

"Colonel Smith!" he gasped. "It is, ain't it?"

I recognized the orderly who had driven General Fernshawe to our rendezvous at the Pyramids.

"Correct!" rapped Smith. "And I must see the general at once. Get him!"

"Oh, my Gawd, sir! 'E's in bed and asleep—I 'ope."

"Get him up, or I'll drag him out with my own hands!"

A look at my friend's face convinced the orderly that he meant it.

"This way, sir," he said hastily. "This way."

He led us along a corridor to a room appointed as a study, switched on the lights, and withdrew, closing the door behind him. I remembered from what Smith had told me that General Fernshawe had taken over the place as his personal headquarters from the prosperous owner of a German restaurant, now accommodated elsewhere. The massive furnishings were reminiscent of Potsdam, and a framed portrait of Wilhelm II still decorated one wall. Displaying a sense of humour with which I would hardly have credited him, Fernshawe had not removed it but hung a portrait of King George V beside it.

From some upper part of the house came a confused sound of bull-like roaring, succeeded by bangs and thumps. Smith grinned mischievously. Several minutes passed; then the door of the study was hurled unceremoniously open and General Fernshawe appeared, wearing a gaudy silk dressing gown—a formidably angry figure, but sadly devoid of dignity, with streaks of greying hair plastered down over a scalp as red as his face. He stared at us with bulging eyes, and I realised that we, in our torn and dishevelled clothes, made no better impression upon him.

When he spoke, his voice was a snarl, rumbling through his huge moustache. But, for the sake of clarity, I will hereafter desist from

*British Army slang for a military prison.

any attempt to reproduce his speech as we heard it.

"What—what is the meaning of this, Colonel?"

"That is what I am here to ask you," countered Smith. "We have been in the hands of Fu Manchu and narrowly escaped with our lives—"

"What!"

"I cannot blame you for that, but you have made fools of us in his eyes—and that I resent most of all. You have lied to us! You told me that those men were couriers!"

"No," answered Fernshawe stiffly. "It was *you* who assumed that they were."

"And you allowed me to believe it, which I call tantamount to a lie!" Smith faced up to his angry superior with such scant respect that I feared for the outcome. "Well, I have news for you, General. Richard Brooker has not been kidnapped. He escaped in the confusion during the fire at the Hotel Iskander and now, if he still lives, he is in hiding—not from Dr. Fu Manchu, of whom he has probably never heard, but from *you!*"

Fernshawe's whole frame seemed to sag, giving him the absurd appearance of a partially deflated balloon.

"Why—why do you say that?" he stammered.

"Because Brooker is of German extraction and was there to meet the man whom you are holding at the Kasr en-Nil—a German agent, named Kurt Lehmann, as I suspect you already know."

"I did not know," said Fernshawe thickly. "But—but I feared it. . . ." He walked behind the desk and slumped heavily into his chair, resting his head on his hands. "Oh, my God!"

I looked at Smith, who shrugged eloquently. The general was obviously a badly shaken man. Straightening himself like a victim of arthritis, he stood up again, crossed to a cupboard, and took out a glass and a bottle of port wine—then, as an afterthought, added two more glasses and, placing them upon the desk, filled all three. His hand trembled and the neck of the bottle clattered on the rims, spilling dark splashes on the finely leathered surface.

"Sit down, gentlemen," he said. "You have been through a harrowing experience, and I owe you more of an explanation than I dare give you."

Smith picked up two of the glasses and passed one to me, setting the other on the small walnut table between our chairs, and accepting the peace offering with reservations.

General Fernshawe reseated himself and drank deeply, then

opened a drawer and produced a small sheet of paper.

"We had no clue to the identity of the man who has lost his memory," he said, "but we found this on him."

He handed it to me, since I was the closer. The paper was stiff, curiously resembling papyrus, and bore two lines of typescript set below a stylised Chinese ideograph.

Your purpose is known. Leave Egypt within forty-eight hours, or your life is forfeit.

"I see," said Smith slowly. "As a trained espionage agent, Kurt Lehmann would certainly have recognized the Great Seal of the Si Fan. So *that* is how he knew who had struck him down—and this is the evidence on which I was sent for."

We were all silent for a moment. Smith's hand went automatically to his pocket, searching vainly for the pipe which he had left in my study, followed by an impatient gesture as he remembered.

"General," he said quietly, "I understand your reluctance to confide in me beyond the limits of necessity. But it may be easier for you if I tell you what you are afraid to tell me. Professor Richard Brooker is the inventor of a device known by the fanciful name of the Midnight Sun, which he intended to sell to the Germans."

Fernshawe shook his head. "No, it is worse than that. The secret is not his to sell. The Midnight Sun is the code name of a Government project, of which Professor Brooker has been in charge. We had no reason to distrust him. He has no known connections with Germany, and does not even speak German. His father died before he was born. But blood will tell, I suppose."

Pausing to refill his glass for the second time, he drank down half the contents at a gulp, glanced at me, and raised the bottle interrogatively. But I smiled politely and declined. It was not an hour at which I could relish vintage port, though, to the general, it was evidently as whisky to most others.

"Professor Brooker asked for leave to come up to Cairo for a medical appointment, and to be accompanied by his chief assistant and friend, Adrian Crawford, as he had several times done in the past. He is not a young man, and is in poor health. My office made the arrangements. But it was not until the day after they had failed to keep them that we learned of the fire at the Hotel Iskander, and later still when we found that they had removed, and brought with them, Government property to which they had access."

"I see," repeated Smith. "That, at least, makes some sense, and I am obliged to you. I have only one further question to ask—one which I have asked before. What are these papers which Brooker has stolen? What is this Government project?"

General Fernshawe hesitated so long that I thought he would not answer. But, at length, he turned, not to Smith, but to me.

"You have heard of the solar energy experiments at Meadi?"

"Yes," I said. "I believe they were started in 1912. But I understood that they had recently been abandoned."

"That is what you were expected to understand." Fernshawe favoured me with a sly smile, and turned back to Smith. "I am sorry, Colonel Smith, but I cannot say more."

I could see that my companion was still far from satisfied.

"Very well," he said finally. "The question, then, comes back to this: Where did Professor Brooker go? And how? Had he any friends in the vicinity?"

"None that we know of."

"And you told me, previously, that neither he nor his partner was well acquainted with Cairo."

"That is correct. Both had been in Egypt for more than two years, but they rarely left the project."

"H'm!" Smith's eyebrows knit in a prodigious frown. "The fire occurred before midnight. . . . He may have gone to some other hotel. But what after that? Could he speak Arabic?"

"No, certainly not. Crawford could, to some extent—which was why he usually accompanied the professor on his visits to Cairo."

"But at the time of the professor's escape from the fire, Crawford was already dead," I added.

Nayland Smith drew a deep breath.

"Brooker has been missing for a month now," he said, "and even

Dr. Fu Manchu thought that you had recaptured him. I'm afraid there is only one likely explanation. He has been murdered, and your precious dispatch case thrown on the nearest rubbish heap as soon as it was found to contain nothing more than papers."

This was clearly a conclusion which Fernshawe did not enjoy.

"In that event," he said pointedly, "you have come here to no purpose. If Richard Brooker is not in his hands, we have no quarrel with this mad Chinaman of yours."

Smith, in his turn, hesitated and I saw that it was on the tip of his tongue to ask to be relieved of his mission and sent back to Burma. But I knew also that, while any chance of coming to grips with our ancient enemy existed, he would never give up the pursuit.

"You make a grave mistake," he said quietly. "Fu Manchu is a greater threat to civilisation than Kaiser Wilhelm."

"The Yellow Peril?" sneered General Fernshawe.

"Dr. Fu Manchu *is* the Yellow Peril! It is not China that we have to fear, but the Si Fan—an organisation of outcasts and malcontents, committed to the destruction of all law and order as we know it, and led by a man with the scientific genius of a future age. Every defeat which we inflict upon Germany, every defeat which the Germans inflict upon us, is a victory for Dr. Fu Manchu!"

I doubt that I had ever heard Smith speak more passionately, but his words made little impression on our host.

"We have other things to do," he replied curtly, "than to help Scotland Yard clear up their unfinished business."

"You forget, General," said Smith earnestly, "that Fu Manchu is also looking for Professor Brooker, and, if he is alive, may find him before we do. He will be assisted by all the criminals to whom our rule is obnoxious—the slavers, the drug traffickers, the corrupt officials whom we have deposed, every thief and beggar who will do anything for as little as a *nuss-faddah* excepting an honest day's work—in short, the very people among whom Brooker must have taken refuge."

Fernshawe looked thoughtful and chewed at his moustache.

"There is something in what you say," he admitted. "Let us, then, leave things as they are. You may continue your efforts to locate Dr. Fu Manchu, without prying into military matters which do not concern you, and we will give you the same help as before."

I was not aware that we had had much help. But little more was to be said just then, and, since we did not enjoy each other's company, the meeting broke up shortly afterwards.

The first streaks of dawn were in the sky as we came out upon the road, to find the car where we had left it—Achmed asleep at the wheel, and Greba still seated beside him.

"Oh!" she exclaimed. "I'm so glad you're back! I've been so scared. . . ."

"Why?" I asked, smiling. "Did you think General Fernshawe would have us locked up?"

"No. It was . . . something which happened."

"Happened?" demanded Smith. "What?"

Greba swallowed audibly, looking embarrassed.

"About half an hour after you'd gone inside, a woman walked up from behind the car, leaned right in, and spoke to me. I recognized her voice immediately. It was the woman who called on the telephone!"

"She spoke to you? What did she say?"

"She said—" Greba broke off in confusion and blushed furiously. "Oh! How can I tell you?"

"You must!" insisted Smith sternly.

"She—she said, 'I did not save him for you, little fool! Be careful how you cross my path.' Then she walked on quickly down the road and disappeared. Oh, how dare she!"

Nayland Smith glanced at me and laughed.

"Your fault, Petrie," he said sardonically. "It is most unlikely that Fu Manchu's daughter would permit you to make love to her, but she expected you to try!"

10

AN ODD CASE OF HEATSTROKE

We returned to Zamalek, tired and depressed, and collapsed into armchairs while Greba fussed about us with iodine and sticking plaster, tending our minor hurts.

"If Brooker was working for the Germans," I said, yawning, "wouldn't he most likely have gone to them after escaping from the fire? They must, surely, have more than one agent here."

"No doubt—but if his only contact had been through Kurt Lehmann, he had no idea how to get in touch with them."

"But where, then, could he have gone?"

"Where indeed?" echoed Smith. "And how? He could only have left Cairo by train, and, since he spoke no Arabic, he couldn't even buy a ticket without going to Thomas Cook's."

"Never mind," said Greba, closing her medical box with a snap. "*You're* not going anywhere till those cuts heal."

She seemed, unfortunately, to be right, for, the following day, I found that I could not put my shoes on and was forced to cancel a tentative engagement to lunch with Rex Engelbach. Lacking more useful employment, I spent the afternoon going through a stack of old magazines and trying to find the photograph of Professor Brooker, published at the time of his award from the Royal Society. Eventually, I succeeded, but, to my disappointment, there was no accompanying article—merely a few lines of print beneath.

"Apparently," I said, "he received the Rumford medal—which is for outstanding discoveries in heat and light—on the strength of some erudite work on the nature of sunspots."

"Well," muttered Smith, "that appears, at least, to check with what Fernshawe told us. What *is* this solar energy project? Do you know anything about it?"

"Only what I have heard. It was the biggest experiment of its kind ever made anywhere. They had over ten thousand square feet of reflecting surfaces, more than two hundred feet long—"

"Yes, but could it have any military application?" he interrupted impatiently. "I believe Archimedes once employed burning glasses to set fire to the sails of a Roman fleet, and somebody or other in the Old Testament ordered his men to burnish their shields, so as to blind the enemy, but . . ."

"Smith, you are too warlike," I said, laughing. "It does not have to be a weapon in order to have military significance. A limitless source of power would be of as much value to Fu Manchu or the Germans as it would be to us."

"I suppose so. Did they have much success with it?"

"Very little, I'm afraid. I think the most they managed was to run a steam engine for a few hours."

"H'm!" he grunted. "With the amount of sun that we get in England, it would take them a year to boil an egg!"

Turning away, he stood for a while at the window, peering out into the little courtyard, where Hassan was making half-hearted attempts to sweep the sandy dust from our doorstep with a palm branch.

"Mystery upon mystery," he said savagely, "and half of it unnecessary! Brooker came up to Cairo on the excuse that he wanted to see a doctor, and accommodation was reserved for him at Shepheard's. But, if he was working at Meadi, which is less than a half hour's train ride, why the devil did he need to stay at a hotel?"

I could think of no reply, but clearly we were far from receiving all the co-operation that we had a right to expect.

Once again, time passed uselessly. We felt tolerably sure that Fu Manchu was not in Cairo, and though we knew that his daughter had been there recently, the police could find no trace of her.

Midway through the week, I lunched at the St. James's with Engelbach, to whom we had promised an explanation of our escapade at the Step Pyramid, fearing that he would ask questions which I dared not answer. However, as soon as I described the apartment in which we had seen Dr. Fu Manchu, he promptly lost all interest in our abduction, declaring that this was not the blue-tiled chamber discovered by Lepsius, and ending by becoming quite displeased with me because I flatly refused to go down and help him to find it.*

Nayland Smith tramped restlessly about the house, scattering spent matches and smouldering shreds of tobacco to the detriment of my carpet, and tugging at the lobe of his left ear till I feared he would do it a mischief. Meantime, in France, the guns boomed their ceaseless song of hate, while the fleshless fingers of Death chalked up fresh figures on the scoreboard of history—British: 300,000; Germans: 200,000—and, somewhere in Egypt, Fu Manchu smiled. . . .

Thus the week ended and, when a hint of action came at last, it was neither from the police nor from Army Intelligence, but in the unexpected form of a telephone call from my professional acquaintance Major Jack Lindsay of the R.A.M.C., to whom neither of us had spoken since our meeting at the Kasr en-Nil.

"I am wondering," he said diffidently, "if you and Colonel Smith would meet me for a drink at Shepheard's to-night. One of our young officers has been killed—murdered, I believe—and I don't see how anybody but your Dr. Fu Manchu could have done it."

"How did he die?" I asked quickly.

"Well, that's what I'd like to know! At the moment, the best answer I can give you is a singular kind of heatstroke. . . ."

How eagerly, and with what impatience, did we await the coming of nightfall! The sun was scarcely below the horizon when, seated side by side in an 'arabîyeh, we drove through the Shâria' Abu el-Ela, with its innumerable alleyways of tiny native shops and cafés, and on into a quarter of brightly lighted shopfronts, restaurants, and theatres, where, as some say, prosperous New Cairo offers a prospect of Paris rebuilt on the Nile.

Even in wartime, the world-famous terrace of Shepheard's Hotel continued to be the meeting point of the transient, cosmopolitan throng which here passes for Society—though army tunics now prevailed over dinner jackets and the strident voices of American ladies were stilled—but we had no difficulty in locating Major Lindsay. As we mounted the steps, he rose quickly from a cane-topped table by the railings and waved to us. We exchanged greetings and sat down.

"How is your patient at the Kasr en-Nil?" I asked.

Lindsay smiled, a shade whimsically. "Kurt Lehmann has ceased

---

*It was ultimately discovered by C. M. Firth in 1924, Fu Manchu's agents having in the interim removed the table and chairs. [Ed.]

to be my patient. The man was a spy, but we can hardly shoot him for what he did in a former existence, as it were. So they've transferred him to the Citadel, where the officer prisoners are confined, and started teaching him to speak."

I wondered whether they were teaching him English or German.

A white-robed waiter came to take our order, and, till drinks had been placed before us, we postponed our conversation, so that it might proceed uninterrupted. Unlike Fernshawe, who had chosen the solitude of the desert, Lindsay had preferred this populous rendezvous, where, beyond the range of our table, overhearing was impossible. At the level of our feet, a swarm of ragged hawkers clamoured about the railings, holding up bright scraps of jewellery, spurious antiques, and bunches of sweet-smelling jasmine, the feverish din of their voices punctuated by the sharp, staccato sounds of horses' hooves and motor horns in the Shâria' Kamel.

Smith loaded his pipe methodically and lighted it with unusual care, using only one match. Then:

"Who is the victim of this new outrage?" he inquired.

"A junior officer," answered the major. "Reginald Courtney Desmond, age twenty-six, rank, captain."

"British Army Intelligence?"

"No. Royal Engineers."

Smith glanced at me and frowned.

"Then there seems no obvious connection with Fu Manchu."

"None," said Major Lindsay, with a slightly malicious smile. "But let me tell you what happened. Captain Desmond had come up from Akaba, on a week's leave. This was his first visit to Egypt, and he wanted to do some sightseeing."

"Then he was really just a tourist," I put in.

"Quite! A tourist in uniform, with no motive but to see the sights and have a good time." Lindsay sipped at his drink and cleared his throat. "Well, on the night of his arrival in Cairo, he was lucky enough—as he thought—to fall in with a brother officer he had known in cadet school, who agreed to show him around, although they were not close friends. So, next morning, they began in the usual fashion by visiting the Pyramids. Then they decided to go on to Abûsir and Saqqara. . . ."

I shuddered involuntarily. Even now, that name sent an icy trickle down my spine.

"They obtained camels and proceeded by the direct route across the desert"—Lindsay flashed me a quick look—"which, as you know, would take two or three hours. However, they had gone only a mile or so when Desmond all at once tumbled from the saddle and fell to the ground. He was, incidentally, an experienced rider and, for the past few months, had been galloping about Northern Arabia, blowing up railway lines, so that there was absolutely no reason for him to lose his seat in such a manner. He gave no cry, and the incident occurred so swiftly and silently that his companion, who was riding a little ahead, remained unaware that anything was amiss till, chancing to look back, he saw the camel wandering riderless and Captain Desmond lying face downwards on the sand."

"A minute, if you please," interjected Smith. "If his friend had his back turned, how do you know exactly what happened?"

"There were several witnesses—some who were also out riding, but none closer than a hundred yards," replied Major Lindsay. "His friend rode back quickly, of course, dismounted, and was shocked to find Desmond quite dead, apparently without a mark on him. Unlikely though it seemed, it could only be assumed that he had suffered what is commonly known as a heart attack."

"But which rarely terminates so abruptly," I added.

My colleague smiled and nodded. "Exactly so. Yesterday, I had the unpleasant job of performing a post-mortem—the results of which have led me to communicate with you. On making a preliminary examination of the body, I observed a tiny spot of inflammation, like an insect bite, situated roughly midway between the shoulder blades. Something—call it an instinct, if you like—prompted me to inspect the victim's clothes, and on the corresponding part of the shirt I found a minute hole, closely resembling a cigarette burn. A further examination quickly revealed—though totally failed to explain—the cause of death. In simple, non-technical terms, the condition of the heart, together with the intervening organs and tissue, was precisely as if the man had been stabbed with a white-hot needle!"

"Good Lord!" murmured Smith, and Major Lindsay grinned in my direction.

"You see the problem? Since there is reliable testimony that no one was within striking distance, he could not have been stabbed with anything! The inference was, then, that he had been shot. But there was no trace of a projectile, and no exit wound. Fantastic though it seemed, I was forced to imagine something like a bolt of pure energy—"

"And not only that!" broke in Smith. "My knowledge of anatomy is rudimentary, but I gather that the wound was inflicted from behind and at a relatively steep angle. Now, the head of a man seated on a camel is at least ten feet above the ground. . . ."

He paused, looking meaningly at our informant and allowing him to draw the conclusion.

"Yes," said Lindsay. "You know the place as well as I do. Where had it been fired from? Judging by the angle of the wound, it could only have been from a point halfway up the Great Pyramid!"

Smith nodded. "Or, possibly, the Second Pyramid, though I grant you that the other is easier to climb."

"But," I gasped, "that would mean that this diabolical weapon has a range of two miles!"

"Apart from which," added Lindsay, "it operates silently and invisibly. Nothing was heard or seen. I thought at once of Kurt Lehmann, who slipped from one life into another with the name of Fu Manchu upon his lips. Who other than he might have such a thing?"

"H'm! Reasonable," agreed Smith, frowning, "but rather a case of what Petrie calls negative evidence. For want of a more likely suspect, we turn to Fu Manchu. But, at the moment, I can see no possible motive. Do you have the name of the officer who was riding with Desmond at the time of his death?"

"Yes, I have it somewhere. . . ." Major Lindsay produced a large notebook, bulging with odd slips of paper thrust between the leaves. "But, as I have told you, he did not see his friend fall."

"True. But it is possible that he knows something about him which would account for Fu Manchu's interest."

"Yes, perhaps."

Lindsay thumbed through his untidy notebook, scattering loose papers, which included a few currency notes of trivial denomination. One slipped from the table and drifted between the railings, promoting a scuffle among the hawkers.

"Here we are!" announced Lindsay triumphantly, finding the page which he wanted. "He is a Captain Holt-Fortescue—an Intelligence officer, now stationed at the Citadel."

Something in the name was vaguely familiar, and I looked at Smith, who smiled mysteriously.

"Ah!" he said. "Your guess seems to have been a good one, after all, Major. Captain Holt-Fortescue is one of the two young fools who was seen going about the town with Fu Manchu's daughter. We will see him again to-morrow—and this time, by God, we will get something out of him!"

11

AT THE CITADEL

East of the Ezbekîyeh Gardens, New Cairo gives place to the old. Past the corner of the Midan Ataba, our army staff car, en route to the Citadel, merged with a tumult of vehicles and pedestrians—black-robed women bearing loads upon their heads, two-wheeled donkey carts, and flat, four-wheeled drays drawn by a pair of horses or, sometimes, by a horse incongruously harnessed with a donkey.

Since our business was official—a matter of discipline—we had been graciously provided with transport. Our driver cursed, and braked to avoid collision with a runaway cow, hotly pursued by a boy on a bicycle. Shouts and bellows faded into the bedlam of traffic.

"What, I wonder, can this devilish contraption be?" mused Smith. "It's hard to imagine a thing powerful enough to be effective at such a range, yet small enough to be lugged up the Great Pyramid."

"Perhaps," I said slowly, "it works by reflection through some unthinkable system of lenses. Consider the full force of the sun concentrated to a point less than an inch in diameter. . . ."

Smith nodded brusquely. "Something, no doubt, dreamed up by Henrik Eriksen—the genius in electrostatics who was supposedly drowned in a fjord, two or three years ago. I strongly suspect that he is now in China—that it is he whom we have to curse for that explosive fireball which nearly burst our eardrums. I can't say," he added sourly, "that I am enjoying this new phase of Fu Manchu's activities. He is by way of becoming a pyromaniac!"

"Would you prefer his exotic drugs and venomous reptiles?" I inquired, smiling.

"I should prefer neither!" he grunted.

I glanced out at the street of small shops and high, plaster-fronted houses through which we were passing. Occasionally, where an upper floor was built out over the pavement, open archways made dim caverns in which stall keepers traded their wares by candlelight. It was Sunday afternoon, but in Moslem Egypt, churchbells yielded to the voices of the *mueddinîn,* echoing in relay across the city.

"What sort of man is this Captain Holt-Fortescue?" I asked curiously.

I had not been present at their earlier interview.

"A nonentity," said my friend. "The typical, well-to-do young imp who would have a name like that and get a job in British Intelligence."

At the end of the street, the shallow domes and pencil-thin minarets of a Turkish-style mosque marked the end of our journey. It stood high above the prisonlike walls of the Citadel, the ancient fortress of Saladin, our old enemy of the Crusades—now, by an odd turn of fate, the stronghold of an infidel army, and as dark with the wickedness of history as the Tower of London.

Though I had seen it often, I had never had previous occasion to go inside. We entered by the Bab el-Azab, crossing a complex of courts and passages—wherein Mahomet 'Ali, the pious builder of the mosque above, had treacherously murdered four hundred and seventy Mamelukes, to make himself lord of Egypt—and were conducted through a yard enclosed by cloisteresque arches to an upstairs office, made ready for our use and simply furnished. Our khaki-clad guide saluted and left us.

Nayland Smith seated himself at the desk, waving me to one of the two chairs set before it.

"Sit there, Petrie," he directed, "and, when our man shows up, feel free to ask any questions you like."

I sat down as instructed and, while we waited, stared idly around. The room was a cheerless place, the drab walls painted in eau-de-nil—a colour which, for some reason, the British Government seems to favour—and indifferently cooled by an electric fan which buzzed like a beehive. Through the open window, I could hear the voice of a drill sergeant bawling orders—though whether in English or in Turkish, as of yore, I was unable to determine.

Smith took his pipe from his pocket—a reflex action—contemplated it ruefully, and replaced it.

"No," he muttered. "I suppose we shouldn't smoke."

Even as he spoke, the door opened, and a slim, flaxen-haired young man entered. He saluted and came stiffly to attention.

"You sent for me, sir?"

"At ease," ordered Smith. "You may sit down."

"With your permission, sir," said Captain Holt-Fortescue, "I pre-fer to stand."

I eyed him curiously, putting him down as a run-of-the-mill prod-uct of Sandhurst—pallid, breathing too rapidly, and clearly on the defensive.

"As you please," answered my companion. "Captain, I have sum-moned you here to repeat the question which I asked you before. What were your relations with the Chinese woman whom we are seeking?"

"My answer must be the same, sir. There was no such woman."

"I cannot accept that." Smith spoke in a deceptively mild tone. "The situation has become serious, and, though you may have rea-sons for your silence, it is imperative for me to learn the truth."

"I—I am sorry that you doubt my word, sir."

Holt-Fortescue licked his lips nervously, but was adamant in his defiance. I looked at Nayland Smith—saw his grey eyes hard and angry, and knew that his patience would not hold out much longer.

"Captain," I said earnestly, "a man, your friend Captain Des-mond, has been killed, and you were the last to see him alive."

Captain Holt-Fortescue, who had so far cast not a glance in my direction, stared at me in amazement.

"What!" he protested. "*Killed*? I was told that he died of a heat-stroke!"

"He was murdered!" said Smith. "And you are responsible! Will you continue to deny that you know this woman—even though you were seen in her company and identified by waiters at two different hotels, both of whom know you by sight?"

"I can only say that they are mistaken, sir. One officer in uniform looks very much like another."

Smith's chair creaked as he sat bolt upright, and he brought his fist crashing down upon the desk.

"Quite! A fact to which you owe your miserable life! You young imbecile! Don't you realise that Captain Desmond was murdered in mistake for you? In some way or other, you have incurred the enmity of the most dangerous woman in Egypt!"

I started slightly, this evident explanation of Captain Desmond's death having somehow failed to occur to me. Holt-Fortescue paled till he looked altogether ghastly. His hands shook, and I thought that Smith had won his point. But after a brief hesitation, the captain recovered his composure and drew himself up stiffly.

"I am sorry, sir," he repeated, "but I have no more to say. Have I your leave to go now?"

"Yes, go!" cried Smith angrily.

Captain Holt-Fortescue saluted again and withdrew, closing the door quietly behind him. Smith leapt up and began pacing the room with long, furious strides before our visitor had barely had time to descend the stairs.

"He is lying," I said. "I never saw a man who looked more guilty."

"Lying?" he returned. "Of course he is lying! But what can I do? I would willingly have him locked up in a cell and hammer the truth out of him—but this is the British Army, not the Turkish. If only—"

He got no further, for at that instant a clamour broke out below—a confusion of shouting and of heavy army boots pounding to and fro. Smith and I looked at each other, and the same thought crossed our minds as we hurried to the window and leaned out. Soldiers were running this way and that, pointing in opposite directions, while, almost immediately beneath us, a dozen or more were assembled in a tight knot, like a Rugby football scrum.

"What is going on down there?" shouted my friend.

A Cockney voice, anomalous in that setting, shouted back.

"Cap'n 'Olt-For'escue's bin shot, sir!"

12

THE WAYWARD GODDESS

Smith tore open the door and we raced down the stairs. As we emerged from the covered walk beneath, my foot struck against something which rolled away across the sun-drenched stones—an officer's peaked cap. Smith stooped swiftly and snatched it up.

"Look!" he said.

I looked and saw a small, round hole just under the brim. The edges were smouldering. Holt-Fortescue lay flat on his back and someone was bending over him, trying to unfasten his collar.

"Leave him to me!" I said, dropping to my knees.

I detected a sweet, acrid smell of singed hair and observed a livid red furrow running across the crown of his head. I put my ear to his chest, and found him to be breathing.

"He is not dead," I announced. "Only stunned."

Behind me, a man with corporal's stripes on his sleeve—he of the Cockney voice—was talking excitedly to Smith.

"I was right beside 'im, sir! 'E went down like a log—I never 'eard nuffink! Where'd it come from, sir?"

"Up there," answered Smith.

He pointed to the tall, graceful minarets of the adjacent mosque, towering above us.

The victim was already groaning and moving his limbs feebly. I assisted him to sit up, and he fell back against my arm, peering wildly about him and gasping like a man half drowned.

"Stand away there!" ordered Smith, clearing the crowd. "Let's get him to his feet and back up to the office."

Together we lugged him upright. Holt-Fortescue was as yet unable to support himself, but we got his arms over our shoulders and, between us, half dragged, half carried him to the stairs. With three of us jammed into the narrow stairwell, it was not easy to ascend, but we managed, the Cockney corporal trailing up behind and helping to lift the injured man's feet upon the steps.

"Get me a first aid kit!" I directed.

"And a bottle of whisky!" added Smith.

"Right, sir! On the double!"

We eased our patient into a chair and into a reclining position with his legs extended, while I made a more detailed examination. He was conscious now, but muttering incoherently.

"How is he?" inquired Smith.

"In the same state that you might be," I said shortly, "if you'd had a red-hot iron laid on your head."

I heard heavy footfalls clumping up the stairs, two at a time, and the corporal burst in, carrying a bottle in one hand and a tin box marked with a red cross in the other.

"Couldn't find no whisky, sir," he panted. "Will this do?"

He held up a half-emptied bottle of Three Star.

"Probably better."

I took the box from him and busied myself with surgical scissors and a burn dressing. The corporal's left-hand pocket was bulging with a half-pint tumbler. He hauled it out and, still holding the bottle in his right hand, extracted the cork with his teeth.

"Just a minute," I warned.

Holt-Fortescue's skin had taken on a waxen hue, and he was trembling so violently that I feared he might go into shock, in which case alcohol was counter-indicated. I checked his pulse, finding it too rapid but strong.

"All right," I said. "Give it to him."

I thrust the glass into the captain's hands, keeping my fingers clasped around his while he drank, since otherwise he would have dropped it. I will not malign Holt-Fortescue by calling him a coward, but he was understandably in a bad condition of fright.

"Pull yourself together!" I said sternly. "You are not seriously hurt. But," I added viciously, "you will probably have a bald streak across your scalp for the rest of your life."

"An inch lower, and it would have seared through what little brain you've got," snapped Nayland Smith. "Well, I warned you. That was the second attempt."

Holt-Fortescue looked up at him with a blank expression of horror on his face.

"No, sir," he whispered. "It—it was the *third*! Oh, God! What can I do?"

"You can begin by confiding in me." Smith glanced aside at the corporal, who stood watching us curiously. "That's all, Corporal. You may leave us now."

The man saluted and retired.

"You—you don't understand, sir," stammered Holt-Fortescue, regarding my friend with a pathetic look of entreaty. "My father commands a regiment in France. If I were disgraced—court-martialled—I believe he would kill himself. . . ."

"You are wrong," said Smith quietly. "I do understand."

Taking the chair which I had earlier occupied, he turned it to face Holt-Fortescue and sat down in it, indicating by a jerk of his head that I should take his place at the desk.

"Forget this uniform that I am wearing," he continued. "If you have committed no crime in the eyes of the law, I give you my word that no entry will be made in your service record. Now answer me frankly. When, and how, did you first meet that woman?"

Holt-Fortescue hesitated an instant longer. Then:

"It was . . . more than two months ago," he replied, "at a costume ball at Shepheard's Hotel." Though his voice was unsteady, it gained strength as he talked. "She was wearing an Ancient Egyptian costume which some of the ladies considered rather improper—though, personally, I could see nothing the matter with it. I danced with her a few times, and we arranged to meet again."

"You knew that she was Chinese," challenged Smith.

"Yes, sir. But what of it?" Holt-Fortescue faced him with a brief resurgence of his defensive manner. "We are not at war with China. She—she told me that her name was Kwan Yin."

Smith raised his eyebrows and smiled.

"Somewhat unlikely," he murmured. "Kwan Yin is the Chinese goddess of mercy."

Two bright spots of colour appeared on the young man's pale cheeks. Seated behind the desk, and feeling oddly like a judge advocate, I followed the conversation eagerly.

"What did you find out about her?" I asked impatiently.

"Very little, I'm afraid, sir. I took her out to dinner two or three times, once to a theatre, and once on a drive out to Heliopolis. She seemed to be very well off, but, apparently, she didn't live in Cairo. She was always at a hotel."

"And what did *she* find out about *you*?" queried Smith.

"Nothing at all, sir. She knew that I was with Army Intelligence, of course, but she never asked me anything about my work."

Nayland Smith frowned. "Not that you noticed, you mean. But a skilled agent can ask questions without appearing to. What did you tell her concerning Professor Brooker and his assistant?"

"Nothing, sir." Holt-Fortescue looked startled. "How could I, sir? I had never heard of either of them until I was instructed to make hotel reservations and buy rail tickets for them."

"Eh?" exclaimed Smith. "Rail tickets from Meadi?"

"No, sir," said Holt-Fortescue, in a puzzled tone of voice. "They were first-class return tickets from Luxor."

"Luxor?" I burst out. "But what were they doing there?"

"I'm sure I couldn't say, sir."

Smith shot me a quick glance and I realised that we could not pursue the subject, since we were clearly expected to be fully informed upon it.

"So this," he insisted relentlessly, "was the information which you passed on to your goddess!"

"No, sir. I didn't. I swear it. . . ." Holt-Fortescue ceased speaking and, all at once, became paler even than before. "Oh, my God!" he faltered. "In—in a way, perhaps I did. I told her that I couldn't see her that Sunday night, because I was to meet two distinguished visitors at the station and escort them to a hotel. But I didn't even mention their names."

"She already knew their names," said Smith tersely, "and, you may depend on it, she knew it was your job to make travel arrangements of that sort. Well—how did she take it?"

"In a manner which I thought quite unreasonable, sir. She became extremely angry, and said that, in that case, I need not attempt to see her again. Of course, I had to carry out my assignment. I went to the station, but, as you know, they didn't turn up. . . ."

"What did you do then?"

"Since I was not familiar with either gentleman, I thought that, somehow, I might not have seen them. So I went to Shepheard's Hotel and waited for them there. But after an hour, with no sign of them, I could only conclude that they had missed the train. I wasn't able to telephone to Luxor to find out if they'd been on it, because I didn't know exactly where they'd been staying."

"Did you report this to anybody?"

"No, sir—not then. Major Middleton, who had given me my instructions, was away for the weekend, and I didn't know whom else

I might get in touch with. There was no further train from Luxor till the next morning, so I just had to give it up. In the circumstances, I tried to phone Miss—er—Kwan Yin, and patch it up with her. She was at the Continental, but she refused to speak to me."

Nayland Smith nodded. "So you made your report at the office next day, and nothing more came of it till news was received about the fire at the Hotel Iskander."

"That's right, sir. But even then it didn't for a moment occur to me that the Chinese girl had anything to do with it. Why should it? Later, I went round to the Continental and tried again to make contact with her. But she had already left, and I neither saw nor heard any more of her till the day you asked me about her."

Holt-Fortescue sipped nervously at his brandy, looking anxiously at Smith, while I watched from my position at the desk, feeling rather disappointed—for, if this was the extent of the information which he had to give us, we had learned little. Silence ensued for some seconds. Then Smith leaned forward in his chair.

"Captain," he said, in a low, dangerous voice, "I believe you have told me the truth, but not all the truth. You have seen her again since I spoke to you."

Holt-Fortescue tried to sustain the regard of those cold, intransigent eyes and failed.

"Yes, sir," he said hopelessly. "I admit it. It was on Saturday—a week yesterday."

I started. Saturday! That was the day on which we had returned from our adventure at Saqqara—the day on which Greba had been accosted in the Garden City. . . .

"Tell me!" demanded Smith.

"It was late in the afternoon, sir, while I was on my way back here in a staff car, passing through the Shâria' Imad ed-Dîn. There were carts and donkeys mixed up with the traffic, and people walking about in the road, and we had almost come to a standstill when, just ahead, I saw her leaving one of the big shops, carrying some parcels. She got into a black limousine, and I ordered my driver to follow."

"Did you take the number?"

"Er—no, sir."

"No, I don't imagine you did!" said Smith acidly. "Go on."

"It was what they call a *hârem* car, with curtained windows, so she couldn't see us. We came down to the Nile, crossed the bridge, and turned off into the road leading to the Pyramids. I thought she might be heading for Mena House—she had stayed there once—but soon I saw that we were going clean out of the city. My driver got a bit anxious, because he had an appointment to pick up another officer and was afraid he might be late, but I told him to continue. We drove on for about half an hour, and finally reached Bedrasheyn."

This was the same route which we had taken, in reverse, on the way back from Saqqara.

"The car passed through the village," went on Holt-Fortescue, "and stopped just short of the river. She got out and began walking down to the bank. Her chauffeur—a fat, ugly Nubian in a white uniform—went with her, carrying her parcels. I got out too, determined to follow, and sent my driver back, telling him that I would find my own way home to Cairo. By the time I caught up with them, they were at the bank, just beyond which a *dahabîyeh* was moored. She had her back to me and was talking, in Arabic, to some of the crewmen. Though I couldn't understand what they were saying, I got the idea that she was not just a passenger, but the owner of the vessel."

"Describe it!"

"It was a big boat—the biggest I've seen of that sort—a hundred feet long, and very new-looking, all painted in white with gold trimmings. I saw the name *Nitocris* on the prow and just above it was an Egyptian symbol, like an eye."

"A quaint idea," commented my friend, smiling whimsically, "after the fashion of a traditional Chinese junk. What did you do?"

"It seemed that she was about to go aboard. But, before she could do so, I walked up to her and seized her by the arm. She was furious and I thought she would order her servants to throw me in the river. I said, 'You have got me into a lot of trouble, and I must talk to you. The authorities want you for questioning.' "

"And how did she respond?"

"Not as I expected. She smiled and said, 'So you mean they are going to hurt me, like they did in Shanghai. Well, you are an Intelligence officer. Come aboard with me, then, and do it yourself!' " Captain Holt-Fortescue stared at us both, groping desperately for a straw of defence and clutching at the empty tumbler so fiercely that I thought he would break it. "Why not, sir? After all, I still didn't know that she'd done anything criminal—you didn't tell me— but I knew that you wanted to see her."

"Quite!" rapped Smith. "But you didn't know what I intended to ask her. The plain fact is that you threatened her in order to further your own despicable ends. What occurred?"

"She—she owed me something," muttered Holt-Fortescue. "She took me into a huge salon full of armchairs and couches—there was even a piano in it!—with vases and bowls of flowers everywhere. Then she said"—he flushed—"she said, 'You can *question* me in here, if you like, but if you want me to be naked, we had better go into my cabin.' "

"A typical offer!" I said, reminiscently. "Did she . . .?"

"She was just making fun of me." The young man's flush deepened to a turkey-cock red. "Good God! You don't imagine I'd—"

"No matter!" interrupted Smith. "I don't care what you did. All I am anxious to know is the outcome of this interview."

"I—I don't know, sir."

"What do you mean, you don't know?"

"Just that, sir." The nervousness had gone from his voice, but the glazed look of horror had come back upon the captain's features. "I—I think we had a drink and a cigarette. Perhaps we even had dinner together. She must have doped me with something. I don't remember passing out or waking up, but all at once it was hours later—the moon was up, and, somehow, I was stumbling along a rough track between the fields, a long way inland. . . ."

"Give him another drink, Petrie," recommended Smith, stretching out his arm for the bottle.

"I—I couldn't seem to think," resumed Holt-Fortescue. "I didn't understand how or why I was there, but just kept going, like walking in my sleep—and then, presently, I realised that . . . that *something* was after me!"

"You mean that you saw something?"

"Not immediately, sir. In a way I can't explain, I just *knew* it was there before I saw it. I started to walk faster, glancing back all the time, and then, at last, I did see it. Oh, my God! It wasn't an animal, and it wasn't human! It was a hundred yards behind me—bounding from side to side of the path, from one patch of shadow into another—about the same size as a man, but sometimes it went on two feet and sometimes on all fours—"

Holt-Fortescue gulped at his refilled glass and, after a moment, continued:

"Every time I looked back, it was nearer, and—and I knew it meant to kill me. I took to my heels and ran. There was a small plantation of sugar cane ahead, on my left. I dodged around it, and made off across country. And then I heard the thing coming at me, crossways, straight through the sugar cane—and you know how close the stuff grows, sir—crashing its way through like a tank. I made another fifty yards or so, too scared to watch where I was going, and fell headlong into an irrigation ditch with about a foot of water at the bottom. I thought, then, that I was done for, but it saved my life."

Smith nodded. "The creature lost the scent."

"Yes, sir! For a long time, while I lay flat on my face, I heard it rooting around on the bank, grunting and snuffling, and making dreadful, half-articulate sounds, like an animal trying to speak. But it couldn't find me, and finally it went away. I lay there till I felt sure it was gone. Then I crawled out and went on across the fields till I reached a village—Mitrahîneh, I think it was. Everybody was asleep, and it was ages before I could find any transport to take me back to Cairo. It was dawn before I arrived."

"However," said Smith, frowning, "you still did not feel it necessary to report this incident!"

"No, sir. But I'd had a bad scare, and my uniform was ruined. I had scheduled duties to perform, but, as soon as I was able, I got hold of a car and went down to Bedrasheyn, meaning to have that woman arrested. But when I got there the ship had already sailed, so I decided that there was nothing for it but to give it up—"

"Realising that you could not pursue the matter without revealing your own part in it!" Nayland Smith stared at the speaker with a contempt which he found hard to conceal. "Well, Captain, I shall keep my word, and this conversation shall remain between ourselves. But your conduct has been less than that of an officer and a gentleman, and the penalty may be your life. We have reason to believe that the woman upon whom you tried to force your attentions is none other than the daughter of Dr. Fu Manchu, and, if she has decided upon your death, I would advise you to volunteer for active service in France—for you will be safer in the trenches than in Cairo!"

13

OUR QUEST BEGINS

By six o'clock that evening, Nayland Smith had converted my study into a campaign headquarters, busying himself with stamp paper, and decorating one wall with a map which stretched almost from floor to ceiling. The map of Egypt is, I imagine, the only one of its kind—ten times as long as it is broad—for, as Herodotus remarked twenty-five centuries ago, Egypt is the Nile.

"We know now how Professor Brooker escaped from Cairo," said my friend. "He had the return half of a ticket from Luxor!"

"But what on earth was he doing there?" I asked.

Smith shrugged. "The fact that his base was at Meadi doesn't mean that he couldn't have had business elsewhere. Therefore, Fu Manchu and his daughter have split forces and are now making their way up the river, seeking news of a madman with a briefcase chained to his wrist. He is probably concentrating on the west bank, where the railway line runs two thirds of the distance, while she employs the *dahabîyeh* to visit villages on the east bank. . . ." He smiled wryly. "In England, his highway was the Thames—here it will be the Nile."

Breaking our homeward journey from the Citadel, we had stopped off at the Bab el-Khalk police station to initiate inquiries of our own, and, in less than an hour, every post north of Assiut had been alerted. A hundred-foot *dahabîyeh* is not an easy vessel to hide; but, thus far, we had learned only that the *Nitocris* had anchored off Beni Suef on the Monday night.

I sat down in an armchair and, following my companion's example, lighted my pipe.

"General Fernshawe knew that Brooker and his assistant came from Luxor," I said thoughtfully, "though he chose not to tell us. But, in that case, how did they arrive in Cairo with papers which were, presumably, stolen from the plant at Meadi?"

"You find that mysterious? Look at the map!" Smith pointed with his finger. "They left the express at Bedrasheyn, crossed the river by ferryboat, and went to Helwan, from which the local line goes to Meadi. Since it was Sunday, no work was being done there, and they had the run of the place, to find and take what they liked. Having done so, they got back on the same train and off it at Bab el-Louk, while Captain Holt-Fortescue was still waiting for them at the Rameses Square station."

He paused to re-light his pipe, as he did every few minutes. His consumption of matches was enormous.

"When I come to think of it," he continued, "that may also explain the inane business of the dispatch case. Since Brooker was in charge, the security guards at Meadi would never have questioned his right to carry off documents, but it might have appeared odd if he had carried them loose. So he deliberately put them into an important-looking dispatch case and locked it to his wrist."

"But why didn't he take it off afterwards?"

"Perhaps he couldn't!" Smith grinned boyishly. "If Professor Brooker is the kind of man that I think he is, he may very well have snapped the cuff on his wrist without realising that he needed a key to get it off! That reminds me," he added, "I must see to it that I have a key of the right pattern, in case we should ever catch up with him."

From the tone in which he spoke, however, I knew that he considered it unlikely. Our present concern was to catch up with Dr. Fu Manchu, and we no longer had the resources of Scotland Yard at our disposal. Not without reason, we had little faith in Army Intelligence, and must, therefore, rely upon a rudimentary police force—which, only a few years ago, as I remembered, had consisted of less than nine thousand men to cover the entire country, under the supervision of sixty-two British officers.

No further word of the ship had reached us by bedtime, but we retired in better spirits, now that we were actively in pursuit of our quarry, if only by telephone.

Breakfast next morning brought no change in the situation but a welcome surprise in the shape of two letters from Kâramanèh—the first indication which I had had of her safe arrival in Capri, written at a week's interval, but delivered simultaneously, through the wartime vagaries of the post. I was eager to write a reply.

"Do so," said Smith. "I am going out to see what I can dig up concerning the *Nitocris,* and there's no reason for you to come with me. Write your letter, and stay by the telephone."

Thus matters were arranged and the day passed without event. I finished my letter and lunched alone, Smith being still absent. The telephone failed to ring, and nothing more disturbed me while I sat reading in my study till, presently, a harsh sound of scrubbing reached my ears. Wondering what member of my household was engaged upon such an unlikely activity, I closed my book and descended the stairs, to find Greba on her hands and knees, working on the tiled floor of the *durka'ah.*

"You should let Hassan do that," I said.

"*Let* him?" she flashed back. "I can't *make* him! Hassan is about as much use as a mummy!"

She sat back on her heels, brushing up a strand of tousled hair from her forehead. She had taken off her blouse, substituting a pinafore apron. Hot and flushed, with her rounded arms and bare shoulders, she looked so delightful that I felt a pang of temptation and was ashamed.

"All the same," I muttered, "you needn't do the housework and you shouldn't go around like that. What if Smith comes in?"

"What if he does?" she demanded. "He's seen my chemise on the washing line. Why can't he see it on me? When Kara does this, she often wears no top at all!"

"Kara is my wife," I reminded her.

At that moment, Smith *did* come in and stood grinning at this domestic scene with paternal amusement.

"Doing a little scrubbing, Greba?" he murmured. "Good for the figure!"

"Mr. Smith," she said severely, "you are not supposed to talk about my figure."

He laughed. "Why not? It's a very nice figure!" Catching my arm, he piloted me towards the surgery. "Let's go outside. Greba, will you do the honours, and bring us some drinks? One for yourself too."

"And put your clothes on!" I said.

We sat down in the shade of the stately *lebbekh* tree which occupied the centre of my small garden, Smith still grinning broadly.

"Don't look so disapproving," he said. "To-day's standards are not yesterday's—the war has seen to that—and, unless we learn to live with them, we shall be old before our time." Taking out his pipe and tobacco pouch, he laid them on the table. "The *Nitocris* has been tied up at Bedrasheyn for the past fortnight," he went on, "so that, no doubt, is where Fu Manchu's daughter was while we were searching for her in Cairo. The crew numbers eighteen."

"Eighteen! That sounds like an ominously large force."

"No," he replied, fiddling with matches. "They are all professional river boatmen, hired to work the ship, and have nothing to
do with the Si Fan. But, of course, there will also be a few of Fu
Manchu's own people aboard. The *Nitocris* is a sailing *dahabîyeh* of
the kind which used to be chartered by affluent foreigners, some
thirty or forty years ago, before Cook's steamers took over. She is
privately owned, but the precise ownership seems difficult to estab-
lish, since the vessel has recently been extensively re-fitted and
re-named."

"I can guess who re-named her!" I said grimly. "Nitocris was a
queen of the Sixth Dynasty, who invited her enemies to a banquet
in an underground chamber, and let in the Nile on top of them!"

Greba reappeared, carrying a tray with three glasses upon it, and
wearing a prim white blouse buttoned up to the neck.

"Beer for you, and mango juice for me. Thank the Lord we have
ice!"*

Flicking the eternal dust of the desert off the seat of the third
chair, she sat down facing us. Smith sipped at his beer.

"According to our friends at Bab el-Khalk," he reported, "the
dahabîyeh has left Minieh. How does a spot of piracy appeal to you?"

"Irresistibly!" I said, smiling. "I can't say that I've thought about
it lately, but every schoolboy who reads *Treasure Island* feels some
urge to be a pirate, I imagine. What had you in mind?"

"The last thing that Fu Manchu's daughter will expect. I intend
to board the ship and take her into custody." He laughed shortly.
"Oh, we shall have the law on our side, so it won't really be piracy,
but she will regard it as such. She is confident that we have no
evidence against her—and, but for the extraordinary conditions of
wartime, she would be correct."

"Very well. When do we leave?"

"To-night. I've already reserved places on the train for Assiut. We
have sleepers, but shan't get much use of them, as we shall reach
there in the middle of the night."

"Shall we be away long?"

"Possibly. I don't know."

"Can I come too?" asked Greba. "I've got something to say to
that woman—"

---

*There were no kitchen refrigerators in 1917, but we had ice machines. [P.]

"And give you both a chance to scratch each other's eyes out? Certainly not! I want you to move your things back in and hold the fort for us. We will keep in touch by leaving word for you at Shepheard's, where you will call each afternoon, and you will convey any messages, in person, to General Fernshawe. Don't telephone us unless it is unavoidable, and, if you must, do it from one of the larger hotels. This line is not to be trusted."

"All right." Greba stood up, her face registering her disappointment, and turned towards me. "I'll go and pack your socks and your linen. Kara would never forgive me if I let you go off like some careless old bachelor. . . ." She hesitated. "Oh, you will be careful, won't you? You're going out after Dr. Fu Manchu—"

"No," I said. "We are going out after his daughter."

"I'm not sure that isn't worse!" she retorted.

"She's right, Petrie," said Smith, frowning after Greba's departure. "We shall be dealing now with a vicious and dangerous enemy—vindictive, and prone to do the most outrageous things at the least provocation. Think of what she did to young Holt-Fortescue, simply because he tried to coerce her." His frown changed to a saturnine smile. "Well, what else could you expect of a woman who, if the tale told in the bazaars is true, was brought up in seclusion in a Tibetan monastery and taught to believe herself a goddess?"

I paid little heed just then, but later, while the Luxor express thundered southwards through the night and I lay sleepless in the upper berth of our first-class sleeping compartment, I remembered how often we had set out boldly eastwards, following the grey, oily swell of the Thames, to a battle with the Si Fan—and how often it had ended in a scramble for our lives.

In the squalid suburbs of London, the alien presence and evil deeds of Fu Manchu had seemed, perhaps, doubly shocking. Now the soft current of air stealing in through the slats of the shuttered window was no longer clammy with the rancid smells of the East End, but dry and spice-laden, reminding me that, here, we were the aliens, while Fu Manchu, if not on his home ground, was at least closer to it. Our British justice condemned him as a murderer and worse; but the dark gods of Egypt would surely fight on his side. . . .

14

PIRACY ON THE NILE

The unassuming New Hotel, where we had finished our night's sleep, had no facilities to offer meals. We ate at a native café opposite, from which we could watch the entrance and await the arrival of our official friends from the local police, while we breakfasted off Turkish coffee and thick, soft pancakes of unleavened bread, gritty with sand.

During our passage from Cairo, our inquiries had met with some success. We knew now that the *Nitocris* was tied up for the night close to Tell el-Amarna, where cruise steamers stopped to visit the ruins of Akhnaton's city—not that I supposed *they* were there for that purpose. In accordance with Nayland Smith's instructions, nothing had been done to interfere, but we had a man on watch, with orders to inform us the moment they weighed anchor.

"I gather that you mean to take them in midstream," I said doubtfully. "But won't it be difficult to get aboard?"

"Possibly. But it will be equally difficult for Fu Manchu's daughter to get ashore!"

I said no more but sat staring across the street, listening to the clip-clop of hooves and the jingle of harness bells. In Assiut, the fashions of a more leisured age persisted. European faces were few, and the passers-by traditionally clothed in drab, shapeless garments, with a turban cloth wound anyhow about the forehead. Egypt is exotic, but not colourful.

Some minutes elapsed till, at length, a light motor van—the first I had seen—pulled up before the hotel and a man descended from it. He wore a khaki tunic with a gold crown on the right cuff, and I recognized Sergeant Henley, who had met us off the train. We paid our bill and hurried to join him.

"Been waiting at the telegraph office since dawn," he said breath-

lessly, his face flushed with excitement. "Let's go! They sailed half
an hour ago."

"Where are we going?" I asked.

"Manfalut. We'll pick up a boat from there."

"Why not from here?"

"Too far." Henley grinned at my ignorance. "It's only about
seventeen miles by road, twenty-seven by the river."

We left him to ride in front and climbed up into the canvas-
covered body of the van, finding it already occupied by four Egyptian policemen, who moved up to make places for us on the narrow
wooden benches fixed along both sides. They carried Lee-Enfield
rifles and were, I supposed, to constitute our boarding party.

Beyond the town, we came out upon a track yet to be made fit for
wheels, following the left bank of the Ibrahîmiyeh Canal. From the
dim, windowless interior of the van, peering through the open back,
I had glimpses only in retrospect of rural life unchanged by the
centuries. At every few hundred yards, between the thorn trees, I
saw a *shadouf,* counterweighted with a gross ball of dried mud and
stones, where two men clad in loincloths laboured at the ancient,
cranelike device to draw up water. Sometimes they paused to stare
at us—sometimes to curse and shake their fists as our precipitate
passage engulfed them in choking clouds of dust.

Ours was the only vehicle upon the road. This was a page of the
Old Testament, across which patient donkeys made their way, their
owners seated side-saddle on green bales of *barsim*—the long-
stemmed clover which, in the absence of pastureland, served to feed
livestock. The van lurched and bumped, forcing me to cling tightly
to the edge of the seat on both sides. Once or twice, I was thrown
so violently upwards that my head struck against the canvas roof.

Smith muttered an imprecation. It was impossible either to talk
or to smoke.

Though we had but seventeen miles to cover, it took us an hour
to do it. Then, at last, the road became briefly level as we passed
through Manfalut—a single street of flat-roofed houses several
storeys high, plastered mostly in shades of yellow, but a somewhat
bigger place than I had anticipated, with large estates and attractive
villas in the vicinity.

"This is where Mahomet 'Ali had a training camp for his army of
black slaves from the Sudan," growled Smith, "but they died like
flies. . . ."

The town lay back at some distance from the river. We crossed the canal by a rickety bridge and continued on Nilewards. The lane—for it was nothing more—ceased to be rough and became unspeakable. Soon after, to my profound relief, the van stopped. Henley's flushed face appeared around the corner of the canvas.

"Everybody out!" he said. "This is it!"

We climbed down thankfully. Hitherto invisible from the back of the vehicle lay a gently shelving, reed-covered bank and the wide expanse of the Nile, placid as the surface of a lake. The craft which was to serve as our police boat was drawn close up—a felucca with a triangular sail suspended from a slanting yardarm longer than the mast which supported it. Our crew consisted of a boy who wore only a rag about his middle and an old man dressed in a soiled white *gallabieh,* like a nightshirt, and a grey felt skullcap; he was toothless save for two yellowed incisors, which gave him the appearance of an aged rabbit.

The vessel was the largest to be found in the locality, but with nine aboard, it was a tight squeeze. We, the officers, disposed ourselves on the plank seats amidships, while our men squatted in the stern sheets, chattering incessantly. Clearly, they looked upon this outing on the river as a pleasant break in their daily duties. I glanced at them dubiously, and then at Nayland Smith.

"I'd give a month's pay," he said sadly, "for a launch from Wapping station and a half dozen of Ryman's river police."

"I think they'd be a bit out of their depth here, sir," answered Henley, "if you'll pardon the expression."

Smith laughed and clapped him on the shoulder.

"You are right, Sergeant," he agreed. "This is your territory, and I shouldn't have said that."

All the same, looking around at those grinning brown faces, I could only reflect that, if this was all we had to pit against the forces of Fu Manchu, the outcome was doubtful. We were counting on it that the hired crew of the *Nitocris* would yield to authority. But what if they did not?

The first part of our journey was uneventful. Beyond the patchworked fields to our left, the Libyan mountains lay hidden under the heat haze, giving the illusion of an endless plain—an illusion since, from Aswan to Cairo, the Nile runs between high ranges through a winding valley rarely more than twelve miles wide. Eastwards, as we proceeded, the mountains of the Arabian desert drew ever closer to the shore, limiting the horizon, till the narrow belt of cultivation beneath vanished altogether. Unlike those of Europe, with verdant slopes rising to a snowline, these were stark and sand-coloured, like the mountains of a dead planet.

An hour passed. While the boy plied a steering-oar at the stern, our deceptively senile pilot sat perched on the starboard thwart, grasping the simple rope with which he controlled the sail, and guiding us on an erratic course through the treacherous shoals and currents which here abounded. His memory was fantastic, for he had no map, and such landmarks as he followed were visible only to his sharp old eyes. Ahead of us, where the river turned, the flat-topped mass of Gebel Abufeyda appeared to block all further progress, like the wall of a stupendous dam.

Nayland Smith snapped a question in Arabic. The old man looked up at the sail, tested the wind against his hand, and yammered a reply. Smith nodded and glanced at Henley, whose knowledge of the language was as yet inadequate. He had been in Egypt only a year.

"He says that we shan't meet up with the *Nitocris* before we round the bend."

Now to our right, as we turned, the barren heights of the mountain loomed above us, rising tier upon tier in long, parallel courses, less resembling a work of Nature than the ramparts of some colossal fortification. At each successive level, the whole face was perforated with the black, square-cut openings of ancient tombs hewn in the rock, contributing the effect of windows and loopholes. Not a scrap of vegetation lent a splash of added colour.

Still there was no sign of our quarry, but we were not alone upon the river. Here and there, the white sails of small craft like our own dotted the surface. We passed a slow-moving barge piled high with earthenware of all shapes and sizes from the kilns of Keneh—then, soon after, rolled in the wake of the daily steamer heading upstream from Deyrout.

Nayland Smith, hatless, and with one hand raised to his forehead, strained his eyes impatiently, but the sinuous course of the Nile made it impossible to see very far. Though the sun was almost at zenith, there was a stiff breeze and I shivered slightly, wishing that I had put on a jacket. Later, however, I was to feel thankful that I had not. . . .

The terraced wall of cliff on the starboard side—which here fell sheer to the water, and so continued for the next twelve miles—opened up abruptly in a great, V-shaped chasm, filled at the base by a steep pitch of white sand, glittering like a glacier. Our boatman watched it warily, mindful of the sudden gusts which might howl down through it to capsize such frail vessels as ours. Gebel Abufeyda had a bad reputation. But we glided past in safety. From the opposite shore, the tranquil vista of fields extended, unchanged, to the distant, pearl-grey skyline, the foreground here and there occupied by clusters of tiny, mud-brick houses, half hidden among date palms.

Smith jerked upright, his hand brushing against me as he raised his arm and pointed.

"Look!" he cried. "There she is!"

Only six hundred yards away, a ship was just clearing the bend which, hitherto, had concealed her—a *dahabîyeh* with sails set fore and aft, lateen-rigged, like all craft on the Nile.

"Put about!" shouted Smith. "Let her overtake us!"

A buzz of excitement broke out behind us. The old man hauled at the *shughool*—the sail flapped, went slack, and filled again as our boat veered and heeled over so steeply that I feared it would be swamped. Then we were back on an even keel, facing upstream, and I was staring over my shoulder.

The lines of a *dahabîyeh* are not graceful, resembling nothing so much as a Thames barge with a shed loaded upon the stern. But by reason of her size and her fresh white paint, the *Nitocris* was impressive. Suspecting nothing, she sailed majestically on till I could make out the gold lettering on the bow, with the Ancient Egyptian representation of an eye stencilled above it.

Smith, waiting patiently till the vessel came within hailing distance, snatched up a tin megaphone—a part of our equipment—and sent a Stentorian shout ringing across the water, first in English and then in Arabic.

"Police! Take in your sails, and heave to!"

There was no response. The *Nitocris* continued to bear down upon us. I looked up at our mast, wondering if we should haul up the Jolly Roger or the White Ensign—not that we had either aboard.

Smith lifted the megaphone again to his lips and repeated the demand—still without response. Our rabbit-faced boatman cursed and laid hold upon the rope, ready to turn us adroitly aside if she attempted to run us down or force us into the cliff.

"If she passes and makes a run for it," said Henley, anxiously, "she can outsail us."

Less than a hundred yards now separated us. Smith barked an order, using the Turkish words of command, since he was unfamiliar with the current practice, and I heard the clatter of rifle bolts.

"I'm prepared to give her a broadside if she tries!" he declared. "It won't sink her, but a dozen holes below the waterline will slow her down quite a bit."

He spoke confidently, but it occurred to me that, if it came to a fight, the *dahabîyeh* might well be the better armed. I thought of the mysterious weapon that fired invisible shafts of heat—which could pick us off, one by one—and looked up at the deck of the approaching vessel, half fearing at any moment to see a fireball float up from it.

Still the *Nitocris* came on.

"We have no cannon," said Smith, between his teeth, "but a rifle will serve just as well." He turned to the nearest of our men. "*Shâ-weesh!* Put a shot across her bows."

The man addressed grinned broadly, swung his rifle to his shoulder, and, obeying the order more than literally, fired a shot directly through the mainsail. Small though the bullet hole was, the wind caught it, tearing a long rent in the canvas.

The result was immediate and gratifying. A clamour broke out aboard the *Nitocris* and a horde of figures went swarming up the rigging, gathering in and furling the sails. An anchor splashed overboard, and the ship drifted to a standstill, swinging lazily in the current. Instantly, we were alongside, the side of our boat thumping against the other.

"Up we go, Petrie!" said Smith.

Setting one foot upon the thwart, he seized the rail above and swung himself up.

15

NITOCRIS

Like all such vessels, the *Nitocris* was low in the water. From the felucca, it was no more than a strong pull and a broad step up. I clambered aboard, feeling as I did so that there should have been gold rings dangling from my ears and a cutlass between my teeth.

Sergeant Henley and the four Egyptians followed. No one made either to assist or to impede us. Staring around as my feet touched the deck, I saw the crew of the *dahabîyeh* gathered about in threes and fours, watching us with a sullen apathy. In common with most of the river boatmen, they were *fellahîn,* with the sturdy figures and tight-curled hair of the tomb paintings—not Arabs, but abject descendants of the once-proud race which built Memphis and Thebes.

Smith thrust a brown paper package into my hand and I took it automatically.

"*Mîn er-Reys?*" he shouted.

A tall man wearing a long blue *gallabieh* and a neat white turban stepped forward with dignity.

"I am the captain, *effendîm.*"

"*Ismak eyh?*"

"Suleyman ibn Sayyid."

"How many passengers do you carry?"

"None, *effendîm*—only the Princess, who employs us."

"Princess!" muttered Smith. "Good God! Is there no limit to her arrogance? Where is she?"

"Up there, *effendîm.* I will take you to her. . . ."

Suleyman ibn Sayyid pointed as he spoke to the after part of the vessel, where two narrow staircases led up to the roof of the cabins, corresponding to the quarterdeck of a mediaeval sailing ship.

"No!" answered my friend. "We will find her ourselves. You, Captain, will bring your crew list and remain here. Sergeant . . ."

"Sir?"

"Assemble the crew, check each man's name, and detain anybody not listed. Meanwhile, have your men search the ship."

Despite the size of the vessel, there was little to search, apart from the deck cabins which occupied about a third of her length. Below would be only a low-ceilinged hold, intended for stores. The crew slept customarily on deck, under the stars.

Nayland Smith and I headed for the nearer of the two stairways. The railed space at the top was empty but for a long swing-seat, suspended on chains from an iron frame and shaded by a striped canopy. Upon this, reclining on silken cushions, lay the self-styled princess—seemingly so little concerned by the assault that she had not even changed her position. We stood staring at her, face to face with the Lady of the Si Fan.

Regal she looked indeed—a Chinese Cleopatra, floating down the Nile in her golden barge to a tryst with Mark Antony. A crewman stood at her side, dressed like a waiter, in white coat and black trousers, and holding in his hand a wicker basket of grapes.

Smith had not seen her before, but, at a glance, I recognized my erstwhile patient. To-day she was completely Far Eastern, sheathed in a green *cheongsam* dress of figured silk embossed with Chinese arabesques and audaciously slit to the hip on both sides of the long skirt, like the outfits worn on the floating restaurants of Aberdeen. Green was, apparently, her favourite colour. As she stretched out a languid hand and took a grape from the basket, I saw that her tapered fingernails were lacquered to match the emerald of her eyes.

She said nothing, regarding us with neither anger nor surprise but, rather, an expression of satirical amusement.

"You are the owner of this ship?" demanded Smith.

For a long moment she did not answer, helping herself to another grape and holding it poised between finger and thumb. Then:

"No," she said calmly, "I am not the owner. But the *Nitocris* sails under my command."

She ate the grape delicately.

"Send your man down to join the others on the maindeck."

The princess shrugged with the undulating grace of a serpent, and spoke a few words in Arabic. The crewman put down his basket, proffered a brass bowl in which she rinsed her fingers, dried them with a napkin as gently as a woman, bowed, and departed. His royal mistress shifted slightly on her couch.

"You are Nayland Smith," she said. "I would welcome you aboard, if you did not come as a pirate."

Her words so exactly echoed his forecast of her reactions that I could not help smiling. But Smith frowned.

"In the matter of names, you have the advantage of me," he replied curtly. "I know what, but not who, you are. By which of the various names which you have used in Cairo should I call you?"

She laughed softly, the icy tinkle of silver bells muted and less cold than I remembered.

"None of them is mine, but those who love me call me Fah Lo Suee. You may do the same."

"As you choose!" he snapped. "But I cannot profess to love you."

She laughed again. "You will, if I wish it. But not *him.*" Suddenly, I was conscious of the lustrous eyes focussed upon my face with such scorn that it startled me. "With him I can do nothing. He is besotted with his Egyptian slavegirl—who once knelt at my feet."

Her savage animosity—which I had done nothing to deserve—warned me that I had made an enemy not to be lightly discounted. But at least, I thought, we at last had a name for her.

"You are Fu Manchu's daughter!" challenged Smith, and again the lazy, serpentine shrug answered him.

"Am I? Perhaps. How can one swear to the identity of one's father? Can you?"

Smith's lips drew together in a hard, straight line. I could see that he hated to trade words with her, but curiosity drove him on.

"They say," he said slowly, "that you were brought up in a Tibetan monastery and worshipped as a goddess."

"That is partly true," she murmured. "But it was south of the Tibetan border—near Kathmandu—where, for a time, I was the Living Goddess of Patan."*

Reaching down among the cushions, she took up a snakeskin handbag, and, opening it, extracted the long cigarette holder which I had seen in my surgery.

"Drop that!" rapped Smith.

She looked up at him with raised eyebrows. "Why? Do you object to women who smoke?"

*The office is still maintained, but the present incumbent spends most of her time at her palace window, looking at, and being looked at by, the tourists in the square below. [Ed.]

"Not at all. But I am well aware that a cigarette holder of that length can make an excellent blowpipe!"

Fah Lo Suee smiled and slipped the suspected instrument back into her bag.

"An interesting thought!" she observed. "I must keep it in mind. . . ."

Glancing back at the lower deck, I saw the crew of the *Nitocris* lined up against the rail, as if for a naval inspection—Henley passing along the line, accompanied by the captain, who carried papers. Our four men were scurrying busily about, diving in and out of hatches, breaking open lockers, overturning boxes, and plunging their bayonets viciously into the sacks piled up outside the cookhouse. Neither they nor we had the least idea as to what they were looking for.

"Give me that, Petrie!" said Smith suddenly, and took from me the brown paper package, which I had forgotten I still carried. Tearing it open, he threw a pair of golden sandals down in front of the swing-seat. "Here are the shoes which you left at Dr. Petrie's house, on the night that you came there to murder me!"

Surprise registered momentarily in the feral green eyes and was gone in an instant. The red lips curled in the same enigmatic smile—mocking and contemptuous. Fah Lo Suee shifted her position, extending one small, ivory foot. She wore no stockings and I saw that her toenails were painted like her fingernails.

"How kind of you!" she said smoothly. "Would you care to put them on for me?"

"I should not!" he retorted. "Let us have no more words. This ship is impounded, and I am placing you under arrest!"

Fu Manchu's daughter—if such she was—started upright, swinging her feet to the deck, her eyes blazing.

"That is absurd!" she exclaimed. "Arrest me? On what charge? Anything I say to you here I will deny in court!"

"You will not appear in court. Under the emergency powers, I have the authority to hold you without trial on suspicion of activities disloyal to the Crown."

For the first time, a shadow of concern clouded the arrogant, patrician features—an empress faced with the brutal reality of armed rebellion. Just so, I thought, must Marie Antoinette have looked on her way to the guillotine.

"You are ungrateful," she complained. "Did I not save your life, when you were lost in Neterkhet-Zoser's tomb?"

"Yes!" said Smith frankly. "And I am still wondering why!"

Fah Lo Suee did not reply immediately, and, when she did so, the words came like drops of ice ringing upon crystal.

"I had heard much of you, and I was curious to see you before it was too late."

Nayland Smith looked sideways at me, smiled, and shrugged.

"Prepare yourself!" he directed. "The *Nitocris* will proceed to Assiut, under police escort. You will accompany us aboard the felucca—in handcuffs. You may either do as I say, or, if necessary, I am ready to use force."

"Yes," she whispered. "I believe you would. . . ." She sprang to her feet. "Very well—I will go with you. But first you must allow me to change into clothes more suitable for a journey to Cairo."

Smith shook his head. "I am sorry, but I cannot let you out of my sight—even for a moment."

"Come with me, then!" she flashed. "But travel in these things I will not!"

Ignoring the sandals at her feet, she swept past us and strode barefoot across the hot planks to the stairway, giving us no alternative but to follow—just as she had done when forcing her way into my premises. Powerless to stay her, short of physical violence, we hurried down after her.

"Be wary of her, Petrie!" cautioned Smith. "Nobody has been found yet, but it's hard to believe that she has none of her own gang aboard. . . ."

At the foot of the steps, Fah Lo Suee turned, conducting us through a low doorway and down a few more steps into a wide salon which I recognized at once as that described by Captain Holt-Fortescue.

My first impression was of an atmosphere heavy with a mixture of perfumes, in which the cloying scent of jasmine predominated. Flowers were everywhere, accommodated in strangely shaped pottery of Chinese origin. Chinese, likewise, were the brightly tasselled lanterns hanging from the ceiling, but the furnishings were an odd blend of East and West, ancient and modern, with softly upholstered divans on both sides of the room and a Steinway piano in one corner. Between the curtained portholes and at the far end, the walls were panelled in light wood, intricately inlaid, as only the Arabian craftsmen can do, with scenes founded on Ancient Egyptian themes, but each with a barbaric and erotic undertone of cruelty absent from the originals.

This, I thought, was an apartment designed to suit the sensual tastes of the owner of the vessel, whoever he might be—not strictly those of Fu Manchu or his daughter.

There was another doorway opposite that by which we had entered, and towards this Fah Lo Suee headed, but did not pass through. She halted, and spun about, facing us with her back to the sliding doors of a wall cupboard decorated with the likeness of a warlike pharaoh braining female captives with a club. The cold fire of her narrowed eyes was chilling but magnificent. Reaching up to her throat, she unhooked the high collar of her *cheongsam* and worked the buttons through the gold-threaded loops.

"I have warned you—" began Smith, but she interrupted.

"Turn your back, or watch me, as you please! I have no secrets to hide from Dr. Petrie, and as little concern for *your* eyes as for those of a common executioner!"

She pulled the dress down from one exquisite shoulder, wriggling out of it in the manner of a snake casting its skin. (Why did the simile of a snake so persistently recur to me?) Beneath it, she wore flimsy garments of so scanty a nature that I wondered what house of feminine fashion could profit from them.

Her disrobing was performed with no trace either of shyness or of insolence—not even gracefully. She did it simply as if we had not been there. Then, stooping to pick up the discarded dress, she straightened herself proudly and, for the first time, deigned to acknowledge our presence.

"Do you wish to search me for concealed weapons," she asked, "before I put on something else?"

"I hardly think that will be necessary," said Smith dryly.

Fah Lo Suee smiled. "You are less prudent than I expected. The weapons of Dr. Fu Manchu may be concealed in less than this."

With the dress thrown over one arm, she turned her back on us and slid open the cupboard. The total indifference and complete naturalness of her movements took both of us off guard. There was just the time for the thought to cross my mind—Why should she keep her clothes here rather than in her sleeping cabin?—just time enough for me to see the gleaming brass blades of a large knife switch mounted on the rear wall of the empty cupboard before she had grasped the handle.

I uttered a warning cry—too late. . . .

Close upon the metallic clash of the switch came a rapid chain of explosions, like a giant Chinese fire-cracker, hammering against the soles of my feet, rolling across the river and echoing back from the cliffs. The entire fabric of the ship shuddered as though in an earthquake. The floor canted up steeply, hurling me back painfully against the wall. Smith shouted, started forward, and fell heavily upon his knees, snatching at the pistol in his pocket. A huge bowl of roses crashed down beside him and shattered, showering him with sharp fragments of porcelain and multi-coloured petals.

Only Fah Lo Suee remained erect, having thrown herself instantly against the adjacent doorframe, grasping it with both hands.

Even though the sound of the explosions had died swiftly away, noise and movement continued—a creaking, tearing, and splintering of timber, intermixed with the crash of ponderous objects thrown one against another, shouts and screams, while the cabin floor seesawed under me as if in a typhoon. Struggling to regain my feet, I heard Fah Lo Suee's voice and her silvery laugh raised to a peak of hysteria.

"Swim for your lives, fools!"

Releasing her hold upon the doorway, she vanished down the passageway beyond. Smith levered himself up and clutched at my arm, assisting me to rise.

"After her!" he ordered. "God in Heaven! She's scuttled the ship!"

By the uphill slope of the floorboards, it was clear that the forepart of the *Nitocris* was already under water. Most of the moveable furniture—cushions, tables, and chairs—had piled up against the steps. As we staggered like drunkards towards the opposite bulkhead, the piano came hurtling down on its castors, missed us by a fraction, and crashed into the lower wall with a discordant ringing of strings.

We entered a narrow corridor with cabin doors to right and left, and, bracing ourselves with outstretched arms, reached a flight of wooden steps which led up through a hatchway. The dizzy sensation of making our way up, bent backwards, may be understood only by one who has climbed the Leaning Tower of Pisa. At the stairhead, we had a glimpse of Fah Lo Suee as she sprang to the rail—then, balancing herself like a tightrope walker, she threw her arms aloft and dived cleanly into the river with scarcely a splash.

I turned, staring back upon a scene of shipwreck unlike any I had witnessed or imagined. The charges, spaced along the full length of the hull, had torn the bottom out of the vessel from stem to stern. Both the masts were down in a tangle of spars and cordage from which men trapped in the fall fought desperately to free themselves.

Others were leaping overboard. The maindeck, with two great holes blown in it, was now nothing but a raft, awash, and splitting into sections as the planks came apart.

On the port side of the wreck, and a short way off, our felucca lay capsized with the sail outspread on the water like a toy yacht on a boating pond, the bald head of the ancient owner bobbing about, egglike, beside it. Farther off, to starboard, I saw villagers clustered on the bank and some of them scrambling down to a few small boats drawn up among the reeds, intent upon our rescue.

No time was to be lost. All that was left of the *Nitocris* was not precisely sinking but breaking up under us. Smith tore off his shoes, while I followed suit. We dived together—less elegantly, perhaps, than Fah Lo Suee, but without mishap. Except for the risk of striking our heads on the floating wreckage, there was no great danger. The water was warm and there were no waves to contend with, though the current proved stronger than I had expected.

The right bank was the nearer but offered no landing, where the amber precipice of Gebel Abufeyda came down into the Nile like a harbour wall. We struck out for the left. For two strong swimmers lightly clad in shirt and trousers, it was no great feat, but the scattered débris of broken timbers, ship's stores, and furnishings was a hindrance. The area for some fifty yards about looked like the surface of a flooded rubbish pit. Smith swore as his foot tangled with a half-submerged chair, and a cabbage hit me in the face.

Halfway to safety, we saw a boat heading towards us. Smith grabbed at a plank, raised himself partly upon it, and waved them away, shouting at them to go out to the *dahabîyeh*, where some might be injured and in difficulties. We could fend for ourselves. Once clear of the flotsam, it was little worse than swimming in one's clothes in a swimming pool. But with only a close-set hedge of reeds to guide us, we chose a bad spot to come ashore.

The bank was not steep, but, when we tried to stand upright, our legs sank knee-deep in liquid mud. Somehow, we clawed our way out, clutching at the reeds, falling on our faces as they came away in bunches in our hands, and digging in our fingers, hauling ourselves up the slope till at last we reached firm ground and could sit, turning to look at each other. We were mirror images—two slimy grey creatures more reptilian than human, our clothes sticking to our bodies like scales, and seemingly hairless.

I drew a deep breath and looked out across the river. Only the cabin roof of the *Nitocris* remained afloat, with two men seated disconsolately upon it.

"I said she might do anything," gasped Smith, "but, upon my soul, I didn't bargain for *that*! My fault, Petrie—I should have remembered the behaviour of the original Lady Nitocris."

Suddenly he began to laugh.

"What amuses you?" I inquired. "I can see little to laugh at."

"I am thinking of Fah Lo Suee," he responded, "who can look no better than we do—crawling up the riverbank like a half-drowned sewer rat, and plastered from head to foot in Nile mud. She'll be in no hurry to forgive us for that!"

16

ABU NASRÂNI

I cannot write with much enthusiasm concerning our inglorious retreat. After a brief rest to recover our breath, we trampled inland with our muddied clothes already drying on our limbs as stiffly as though starched, till we came upon a *sákiyeh,* where a buffalo harnessed to a beam walked in circles to draw up water from a well by an endless chain of earthenware pots, and sluiced ourselves more or less clean, watched gleefully by the boy who sat on the buffalo.

The personnel of the two wrecked vessels had swum, or been ferried, ashore at widely separated points all along the riverbank, and had no organised means of getting in touch with each other. We therefore decided to make our own way back to our temporary base in Assiut, leaving Henley and his men to do likewise.

All that afternoon, Nayland Smith and I trekked through orchards of dwarf banana trees and a tea plantation, meeting no one on the way. Eventually, we reached the railway line, but, so far as we knew, distant from any station. We lighted a fire upon the tracks and flagged down a local train, travelling at donkey speed. The driver was outraged, but we invoked our official privilege to get aboard and sank down, exhausted, upon dusty wooden seats in a carriage like a cattle truck.

Every door and every window was broken. The flies were pestiferous and were later succeeded by a hungry horde of mosquitoes. Smoking might have kept them at bay, but the stem of Smith's pipe was blocked solid with dried mud, and I had lost mine. The sun was low on the horizon when our miserable train rattled through Manfalut, and nothing more was to be done that night.

A new day dawned, and, somewhat rested, we forgathered at the police station to assess the extent of our losses. Our piratical expedition seemed to have gained us nothing.

We found Henley safely back at his desk, struggling with a stack of forms printed in French, Arabic, and Turkish, all of which had now to be completed. Casualties had been heavier than we had first thought. One of our four Egyptian policemen—a poor swimmer— had been drowned, and two, at least, of the men from the *Nitocris* killed in the multiple explosions which had torn her apart. As yet there was no word of the old man and the boy who had manned our craft, but the felucca had drifted across the river and been battered to pieces on the rugged walls of Gebel Abufeyda.

Our search of the *dahabîyeh* had, as we now learned, yielded only the discovery of a cell-like chamber below, fitted with a massive wooden door; it stank like the lair of a wild animal. All that it contained was a heap of straw and a few bones with scraps of meat adhering to them. But the meat had been cooked!

Of Fah Lo Suee, needless to say, no trace had been found.

"It won't be hard for her to disappear," said Smith, "in a place like this, where the women cover their heads and shroud themselves up to the eyes like mourners at a funeral."

Grim confirmation was obtained later in the day with a report from Koussieh, where a woman, carrying up water from the river, had been struck down by a savage blow on the head and robbed of the long black winding sheet which was her sole garment.

Henley had men out trying to round up the crew of the *Nitocris*, in the forlorn hope that we might learn something useful from them, but my friend was pessimistic.

"They have only to declare themselves outlaws," he said sadly, "in order to obtain sympathy. The *fellahîn* are no friends of the law—and, in view of what the law has done for them, is it any wonder?"

Contrary to his expectations, however, the search was soon rendered unnecessary by the voluntary arrival of Captain Suleyman ibn Sayyid, seeking compensation for the abrupt termination of his contract. I felt indignant. But Smith smiled.

"There is some justice in your claim," he admitted. "Help us to find your employer, and I will see that it is considered."

Suleyman inclined his head. "Such knowledge as I have shall be yours, *effendîm*—though it is but little."

He sat down, accepted a cigarette, and we called for coffee. He talked and we listened—Sergeant Henley still seated at his desk and doing his best to follow, but without much success. In a land of illiteracy, where story-telling must take the place of literature, *Reys* Suleyman spoke with the poetry of *The Arabian Nights*.

We gathered that the crew of the *Nitocris* had been hired to sail the ship for a period of three months, possibly as far south as the First Cataract, but with no fixed destination or schedule. Day to day, orders were given by Fah Lo Suee.

"We knew that she was no princess," he confessed, "but a sorceress skilled in the wicked arts of *es-sîmiya* and *es-sehr.* Yet what might we do? We are sailors, but these are evil days. When there is no work for us on the river, we must become farmers, and to labour at the *shadouf* is not to our liking." He spread his hands in a peculiarly Egyptian gesture. "She boarded the *dahabîyeh* at Bedrasheyn, and with her came four terrible men. Two were jackals of the desert. Two, whose faces were the colour of dried lemons, spoke a tongue like the twittering of birds, which only she could understand, and, with them, they brought strange and dreadful things, one being a devil-box, with which they wrote words on the air and sent them on the wind to distant places."

Nayland Smith shifted impatiently, fearing that the captain's poetry was getting the better of him.

"*Reys* Suleyman," he said curtly, "you are an old hand at sailing and an intelligent man. Don't tell me that you have never heard of a wireless transmitter!"

Suleyman ibn Sayyid smiled and nodded. "Oh, yes, *effendîm*! I know that you, too, have many devil-boxes in your country." He cleared his throat noisily. "But this was not all. Worse was the thing in the prison below the deck, which howled and babbled and beat upon the walls till we feared that it would break through the sides of the ship and sink us. . . ."

"You don't know what it was?" demanded Smith. "You never saw it?"

"No, *effendîm*, we never saw it. But we all knew what it was. It was an *ifrît*!"

Smith looked at me and I at him, and we shook our heads.

"What happened to these men?" I put in. "They were not there yesterday."

"Allah is merciful!" exclaimed the captain. "On the fourth night, we anchored at a spot where the cliffs are close to the shore. Then a band of brigands armed with guns came down through a *wâdi*, riding upon camels. I could not tell how many they were, *effendîm*—twelve, or perhaps twenty. . . ."

I assumed that there had been at least six.

"We were frightened," he went on. "They were all dressed in

black—bandits from beyond the far oasis of Sîwa, with the faces of eagles and the souls of demons. When they came aboard, none of us dared speak to them. But their leader stayed upon the shore, seated high in the saddle, and watched. His face was not as theirs, but the very face of Iblîsi, and when the moonlight shone upon them, his eyes glowed like those of a leopard—like those of the princess."

I turned towards Smith. "Fu Manchu—on a camel?"

"I see no reason why not!" he answered with a shrug. "There are plenty of camels in Sinkiang. Go on, Captain!"

"When they left," said *Reys* Suleyman, "the four who had come with the princess left too. With them they took the devil-box and also the *ifrît* in a great wooden chest bound with brass, after they had subdued it with the smoke of a blue candle—and those of us who breathed what lingered in the hold slept and were sick. . . ."

"But you didn't know who really owned the vessel?"

"No, *effendîm*. It was always the princess who paid us. But, though much had been made new, the *Nitocris* was old. All my life, I have worked on the river, and, as soon as I stood upon the deck, I knew that this was the same ship which I had often seen as a boy—which then had belonged to the Governor of Keneh, long ago, when Tewfik still ruled as Khedive. But who became the owner after Allah, in His wisdom, had taken both him and Tewfik and cast them down into the fiery pit of Jahannum, I knew not. . . ."

We questioned him further, but he had no more to tell us. Convinced of his sincerity, we offered him money for his immediate needs, but he would not take it. Saying only that he would wait till his claim was settled, he saluted us gravely and departed. He was a dignified type of Egyptian, whom the peddler and the beggar disgrace.

Sergeant Henley threw down his pen with a curse.

"I wouldn't so much mind being blown up and shipwrecked," he grumbled, "if it didn't make all this paperwork! I thought I was well off, coming out here from the Met, but now I wish I'd gone into the Army."

"Why didn't you?" I inquired curiously.

"I tried, but they wouldn't have me," said Henley, and added gloomily: "Flat feet."

We left him to his Herculean task of cleaning the Augean stables, and walked back slowly to our hotel.

"It appears," said Smith thoughtfully, "that Fu Manchu has replaced his dacoits with Senussi. We saw two of them at Saqqara."

"Likely enough," I agreed. "They are allies of the Turks, and, though it's six months since General Maxwell chased them out of Egypt, I daresay there are still a few bands of them wandering about. Fu Manchu may have got control of one—"

"Which he could do! It's a bit odd to imagine him in the rôle of a desert *sheikh,* but I've no doubt he could play it. . . ."

"What shall we do now? Shall we stay here, or go back to Cairo?"

"Neither! It's too late to-day, but to-morrow we will take the train and go on south to Luxor."

"Luxor? Why?"

"It's the opposite end of the trail, where Brooker and his assistant started from, and the direction in which Fah Lo Suee is heading." Without pausing in his stride, Nayland Smith reached down and knocked out the bowl of his pipe on his right heel—an old trick of his, which I was never able to imitate. "Not only that, but the information we received from *Reys* Suleyman may have some significance. Who was the owner of the *Nitocris*? More than ten years ago, when I was first here, the old Governor of Keneh was long since dead, and his son—a young profligate, named Yildiz Bey—had succeeded him. A year or so after I left, our administration got rid of him. He may, of course, have sold the ship to Fu Manchu or somebody else. On the other hand, Yildiz Bey may still be alive and an ally of the Si Fan. He would have every reason to hate us. As a possible base of their operations, Keneh may be worth investigating, and it's not far from Luxor, which is the most convenient base for ours. . . ."

I raised no objection. In Luxor—which, after Cairo, is the second Mecca of the tourist—we should have decent beds to sleep in and food which we could eat without risk to our intestines.

Nothing else of importance occurred during our sojourn in Assiut, and, the following afternoon, I found myself seated once more in the reasonable comfort of a first-class railway carriage, staring from the window at the subtle changes of scenery which betokened our passage into Upper Egypt. Here the riverbanks were screened by the spreading branches of *dôm* palms, furry-looking, and, from a distance, somewhat like the contorted shapes of Asiatic pine trees, the roofs of the cottages—if such they might be called—often composed now of *durra* straw mats, with fences of the same erected in front.

South of the Delta, the centuries roll back and the startled eyes of the traveller are greeted by a pattern of life more in keeping with his ideas of darkest Africa. Each village was the same—a huddle of mud huts, sometimes enclosed by an irregular wall, above which rose the pepperpot-shaped tower of a pigeon house, chequered with holes and bristling with a *cheval-de-frise* of spikes for bird perches.

Smith, sitting opposite me in a cloud of tobacco smoke, said little. But presently, he put away his pipe and leaned over.

"Fu Manchu is short of men and materials," he remarked. "He withdrew them from the *Nitocris*—to say nothing of the *ifrît!*—because he has need of them elsewhere. Where, I wonder?"

Beyond Farshut, the train thundered across a long iron bridge, crossing to the east bank of the Nile, where, for some obscure reason, the line is worse, and our carriage swayed and jolted so alarmingly that we often seemed in danger of derailment. It was dark before we reached Luxor, where, descending from the train, we summoned an *'arabîyeh* to take us down to the waterfront and the hotels which furnish an oasis of civilised living for the modern pilgrim to ancient Thebes.

Though the Winter Palace holds first place, the formal society of titled tourists, senior officers, and their wives made no appeal to us just then, and we had chosen the more modest Savoy. Here, at least, I was able to enjoy the luxury of a private bathroom, after three nights in Assiut—where we had shared the washing facilities with all the tenants of the fourth floor and an indefinite number of small green lizards.

Troubled by no immediate worries, I slept peacefully. Smith's first intention was, as I knew, to visit Keneh and discover what he could concerning Yildiz Bey—who might, or might not, be a supporter of the Si Fan. This plan, however, was one which was destined to be postponed and ultimately achieved in a manner vastly different from any that we might foresee. . . .

My seven hours' rest under a pyramid of mosquito netting had the desired effect, and I came down early, feeling better than I had done for some time. Finding, however, that Smith was still in his room, I went out on the terrace and sat down to wait for him, so that we might have breakfast together.

Luxor has always something of a holiday atmosphere, with the endless stream of *'arabîyat* passing to and fro along the broad,

tree-lined concourse between the hotels and the riverbank. Sipping
at a glass of iced pomegranate juice, I stared across the road, finding
it hard to remember that the Nile, and not the sea, lay beyond. The
peaks of the Theban Hills surrounding the Valleys of the Kings and
the Queens looked like an island offshore—the pointed sails of the
feluccas like those of yachts at a regatta.

Strange, I thought, that a cemetery should become a play-
ground—yet, at the same time, I reflected that those who slept
yonder had got exactly what they wanted. Their names were remembered, their monuments visited, and their earthly remains pre-
served from decay by all the means of modern science.

The sound of a footstep ended my reverie and I turned, to find
Smith at my side, frowning down at an envelope in his hand.

"What have you there?" I asked.

"Seemingly, a letter," he replied, "addressed to me, and handed
in this morning at the desk. . . ."

"But nobody yet knows that we are here!"

"Quite! So far, I haven't even informed Greba—though I must do
so this afternoon." Smith dropped into the chair opposite, tore
open the envelope with impatient fingers, and scanned the single
sheet of notepaper which it enclosed. "Good God!"

"Who is it from?" I inquired.

"An old friend," he said slowly, "or I suppose I should call him
that, though I never expected to hear from him again. . . ."

For some seconds, he scowled over the missive, pursing his lips,
and obviously finding it difficult to read. Glancing at it upside down,
I saw that it was written in sinuous Arabic, with so many points and
flourishes that it looked like a page from the Koran.

"Your friend writes a classic style," I commented.

"His *kâtib* does!" answered Smith dryly, and threw the letter
across to me. "Here! See what you make of it. My Arabic is strictly
colloquial."

I picked it up and studied it carefully.

"It begins with greetings to Nai'man es-Samit," I announced after
a moment, "which, I suppose, means you, and it reads: 'It has come
to my ears that you seek a traitor to your king, who carries a great
treasure. Visit me at my camp this night, where there shall be feast-
ing and rejoicing, and I will help you to find him.' " More was
written, but my eye passed on to an illegible scrawl at the foot
of the page. "It is signed in a different hand, which I can't make

out. . . . For Heaven's sake, Smith—who *is* this man?"

"Abu Nasrâni," he said quietly, "a merchant and a smuggler, and said to be head of the legendary Guild of Thieves and Receivers. . . ."

17

AN EGYPTIAN NIGHT'S ENTERTAINMENT

Abu Nasrâni . . . It sounded suspiciously like a nickname.

"He is a Christian?" I exclaimed.

Smith laughed. "Hardly! They call him that because he's a colourful old rascal who ignores all the restrictions of Islam which he finds inconvenient, and his network of underhand information is almost as extensive as that of Dr. Fu Manchu. They say that if a copper coin is stolen from a blind man's bowl, Abu Nasrâni hears of it. In other words, if anyone knows what has become of our fugitive professor, he does."

"But why should he offer to help us?"

"Because, as it happens, I was once able to do him a service. Have I never told you?"

"No, never."

"Well, it was long ago, when my world was young and justice still seemed to mean something. . . ." Smith paused, gestured to a waiter, and joined me in my choice of fruit juice. "The details don't matter," he continued, "but it was a nasty business, connected with the slave trade, and Abu Nasrâni was to be made the scapegoat. He traded in all sorts of dubious merchandise, but neither in drugs nor in slaves. I determined to get to the bottom of it, and it ended with the hell of a scandal, involving several highly placed officials, both Turkish and British. . . ."

Again my friend hesitated, staring out at the concourse with narrowed eyes and a thin smile on his lips.

"I was personally congratulated by Lord Cromer and, very soon afterwards, transferred to Mandalay—whether as a reward or a reprimand, I've never really known." He shrugged. "At all events, Abu

Nasrâni was amazed because I had supported him against my own kind, and swore that one day he would repay me. I thought little of it then, and have never met him since—but a vow is remembered longer in the East than it often is in the West."

"Will you go to see him?"

"Of course—though it will mean a bit of an expedition. Abu Nasrâni prefers the desert life—he was born in the Bishârîn settlement at Aswan—and lives in a sort of semi-permanent encampment, miles from anywhere, on the road to Koseir. You may accompany me if you wish, but—"

"Why should I not?" I demanded.

Smith grinned like a satyr. "You may find our reception a trifle too Bacchanalian for your tastes." Reaching over the table, he took the letter back from me. "If I'm not mistaken, it says here that an escort will be waiting for us at sundown behind the Karnak Temple, and transport will be provided—presumably camels. Do you think you can manage one?"

"As well as you, I expect!" I said warmly. "You forget that I was riding camels before you ever saw one outside a zoo!"*

Having some idea of what was to come, we lunched sparingly. Then, leaving Smith to do the same, I went upstairs and lay down on my bed to rest before our journey and await his summons.

When he tapped upon my door, the room was already dim and the sun sinking below the frowning peak of She Who Loves Silence. We crossed the road and hired an 'arabîyeh from the stand opposite the hotel, telling the man to take us out to Karnak. Abu Nasrâni's wild men of the desert could not bring their animals into the town without creating a sensation, but it was only a twenty-minute drive to the Temple of Ammon, where the great pylon of the principal gate towered a hundred feet above our heads, golden in the setting sun—a spectacle less ancient than the Pyramids, but equally impressive. Karnak, the symbol of the New Kingdom, had dwarfed the achievements of architects and masons for a thousand years to follow.

In a clump of date palms at the back, we found our promised escort—six fierce-faced men, with striped kafîyâh draped about their heads in place of the townish turban or tarbûsh. Two sat shading themselves, desert fashion, under their long riding cloaks, drawn

---

*Though Dr. Petrie took his medical degree at Edinburgh, he was born in Egypt, when his illustrious father was excavating at Tanis. [Ed.]

forward over the head and held tentwise by a camel-stick grasped
in the wearer's hand. All sprang to their feet, saluting us with a
sweeping motion of the hand, touching fingertips to breast, lips, and
forehead.

They appeared to be unarmed, but our 'arbâgi clearly did not like
them. He took his extortionate fare without the usual argument for
double the agreed sum, and drove off quickly.

Our camels, kneeling with their legs tucked under them, looked
prehistoric, like small dinosaurs. I mounted swiftly, sitting sideways
on the high wooden saddle and hooking my right knee around the
pommel—glad to find that, despite a recent lack of practice, I still
had the trick of it. Nayland Smith rode astride, keeping his feet in
the rope loops which served as stirrups.

A tap of the stick brought my camel to her feet in the awkward,
but familiar, three-stage motion, pitching me forwards, backwards,
and forwards again. Smith kicked his inexpertly with his heel, and
she bounded ahead, nearly throwing him. I followed, grinning mali-
ciously, since there was little that I could do more skillfully than he.

Leaving touristland behind, we rode out into the stony wilderness
which separates the Nile from the Red Sea. Soon we were passing
through a ravine floored with loose flakes of stone, the cliffs rising
steep and high on either side—an excellent place for an ambush, I
thought, if Fu Manchu had, by some occult means, learned of our
journey. Our escort produced long-barrelled revolvers of Boer War
vintage, which, till now, they had kept tactfully hidden in their
saddlebags. Happily, it was a needless precaution.

Our animals were sleek-coated and vastly different from the
wretched beasts of burden kept by the peasant farmers. I remembered that the Bishârîn had a long-standing reputation as camel
breeders. We rode at a steady canter, more smoothly than on
horseback, our mounts advancing their hind legs in step with their
forelegs, like men on the march. Darkness followed swiftly upon
twilight, but, in the clear air of the desert, the lamplight of the
heavens was all that we required.

For two hours or more, we rode on, seeing nothing but the stars
above. Looking up, one easily understood why the Ancient Egyptians had conceived the earth as a saucer-shaped depression covered by a star-spangled dome. All about us, the desolation was
complete. Nothing changed till, presently, a high ridge of limestone
loomed up before us like a wall, and, as we drew closer, the leader
of our party lifted his cumbersome pistol and fired a shot at the sky.

Instantly, a score of women swathed in black appeared atop the ridge, uttering the shrill, ululating *zaghareet* of welcome.

To this eerie accompaniment, we rode into the camp of Abu Nasrâni, which looked like that of an army—save that the tents were black, hut-shaped structures of coarse-grained cloth stretched over a square framework of timber. Here and there, campfires glowed. A horde of figures surged towards us, greeting our arrival with shouts and a firework display of antiquated muskets, the orange flashes stabbing blades of fire into the night. Laughing and chattering, they surrounded us, clutched at the halters, and led us to a tent—or, rather, a marquee—somewhat separated from the rest.

As our camels sank to their knees, three men rushed out, two holding lanterns and preceded by the other—a powerfully built man in late middle age, with a thick beard shaped like a headsman's axe, the points curling upwards. He wore princely robes and carried a dagger at his belt, encrusted with gems too big to be real.

"*Ahlan! Ahlan wa sahlan, ya akhi!*" he cried, and embraced Smith, kissing him on both cheeks. "Praise be to Allah, who has given me the years to behold thy face once more!"

I noted that he addressed my friend not by the Turkish title *effendîm* but as "my brother," and so warm was his welcome that a cynic might have doubted its sincerity. When we were introduced, he greeted me with a like cordiality, but, to my relief, less effusively.

The tent into which we were conducted was a huge, rectangular affair, one wall being raised upon poles, so as to leave the whole of that side open to the air. It was made not of canvas but of woven goatshair, and the number of goats which had contributed to its making defied my imagination. Of furnishings there were virtually none—solely rugs and carpets, and a number of wooden chests. Incongruously, however, it was lighted by bare electric bulbs which, throughout the evening, dimmed, brightened, and occasionally went out, in response to the eccentric behaviour of an unseen motor, humming and choking in the near vicinity.

We sat down and reclined, resting our elbows on camel saddles, and surrounded by a dozen of our host's principal retainers. Each wore a bandolier of brass-tipped cartridges, and a more villainous-looking crew I had never seen.

"I am ashamed that this is all I have to offer," declared Abu Nasrâni, "but I think that, if a man cannot load his worldly goods on his camels, then the earth owns him and he owns nothing."

"Be comforted," answered Smith. "We ask only your friendship."

"Yet," insisted his friend, "I am not ignorant. I can write my name, and I have been to Paris!"

He added a short description of that city which might have astonished a Frenchman.

Two servants lugged in a case of champagne. Contemptuous of wired corks, they dashed the necks from the bottles with a stone and poured the foaming contents into tankards made from old tin cans. Their lord led the drinking, and most of his band followed suit, though some bowed to Islam and contented themselves with sherbet.

Here, Abu Nasrâni lived like a king. Outside the tent, two of his subjects stood on sentry duty, leaning on ancient, muzzle-loading weapons.

While we drank, he talked of his affairs—of his caravans bringing ostrich feathers, lion skins, leopard skins, henna leaves, and ivory from the Sudan, salt and soda from the Wâdi Natrûn, and dates from Dakhla. Of other things—smuggled spirits and tobacco, and items pilfered from army stores—he did not speak, neither did we ask.

Anxious though we were to begin the business on which we had come, I knew that it could not be done until we had dined, and, in due course, four men staggered in, carrying a brass tray the size of a small dining table, loaded with a mountain of rice in a sea of clarified butter, the slopes strewn with pieces of mutton and the summit crowned with a sheep's head.

The meal which ensued, clustered around the enormous platter, did little to aid the digestion. We wadded the rice into balls, tossed them into our mouths, and tore off strips of meat with our fingers. The sheep's head had two eyes, and they were meant for us. While Smith chewed manfully through one, I contrived to slip the other into the neck of my shirt, where it slid down and rested, cold and sticky, against my stomach. But it felt better out than in.

At length, when we were all bloated to capacity, the leftovers were carried out to feed those of lesser rank. But the lavish hospitality of Abu Nasrâni was still far from exhausted. Three men and a woman made their appearance, armed with musical instruments, and settled themselves down. One man bore a *darabukkeh*, shaped like a gross earthenware jar with a skin stretched over the mouth, another a *kemengeh*—resembling a one-stringed fiddle, save that it had two strings and a soundbox made from a coconut shell—while the third carried a double reed pipe, or *arghool*. The woman had only a tambourine.

"In this miserable place," said Abu Nasrâni, "there are no *ghawâzî* to delight the hearts of men. But I have four daughters, and to-night, by God, they shall dance for you!"

I was aware of a subtle disturbance in the background—a stir of expectancy. I jerked my head round and saw that the goatshair curtain separating the main part of the tent from the women's quarters had been partially drawn aside, and within the opening stood four dark-skinned girls, giggling nervously.

"Good heavens!" I muttered. "Even the women in the Square of the Fountain wear something besides their jewellery!"

The girls advanced and formed up into a line, facing us. They wore anklets trimmed with tiny silver bells, numerous arm bangles and necklaces. Apart from these items, the costume of each was completed by a sort of apron composed of a dozen strings of gold coins linked edge to edge and suspended from a chain girdle.

That this was a unique performance, staged for our benefit, was confirmed by the behaviour of the aged *kemengeh* player, who stared at them open-mouthed and goggle-eyed. Abu Nasrâni frowned, reached out, and thumped him on the head with his fist.

"Play!" he snarled.

The old man set the foot of his fiddle hastily to the ground, drew his bow across the strings, and the dancing commenced. The girls raised their arms, clashing miniature brass cymbals attached to the thumb and second finger of each hand, oscillating their hips so that the strings of coins swayed and jingled, to a furious pounding of the *darabukkeh* and a wild cacophony of sound from the other instruments. The *kemengeh* squealed and the *arghool* whined like a small bagpipe. I leaned towards my companion.

"His own daughters?" I murmured. "The old villain!"

"Do you suggest," asked Smith acidly, "that it would be more proper for him to employ someone else's daughters?"

All four appeared to be the same age—which, I supposed, was possible, since Islam allowed him four wives. They were fine-looking girls, though not good dancers—indeed, I doubt if they had ever done it before—but what they lacked in technique they made up in audacity, posturing with a calculated immodesty rendered all the more shocking by their artlessness.

Outside the tent, a wave of shadowy figures appeared, summoned by the sounds of revelry and the swift spread of rumour. Our sentries lifted their muskets, fired admonitory shots above their heads, to advise them that this was a private entertainment, and they drew back, watching from a safe distance.

Abu Nasrâni clapped his hands, shouting encouragement, and the four dusky Corybantes responded. They knelt, and threw themselves backwards across our knees. They leapt across our extended limbs—neither Smith nor I being able to sit cross-legged—and shook their absurd, fringelike aprons in our faces.

For half an hour they kept it up, one or another sometimes dropping out to lean against a tent post, fanning herself with one hand, while the man with the *arghool* blew till his face was purple, his cheeks puffed out like balloons. But, at last, it was over and the girls retired to the curtained rear of the tent, panting and glossy. The musicians gathered up their instruments and withdrew.

At a sign from Abu Nasrâni, the rest of our companions followed them out, leaving the three of us alone. A servant entered, bearing a beak-spouted coffee pot and little silver *fanâgîn* on a tray suspended from an arch-shaped handle. Tall brass *marâghîleh*, like ornate candlesticks, were placed beside us, gurgling horribly as we drew the perfumed smoke through the water.

Now, and no sooner, the real purpose of our visit might be accomplished. Abu Nasrâni smoked silently for a time, then, at last, turned towards Smith.

"The name of every thief from Aswan to Iskanderiyeh is known to me," he began, "yet I speak against none. But, for your sake, Nai'man es-Samit, I would denounce my own parents—were they not already in Hell. . . ."

Again he was silent, scowling till his hirsute eyebrows almost met.

"There is a man named Joseph Malaglou," he said finally, "a dealer in *hashîsh* and worse. He calls himself a pure Greek from the island of Cos, though in truth he knows not the name of his father—neither he nor his mother. Once, he claimed to have cotton interests in the Delta. But, now that your soldiers are active in the Sinai, he has moved to a plantation north of Esneh."

I listened quietly, making a pretence of smoking with enjoyment, but finding the flavour of *tumbakh* mixed with honey mild and insipid to a confirmed pipe smoker.

"On the fourth day of Shâban," resumed Abu Nasrâni, "this man came to me, offering money if I would help him to find one of those who worked for your enemies. There are many such in Egypt, and some I know, though I do not speak. I love the British no better than I love the Germans. No matter who wins, it will be the worse for us."

"But why," inquired Smith, curbing his impatience with an effort, "did Malaglou wish to get in touch with them?"

"This he was reluctant to tell me. But, seeing that otherwise I would not help him, he confessed that he was acting for another—a strange man, old and mad, who had robbed your people of a secret for which your enemies would pay much."

"Brooker!" I burst out. "Then it was Brooker himself who made the approach!"

"So it seems." Smith shrugged and addressed Abu Nasrâni. "Did you do as he asked?"

"No. He left unsatisfied." Our host paused, staring gloomily at a cockroach, which was busying itself with a food stain on the carpet at his feet. "I love the Germans no better than I love the British. Besides, he has cheated me twice already."

Taking the mouthpiece from his lips, he spat viciously and accurately upon the cockroach.

"Yet," he went on, "I heard later from my spies that, even without my help, Malaglou had succeeded and entered into a compact with one who lived in Luxor, disguised as a Frenchman. . . ."

"Kurt Lehmann, alias François Duhamel!" I said.

"*Aiwa!* That was his name. This man became his confederate, and gave to him a wireless machine, such as the Germans have, that they might talk secretly to each other. Somehow, though I know not how, their plans miscarried. You learned of them—the old one fled, and now you pursue him."

"This is all that you know?"

"All that I know—yes." Abu Nasrâni nodded. "Yet this I say to you. Having no other place to go, he whom you seek may now be hiding in the house of Joseph Malaglou—or he, if any, may know where he is. . . ."

I glanced at Smith. This seemed like a plausible hypothesis, but before we could discuss it, we were interrupted. The curtain at our backs twitched open and the four daughters of Abu Nasrâni reappeared—more strangely, and no less disturbingly, clad in filmy nightgowns from the Rue de Rivoli. One of them came forward, bent to her father's ear, and murmured something. Our host turned to Nayland Smith, added a few words which I did not catch, and Smith turned to me with a glint of mischief in his eyes.

"It seems," he said tonelessly, "that accommodation has been prepared for us, and he asks which of his daughters we will choose to attend us. . . ."

I stared at him blankly.

"Well, I warned you!" he said blandly. "We can't get back to Luxor to-night, and, after all, you only have to choose *two* of them!"

Words failed me.

18

THE ETHEREAL ENEMY

The wide lobby of the Savoy Hotel was almost unoccupied, for it was midnight, and, in Luxor, sightseeing commences with the dawn. Waiting for Nayland Smith to rejoin me, I sat alone, companioned only by a waiter who moved silently about the tables, dusting them off and emptying ashtrays.

Following our night at Abu Nasrâni's camp, of which I will say no more, we had returned with our plans to pursue Dr. Fu Manchu temporarily shelved. Clearly, our immediate business must be to pursue the villainous Joseph Malaglou, and for this we might now enlist the help of the military, since the charge was one of espionage.

Smith had spent most of the afternoon at a nearby Army camp, in conference with the commanding officer, and come back with a strange story. It seemed that, during the past few nights, clandestine wireless transmissions had already been picked up, emanating from somewhere in the neighbourhood of Esneh, though, for technical reasons which I did not understand, it had so far proved impossible to pinpoint the source.

Had Brooker sought shelter with his confederate? Was it he who called? To-night, we intended to find out. Smith, who had been up to his room to change from dinner things into more suitable attire, reappeared at the foot of the stairs, walking a trifle stiffly—our desert jaunt had left him with camel sores. He lowered himself gingerly into an armchair, grimacing and swearing, and I tried to smile sympathetically, but he took it badly.

"Laugh if it pleases you," he gritted. "An Asian camel has *two* humps, and one doesn't have to perch on it like a gnome on a toadstool!"

I hastened to change the subject.

"According to what we have learned from your friend Abu Nas-râni," I said, "it was not the Germans who persuaded Professor

Brooker to turn his work over to them, but he who offered."

Smith grunted and made no comment.

"Human nature being what it is," I went on sadly, "I think I can understand his motives. Overworked and underpaid by his Government employers . . . unappreciated, and frustrated by a tangle of red tape . . . But what an insane way of doing it! Since he had free access to those cursed documents which he stole from Meadi, why didn't he just copy them? Why did he raise the alarm by going off with the originals?"

Smith shrugged contemptuously. "Scientists are usually half mad—and Crawford, his partner in crime, must have been nearly as mad to let him. . . ." He broke off, glancing impatiently at his watch. "Damn it! It's twenty past twelve, and I said midnight. Where are they?"

"Here now, I think," I replied.

Coincident with his words, a man had entered from the street and stood in the doorway, looking around him—a young man, wearing the ugly khaki uniform of a non-commissioned officer, with breeches and spindle-legged puttees. I beckoned to him, and he crossed to our table, stiffening to a crisp salute.

"Corporal Billings, reporting for duty, sir! Sorry we're late, sir—'ad a bit of a breakdown."

"Sit down," said Smith, "and forget the formalities. Have the signals recommenced?"

"Yes, sir. Ten minutes ago, the same as last night and the night before—just the same group of figures."

Billings, I gathered, was in charge of the direction-finding unit which had first detected the transmissions.

"It's a call sign," he continued, "but 'e ain't gettin' no response."

"If Brooker is there," I said, turning towards Smith, "they may be trying to get in touch with Kurt Lehmann. Perhaps they don't know that he is—well, if not exactly dead, no longer Kurt Lehmann."

"It's took me three nights to get a fix on 'im," added the corporal. " 'E don't stay on long enough. 'E's somewhere north of Esneh and south of Luxor, but I still don't know where."

"Surely," asked Smith sharply, "the sensible thing to do is to use another unit and take a cross-bearing?"

"Right you are, sir," agreed Billings. "But we ain't *got* another one! They've bled us dry and sent everything up north for the push on bloody Gaza."

"It doesn't matter," I said shortly. "We know where he is."

Try as I would, I could not really like Corporal Billings, and the better I came to know him, the less I liked him. Wireless, which he called "radio," was his ruling passion. He neither drank nor smoked and, in civilian life, had spent all his available cash on components and every Sunday tinkering with wires and a soldering iron on the kitchen table. An expert in his limited field, he was one who scared me a little, as I saw in him the kind of technician upon whom our post-war world would depend—uncultured, and disinterested in all but the manual skills of his job.

Nayland Smith rose to his feet.

"Let us get on with it," he proposed. "As Petrie says, we know who your man is. But unless we can catch him in the act, we shall have no case against him."

On a stone bench adjacent to the hotel entrance sat a cross-eyed lad of poverty-stricken appearance, munching at a handful of *tirmis*. This was Awad, who had accompanied us from Abu Nasrâni's camp and sat there all day, uncomplaining, since the management would on no account have him inside. It was his task to lead back the camels, but first to guide us to the premises of Joseph Malaglou.

Billings glanced at him coldly and with ill-concealed scorn. As I have often observed, the class distinction between the lower and the lowest is the widest gulf in the social scale.

Drawn up in front stood a canvas-covered motor van—similar to, but larger than, the one in which we had ridden earlier in the week—with an odd contraption like a child's hoop mounted on the roof. Smith approached and spoke to the man at the wheel.

"Drive straight to the village of esh-Shaghb."

"Yes, sir! Where the 'ell is it, sir?"

"This young man will show you." Smith introduced our guide. "He knows enough English to give you directions."

The driver, whose name was Rigby, and whose former charge had been a London bus, looked at Awad as unfavourably as Corporal Billings had and turned to the soldier at his side.

"Git aht of it, Thompson," he ordered, "and go in the back with t'others." He turned again to Awad. "Awright, then! 'Op up 'ere, you black-faced little blighter, and don't drop your bloody peanuts all over everywhere!"

Awad grinned and, at a nod from Smith, scrambled up, while we crowded into the rear to join our comrades for the night—five khaki-clad men from some border county regiment, as hard and as taciturn as nails. Billings put on headphones and sat down with his back to us at an apparatus which I recognized as a wireless set, though it had more knobs and dials than any I had ever seen, and pear-shaped valves glowing behind a screen of metal meshwork.

"Signals still coming in, sir," he announced.

Outside the well-paved streets of the town, the van bounced heavily, jostling me against the man beside me. The rifle slung from his shoulder struck me on the elbow, and we swore in unison.

Unlike the grinning, chattering Egyptians who had accompanied us down the Nile on our ill-fated expedition against the *Nitocris,* our companions were a surly crew, sullenly resigned to doing as they were told, but resenting and mistrusting the authority of men "in civvies"—since, as usual, Smith had neglected to wear his uniform. Unhappy in their company, I was conscious of a bleak sense of alienation. Billings, crouched over his instruments, with the black pillboxes clamped to his ears and the metal adjusting rods sticking up like antennae, had a peculiarly Martianesque appearance.

South of Luxor, the interior of the van was stifling, and less like a tent than the claustrophobic confines of a submarine, as we moved blindly on, groping with invisible hands for an invisible enemy. From time to time, Corporal Billings reached up to the control which, presumably, rotated the hooplike thing on the roof, muttering something esoteric about vectors and decibels. This, I thought somberly, was war—devoid of the clarion call of bugles, the hoofbeats of cavalry, and the desperate interplay of bright-hued uniforms, which had once made war seem glorious. Ugly and uninspiring, it frightened and disgusted me.

Thus, for an hour or more, we continued on our way, seeing nothing and saying little, till at last the van stopped abruptly. A blind shot up in the partition separating us from the driver's cab, and Rigby's face appeared framed in the opening.

" 'Ere we are, sir!"

The canvas curtains which closed the rear of the vehicle were swiftly unlaced, and all of us got down, to find Awad standing in the road with Rigby.

"*Ahi el-'ezbah!*" Awad said, and pointed.

Below us, a broad valley lay cloaked in shadow. Dimly, I made out the outline of a rough track leading to an extensive property, with fields beyond and bushes dappled with white tufts of cotton, like droplets of snow. Billings handed a pair of night glasses to Smith, who employed them briefly, then passed them to me without comment. Seen through the powerful lenses, the house of Joseph Mala-glou was of an architecture which defied definition and had, I surmised, been built by some prosperous landowner during the preceding century—a confusion of archways, balconies, and outside staircases. Crowning one corner was a Gothic tower with a tall spire shaped like a beer bottle.

"Good place for an aerial!" said Billings.

"Right!" directed Smith. "Get back to your equipment, and train your sights on the house—or whatever it is that you do. Check that the signal comes from it. Then we'll go in."

The corporal saluted fatuously and left us. Awad chewed *tirmis*—of which he seemed to have an inexhaustible supply—and offered some to Rigby, who accepted. Astonishingly, they had made friends. Billings reappeared, flushed and excited.

"That's it, sir!"

"Let's go, then!" Smith glanced at Rigby. "Switch off the head-lights and don't come any closer, or he may hear the engine. This is a hanging offence, and he won't be taken easily."

By starlight, the descent was troublesome and unsafe, but we managed it without mishap. At the foot of the declivity, we came into the shadow of a high adobe wall surrounding the premises. Having left only Awad and Corporal Billings behind, the rest of us—eight in number—skirted the wall till we came to a gap. There was no gate. The house we had seen from above faced us across an open space encumbered by ill-kept bushes and spreading casuarinas. No lights showed.

Smith halted us to issue instructions, briskly taking charge as I had seen him do in our several raids upon houses occupied by Fu Manchu.

"It will take too long to break in the door." He pointed to the shuttered windows. "Force the shutters and, if there is any glass, smash it. Then in as quickly as you can. There are nine or ten rooms in there and our man may be in any one of them. If he tries to escape, shoot—but not to kill. We want him alive."

We approached swiftly but cautiously, the six soldiers crouching over their rifles as if expecting to be met by machine-gun fire. Smith and I took the lead, with pistols ready in our pockets and electric torches in our hands, since we looked to find the interior in darkness. Still there was no sign of life, but ere we had gone halfway, we were startled by a dull crash, loud but distant, from somewhere at the back of the house.

"What was that?" I gasped.

"God knows! It sounded like a ton of bricks being dropped on a woodshed! Come on!"

Abandoning caution, Smith broke into a run and we followed. But, before we could reach it, the door burst open in our faces and three figures—two men and a woman—came hurtling out, yelling, and hoarse with terror. They appeared to be servants, and, from their scanty attire, appeared to have been sleeping.

Oblivious to our presence, they rushed past us, careless of our shouts, and vanished plantationwards—crazed with fear, not of us, but of something at their backs.

"Let them go!" ordered Smith. "Inside!"

At the same instant, I was thrust roughly aside and Awad—who had evidently ignored his instructions to stay with the van—came streaking past in the opposite direction, waving a crescent-shaped dagger, his eyes bright with the lust of battle.

Shrieking *"Allahu akbar!"* he vanished through the open doorway, and was in first.

Smith and I were hot on his heels, switching on our torches as we came immediately into a dark, narrow corridor. At the far end, we saw Awad beating upon a closed door with the hilt of his dagger, while from beyond issued a confused din of furniture being over-turned, woodwork ripped apart, and a high screaming which, as we caught up with him, ended suddenly and horribly. Smith grabbed Awad by the shoulder and dragged him back to make way for the two armed men behind us, who set about the door with their rifle butts.

It was a solid affair, locked and bolted from inside, and resisted their efforts. In the close confines of the passage, the noise of their pounding was deafening—yet insufficient to disguise the crashing and tearing sounds which continued, simultaneously, within the room, as if it were being demolished with a sledge-hammer. Woven into those sinister sounds I detected another—a snarling and incho-ate babbling which surely came from no human throat, yet gro-tesquely resembled speech.

"God in Heaven!" I cried. *"What* is in that room?"

19

THE THEBAN MINOTAUR

Above the tumult, I heard a whistle, pitched so high that it hurt the ears. Then, reduced almost to splinters, the door gave way, disclosing a chaos of destruction. An oil lamp hung from the ceiling by a chain, swinging back and forth, casting eldritch shadows. On the far side was a French window. Though the shutters were hinged to fold outwards, they had been burst *inwards,* as if by a battering ram.

Blood was everywhere—in scarlet pools and streaks upon the floor; splashed even upon the walls. So much had been spilled that one could scarcely believe that all had come from a solitary victim. Yet such was the case. Joseph Malaglou lay in one corner, in a half-seated position, and no medical opinion was needed to pronounce him dead, but I hurried to bend over him.

He had been some fifty years of age, swarthy and strong-limbed. His face, which alone remained unmarked, was that of a man once poisonously handsome. Now, his mouth gaped open in a soundless scream, his eyes started from their sockets—the face of one who had looked not upon the Angel of Death but upon Satan. The wounds which had put an end to his evil life were ghastly beyond description.

"A wild animal has done this!" exclaimed Smith.

"Yes," I said unsteadily. "But these are not the marks of teeth or claws. This is some creature which has horns or tusks!"

Indeed, the state of the room could not have been worse if a bull had been let loose in it. The woodwork was gashed and split, the plaster torn from the walls, furniture ripped apart, the upholstery rent open and the packing scattered. But among the débris there was evidence enough of Malaglou's treachery. Close to one wall lay what was left of a wireless transmission set, the overturned batteries sparking and hissing.

"This is *his* work!" said my friend softly.

He pointed to the blood-stamped impression of a bare foot, the toes splayed fanwise and big enough for a size twelve shoe.

"The thing they took from the *Nitocris*!" I muttered.

Elsewhere, we found the imprint of a hand with fingers as long and as broad as those of a leather motoring glove.

"It has human hands and feet," mused Smith, "but, in Heaven's name, what sort of head does it have?"

"Good God! It must be a monstrosity like the Cretan Minotaur!"

Smith smiled faintly. "A Theban version, perhaps?"

I shuddered, thinking of the beast-headed gods of Ancient Egypt. In that room laid waste by the homicidal fury of a thing beyond our knowledge, it was tempting to think of them as a reality.

On the off chance that our runaway professor might still be somewhere inside, a search of the house was conducted and completed in ten minutes, no trace of him being found, and no evidence that he had ever been there.

"If he was hiding here," said Smith, tugging at his earlobe, "it was probably in some outbuilding—in which case, Fu Manchu has him already. . . ."

I crossed to the sagging shutters and peered out.

"Don't go out there!" he warned. "If that abominable creature is lurking about, it may come at you before you can defend yourself!"

I turned away from the window, but, before I could answer, a fresh interruption took place. Running footsteps sounded in the corridor, and Corporal Billings rushed into the room with the headphones hooked around his neck and the cord looped around his waist. Neglecting, in his excitement, to remove them, he had clearly run all the way from the van.

"The signals!" he panted. "They've started again, sir!"

"What? Impossible!"

"It's the same, sir!" insisted the corporal. "But it's a *different* station! And, judging by the strength, it ain't far!"

I exchanged glances of bewilderment with Smith. Billings stared about him, his eyes widening as they took in the destruction and the still figure slumped in the corner.

"Gawd! We never done this, did we, sir?"

"Of course not!" Smith snapped his fingers at the two men nearest. "You and you! Stay here till we can summon help. This is now a matter for the police, not the military. The rest of you—back to the van!"

Out we ran again, through the neglected garden and alongside the wall, seeing no trace of either the bestial intruder or the panic-stricken servants. The van stood as we had left it. Rigby leapt up into the cab, Awad bounding up beside him like a monkey. As we took our places in the back, Billings jammed a plug into a socket, and listened.

"There he is again, sir!"

The van jerked forward and stopped, the gears howling in reverse, as we made the turn.

"What is he sending?" demanded Smith.

"The same as usual, sir," replied Billings, and added, somewhat superfluously, "but it ain't the same bloke!"

"H'm!" Smith grunted, and scowled. "Well, it might be the man whom he was trying to contact—though it's strange that he should answer at the very moment when Malaglou died. . . ."

"Brooker himself?" I suggested.

"Possibly. But I doubt whether he knows how to operate a telegraph key."

Billings leaned forward, leaving the blind in the raised position, and talking over the driver's shoulder. Now that two of our force had been left behind, there was more room. The three who remained moved farther to the rear, aloof from the "officers," and talking in low, shuddering tones. Murder as conceived by Dr. Fu Manchu was not the same as death on the battlefield.

The corporal consulted his instruments, conferred with Rigby through the partition, and glanced back at us anxiously.

"It's on the other side of the ruddy canal!"

From within the van, I could see nothing, but it seemed that we were following an artery of the system which ran parallel with the Nile, sometimes on one side and sometimes on both.

"Find a bridge, then!" said Smith.

Of bridges there were many—but none constructed for a vehicle such as ours. We reached the first in less than a mile, halted, and got down to inspect it. Like all the rest, it was a wooden structure intended for camels and donkeys, and barely wide enough to accommodate the wheels. Awad ran on ahead, shook the handrail, and stamped on the planks.

"*Gamîd!*" he assured us. "*Gamîd ketîr!*"

"Not that strong, I'm afraid," said Smith doubtfully.

"I'll 'ave a go at it, sir!" offered Rigby. "You'd all best walk across first—then I'll try to git 'er over."

"Do it, and I'll recommend you for a decoration!"

Rigby grinned. "Thank you, sir. But I 'ope my old woman don't git it instead!"

He clambered into the driving seat while the rest of us trooped across in single file. The canal—I think it was the Ma'alla—was broad and deep, and, at this season, filled high enough to drown a regiment. On the far side, we waited and watched.

In the glare of the headlights, I saw the boards bend under the weight of the heavy army vehicle as it inched towards us. The bridge creaked and groaned. At the halfway point, Rigby gunned the motor, and he completed the crossing at a bound. It was well that he did so—for no sooner had the rear wheels gained the bank than the whole flimsy construction went crashing down into the water.

Nayland Smith laughed in sardonic relief.

"Another bit of somebody's property which our Government will have to pay for!"

Rigby leaned out of his cab.

"All aboard for Syden'am and the Crystal Palace!" he shouted.

For the third time that night, we took our places inside and the quest was resumed, but we had covered no more than a couple of hundred yards when our driver braked to a standstill and thrust his face through the square hole in the partition.

"There's no bloomin' road out there!" he complained. "Nothin' but sand and rocks and a bloody great mountain up in front!"

"Do the best you can," said Smith.

Now we were going literally across country, reeling drunkenly over arid ground, where stones pinged off the wheels and hammered at the tyres, throwing us from side to side. We hung on, clutching at each other and at anything for support, till, at length, came the inevitable disaster. The van pitched backwards and sideways, hurling all of us into a heap—save for one man, who was thrown clean out of the back. The rear wheels whirred and screamed, finding no traction. Rigby switched off the engine.

"We're stuck!" he announced laconically.

"Anybody hurt?" I asked, disentangling myself from Smith's legs and standing up.

Billings was. He had struck his head on the instrument panel, hard enough to leave him dizzy, and had a long cut over his left eye. Assuming the functions of medical officer, I applied a field dressing—luckily, we had no lack of supplies—and jumped down to join my companions, who had already descended. We stood in a disconsolate group, staring at our vehicle. One rear wheel had sunk axle-deep in a soft patch of sand, the other pointing skywards.

"We've got a couple of shovels," said Rigby. "Maybe we can dig it out."

"If not," answered Smith, "we can at least use the wireless to call for assistance—"

The end of his sentence was lost in a low rumble, as of distant thunder, and I glanced up at the sky. Contrary to popular belief, storms and even heavy rains are not unknown in Egypt. But, as usual, the night was clear and jewelled with a multitude of stars. For some ten to twenty seconds, the sound continued, rolling remotely back and forth, as one often hears it on a summer night in England.

"Sounds like gunfire!" said someone.

Corporal Billings was standing beside us, with the bandage pallid upon his forehead, and a pocket compass in his hand.

"Where's the bloody radio station?" he stammered. "It should be right out there"—he pointed with outstretched arm—"but there ain't even a ruddy palm tree!"

Ahead of us, there was nothing but a rock-strewn plain, ending in a perpendicular wall of cliffs a thousand feet high, as if we stood at the edge of the world. Awad clutched at the hem of Smith's bush shirt, gesticulating and pointing. Despite their strabismus, his eyes were as sharp as those of a nighthawk.

"Give me the glasses!" said my friend.

One of the soldiers re-entered the van to get them. Now that the thunder had died away, the air was awesomely still—just such a stillness, I thought, as might presage a violent electrical disturbance. Very far off, I heard the ghostly howl of a jackal.

"What do you think, Petrie?" inquired Smith. He handed me the binoculars. "Out there, at the foot of the mountain . . ."

Following his directions, I raised the glasses to my eyes and looked. At first, I could see nothing but a heap of rocks; then, as a lighter patch among the shadows came to my notice, I saw what he meant. I adjusted the focussing screw and the image sprang into sharp relief—a white cube, surmounted by a broken dome.

"It's a *sheikh*'s tomb!" I said.

Such structures were common in the foothills of the mountains bordering the Nile—the resting place of some locally revered saint, such as the ancient ascetic who had sat in holy meditation for fifty-three years, unclothed and unwashed, on the high bank above Hou.

"That's it!" declared Billings. "That's where he's got the transmitter!"

Smith nodded. "Probably. Well—it's no more than half a mile, and we can get there on foot. But he'll see us, and there may be shooting. Unsling your weapons!"

For my uniformed companions, a direct assault on an enemy position was doubtless no new experience, but I followed reluctantly, letting the soldiers take the lead. On the open terrain, bathed in the starlit brilliance of an Egyptian night, we were easy targets. But our bold advance had barely begun before a warning shout halted us in disorder.

Nayland Smith seized my arm, pointing upwards.

"My God! Look!"

High above the hard, flat ridge of the mountaintop, where the night sky spread like the gossamer veil of a dancing girl, bright with sequins, a section of the stars was blotted out by a huge, fusiform shape drifting silently against them—like the underside of a warship seen from below the surface.

"Cripes!" yelled Corporal Billings. "It's a Zeppelin!"

20

THUNDER IN
THE DESERT

Fu Manchu and his bizarre weapons were forgotten while we gaped foolishly upwards. All of us had heard much of the giant airships with which our enemies added a new dimension of terror to warfare, bringing war back to the homes of our men fighting in the trenches. None of us had ever seen one. Now, seen with my own eyes, the reality challenged belief—a Leviathan of the skies, six times the length of the *Nitocris,* deadly with the evil beauty of a barracuda.

"Oh, Gawd! The lights!" shouted Rigby, and went racing back to extinguish the headlamps.

That awesome form drifting silently above was one to panic a city. The bald figures of damage inflicted upon London—relatively slight—had thus far failed to impress me, but now, gazing spellbound, I understood the terror and frustration of unarmed civilians menaced by an adversary against whom they had no defence.

The powerful Maybach engines roared briefly into life and I heard again the sound of muted thunder, as the nose of the airship veered to the south-west. I could see the whole torpedo shape of it, black against the stars, tapering smoothly to angular tail fins, and flying so low that the gondolas beneath were clearly visible.

"They're sailing on the wind to avoid detection," said Smith, "and using the engines only to correct their course."

"*Ana khaif!*" muttered Awad. "This is a battle not of men but of demons!"

"It's the bloomin' signals!" cried Billings. He gestured towards the distant rocks, where the half-ruined shrine lay hidden in the shadows. "They're *guiding* the Zeppelin!"

His face was as pale as the bandage on his forehead. In the

background, the remainder of our force stood grouped together, their voices raised in a senseless babel of oaths and accents.

"Quiet in the ranks!" ordered my friend irritably. "Get back to your apparatus, Corporal, and send out a general alert."

"A lot of bloody good that'll be!" growled a man from the Tyneside, his thick speech angry and contemptuous. "There ain't a thing to fight *that* with no nearer'n bloody Cairo!"

"We must do what we can!" snapped Smith.

What, I wondered, could we do? Now almost above our heads, the great airship was heading inexorably in the direction of Esneh, on its unknown mission of murder. Whence it had come, whither it was bound, or upon what purpose, I had no idea. I could think of no military objective in Upper Egypt to justify such an expedition. But nothing, it seemed, might hinder it.

Yet, if we were helpless, there was one who was not. I did not see what took place till a furious hissing sound, as of a boiler blowing off steam, brought me spinning around, and I saw the *sheikh*'s tomb bathed in a lurid glare—an orange shaft of light streaming up from the broken dome. It lengthened, rising higher amid billowing grey smoke, and the dome collapsed, the walls of the dilapidated building falling in upon it in a shapeless heap, while the arrow of flame streaked up into the sky, gaining speed with each second, and trailing a fiery wake, like a comet.

"Strike, O Lord!" screamed Awad. "Strike down the enemies of the Faith!"

His fervent call upon Allah was spectacularly answered, as the bolt struck full upon the after part of the Zeppelin and exploded in a starshell burst of flashes, so brilliant that I could plainly see the Iron Cross painted amidships. The multiple detonations rang out like gunshots. Darkness and silence supervened; then a dull glow appeared close to the tail section, lighting the ship from within, followed by a corona of bright, spirituous flames licking along the top. They spread rapidly, erupting in vast clouds of fire as the gas cells caught, almost soundlessly, one after another, till the entire length was ablaze from end to end.

In the same space of time, my emotions changed as swiftly, from astonishment to relief—a savage thrill of elation, then a chilling sense of tragedy. Though mortally stricken, the airship did not fall like a stone, but sank with an agonising slowness, writhing in its death throes, as, second by second, it lost buoyancy. The fabric covering had burnt off first, to expose a skeleton of rings and girders, engulfed in a seething inferno of nearly two million cubic feet of burning hydrogen.

"God pity them!" whispered Smith. "They carry no parachutes!"

Bewitched by a dreadful fascination, I watched fixedly, though I longed to put my hands to my eyes and see no more. The metal framework looked like an iron basket of blazing coals. In the eerie light cast down from it, I saw the matchstick figures of men leaping to death, rather than endure the alternative, crushed and broken beneath the ponderous wreckage and cremated while yet alive.

Protracted though it seemed, the end came in less than a minute. At first, I thought that the Zeppelin would fall close to us—close enough, perhaps, to endanger our own safety—but it vanished below the brow of the cliffs and struck at some distance beyond. Thus far, all had happened silently, but now there was sound aplenty, proving beyond doubt that it had carried a full bomb load. A dozen heavy explosions boomed sullenly across the hills, each separate burst throwing up a shower of sparks into the sky, shaking the ground, and sending stones skittering down the mountainside.

I turned away, sick with horror. Not so our companions in uniform. They shouted, cheered, joined hands, and danced like madmen. One of them began to sing "Pack up your troubles," and the rest took it up. I stared at them, unable to share in their rejoicing, and hating them for their callous insensitivity.

"Don't be too hard on them, old man," said Nayland Smith softly, putting a hand on my shoulder. "They have wives and children whose lives are threatened by those monsters."

Awad appeared suddenly beside us, voluble with excitement.

"Henceforth I will pray at the appointed times, and wash first!" he vowed. "Great and wonderful is Allah, the Compassionate, who has saved us from the evil *djinn*! Many times have I seen his lances hurled across the sky to transfix the servants of wickedness.* But never have I seen a *shiháb* rise up from the earth! Truly, it was none other than the avenging spirit of the holy one who lies buried there, called forth from his tomb!"

"I'm afraid," said Smith, leaning towards me, "that our salvation was Satanic rather than Divine! The second station was a decoy set up by Dr. Fu Manchu, and, this time, he preferred old weapons to new. The Chinese did not, it is true, use their knowledge of gunpowder to make guns—but they made rockets!"

*He meant shooting stars—a common Arab superstition. [P.]

For the time being, we had only to notify our army base and await reinforcements. Our news would, I thought, be received with in-credulity—the possibility of a Zeppelin raid in these parts had been considered too remote to consider—but the thunder of the explo-sions must have been heard all the way down to the Nile.

We trooped back to the spot where we had left the van grounded at a steep angle, like a ship stuck on a reef. Fortunately, the wireless still worked, but the interior of the vehicle was useless for occupa-tion. We disposed ourselves on the sand, where the hardened cam-paigners curled up on their sides and went to sleep. I tried to do likewise, but could not. The faceless slaughter of war on the batt-lefield was new to me and more than I could stomach. Each time that I closed my eyes, I saw the burning airship flaring like a torn gas mantle, the crewmen hurling themselves to suicide, and I fancied I could hear their screams.

Sleepless, I sat with my arms clasped around my knees till the first spears of dawn came up from the Arabian desert. When the sun was fully above the horizon, it glittered on the duralumin latticework of the Zeppelin, thrust up like a pointed dome above the edge of the cliffs. Smoke still rose from it.

An hour later, we bestirred ourselves and crossed to the foot of the mountain, to inspect the fallen remains of the *sheikh*'s tomb, from which the rocket had been fired. The entire ramshackle build-ing had caved in, but we shifted some of the stones and found the body of a man, charred beyond recognition. Either he had bungled the firing or immolated himself deliberately—which, in the case of one who served Fu Manchu, was not unlikely.

Army trucks arrived soon afterwards, bringing a large detachment of men. They were officered by a middle-aged major with a tooth-brush moustache and a laugh like a mad horse, to whom Nayland Smith made a terse report while the soldiers prepared to ascend—to search through the débris, carry off anything of interest, and bring down the corpses for burial. We did not accompany them. I had no wish to see the scattered wreckage of the airship at close quarters, and, least of all, the bodies of the victims lying in shallow graves scooped out in the sand where they had fallen.

One of the trucks took us back to Luxor and left us at the hotel. By then, I was dog-tired, but, knowing that otherwise I should still be unable to sleep, I got out my medicine chest and took a tablet, though I hate to use soporifics. Thanks to this, I slept dreamlessly for a few hours, and awoke feeling better. The horror which I had witnessed would, from time to time, haunt me forever, but, to my shame, I realised that I could not feel a lasting concern for men whose names I had never known, and in whose fate I had had no hand.

The afternoon was well advanced when we came out upon the front terrace to sit at our favourite spot, facing the road across a narrow garden and a low stone wall. From scraps of conversation at the adjoining tables, I gathered that rumours of the air raid had reached the town, and Luxor was talking of nothing else. One or two of the more timid among the hotel guests had packed their bags and left.

Smith was silent for a time, smoking rapidly and nervously, constantly knocking out and re-filling his pipe, and expending an even greater quantity of matches than was his habit.

"Our guess was wrong," he said finally. "Malaglou was not trying to make contact with Kurt Lehmann, but with the Zeppelin. His job was to send out his signals nightly, since he did not know for certain when it would come."

"Where were they coming from?" I asked.

"Probably from Aleppo. The Germans are in charge there now. The point is, rather, where were they going? Zeppelins have an almost unlimited range, but their raids on England have been largely a failure, since they never know quite where they are." He hesitated, frowning across the river. Then: "The ship which came last night was flying low," he said slowly, "and trying to locate the Nile. . . ."

"Why? What was their target?"

"There is only one that I can think of—the Aswan Dam!"

I stared at him blankly. "But it's a hundred and fifty feet high; forty feet thick at the top, and a hundred at the base! Could it be destroyed by a few bombs?"

"I don't know. A number of well-placed hits, perhaps, might open up a fissure and the water pressure would do the rest." Nayland Smith's expression became more than usually grave. "They have more than a thousand million cubic yards pent up there—enough to supply all the land throughout the dry season. If the dam were to burst—as certain scientists in Cambridge predict that it inevitably will, one day—the result would be unthinkable. It would sweep away every town and village from Aswan to Assiut, and possibly beyond—flood the railway and the roads, drown men and livestock, and wash the soil from the fields, with famine and pestilence to follow. In a word, it would devastate Egypt! Our offensive in the Sinai would have to be called off—all our manpower and resources diverted to the colossal task of relief and reconstruction."

"Casualties would be numbered in the thousands!" I gasped. "Surely, not even the Germans . . ."

"Wouldn't they, Petrie?" He laughed grimly. "Our enemies are more logical than we tend to be. Is right and wrong a matter of arithmetic? May we slaughter a million in a year, but not in a week? Is it right to kill a hundred, but wrong to kill a thousand? Then what are the acceptable figures? The ultimate blasphemy of war is that it asks questions which no one can answer."

I, certainly, could think of none. Put in such terms, I could only concede that the lives of the Zeppelin's crew—twenty-nine, as we later learned—had been but a trivial sacrifice.

"Dr. Fu Manchu has no greater respect for human life than the Germans," resumed Smith. "But he could not allow them to destroy all the facilities which he has in Egypt. . . ."

Again he lapsed into silence, and I stared riverwards, listening to the lazy clatter of hooves and the sharp, metallic clang of the drivers' warning bell—curiously resembling that of a London tramcar—as the carriages turned out upon the concourse. On the opposite side of the road, an orderly line of un-English trees with smooth trunks supporting an enormous ball of foliage, like the trees in a child's painting, partially masked the Nile. Between them, I could see the white sails of the feluccas ferrying tourists across from the Valley of the Kings. How little they dreamed, I thought, of the fate from which they had been saved—and saved, ironically, by one whose motives were yet more inimical!

Waiters were drifting about the tables in the garden, setting out teacups, and the stream of carriages had changed direction, bringing the sightseers home from their dusty labours. The voluminous black carriage hoods were mostly drawn fully forward against the sun, so that the passengers could neither see out nor be seen. One had just pulled up before the herbaceous archway which guarded the approach to our hotel. Watching with an idle curiosity, I saw a man get out—a coal-black Nubian, massively proportioned and attired in flowing white, with a neatly tied turban. He stretched out his hand to assist his companion, and a woman alighted, stylishly dressed in a beige costume. She wore white lace gloves and a small hat with a half veil, which, at that distance, prevented me from seeing much of her features.

I could not recall having seen them earlier; yet, I thought, they could scarcely be new arrivals. The man—obviously a servant—carried no luggage, and, in any case, no train was due till the evening. Passing under the arch, they walked towards the entrance doors, the woman leading and the Nubian following several paces behind. But, without entering, she turned abruptly and came out upon the terrace, heading directly towards us.

Closer she came, and I leapt upright in my chair with an exclamation. She was Fah Lo Suee.

21

THE SIGN OF KHEPERA

Nayland Smith, seated with his back to the entrance, had not seen her till my cry of amazement caused him to turn swiftly around.

"Good God!"

He had no time to say more. Walking with short, impatient steps, her high heels ringing on the paving stones, Fah Lo Suee approached our table, pulled out a vacant chair, and sat down, eyeing us with a coldly defiant expression.

Smith took the pipe from his lips and laid it down.

"Your visit is unexpected," he said dryly, "but not unwelcome. I was about to call for some tea. Will you join us?"

"No!" came the curt reply. "I shall stay here only a minute, and to-day you will do nothing to detain me. Do you see that man behind you?"

Smith glanced back over his shoulder. Less than a dozen paces distant, the black Hercules stood leaning indolently against one of the pillars which supported the wide balcony above the hotel doors, his hands tucked in his loose sleeves.

"That is Salîm," said our visitor, "and, in his sleeve, he has a repeating air pistol. The darts are tipped with the same venom which once made a raving madman of your Inspector Weymouth—which, but for the clemency of Dr. Fu Manchu, he would be still."

Her reminder of that dreadful episode on the Thames sent a shiver through me. But Smith merely raised his eyebrows and shrugged.

"Nothing would please me more than to give him the sign to fire," added Fah Lo Suee viciously. "You forced me to sink a ship worth a caliph's ransom, and, when the owner hears of it, he will be furious. I shall have to let him whip me."

"Then Dr. Fu Manchu was not the owner?" murmured Smith.

"He was not. I had been in Cairo to have the *Nitocris* re-fitted for the pleasure of one who is a friend to us. But you will not trick me into telling you more than I wish. I have come here only to return good for ill and to offer you advice. You will not find Professor Brooker by chasing Zeppelins. Ask for him at the hotels."

Slipping the glove from her right hand, she opened her flat camel-skin handbag, took out a ring, and tossed it upon the table.

"This is for your protection. So long as you wear it, the Si Fan will not harm you."

Fah Lo Suee stood up and, without a word of farewell, walked away, checking her stride only for an instant as she passed Salîm.

"Come, filth!" she ordered, and swept regally out of the premises to the waiting 'arabîyeh, followed by her grinning bodyguard. Smith turned casually in his chair, watching her depart.

"There are carriages on the other side of the street," I said urgently. "Shall we go after her?"

"No! I, for one, have no desire to have poisoned darts shot at me. She means it, Petrie. Let her go."

"But why did she come?"

"For the reason that she gave. Dr. Fu Manchu could hardly propose an alliance, but that is what it amounts to." Returning his pipe to its accustomed place between his teeth, Smith paused to strike a match. "I think I know now what happened at Saqqara. When Fu Manchu abandoned us in Zoser's labyrinth, he fully intended to leave us there. But, by the time he reached the surface, he had changed his mind, realising that, alive, we might be useful to him. Therefore, he instructed his daughter to secure our release."

He picked up the ring and examined it curiously.

"Be careful!" I warned. "It may be some deadly contrivance with a spring."

"I doubt it."

Smith passed the ring across to me and I took it nervously between finger and thumb. It consisted of a large, greyish-green scarab, like half a walnut shell, crudely set in a broad band of copper.

"She doesn't want us murdered by mistake before we have served our purpose," he said. "But why a scarab, I wonder? You are the Egyptologist. Has it any special significance?"

"Not much," I replied. "It is Khepera, the common dung beetle, which the Ancient Egyptians regarded as a symbol of the sun."

"Preposterous!" he grunted. "What kind of people could believe that the sun was a ball of dung?"

"They did not actually believe . . ." I began warmly, but he was not listening.

Standing up, he slipped the ring into his shirt pocket.

"I will keep it, in case we need it. But I shan't wear it. I detest rings, and men who wear them. Well—we have time before dinner, so let us put Fah Lo Suee's suggestion into practice and go around the hotels. They will open their books to us, but not to her—which is why she wants us to do it."

All the European hotels lay within easy walking distance. We commenced with the Tewfikieh and the Karnak, these being almost next door, and, not to our surprise, drew blank. Brooker and his assistant had been heard of at neither.

"I can't think what Fu Manchu expects to gain by this," observed Smith, scowling ill-humouredly as we made our way south along the concourse, "unless he knows more than we do. Even if Brooker came back here with the hounds on his heels—which I doubt—he wouldn't have gone to a hotel. He may have been mad, but he wasn't a fool."

I smiled, thinking it rather a fine distinction.

We had come to the Great Temple of Luxor, which, for centuries, had lain forgotten and half interred under the mud huts and squalid alleyways of an Arab village. Now, by the tireless efforts of Maspero and his successors at the Department des Antiquités, the majestic ruins stood free once more to worship the sun—a roofless complex of mighty colonnades leading northwards to the twin-towered pylon of Rameses II. But to-day, as we passed by the battered columns, headless statues, and scattered blocks of stone, I could only feel that it all looked like the grim aftermath of an air raid.

"Here, if anywhere, we shall get word of him," said Smith, as we climbed the imposing quadrant of steps sweeping up to the first-floor entrance of the Winter Palace.

I agreed. Like Shepheard's in Cairo, the Winter Palace enjoyed almost a monopoly of official visitors.

I had a slight acquaintance with M. Duvivier, the dignified Swiss manager, who invited us at once into his office and seated us in armchairs. He received us cordially, but the troubled look in his eyes told me that he wished us elsewhere. It was his job to maintain the tranquility of his palatial establishment—ours to disturb it.

"Professor Brooker and Dr. Crawford?" he said. "Yes, I know

both those gentlemen. They stayed here regularly."

"Regularly?" exclaimed Smith.

"Yes—about once a month, over the past two years."

"You mean, they came here from Cairo?" I inquired.

"No, not from Cairo." M. Duvivier looked at me with an uneasy air of surprise. "They came from the opposite direction, stayed here a day or two, and went back the same way. They went on to Cairo on only two or three occasions that I recall." His expression of unease changed to one of positive alarm. "But am I to understand that a crime has been committed?"

"That is what we are here to determine," said my friend, mendaciously. "Let us proceed, if you don't mind. Did you know precisely where they came from, or what they were doing there?"

"Certainly not. For reasons of national security—or so I was informed—I was not permitted to know. But since they came and went by the train from Aswan, I naturally supposed that they had some work in connection with the dam."

"I see." Smith nodded. He pulled out his notebook and checked dates. "Their last visit would, I take it, have been at the end of August?"

"I don't know. I did not see them myself at that time. But we can easily ascertain."

M. Duvivier picked up the telephone and spoke to the front desk, asking for the records to be brought.

"Let me ask you now," pursued Smith, "if you knew the reason for these periodic trips to Luxor."

"Certainly!" repeated M. Duvivier. "Professor Brooker came here to consult our resident physician, Dr. Deane. He suffered from some sort of chronic condition which made him a very sick man."

"You don't know what his illness was?" I put in curiously.

"No. I'm not sure that anyone knew."

While we waited for the books, Nayland Smith lapsed into a thoughtful silence, tugging absently at his earlobe.

"M. Duvivier," he said at length, "I have never had the privilege of meeting Professor Brooker. But you have. What kind of man was he? In your opinion, was he altogether sane?"

"Sane? Yes." The manager laughed nervously. "But he was somewhat absent-minded. Our people were forever running after him with things he had forgotten. Twice, he left his key in his room and locked himself out."

A knock sounded at the door and a clerk entered, bringing the hotel register and a file of papers, laid them upon the desk, and withdrew. We watched silently while M. Duvivier turned the pages.

"Yes," he announced, "they were here on Saturday, the first of September, and left on the morning train for Cairo."

Smith and I looked at each other. This was what we had expected. M. Duvivier continued to turn pages and consulted the file.

"However," he went on, frowning, "I can find no later record and no reservation seems to have been made for them. If they returned to Luxor, they did not stay at this hotel."

"They did not return," said Smith shortly, and stood up. "I don't think we need to trouble you any further, M. Duvivier, but I should like to have a word with your physician, Dr. Deane."

"That can be arranged." M. Duvivier likewise stood up and came around the desk to shake hands. "In addition to his practice here, Dr. Deane is chief medical advisor at the hospital on the corner. He is there now, but he will no doubt be back before long. If you would care to go out on the terrace and wait for him, I will have some refreshments sent out to you, and leave word for him to join you as soon as he comes in."*

Out on the wide, square terrace overlooking the spacious garden, the ritual of afternoon tea was drawing to a close and few of the tables were occupied. Nayland Smith made no remark, though from the grim set of his jaw I could see that he was murderously angry. But, containing his emotions with an effort, he remained silent until the waiter had served us. Then the storm broke.

"Damnation!" he burst out. "Those two men were never at Meadi! Fernshawe is a master of prevarication—I was a fool to tackle him when I was too tired to think. When I asked him about the Midnight Sun, do you remember what he actually said?"

I thought carefully before replying, trying hard to recall the scene in the general's study after our escape from Saqqara.

"I don't think he answered you," I said slowly. "Instead, he asked *me* if I had heard of the solar energy experiment at Meadi."

"Exactly—and we both fell into the same trap! There is nothing going on at Meadi but an attempt to make the enemy believe that something is—to divert their attention from what is going on elsewhere. In short, we have not a shred of evidence that the Midnight Sun project has anything to do with solar energy!"

---

*In 1914, the resident physician of the Winter Palace Hotel was a man named *Dr. Dunn.* Perhaps the same?[Ed.]

"Good heavens!" I muttered. "Then we are back where we started!"

Smith sat glaring into space, hard-eyed and silent, and clamping upon the stem of his pipe so fiercely that he seemed likely to bite through it, till a shadow fell across our table and I looked up to see a man in an old-fashioned frock coat standing beside us.

"I am Dr. Deane," he said, and, at our invitation, sat down reluctantly.

Dr. Deane was conservative of dress, with a manner as stiff as his white starched collar.

"I am told that you are seeking information in respect of Professor Richard Brooker," he began, "and that you do so on behalf of British Army Intelligence. But, as Dr. Petrie will clearly understand, I am not at liberty to discuss the affairs of my patients."

"I appreciate that," replied Smith quietly. "But permit me to explain. The professor and his assistant were involved in an accident. Crawford is dead, and Brooker is missing."

"What!" Deane looked thunderstruck. "Dear me!"

"No one has seen him since early last month," I said. "Anything which you can tell us will be in your patient's interests."

"For what ailment were you treating him?" asked Smith.

A brief hiatus ensued while Dr. Deane struggled with his professional conscience. Then, evidently feeling it more proper to confide in a fellow practitioner, he turned to me.

"In the circumstances, there seems to be no reason why I should not speak. Professor Brooker was suffering from a rare form of pernicious anaemia, which did not respond well to treatment."

"Would it, in your opinion, be fatal?"

"Eventually—yes. Probably in a matter of weeks, if he had ceased to be treated. He required constant medication, and, on two occasions, his condition became so alarming that I was compelled to send him to Cairo for a blood transfusion."

"Only twice?" rapped Smith. "You didn't send him there six weeks ago?"

"No," said Dr. Deane, looking at him in some surprise. "If he went there then, it was not on my advice. His condition at that time was poor but relatively stable."

Smith caught my eye and nodded significantly.

"But you saw him when he was last here?"

"Yes, I did."

Out came Smith's notebook.

"To be precise, on Saturday, the first of September?"

Dr. Deane hesitated, frowning. Then, with an air of complete innocence, he dropped his bombshell.

"No," he said. "If he was here on that date, I could not have seen him, since I was not in Luxor that weekend. It was two days later, on Monday the third, that I last saw him."

I stared, speechless with astonishment. Deane had seen the professor *after* his flight from Cairo! Nayland Smith, equally astonished, but better able to control his emotions, flashed me a quick look, warning me not to panic our witness.

"You are sure of that?" he asked evenly.

"Yes, quite sure. It was the first time that he came to me at the hospital—usually, I saw him here in the hotel—and the only time that I ever saw him unaccompanied by his assistant."

"And where did he go afterwards?"

"I presume that he came back here, since this is where he always stayed."

We, however, knew that he had not.

"Were there any other unusual circumstances surrounding this last visit?" queried Smith relentlessly.

"Possibly there were—though I thought little of them at the time." Again Deane hesitated, obviously finding it difficult to recall events which had occurred six weeks previously. "It was late in the evening when he arrived at the hospital, and it was only by chance that he found me there. He had made no appointment, and I was not expecting him for at least another week. He asked me for a further supply of the capsules which I prescribed for him, though he should still have had plenty. He said that he had lost them."

"Did he, by any chance, have a briefcase chained to his wrist?" I added eagerly.

Dr. Deane started. "Good heavens! How do you know that? Yes, he did. . . . Well, not precisely a briefcase, but a small suitcase, and very heavy. The steel cuff had chafed the skin, and I suggested that he should detach it. He said that he had lost the key."

"What about his clothes?" snapped Smith. "Were they untidy? Dishevelled?"

"He was always very untidy. If he was any more so then, I really did not notice."

Smith pursed his lips irascibly. Dr. Deane's powers of observation left much to be desired, but I sympathised. A hotel physician with a register of transient patients could, I felt, hardly be expected to pay much attention to details outside his profession.

"He appeared nervous?" I suggested.

"He was always nervous. It was partly a feature of his personality, and partly a symptom of his illness." Dr. Deane made a noble effort at concentration. "Certainly," he said slowly, "his manner *was* somewhat strange. As a rule, he made no unsolicited remarks— none whatever. Therefore, I was startled when he suddenly asked me if I thought it possible for a scientist to believe in God."

"How did you interpret that?" demanded Smith.

"A trifle unfavourably. I could only conclude that he feared he had not much longer to live. I tried to reassure him, and he made no further reference to the subject."

"To what other subjects did he make reference?"

Dr. Deane laughed apologetically, but with a hint of derision. "Oh, nothing but idle topics—the current state of the war in France, numerology, the absurdity of women's fashions, the fallacy of the metric system, and, just as he was leaving, some desultory talk about a picture in my room at the hotel—"

"A picture?" echoed Smith. "A picture of what?"

"A rather indifferent watercolour, painted and given to me by one of my patients." Dr. Deane smiled. "It depicts the ruins of an old Coptic church, called Der el-Melik. Some months ago, when they were visiting me here, Dr. Crawford had asked me what it was, but I had completely forgotten the incident until Professor Brooker reminded me. He asked me where the building was situated, and how one could go there. . . ."

22

A SCANDALOUS SITUATION

Dusk was gathering as we came out upon the riverbank, and the reedy voice of a *mueddin* chanting the sunset call to prayer floated across the road from the ugly little mosque of Abu'l Haggag, incongruously stuck on one corner of the Great Temple—an unwitting hymn to Ra descending into Amenti, the western afterworld of the Ancient Egyptian dead. Nayland Smith walked briskly as we headed back towards our hotel in a very different mood from that in which we had left.

"Fernshawe has lost a trick!" he said—and I readily forgave him for the triumphant tone of malice in his voice. "Brooker came back here, to renew the stock of medicine which he had lost in the fire, and get directions to the one place where he thought he could hide."

"Der el-Melik?"

"Of course!" Smith cupped his hands to light his pipe as he walked, talking between puffs. "When he fled from Cairo, his sole object was to seek a hiding place. He had the choice of a thousand empty tombs, ruined temples, and abandoned houses. But how could he find one? Fortunately, there was one that he knew of."

"Amazing, surely, that he should remember it!"

"No, I don't think so. Absent-minded though he was, Brooker was probably the sort of eccentric genius who forgot nothing he had ever heard. He not only remembered the picture he had seen in Deane's room, but was cunning enough to disguise his interest by talking about other irrelevant subjects too."

"It was lucky that you picked the right one!" I remarked.

"Lucky?" Smith's lips curled in a sad smile. "Give me some credit for knowing how to conduct an investigation, Petrie! The other things he talked about were general—the picture was specific. It stuck out like an obelisk. Heaven knows where he spent the night after leaving Deane at the hospital. But, in the morning, he could surely have found an English-speaking guide to take him down the river."

"Is it possible that he is still there?"

"Perhaps." Smith nodded grimly. "Fu Manchu has no doubt learned that Brooker returned to Luxor from someone who saw him here, but he has been unable to discover where he went. Therefore, he decided that it was time to use us as his stalking horses. Now the hunt is on, and every step we take will be covered."

I glanced around suspiciously at the carriages clattering past and the couples strolling hand in hand under the trees.

"No one appears to be following us now," I said.

"No one will *appear* to be!"

Darkness had fallen during our twenty-minute walk from the Winter Palace to the Savoy. Bullfrogs were croaking in the front garden and candles shielded under glass burned on the scattered tables for the convenience of any who cared to brave the mosquitoes. Smith and I did not.

"According to Dr. Deane," he went on, as we turned in under the leafy arch, "Der el-Melik is on the opposite side of the Nile, at some distance from a village called Nagadeh. We will go out there tomorrow and see what we can find."

"Do you think we shall find Brooker?"

Smith's lean jaw shot truculently forward.

"I think it most likely," he said shortly, "that we shall find him dead of starvation and exposure! Could he have kept himself alive for six weeks in a ruined building? Ill, and unaccustomed to hardship . . . camping out like a tramp, creeping out at night to steal food and water . . . no!"

I shuddered slightly, feeling a tremor of compassion for the hunted man who had betrayed his country and paid so terrible a price.

Though we had missed both breakfast and lunch, it was still too early for dinner, so we sat down to continue discussion of our plans in the comfort of the lobby, before going up to our rooms to put on jackets and ties.

"Try at the desk," said Smith, "and see if they've got a copy of Baedeker."

I did as he bid, but they had not, and politely recommended me to the bookstall. There, at some minor expense, I was successful and came back clutching a small, heavy volume of the 1914 edition. Searching the pages, I located the item which we wanted, inconspicuously printed in small type.

"It's an old Coptic convent," I reported, "on the edge of the desert, and dating from the time of the Empress Helena— unoccupied, but still occasionally used for special festivals."

Smith nodded. "In other words, tourists don't go there. They come here to see Ancient Egyptian ruins, not relics of the Holy Roman Empire."

As he spoke, a hubbub of conversation broke out behind us, forcing him to raise his voice. A party had arrived off the morning train from Cairo, shepherded by a man who wore the peaked cap of Thomas Cook. Transatlantic tones still predominated, though the entry of America into the war, earlier in the year, had thinned them out.

"What do we know of the Copts?" inquired Smith.

"They are the Egyptian adherents of a weird religious sect," I said, "an offshoot of the Greek Orthodox Church—persecuted throughout history, and generally regarded as heretics."

"Unorthodox Greek?" he suggested ironically.

"If you wish," I said, smiling. "They speak Arabic, but they are not Arabs. They are descendants of the educated class of Ptolemaic times, who adopted Greek culture and Christianity, just as the *fellahîn* are descended from the peasants, who adopted Islam—"

I broke off, aware that my friend was staring past me with a strange expression on his face, bordering on consternation.

"God Almighty!" he exploded. "What is *she* doing here?"

I twisted around, half expecting to see Fah Lo Suee. Instead, I saw a girl in a white dress and a wide-brimmed hat, standing with her back to us, a few steps behind the Cook's party. Seen even thus, she looked oddly familiar, and then, as she turned her head, so that her face was revealed in profile, our day of surprises ended much as it had begun—not Fah Lo Suee, but my nurse-receptionist, Greba Eltham.

Smith leapt to his feet.

"I'll go and grab her," he said tersely. "Get your key and follow us upstairs—quickly!"

When Smith spoke thus, one asked no questions. I hastened to the desk, shouldering my way with muttered apologies through the throng of tourists. Out of the corner of my eye, I saw him hurrying Greba up the stairs, holding her suitcase in one hand and her arm in the other, as if escorting her under arrest.

By the time I gained the attention of the overworked clerk and collected my key, they had disappeared. I ran up after them and arrived, out of breath, on the third floor, to find them standing outside my bedroom, Smith still grasping Greba's arm.

"Unlock the door!" he instructed, looking up and down the empty corridor. "Quick—before anyone comes along!"

Hustling us inside, he slammed the door and leaned back on it, while Greba turned and stood facing him, rubbing her arm ruefully.

"Now!" he demanded. "Why have you left your post?"

"I—I had something to tell you . . ." she faltered.

As much startled by her welcome as we were by her advent, she looked frightened and ill at ease. I set a chair for her, and glared at Smith.

"Sit down," I said, "and relax."

"Well?" pursued Smith impatiently.

"I thought it was important. You told me not to telephone, and I was afraid to send a letter, in case it got lost or intercepted." She swallowed nervously. "Yesterday afternoon, I had a visitor—the man you questioned at the citadel, Captain Holt-Fortescue—"

"Good heavens!" I interrupted. "What did he want?"

"He expected to find you there, of course, and was quite disappointed when he didn't. He said he wanted you to know that he'd taken your advice and was leaving Egypt. . . ."

"Eh?" jerked Smith. "He's really going to France?"

"Not exactly," murmured Greba, with an arch smile. "He's been appointed military attaché to our embassy in Washington."

"God, how the wicked prosper!" groaned Smith.

"I think he came to Zamalek just because he wanted to show off—to get back at you for the way you treated him. And then, finally, he said—well, I'll try to tell you exactly what he said, because it's so queer and so important—he said, 'Tell Colonel Smith that I am not the only officer whose conduct bears investigation. Last June, Brigadier-General Fernshawe was away from Egypt for several weeks. He was supposed to be on leave in England. But I have a cousin who works for the Swiss Red Cross in Geneva, who saw him there, having dinner in a restaurant, with two men from the German Embassy!' "

I gasped, looking properly amazed. But Smith continued to regard her with no change of expression.

"You—you don't think it's important?" she asked.

"Frankly, I don't. Fernshawe a traitor? Nonsense! And, even if he were, would even he be fool enough to go dining with Germans in a public restaurant?"

"Oh!" said Greba, in a pitiful tone of disappointment. She stood up, making a helpless little gesture, and turned towards me. "I'm tired and I'm grubby. Can I clean up in your bathroom?"

"It's this way," I said.

I closed the door on her and turned back to Smith.

"Smith," I said earnestly, "what can it mean?"

"Nothing!" he responded. "Holt-Fortescue is either lying or mistaken. And if, by any chance, Fernshawe *was* there in Geneva, he had some perfectly sound excuse."

"Negotiations for peace?" I hazarded. "There's been talk of an armistice ever since the collapse of Russia. I pray to God that it might be! Though," I added sorrowfully, "if an armistice were signed now, it would be in favour of Germany."

Nayland Smith shook his head brusquely. "There's no reason why Fernshawe should be involved. He's not a diplomat. He doesn't even command an army in the field. . . ." He paced the room, stopped, and pounded his right fist into the palm of his left hand. "Confound it! Why does she have to turn up now, when we're on the verge of going into action? What the devil are we going to do with her?"

"She was only trying to help," I protested.

"Help?" He stared at me angrily. "So long as Fu Manchu believed her to be just a servant in your household, she was reasonably safe. But once he discovers that she is anything more, he will take the first opportunity to seize her and hold her as a hostage." He broke off, frowning down at the carpet. "Well, we can't get her back to Cairo to-night. Here she is, and here she will have to stay."

"I'll go downstairs and see about a room for her," I offered, moving towards the passage.

Smith stepped in front of me, barring my way.

"You will do nothing of the sort! She will stay *here*—with you!"

"What!" I exclaimed. "Smith—that's impossible!"

"Is it?" he challenged. "Why? You have three beds in your room, and whether you share a bedroom or a bed concerns only yourselves. But I don't want her out of your sight—not for a minute! Three years ago, when we were staying at Greywater Park, you almost lost Kâramanèh because you occupied separate rooms."

I could think of no immediate reply. Then:

"You also have three beds in your room!" I reminded him.

This, in fact, was a usual arrangement. When an Egyptian goes to a hotel, he expects adequate provision for his family.

"I shan't be in my room!" he retorted. "I have other plans." He strode briskly to the door, unlatched it, and turned. "Wait in here till I get back."

He went out, leaving me with no hint as to where he was going. I sat down weakly, in a turmoil of mental and moral confusion. Altogether too much was happening in too short a time. Splashing sounds emanated from the bathroom, continued for a while, and presently ceased. Then, after a further interval, Greba reappeared, voluminously clad in my bathrobe, with the hem sweeping the floor, and her hair hidden under a high Persian turban of hotel towelling.

"Mr. Smith doesn't seem very pleased to see me," she said mournfully. "I think he hates me."

"No," I replied, hastening to reassure her. "He's just worried. He wishes you'd stayed in Cairo, where you were safe."

"How can you be sure that I was safe there?" Greba sat opposite me, drawing the robe decorously about her knees. "Fu Manchu has attacked the place twice already, and Hassan says the house is surrounded by demons. He says they come up at night and leer at him through the windows."

"If he's been at my whisky again," I said sourly, "I shouldn't be surprised."

While we waited for Smith, I told her of our recent adventures— the Zeppelin, Fah Lo Suee's visit, and what we had since learned. Finally, and with some embarrassment, I mentioned Smith's intentions regarding our accommodation for the night.

"I don't mind," said Greba, looking at me with a sort of wicked innocence. "Do you?"

More than an hour had passed before we heard the peremptory triple knock at the door which identified Nayland Smith, and I sprang up to admit him. He carried a suitcase.

"Now," he began, looking at us fiercely, as if he expected opposition, "you will both do exactly as I say."

"Yes, Colonel!" murmured Greba. Smith glanced at her, raising an eyebrow at her informal attire, and she flushed. "I washed my dress," she explained, "and hung it out of the window."

"Mistake number one," he growled, "thereby announcing to the world that you were in here!"

Going to the nearest bed, he swept aside the mosquito curtains, threw down the suitcase, snapped it open, and tipped out a suit of clothes.

"I trust the hotel management with our lives, but I can't be sure of the rest—the waiters, the porters, and the boys who make up the beds. With the assistance of Cook's office—and, if we can't trust Thomas Cook, our world has really come to an end!—it has been made to appear that we left on the night train to Cairo. This room has now been allotted to the Reverend Ezra Caldwell and his wife, a couple from Springfield, Minnesota, who complained about the room they had first been given. . . ."

"Oh, Lord!" said Greba faintly. "I was a missionary's daughter, and now I've got to be a parson's wife!"

I picked up the clothes which Smith had tumbled on the bed and examined them curiously.

"Where on earth did you get this outfit?"

"From the real Reverend Caldwell!" He laughed shortly. "Oh, yes—he really exists. He came in with the Cook's party. I had no difficulty in securing his co-operation, since he believes that Fu Manchu is an incarnation of the Devil. He and his wife have been moved quietly down the road and installed in a luxury suite at the Winter Palace, at the expense of His Majesty's Government."

"I'll look ridiculous in these things," I grumbled, "and I doubt if they'll fit."

"We don't have Scotland Yard's wardrobe to choose from, so we must make do with what we can get. The Reverend Caldwell is somewhat larger round the middle than you are, but if Greba has a needle and thread handy, she can probably manage with a tuck here and a dart there."

"I'm not sure that it isn't sacrilege," said Greba dubiously, "but I suppose we'll be forgiven, if it's all in a good cause."

"We've no facilities for make-up," continued Smith, "but you can tone down your complexion a little with her face powder, and, luckily, it doesn't look odd to wear dark sun glasses in Egypt. Don't go down to dinner to-night. Have something sent up here. When the waiter brings it, disappear into the bathroom, and let her take it in. Nobody here has seen her yet—I hope! Likewise breakfast."

He glanced at us sharply, as if inviting comments, but neither of us ventured one.

"I can't see that you've much to complain of," he concluded. "You two will spend the night in a comfortable hotel, while I spend it in some flea-ridden little bug hutch around the station. When we go out to-morrow, Fah Lo Suee's agents will be on the lookout for two Englishmen in tropical drill clothes. They won't pay much attention to a minister of the Lutheran Church, accompanied by his charming wife and an Egyptian dragoman. I," he added, with a wan smile, "shall be the dragoman. . . ."

23

DER EL-MELIK

When Greba and I came down into the lobby at nine o'clock next morning, we found our dragoman seated near the door on the bench reserved for those of his lowly occupation, his hands clasped on the knob of a stout walking stick. He stood up to greet us with a bow.

"*Naharak sa'îd, 'ustadh!*" he cried. "I am Mohammed. I have carriage for you. Now I show you places most wonderful!"

I stared hard at him. I might not have failed to recognize Nayland Smith under his disguise, but one less well acquainted with him must surely have done so. He wore a long, striped caftan under an open *gibbeh* of dark blue cotton, and a white muslin turban, loosely wound around a lace skullcap. These things, I supposed, he had purchased in the bazaar the night before, and, by some means, he had darkened his coffee-coloured skin to the hue of a coffee bean.

Conducting us out to the *'arabîyeh,* he helped us to climb up and sat opposite, with his back to the coachman. A boy followed us out and handed up a small wicker hamper, packed with our lunch; then we set off at a jog-trot, northwards along the riverbank. It was a slow form of transport, but, as Smith had pointed out, leisured sightseers such as we pretended to be would not put up with the dusty discomfort of a local train—not that an *'arabîyeh* offered much better. Ours was as poorly sprung as the worst of its kind, squeaked, and smelt pungently of horse and harness.

Beyond Karnak, we lost sight of the Nile, where it made a long, lazy bend to the west, and continued on alongside a canal bordered by *dôm* palms like giant candelabras and feathery tamarisks, amid which brown backs bent to the busy creak of the *shadouf.* Barnyard fowls ran about, clucking and squawking, under the horse's hooves, avoiding the carriage wheels by a miracle. Here and there, we passed long-legged Arabs riding short-legged donkeys, so that they

seemed in danger of stubbing their toes on the stones which everywhere encumbered the route, and Greba laughed delightedly.

Smith, acting his part with consummate skill, pointed out objects
of imaginary interest, entertaining us with a comic introduction to
a business which, I feared, was likely to be grim.

"Look, my gentleman!" he urged. "People here rich—have many
hens and cock-a-doodle!"

I envied him his artistry, feeling hopelessly miscast in my ill-fitting
minister's black, with a clerical dog-collar clasped around my throat
and the Reverend Caldwell's hat jammed upon my head like an
inverted soup plate. Greba, whose conduct during the night had
been somewhat mischievous, leaned close to my ear.

"Play up to me! You're supposed to be a pastor, not a monk!" she
hissed. My self-conscious response earned me a scowl, and, leaning
closer, she whispered something sulphurous about "pyjama
strings," which I hoped Smith did not hear.

A wagon lumbered past, drawn by two hump-backed oxen.

"Buffalo," said Smith. "You have buffalo in America?"

The town of Kous, where barking dogs ran out to greet us, was
situated at a safe distance inland—for the Nile, which is the lifeblood
of Egypt, can also destroy in years of excessive flood. Turning
westwards, we made our way down to a crude landing stage, from
which an infrequent ferry service crossed to and from Nagadeh. We
had, as it transpired, half an hour to wait and the place was colour-
fully thronged with other would-be passengers, bearing goods of
every description and accompanied by their livestock.

Smith, as solicitous for our comfort as a Swiss mountain guide,
found a bench for us to sit on, obtained coffee from a wayside
kahweh, and, while we drank it, went off to argue with our coachman.
From the manner in which the discussion was conducted, they
seemed likely to come to blows—but, as usual, it ended with hand-
shakes and an exchange of money, and our dragoman rejoined us.

"I tell him be here at four o'clock," he said loudly, and added, in
an undertone, "but God knows if we'll be back!"

The ferryboat which presently appeared proved to be not a sailing
vessel but a fair-sized ironclad, constructed of boiler plate, and
powered by a Diesel engine amidships, so that it must have been
relatively modern, though it looked more like one of Isambard
Brunel's nineteenth-century rejects. Its arrival was followed, inevitably, by an untidy scramble to get aboard, in which Smith, alias
Mohammed, used his elbows to evil effect, shouting curses and

demanding priority for his distinguished patrons. When we stepped
upon the deck, it boomed like a drum.

The after part of the boat was raised somewhat above the rest and
shaded by a tattered awning of canvas. Smith quickly secured places
on the wooden seats which ran along both thwarts, leaving our less
fortunate companions to sit upon or stand about the deck. The
lower level was soon occupied to capacity by a flock of the shaggiest
and dirtiest sheep I had ever seen, mixed up with a few goats. Then,
to a noisy chorus of baaing and bleating, we moved out upon the
river.

Nagadeh lay not directly opposite but some way upstream. Here
the Nile was broad, and divided by a long, narrow island, or sand-
bank, completely covered in reeds. To either side, the mountains
had receded into a pearly heat haze, and nothing appeared above
the skyline but the smokestacks of a sugar factory somewhere near
Kous. Nayland Smith gestured this way and that, chattering nonsense.

"Look, my lady! Look, my gentleman! Here, long time before, is
many crocodile and hippy-potamus!"

Our crossing took about thirty minutes. The engine chugged
busily, the note changing occasionally in response to hammerlike
blows on the tin roof of the shed which housed it, as the helmsman
telegraphed orders with a long line of string joined to a piece of
scrap iron, hinged like a door-knocker. This rough-and-ready device had one advantage over much of our more complicated equipment—it worked. Rounding the south tip of the reed-clad island,
our uncouth craft now crossed the river and followed a course
parallel with the shore. At the summit of a high, shelving embankment, we saw a ragged line of houses, palm trees, and a number of
pigeon towers.

We landed at some distance from the village, but did not immediately enter it. Already, it was past midday and time to think about
lunch. We might not appear to be in any hurry—nor was there need.
If Brooker had somehow survived six weeks at Der el-Melik, he
could wait another hour or so to be captured.

Making ourselves comfortable in the shade of the trees, we un-
packed the hamper, spread a cloth upon the ground, and weighted
it down with stones. The hotel had provided us with paper plates
and cups—even a thermos flask filled with white wine—naturally
assuming that Nagadeh would furnish nothing palatable to American visitors. In accordance with custom, we did not invite our drago-

man to share our meal and, while Greba and I ate turkey sand-
wiches, Smith went up into the village to secure information for our
onward journey.

A group of five or six raggedly clad urchins gathered a short way
off and sat down on the bank to watch us, laughing and pointing.
Here, we were the curiosities. In a place such as this, tourists were
undoubtedly rare; but I eyed them suspiciously till Smith returned,
carrying a handful of dates wrapped in newspaper, and sat down
beside us to eat them.

"All the people of Nagadeh seem to be Copts," he announced.
"I've arranged for a guide. He'll be along shortly."

Greba bent suddenly, seized his wrist, and sniffed at the back of
his hand.

"I guessed as much!" she said gleefully. "Boot polish!"

Smith grinned and nodded.

"You'll have an awful job to get it off," she murmured.

Our meal concluded, she folded the tablecloth and neatly re-
packed the used things in the hamper, fastidiously refraining from
adding to the litter which was everywhere apparent. Looking up, I
saw an ill-favoured youth approaching us. In his left hand, he carried a bunch of keys; in his right, a length of sugar cane, munching
at it, and spitting out the pieces.

Smith stood up quickly.

"What is your name, boy?" he demanded.

"I am called Youssuf, the Cleaner of Pipes," said the boy, staring
at us uncertainly with his one good eye. The other was white and
sightless. "Also, I clean the church."

From the revolting state of his torn *gallabieh,* I judged him to be
in his working clothes. Smith put his hand on my shoulder.

"This is my gentleman—a great *'ustadh,'*" he said, "a very holy
man from the great and wonderful land of America, who comes to
see the places of your horrible religion."

"I will show you," promised Youssuf—somewhat unwillingly, I
thought. "Give me money!"

"Afterwards!" snapped Smith. "Lead on!"

The pipe cleaner shrugged ungraciously, threw aside the last ten
inches of sugar cane, scrubbed his sticky hand on his robe, and
turned towards the village.

"Follow!" he directed.

"Mohammed," said Greba, pointing to the hamper, "carry this,
please!"

"Yes, my lady," replied Smith meekly, and picked it up.

Nagadeh was a deserted street of shuttered shops—the siesta hour having commenced—with a few dark alleyways leading off. Like all Nile towns and villages, it looked to be half in ruins, partly because the flat-topped houses appeared roofless from below, and partly because of their tumbledown condition. The Egyptians, who swiftly break everything and repair nothing, live in a land of dun-coloured ruins dating from the first pharaoh to the last khedive, all covered with the timeless dust of the desert, and it is difficult for the unpracticed eye to distinguish which is which.

Youssuf walked ahead, swinging the keys like a playful ape, and walking with the shambling gait of the half-witted. At the corner of an alley, we came to a *sebîl*—a huge earthenware vessel resembling an enormous carrot, supported in a rusty iron stand. Smith paused briefly, lifted the cover, and, ignoring my warning shake of the head, helped himself to a dipperful of tepid water.

At the far end of the street, our guide halted before a building like a commonplace mission hall, and unlocked the door.

"This is our church," he said.

The interior was a dim place of many pillars and arches, with an altar inconspicuously placed and surmounted by a rudimentary cross. In the walls there were deep niches with half-domed ceilings, elaborately fluted in the Byzantine manner, and, between them, garishly painted pictures of saints—sacred ikons which, to me, looked more like the blasphemously macabre designs of the Tarot cards. I bent to examine them, feigning an interest, while Smith, for a moment, did nothing, then turned abruptly to the boy.

"This is not what we would see," he pronounced. "Take us to Der el-Melik—the old *knîseh* on the edge of the desert."

Youssuf looked at him in dismay.

"No, no!" he protested. "It is too far. Nothing to see there. Besides," he added hopefully, "there is no such place!"

"We will see it!" insisted Smith. "And no money shall you have till you take us there!"

"The *Kasîs* has the key . . ." mumbled Youssuf.

"Get it! And bring donkeys!"

Acting with the authority of his patrons, the typical dragoman inclines to be arrogant towards his fellows, but Nayland Smith was, without doubt, the most arrogant dragoman who had ever set foot in Nagadeh. Youssuf dared to protest no more, but departed, while we sat down in the shadow of the open doorway to await his return.

"Smith!" I said reprovingly. "You should not have drunk from the *sebîl.* Even with your stomach—"

"I only *pretended* to drink!" he answered curtly. "Don't talk to me now. We are certainly being watched, even though it may not be by the Si Fan."

No one was visible in the street facing us but an old man squatting at the corner and smoking a *shibouk* with a pipe stem four feet long. But I had no doubt that curious eyes surveyed us from behind the fretwork-screened windows of the surrounding houses.

Smith, whose well-worn briar would not have been in character, contented himself with chain-smoking cheap cigarettes, holding them between finger and thumb like the mouthpiece of a *narghileh,* with his fingers turned towards his lips. Half an hour passed without event.

"I don't like this," he muttered. "He doesn't want to take us. The little squirp may just be bone lazy, or he may have some other reason. . . ."

I nodded. In dealing with Egyptians, delays of this nature were not uncommon, and not necessarily significant. But when a second half hour had gone by, still with no sign of our guide, it was plain that we could wait no longer. Smith, having smoked the last of his cigarettes, crumpled up the empty packet and threw it into the road.

"He's not coming back," he said tersely. "Let's go and look for him."

"Shall we take the hamper?" inquired Greba irrelevantly.

"Leave it there," he retorted. "We don't want it, and, with reasonable luck, somebody will steal it while we're away."

We set off along the street. The village was easy to search, and we doubted that Youssuf would make much attempt to hide. Oriental etiquette expected us to accept his defection with a shrug and importune him no further. But we persisted, and, soon enough, came upon him in one of the side alleys, crouching on his heels and playing a game of *táb* with three other youths, grouped around a "board" of shallow holes scraped in the dust, with pieces of stick for counters.

Seated with his back to us, he was unaware of our presence till Smith lifted his foot and, without actually kicking him, gave him a shove between the shoulder blades, which sent him sprawling across the improvised board, scattering the counters. His companions scrambled up and disappeared precipitately in three directions. Youssuf rolled over and sat up, supporting himself on his hands.

"O stench! O dreadful mistake of thy father!" shouted our irate dragoman. "Did I not tell thee to bring donkeys?"

"Lord, there are no donkeys in Nagadeh. . . ."

Smith, brandishing his stick within an inch of Youssuf's nose, answered with a classic tirade of Arabic worthy of the best in Islamic literature.

"Thou liest, foul insect!" he bawled. "While we waited and thou camest not, vile reptile, a hundred have passed before my eyes! The walls shake with their braying! Now may Allah—in Whom thou believest not, thou left-handed eater of hog's flesh—afflict thee with an itch thou canst not scratch! Go! Get donkeys!"

Youssuf scuttled off, saying nothing, and was back in some fifteen minutes, leading four donkeys tethered in single file, and having, in this remarkably short space of time, picked out the worst in the village. Mine was lame.

Leaving the houses behind, we rode out on a rough, stony track winding between fields golden with wheat, green with *barsim*, and brown with *durra*. At this hour, in the full heat of the afternoon, no one was working in them. Youssuf went ahead, riding with hunched shoulders and his head tipped forward in a way which suggested that he was asleep—as he probably was, leaving the donkey to do the leading. Greba followed, and I came next, our beasts ambling at a walking pace. Nothing, it seemed, could urge them to greater endeavour. We belaboured them with palm sticks and kicked with our heels, all to no avail, till we felt sorry for them and gave up.

Only our reluctant guide knew just how far we had to go. Der el-Melik guarded the site of the Coptic cemetery, where the cultivated land gave way to the desert. Smith cantered up alongside me.

"Careful!" he warned. "We've no idea what we shall find when we get out to this place—though I think that wall-eyed little devil in front knows. If Brooker is there and alive, he may be completely off his head and as dangerous as a mad rat. . . ."

Owing to the more or less flat level of the terrain, it was impossible to see far ahead, but, at length, the rampart of barren mountains marking the approach to the Western Sahara materialised on the skyline, cloudy and indistinct. Soon afterwards, the green fields ended, starkly and dramatically, where the desert began. Here, as often in Egypt, one might stand, literally, with one foot on the soil and the other on the sand.

Camouflaged against that background of eternal desolation—like a landscape on the moon—a building appeared, or, rather, a group of ruined buildings, enclosed by a wall. Der el-Melik . . . As we drew nearer, I saw that the largest was a square structure, rising high above the others and crowned by row upon row of beehive-shaped cupolas, so that the roof looked like an egg box turned upside down. Many of them were broken, and the whole ensemble, both wall and buildings, composed of crude brickwork.

The arid plain beyond, extending to the distant mountains, closely resembled that upon which we had witnessed the destruction of the Zeppelin. But here it was dotted about with scattered tombs—not the domed sepulchres of a Moslem graveyard, but massive, rectangular mastabas, like those of the Old Kingdom, before the age of the pyramid builders.

We dismounted. The wall, twelve to fourteen feet high, was pierced by an archway with iron gates, chained and padlocked. Youssuf bent to them, fumbling with keys.

"How did Brooker get in?" asked Smith, in a whisper. "An active man could climb that wall. But one who was old and sick . . ."

Youssuf unlocked and threw open the gates.

"This is the Church of St. Michael—"

"Wait here!" interrupted Smith. "Stay with the donkeys. I, Mohammed—best dragoman in Egypt—will guide my lady and gentleman!"

Close upon his heels, we entered an empty courtyard, with the principal building of the ancient convent standing to our left. In the wall above, there were barred windows, and the heavy wooden door stood a few inches ajar. But, as we turned towards it, Greba caught at my sleeve, pointing upwards.

"Oh, my God!" she said unsteadily. "Look, up there!"

Circling about the roof, cawing raucously, carrion crows were flying in and out of the shattered domes.

24

THE HERETIC PRIEST

The ghastly portent of that sinister sight brought a qualm of nausea to my stomach. Though we might have expected it, anticipation did nothing to mitigate the horror of the reality.

Nayland Smith thrust open the door, which creaked dismally, revealing a shadowy interior.

"Stay here!" he snapped, and plunged inside.

I seized Greba's arm, holding her back as she would nonetheless have followed, and she struggled.

"You don't have to worry about me," she protested. "I've been a nurse—"

"I know," I said tactfully. "But why distress yourself when it's not necessary?"

Less than a minute passed before Smith was back again, standing in the doorway with a strange expression on his face, oddly compounded of disappointment and relief.

"You can come in and see for yourselves," he said shortly, "not that there's much to see. It's not what we thought."

He turned, leading the way. Seen from within, Der el-Melik resembled the local church at Nagadeh, dimly lighted by shafts of sunlight striking at random through a few small windows set high in the wall and the broken domes above. I saw that the multiple cupolas formed a high, vaulted ceiling, the arches not serving to support the roof, but merely projecting above it.

The place reeked with an odour of putrefaction; but it was not the dreadful smell of human mortality.

Smith, who had a surprising number of useful items under his loose robes, produced an electric torch and directed our steps to what had evidently been some kind of side chapel, dark and windowless. He cast the light downwards, revealing the carcass of a sheep or a goat, upon which two crows perched, pecking at the flesh which still adhered to it. They took fright and rose, fluttering about our heads, screeching, and beating their wings against the walls. Greba uttered a small scream and cowered, throwing up her arms to protect her face.

"This is where he was," said Smith tonelessly. "But it was weeks ago. The birds have picked the bones almost clean."

Among the rubbish which carpeted the floor lay a heap of rotting vegetables. Ashes and some blackened sticks indicated an attempt at cooking, but there were no utensils. The fugitive had been able to do no more than to cut a few pieces of meat and grill them roughly over the fire. Smith picked up a bulging goatskin of the type used by a *sakka,* and poured out a stream of stagnant water.

"Half full," he observed. "He wasn't here very long."

"He has found some other hiding place," I said.

"Perhaps . . ." Smith hesitated, then turned abruptly on his heel. "Let's go. There's no more to do here."

Leaving the crows to their disgusting feast, we went out into the courtyard and out again through the rusty iron gates—then halted, staring about us in stupefaction. There was no sign of Youssuf or of our donkeys. Searching farther afield, I saw a cloud of dust, six hundred yards away, on the path back to the village, and, half hidden in it, our miserable mounts going like racehorses.

"Hell and damnation!" burst out Smith. "He's run off! He knows the game's up, and he's gone to warn them!"

"Warn whom?" I inquired stupidly.

"The Copts! Isn't it obvious? They found our man here, killed him, if he wasn't already dead, and took his briefcase!"

"Why? If it contained only papers . . ."

"They didn't know that till they had it open!"

"What do we do now?" asked Greba.

"Walk!" grunted Smith. "What else? It's not all that far. But it'll be nearly dark before we get there."

With the sun at our backs, it was a long, hot tramp back to the village, in which Greba came off best. In her cool white dress, she was the most suitably clad, and she had sensibly provided herself with a stout pair of walking shoes—a plain indication that, when leaving Cairo, she had not intended to return. I fared the worst, wrapped up in the stifling black outfit of a Lutheran minister from Minnesota. Without looking even more absurd and out of character than I already felt, I could not even take off my jacket.

Smith strode grimly ahead. As the sun declined, a few men had come out into the fields, scraping at the earth and tending crops with rude farming implements identical with those to be seen in the wall paintings of an Egyptian tomb. Some of them paused in their labours to stare at us foolishly, and sometimes to shout vulgar pleasantries, to which Smith responded curtly and in kind.

"We are in no danger from these people," he remarked, "but by the time we arrive, the whole village will know about us. Every man who had a hand in the crime will have made himself scarce, and the rest will pretend to know nothing. . . ."

A mile outside Nagadeh, three camels plodded solemnly past, loaded down with *barsim* and led by a man on foot, who seemed wholly unaware that the second and third were each eating the load carried by the camel in front. Greba, tired though she was, burst out laughing. But Smith and I were in no laughing mood.

The sun was down over the distant mountains when, at long last, we came into the solitary street of dilapidated houses. Lights glowed in the open shopfronts, and neighbours sat upon chairs ranged outside their doors, smoking, and drinking coffee. Smith, resuming his rôle of dragoman, seized upon the first man whom we met.

"Take us to the house of the *Kasîs!*" he ordered.

On the tacit understanding that a reward was forthcoming, the fellow turned immediately and conducted us to a dark alley and a wooden door set in a high wall. Imprinted in the plaster above I saw a Coptic cross inscribed in a circle. Smith raised his fist and beat heavily on the boards.

Now we, who had received so many surprises of late, were to receive yet another. At once, there was a sound of bolts withdrawn, and the door was opened to us—not by the cunning, shifty-eyed priest we had half expected, but by an old man with white hair falling to his shoulders, who wore a black robe and a narrow headband patterned in red and black, and who welcomed us with a smile.

"I am Kyrilos, the *Kasîs,*" he said, in soft-spoken Arabic. "Enter, and be at peace."

Even Smith seemed taken aback. I have spoken of the tangible aura of evil which hovered about the gaunt form of Dr. Fu Manchu. Now, in the presence of this frail figure, I was conscious of an aura of sanctity which made me ashamed of my borrowed vestments.

Beyond the gate, we found a small, square courtyard, floored with earth, and bounded on two sides by a mud-brick house with an open staircase. The lower part of the building was given over to the accommodation of domestic animals—goats, and a small flock of hens. Kyrilos closed and barred the door behind us.

"Youssuf should not have deserted you," he said. "But he was afraid. You are weary, and you are thirsty. Sit down and rest." He pointed to a wooden bench against one wall and a table set before it. "My wife will bring fruit and something to drink."

"First," said Smith, "let me make it clear that I am not what I seem, but a British police officer."

"This I had supposed."

"I, too, am here under false colours," I confessed. "I am not a man of the cloth."

"This also I had supposed." Kyrilos glanced at me, still smiling. "No matter. We all worship the same God, even though you think me a heretic."

An elderly, grey-haired woman in a simple cotton print dress descended the rough flight of steps, bearing a tray loaded with plates and glasses—for marriage is permitted to the Coptic clergy, though it must be but once. Yielding to our host's urging, we sat while she served us with juicy pink segments of the big, zebra-striped melon which the Arabs call *batîrkh,* and glasses of cool green sherbet made from violets. Then, since the light was almost gone, she lit a lantern, hung it on a pole close to the table, and left us. Kyrilos drew up a stool and seated himself, facing us.

"I know why you are here," he said calmly. "But you come too late."

"He is dead," answered Smith flatly.

Kyrilos nodded gravely. "Yes—an hour before the dawn."

"What? You mean that he died only last night?"

"Yes." Again Kyrilos nodded. "But, for many days, he had lain without speech. Presently, if you wish, you shall see him."

For a while there was a solemn silence, as though in respect for the dead. I do not know why the personality of that old priest of a half-forgotten faith made so profound an impression. In his eyes there was neither sententiousness nor the burning fervour of the Reverend J. D. Eltham, eager to drag lost souls to salvation by the scruff of the neck. There was only a sense of quiet conviction and a plea for understanding.

"In the month of Misra, when my people went to the Church of St. Michael to make preparation for the Festival of the Cross, they found him there—whither he had fled to take refuge with God and to seek His forgiveness for some great sin. He had injured his knee, and could not walk. I think he had fallen when he climbed the wall.

By my orders, he was brought here, where he might be cared for."

I smiled, half in sympathy and half in amusement, as I reflected that they had, nevertheless, neglected to clear up the telltale traces of Brooker's occupation. Since, apparently, that corner of the building was not to be used in their ceremony, Youssuf, the Cleaner of Pipes, had felt this to be superfluous; I hoped he cleaned pipes better than he cleaned churches.

"There is no doctor in Nagadeh," went on Kyrilos, "but I have a little skill. I bound up his hurt, and it healed. But he never walked again. Already, he was very weak, and I saw that the hand of death was upon him. He knew no language which we could understand, but, seeing the cross which hung upon the wall above my bed, he touched it and spoke the Greek words *Alpha* and *Omega*—the Beginning and the End—by which I knew that he had found God."

"But it was your duty to inform the police!" said Smith sternly. "The ancient right of sanctuary is no longer recognized."

"It was recognized in the fourth century," replied Kyrilos, gently but firmly, "and extended to all church property, more than fifty years before the Council of Chalcedon separated us from the Church of Rome. It is recognized by me. I cannot admit that the decrees of Man may supersede those of God."

Greba, who had understood no word of the discussion, turned anxious eyes upon me.

"What are they saying?" she whispered. I told her, and she added: "Please tell him that my father thought the same!"

I did so, somewhat to Smith's annoyance. He glanced at me sharply, frowned, and then, still speaking in Arabic, so as to avoid hurting Greba's feelings, turned back to Kyrilos.

"And he paid for it with his life!" he said.

"As I am prepared to do," answered our host impassively. "All in this village knew of the man who lay helpless in my house, but I charged them that they should say nothing, and none would betray me. Whence he had come, or what he had done, I did not know. At first, he spoke often, and I thought that he was praying. Therefore, I prayed with him, and, at the last, when he could speak no more, I prayed for him. Now he is with God, and your law cannot touch him."

"I appreciate and respect your motives," said Smith severely, "but the fact is that you were harbouring a fugitive from justice—"

"Smith!" I interceded. "Kyrilos could not *know* that Professor Brooker had committed any crime—"

"There is no need for you to act as his advocate!" He glared at me, then shrugged. "Well, the man is dead, and I am here neither to prosecute nor to persecute." Again he turned to Kyrilos. "What of the property which he had stolen—the case which he bore shackled to his wrist?"

"He has it still. I would have brought tools and relieved him of his burden, but this he would not suffer me to do. Neither would he suffer me to open it. Though I knew not what it was, I saw that it must be in some way connected with his sin, and I thought that he might carry it as a penance. Even to the last, he clutched it close to him, and I believed that he wished it to be buried with him."

A silence ensued, longer than the first. Smith administered a savage tug to his earlobe and winced. Then, at length:

"Father Kyrilos," he said earnestly, "—or however I should address you—the burden which this man carried belonged not to him but to our Government. Others seek it also—others who would burn down this village and desecrate his grave to obtain it." He paused and, either by guile or by inspiration, continued: "Should it be lost, or fall into their hands, many lives will be forfeit. Therefore, I beg you to let us take it."

Kyrilos stood up.

"Take it, then," he answered. "If it is yours, you may have it. But the man belongs to God, and he shall have Christian burial in our cemetery."

Indicating that we should follow, he crossed the courtyard to the flight of steps on the opposite side—a solid but clumsy construction which we ascended with care, since it had no handrail. At the top was a kind of balcony, along which Kyrilos led us past several dim, cavelike openings to a small apartment in which candles flickered, open to the sky and roofed only by mats of palm sticks laid edge to edge and loosely bound together.

A spartan couch, consisting of a wooden frame and interlaced strips of webbing, stood in one corner, and upon this lay the body of a man, shrouded in a clean white robe. I bent over him, and stared into a face impossible to recognize as that which I had seen in the photograph.

"Can this be he?" I exclaimed.

What I saw was no more than a skull with the waxen skin stretched taut over the bones—the whole form so shrunken that it seemed less than human, like the desiccated remains of Ancient Egyptian commoners, roughly interred in the sand.

"Yes, it's Brooker," said Smith shortly.

He pointed to the withered hands joined upon a small leather suitcase. Kyrilos had seen nothing else to do with it.

"God knows what he died of!" I said doubtfully. "Deane called it anaemia, but I know of no disease which would result in an emaciation of this character. . . ."

Smith shook his head impatiently. "Who can say? We don't know exactly how he escaped from the fire at the Hotel Iskander. He may already have been infected with some diabolical stuff prepared by Dr. Fu Manchu. . . ."

Searching under his dragoman's robes, he took out his notecase and extracted a key. Hitherto, I had imagined that Brooker's dispatch case would be of the sort carried by bank messengers, with a chain joined to the wrist by a single cuff. Now, however, I saw that it was an ordinary suitcase, about twenty-four inches across, with a pair of police-pattern handcuffs attached to the handle.

"Yes," said Smith absently, fitting his key to the lock. "I found out that much when I got the key. Brooker borrowed a pair of handcuffs from the security guards—though Fernshawe didn't see fit to inform me that it wasn't at Meadi!"

The steel band hung so loosely about the wrist that the skeletal hand might almost have been withdrawn through it. Smith unlocked it, with some difficulty, since the wards were corroded; then, watched anxiously by Kyrilos, we slid the suitcase out carefully, almost reverently, from beneath the dead man's fingers—which, fortunately, were not closed upon it in a death grip but merely rested upon it.

"Let him take this instead," said the priest solemnly, "and let it be the sign of his forgiveness."

Taking down the plain wooden crucifix from the wall above the bed, he laid it under the empty hands, bowed his head, and murmured sonorous words in the language of the last pharaohs.

"Now let's see what we have!" urged Smith, and, for once, even his iron control failed to keep the excitement from his voice. "We have no keys, but the locks shouldn't be hard to force. . . ."

To our surprise, however, it proved unnecessary to force them. The suitcase was not even locked! Though they operated stiffly, the buttons turned and the catches flew up, allowing us to raise the lid. Contrary to Fernshawe's statement, it was not steel-lined—but for this he might be pardoned, since he had never seen it. The interior was tightly packed with scraps of newspaper, which, on further examination, we found to have been torn from issues of the *Egyptian Gazette* and the *London Times*.

Cushioned in this makeshift packing was a metal cylinder, some three inches in diameter and twenty in length. Save for the weight—which was extraordinary—it resembled the containers commonly employed by draughtsmen for the storage of drawings and plans, and was stamped with the broad arrow of Government property.

"The Army likes to have everything ten times as heavy and cumbersome as necessary," commented Smith, as he drew it out.

I came close to holding my breath as he endeavoured to open it. At last, the secret of the Midnight Sun lay—literally—in our hands. Yet it was destined to remain a secret. The hairline crack two inches below one end of the cannister indicated that it was closed by a cap—but, despite our utmost efforts, we could neither pull it off nor unscrew it.

"It seems to be sealed," I said, disappointedly, after I had tried and failed.

"Quite!" rejoined Smith. "So *that's* why he took the originals—why he didn't just copy them. He could steal the container, but he couldn't open it!"

On closer examination, I saw that the smooth surface of the cylinder—which was of some dull grey metal unfamiliar to me—was broken at either end by two square notches, presumably intended for the reception of tools by which the cap could be wrenched off. Smith grunted ill-humouredly, and, abandoning the attempt, set about re-packing the suitcase.

As he did so, a small piece of stick fell from above and settled lightly upon the pallid features of the man lying on the bed. Kyrilos leaned over to brush it off—and, at the same instant, we were startled by a cry of alarm from Greba, who, till now, had stood quietly in the doorway. I spun around and saw her wide-eyed with shock.

"There was a man looking down through the roof!"

Both Smith and I stared up at the simple ceiling—a Biblical roof, such as that through which the people of Capernaum lowered down the sick of the palsy to Jesus of Nazareth. Between the palm sticks, where there were gaps, we could see the sky, not yet completely dark, but dotted with stars. That was all.

"Are you sure you're not mistaken?" rapped Smith.

"I saw him!" she insisted, and shuddered. "The light of the candles was shining directly on his face—a dreadful face, all pockmarked, like I saw once before—"

Before she could say more, her words were dramatically verified.
From some point in the near distance came an eerie, wailing sound,
like and yet unlike the howling of a dog—a sound which stiffened
the hairs on the back of my neck, as it recalled memories of the night
when first I had heard it—the cry of a Burmese dacoit, signalling to
his fellows. . . .

25

HARE AND HOUNDS

"Fury!" cried Smith. "They've found us!"

He crammed the metal cylinder down into the suitcase, scattering scraps of newspaper, and slammed the lid shut. Greba moved closer to me, clutching at my arm with nervous fingers.

"Redmoat . . ." she whispered, and I nodded.

I, too, was thinking of that summer night, now distant in time and space . . . besieged in the old priory on the banks of the Waveney. . . .

"They'll be down on our necks the moment we go outside," said Smith, gritting out the words between his teeth, "and, if we don't go out, they'll break in! Why should they bother with subtlety? There's not so much as a village constable to stand in their way!" He turned quickly to our host. "Can we get out of here by any other means than the door we came in by?"

Kyrilos, who stood passive as before, with his arms folded, smiled faintly.

"Yes," he replied. "Over the wall!"

Leading the way, he escorted us back along the balcony and down the steps, impeding our haste by his unhurried descent. In the courtyard below, he left us for a moment, disappearing into a dark recess where goats bleated, and reappeared with a short ladder, which he set up against the wall at the rear of his premises.

"God go with you!" he said. "To your left is a dead end. Turn to your right, and you will come into the main street. The river lies close by and, somewhere along the bank, you will find boats. . . ."

"You first!" directed Smith, and I climbed up, seating myself atop the wall to help Greba. But as Smith set his foot to the ladder, the door at the far side of the courtyard shook to a furious assault. "Come with us!" he urged, glancing back over his shoulder. "Those devils will show you no mercy when they burst in!"

But Kyrilos shook his head solemnly.

"There is One who will defend me!" he said, and, as Smith gained the top of the wall, took away the ladder.

We had no time to argue. The wall on which we sat, like roosting fowls, was about eight feet high; it was an easy matter to swing over and drop down into the alley. I went first, assisting Greba to follow. Smith threw down the suitcase, took the descent at a leap, landed badly, and picked himself up, swearing. We stood in a narrow passageway, closed at one end by an enormous pile of rubbish. At the opposite end was the street, but, as we reached it, he paused.

"It's no good!" he declared. "Come what may, we must fight it out. We can't leave him to be murdered."

Turning away from the Nile, we ran back to the corner of the next alley, which gave upon the premises of Kyrilos the *Kasîs*. The shadows of overhanging balconies made it too dark to see clearly, but, halfway along, a group of five or six men crowded around the courtyard door. Two, at least, were dacoits, wearing only loincloths and armed with knives. Smith dropped to one knee, lugging out his pistol. But before he could aim and fire, there was an interruption.

A grey, ghostlike form sped out from nowhere, and Youssuf, the Cleaner of Pipes, launched himself upon the back of the man nearest, clutching him around the neck. It was one of the bravest actions that I have ever seen. The dacoit threw him off with a sweep of his arm, not troubling to employ his knife, and the boy crashed back against the wall of the house behind, slipping down into a seated posture in the road.

Smith's pistol cracked, and the same man fell, clasping his thigh. The rest sprang back, turning to face this new attack, and I fired also, but hit no one. Simultaneously, Youssuf dragged himself dizzily to his feet and ran, staggering, down the alley, hammering on the doors and screaming at the top of his voice.

"Help! Help! They are killing our father!"

The response was immediate and unlike anything in my experience. Out from every door they came—some, I think, from the windows—and, in seconds, the narrow space between the houses was packed with a horde of struggling figures. No free-for-all in a Wild West saloon was ever accomplished more rapidly or completely. In the heat of the encounter, they fought the enemy and each other. In the midst of the mêlée I saw a curved blade raised on high—and disappear as the man who wielded it was smitten in the face by an iron cooking pot. The shutters above were thrown open, and women leaned out, shrieking abuse and hurling down refuse on the heads of the combatants.

"Out of it!" shouted Smith.

We had no clear targets, and it was mutually impossible to distinguish friend from foe. Leaving our heroic allies to cover our retreat, we ran down towards the river. But ere we reached it, a fresh clamour broke out behind us, and, turning my head, I saw black-robed men forcing their way into the far end of the main street, mounted on camels—Fu Manchu's desert raiders. More swiftly than we had dreamed possible, the full force of the Si Fan had been loosed upon us.

Due to the narrowness of the street, they could not sweep through it at a gallop, but they pressed on ruthlessly, overturning the tables set outside the shops, trampling men and merchandise underfoot, and striking down the textiles hung above. Clearly, they would make short work of the villagers, but there was nothing which we could do to stop them.

Out on the high, tree-bordered embankment where we had lunched, we turned left and ran for our lives. Now, as we ran, I was thinking no longer of Redmoat but of another night, when Smith and I had run a bizarre, life-or-death race across the Thames marshes, pursued by three dacoits. Now, as then, we had a start of three or four minutes before they came after us.

Below us, to our right, the Nile lay dark and silent. Kyrilos had said that there were boats, but, in the gloom, we did not see them until we were almost upon them. Beyond the village, the lights of a few outlying houses gleamed through the trees. Coming abreast of them, we saw an orderly patchwork of mud bricks laid out on the bank to dry in the sun, fishing nets, and six small rowing boats drawn up stern first just above the water's edge.

There seemed to be no steps. Sliding, rather than walking, we descended the slope and arrived, breathless, at our destination. Seizing upon the nearest boat, and pausing only to make sure that there were oars in it, we got it afloat. Luckily, since the Nile is not tidal, it had been unnecessary to pull them up very far. Smith threw in the suitcase and snapped a command at Greba, who leapt aboard with the grace of a young fawn, disposing herself in the bows.

"Help me to get rid of the others!" he demanded.

I saw at once what he meant. With the enemy only minutes behind us, we could not afford to leave our pursuers with the means of pursuit. Between us, we dragged the next boat down, launched it upon the river, and shoved it out till the current took it and it drifted away downstream—likewise a second and a third. As we did so, I glanced back at Nagadeh, where a dull red glow was rising above the rooftops, suggestive of a house on fire, and I hoped anxiously that it was not the house of the *Kasîs*.

So far, the disturbance in the village had not communicated itself to those who dwelt in the houses adjacent to us. But, by some ill chance, we were detected, and the fishermen whose boats we were casting adrift came rushing out upon the bank, yelling outrage. We had no leisure for apologies. As they ran toward us, Smith fired a warning shot and they drew back, chattering fearfully and angrily.

But the shot and the shouts had given away our position. Even as we set about the last two boats, I saw dark shadows racing along the embankment. In ninety seconds, they were halfway, but, by then, our work was complete. I scrambled into our boat and unshipped the oars. Smith waded out, grasping it by the stern and helping to push us off before he, too, embarked.

I pulled hard at the crude baulks of timber which served as oars. Ten—twenty—thirty yards separated us from the shore, and, temporarily, we were safe.

Our pursuers had reached the spot at which we had embarked and stood clustered on the bank, baffled, and yelling like madmen. But now, as I stared back towards the beleaguered village, I saw elements of the Si Fan's camel corps streaming out to join them. Seconds later, there was a rattle of antiquated musketry, and a fusillade of shots splattered into the river all around us, kicking up tiny waterspouts, like drops of rain bouncing off a road in a thunderstorm. But we were almost out of range, and it would be only by chance if any hit us.

Rowing as I had not rowed since college days, I headed for the shelter of the long, narrow island of reeds downstream.

Yellow tongues of flame sprang up at the top of the embankment. Some of the Senussi had dismounted and lighted a bonfire, feeding it with handfuls of dry palm leaves. Their purpose was obscure, unless it was to provide themselves with a better illumination for their operations. Two of them seemed to be unloading something, watched by a leader who had not dismounted but sat upright on his lofty saddle, a little removed from the others. Though at that distance I could see nothing else about him, the proud bearing of that motionless figure convinced me that it was Dr. Fu Manchu himself.

By the lambent light of the flames, I saw that they were setting up a tubular apparatus which looked suspiciously like a trench mortar. Such, indeed, it proved to be, or a device somewhat similar—for, a moment later, a ball of fire shot up skywards at a steep angle and plunged down towards us. Greba uttered a cry of fear and my heart pounded wildly as I remembered the unearthly thing which had been launched against us in Cairo. This, however, was a more primitive missile, which flared luridly, turning over and over as it came, fell ten feet short, and continued to burn as it floated on the water.* A second shot sailed over our heads and struck the same distance in advance.

No one, I thought, had been under such an attack since the days of Alexander, for this, beyond doubt, was Greek fire—the composition of which has been disputed by scientists and historians. But it was known to Dr. Fu Manchu.

"They are mad!" I said, pausing between strokes. "If they sink us, the secret of the Midnight Sun will go to the bottom."

"But they can send down divers to recover it!" answered Smith tersely. "Pull! Save your breath for rowing!"

Only one more burst was fired, and this with no greater accuracy. Then we had passed around the southern tip of the island, and were drifting down with the current under a dense screen of rushes rising high above our heads. It was so dark now that I could not see the opposite bank—only a few pinpoints of light from isolated houses on the way to Kous.

"Where did we go wrong?" muttered Smith. "I could have sworn we weren't followed. Nobody suspected us—at least until we went out to Der el-Melik. How did they catch up with us so quickly? And how, by all that's wonderful, did Fu Manchu know where to assemble his storm troops?"

I had no answer, nor did he expect one. This was not the first time in our experience when the powers of Fu Manchu had seemed to suggest sorcery. All that I could think of just then was that, having been the hunters, it was now our turn to be the hunted. Brooker's suitcase was a dangerous prize which exposed the possessor to assault from all quarters—from enemies both known and unknown.

Under Smith's direction, I rowed on downstream, keeping close in to the black wall of reeds. Visibility was nil, but, with the shallow draught of our vessel, there was little danger of running aground.

---

*We later discovered that Fu Manchu's "electrostatic vortex" required a truckload of complicated equipment to produce and control it. [P.]

Smith took out his pocket torch and shone it alongside. He appeared to be looking for something, but I did not know what it was until, presently, he ordered me to rest on the oars, and, looking down, I saw the derelict remains of a small boat similar to ours, stranded among the rushes and half filled with water. A shapeless heap of flotsam in the thwarts might once have been fishing gear.

"I noticed it on the way out," he said, and, without further explanation, began to divest himself of his outer and inner robes. Beneath them, he wore his customary bush shirt and slacks, rolled above the knee. "Hand me that damned suitcase!"

Greba passed it over my head. Smith took it, opened it, and extracted the metal container.

"I'm strongly tempted to pitch it in the river," he continued savagely, "since I can't see any reason why Fernshawe should want it! So long as he's sure that neither Fu Manchu nor the Germans can get hold of these confounded papers, isn't that sufficient? It's unthinkable that even the British Army would keep only one copy!"

Wrapping the cylinder in his discarded clothing, he unwound his turban, used it to tie up a tight bundle, and, leaning out, thrust it into the decaying rubbish heaped in the other boat.

"There! It should be safe there, for a few days."

"Why?" I asked wonderingly.

"Because we haven't a chance of getting it back safely!" he snapped. "We've thrown them off for the time being, but they'll signal across the river and be waiting for us on the other side—where, if I'm not mistaken, Fah Lo Suee is in command!"

This was an unpleasant thought, which had not previously occurred to me.

"It's no use making for the landing stage," he added. "Even if they don't have men there, our coachman will have given us up hours ago. He had to, if he was to get home before nightfall, and he'll be round at the Savoy to-morrow, looking for his money."

"Then how are we to get back to Luxor?" I inquired.

"That's where Fah Lo Suee will expect us to go! She will put her agents at the railway station and the hotel—or, since there is only one road, try to pick us up on the way."

I made no answer. Not for the first time, we were fugitives on our own ground. For all that the sparse network of police and military services could do to assist us, we might as well have been in China. Now we had nothing to rely upon but the ingenuity of Nayland

Smith, and I pulled mechanically at the oars, waiting patiently for him to speak. At last, he did so.

"Carry on past the landing stage," he instructed. "We'll go ashore a mile farther down the river, where the railway line runs closest, hike across the fields, and follow it back to the station. We shall be too late for the day train to Luxor, but we should be in time for the night express to Cairo."

"But it will not stop here!" I objected.

"It will to-night!" said Smith grimly. "I have the necessary powers!"

26

KENEH

"But, look here," protested the man from Cook's, regarding us dubiously. "I thought the Fu Manchu business was all over and done with before the war broke out!"

"So did we," said Nayland Smith grimly. "But, unfortunately, we were wrong."

At the double row of tables behind us, dinner was in progress. Silk-shaded lamps gleamed on spotless napery and silverware, and two Egyptian waiters moved up and down the aisle, skilfully dispensing salad with a fork and spoon clutched in one hand. There was quiet conversation and laughter. None of the passengers on the Cairo express that night had noticed the unscheduled halt at Kous, or suspected the desperate reasons which had occasioned it.

Following our precipitate retreat across the river, all had been accomplished with an ease which surprised us. We had found a good place to land and a tolerable track through the fields. En route, we met no one, arriving at the station ten minutes before the train was due to pass through. There, after much shouting in Arabic, the signals had been set and the express brought to a standstill, overlapping the platform.

Five minutes later, when the interrupted journey was resumed, Nayland Smith was unobtrusively but effectively in control. We spoke with the guard, but the functions of that eminent official were nominal in comparison with those of Basil Sorensen, the representative of Thomas Cook & Son—a sandy-haired young man, currently engaged in shepherding his party back from their homage at the tombs and temples of Luxor, who now acted as our liaison officer.

"We are still far from safe," continued Smith. "It will be nearly twelve hours before this train reaches Cairo. Meanwhile, they will try to get somebody aboard. . . ."

Sorensen stared at him with an expression of polite incredulity, to which he responded with a frown.

"Make no mistake!" Smith growled. "We always knew that the Si Fan had a well-organised branch in Egypt, which was left more or less intact when they withdrew from England—and which Dr. Fu Manchu is now personally directing."

Greba, seated opposite me beside the Cook's man, gave me a tired smile, picked up the whisky bottle, and refilled my glass. Dinner had been offered, but our digestive systems were in no state to cope with it. Smith went on talking, rapidly and incisively.

"It won't take them long to find out that we stopped the train at Kous. We were lucky to get there ahead of them. Orders will be sent out to every point along the line—by telephone, telegraph, possibly by wireless—to recover this object"—he pointed downwards to the battered suitcase, tucked between our seats—"with or without murdering us in the process!"

Knowing that it now contained nothing but newspaper, I glanced at him in some surprise.

"Why are we keeping it?" I inquired.

"In the first place, to lay a false trail. In the second, as a possible means of saving our lives, since they are more interested in what we are carrying than in us. We may find it expedient to let them take it, and buy ourselves a chance to escape before they open it. Meanwhile, our main concern is to report back to General Fernshawe and tell him what we have done with the original contents."

"Why not phone him, then?" suggested Sorensen laconically.

"Because Dr. Fu Manchu has some way of listening in to one's telephone conversations without even touching the wires!"

Our new friend looked blank for a moment. Then:

"If you say so, I believe you," he said, and, hesitating, added, a little too cleverly for his own good: "But, hang it all, there are thousands of telephones in Egypt! How could he know which one you might use?"

This was the kind of quick-witted but inane observation of which I, too, had often been guilty, and it met with the same biting rejoinder from Smith.

"The number of telephones in Egypt has nothing to do with it! There are only a dozen or so long-distance lines between Luxor and Cairo, and he can monitor them easily enough."

The sprucely uniformed guard came pacing down the length of the dining car and halted at our table.

"Keneh in ten minutes," he announced.

"Good!" replied Smith. "Anyone to pick up there?"

"Yes," said Sorensen. "A Canadian couple, who've been out to see the Temple of Hathor."

Smith addressed the guard: "Pick them up, then—but no one else! When the train stops, every door must be locked, save one by which passengers will be allowed to disembark."

The guard nodded gravely and departed. One or two of the diners seated nearest to us looked up with a mild curiosity and went on eating. Needless to say, our first business on boarding the train had been to render ourselves less conspicuous. Smith had scrubbed the stain from his face and hands, and Basil Sorensen, with the ready resourcefulness demanded of a Cook's courier, had somehow found me a passably fitting suit of clothes to replace my soiled clerical garments. Now those who noticed us in conference with the guard assumed that we were probably railway officials.

"We won't make it too easy for them," resumed Smith. "Apart from the people already on your list, nobody is to get on at any of the stations between Keneh and Cairo."

Sorensen shrugged lightly. "No problem, Colonel. Nobody much wants to get on after midnight. If anybody does, we'll say we're full up—though, as a matter of fact, we're half empty. How many sleeping compartments do you need? Two, or three?"

"Only one—for Miss Eltham. Petrie and I are getting off at the next stop."

"Are we?" I asked vaguely.

"Yes!" Nayland Smith looked fiercely across the table at Greba, anticipating and cutting short her protest. "Listen, and don't argue! I have a job for you. We will try to draw off the hounds while you get through with the information. When you reach Cairo, go straight to General Fernshawe and tell him exactly what has happened. In the event that Petrie and I don't make it, do you think you could guide him back to the place where we left the material?"

"I—I suppose so," she said doubtfully. "But—"

"No 'buts'! Impress upon Fernshawe that a strongly armed escort will be needed, whether we go to collect it or whether you do. After you have seen him, I shall get in touch with you as before, but not at Shepheard's. The Si Fan may already know about that. Go to the Semiramis. Assuming that we haven't been captured or assassinated in the interim, I shall phone between two and four to-morrow afternoon. I want to know what my orders are. That is"—Smith raised his right hand, ticking off the items on his fingers—"am I to come up to Cairo, stay in Luxor, or go elsewhere? Is all that clear?"

"Yes," murmured Greba.

Smith gave her a tight-lipped smile of approval and again addressed Sorensen.

"After we leave, can we count on you to look after her?"

"Looking after people is my business. In this case, it will be a pleasure."

Sorensen glanced sideways at Greba with a look on his face which caused me to feel a ridiculous pang of jealousy—forgetting that I was no longer the Reverend Caldwell, and she no longer my wife.

"It will also be a grave responsibility, and, possibly, a dangerous one," warned Smith. "If we succeed in keeping Fu Manchu's agents off the train, you will be safe as far as Cairo. The worst stage will be to convey her safely from Rameses Square to General Fernshawe's headquarters. We know from experience that the Si Fan doesn't hesitate to operate in the street and in broad daylight. Petrie—what is the name of your man who runs the car-hire service—who came out to rescue us at Saqqara?"

"Achmed Da'ud," I said.

"Ah, yes! So it is." Smith turned back to Greba. "You have his telephone number, of course. Call him from the station, and have him pick you up there. Unless the car is driven by somebody you know, you can't be sure that it doesn't belong to the Si Fan!"

"I'll go with her," volunteered Sorensen.

"Yes—do that," I said earnestly.

Little though it pleased me to hand Greba into his care, I felt no qualms concerning his capability. Basil Sorensen was no shirker, avoiding military service while ministering to the needs of the idle rich—as I sometimes feared I was. He had joined up and "done his bit" early in the war—early enough to become a victim of the first gas attack at Ypres—and now lived in the dry climate of Egypt for the sake of his permanently damaged lungs.

The rhythmic clatter of the wheels dropped to a lower pitch, and the train slowed, jolting over points. I twitched aside a corner of the window blind and saw the lights of Keneh sliding past.

"I take it that you'll stay here to-night?" queried Sorensen. "Try the Hotel Denderah. It's the only place that's half decent. Clean rooms, but no meals."

The express ground to a halt, unaccompanied by the bustle and shouting which one associates with an English railway station.

Rather, it seemed that the ripple of conversation in the dining car became oddly hushed. The engine panted, and, in accordance with my companion's instructions, a solitary carriage door banged open. Sorensen stood up.

"Must go and collect my people. Nobody else gets on—right? What about the mail? Do we load it, or leave it behind?"

"Leave it. It's not beyond the resources of Fu Manchu to have a dwarf stuffed into a mailbag!"

Sorensen grinned and nodded. "See what you mean. Well, then, we'll leave it. The Post Office will play hell about it—but that'll be your headache, not mine."

He hurried away. Nayland Smith, standing likewise, gathered up the accursed suitcase and prepared to follow, while Greba and I glanced at each other in that embarrassing moment of seeing off a friend, when neither can think of anything to say but the banal phrases of parting.

"Take care of yourself!" I muttered.

"You too!"

Halfway along the corridor, we encountered a porter burdened with luggage and a middle-aged, respectably dressed couple who murmured polite words of apology as we flattened ourselves against the windows to give them passage. Basil Sorensen brought up the rear.

"Glad you enjoyed yourselves . . . sorry to hear about the donkeys. . . . Go right ahead, sir. I'll be with you in a minute." He looked back at us. "Goodbye, and good luck! Don't worry about Miss Eltham. I won't take my eyes off her. . . ."

Outside the train, we saw only the guard in a furious altercation with two postal officials. No one, other than Cook's passengers, had attempted to get on. We stood watching, till presently the guard waved his lantern, blew his whistle, and swung himself up. The line of lighted windows flashed past us, gathering speed, and vanished into the night like a luminous caterpillar, leaving us alone on the platform.

"I hope to God she's safe!" I said anxiously.

"Safer than she would have been with us!" answered Smith. "We are dangerous company. Why, otherwise, do you think I chose to risk our necks in the lions' den? In case you've forgotten, Keneh is—or so we suspect—the local headquarters of the Si Fan. . . ."

27

'ALI OF ISTANBUL

We slept at the Hotel Denderah, dividing the night into watches—as we had often done before—with a pistol handy and an eye on the open window, wondering who or what might come through it. Yet, save for a hideous caterwauling which ended, conventionally, in an explosion of snarling and spitting, nothing disturbed us, and, much to our surprise, the day dawned with no trace of activity on the part of our enemies.

Our room was not supplied with running water, and the communal washroom so poorly appointed that it possessed not even a coat hook, so that we were compelled to leave our things behind and go shirtless down the passage. Returning from this expedition, Smith picked up his bush shirt and shook it vigorously to brush off the dust. As he did so, something fell from a pocket and tinkled on the stone floor.

He stooped to retrieve it, glanced at it, and shook his head.

"Fah Lo Suee's ring," he said, "which was supposed to protect us. It's broken—the stone has come out of the setting. Well, we have had no use for it, and certainly we shall have none now—" Suddenly, he ceased speaking, whistled softly, and laughed. "My God! You were right, Petrie—I should have thought twice before accepting gifts from Fu Manchu. Look at this!"

He held out the scarab, turning it over in his fingers, and I saw that it was hollow—the interior packed with tiny metallic globes and cubes, joined by an intricate network of hairlike wires.

"What is it?" I gasped.

"Some kind of wireless device," he replied, "emitting a signal by which they were able to trace us. It worked well enough till we left Nagadeh, but somewhere during last night's scramble, I must have broken it. That's why they have lost us."

"Do you think they could hear what we were saying?"

"That hardly seems possible."* Smith hesitated, frowning. "Yet, if it *is* possible, that would explain how Fu Manchu knew that we were going to Der el-Melik. . . ."

In view of this strange discovery, our painstaking attempts to confuse the enemy appeared to have been both futile and unnecessary. Going downstairs, we left Brooker's suitcase at the desk, saying that we would be back for it later, and went out into the street.

Seen in daylight, Keneh was a nondescript town, combining the worst of old and new—the starting point of caravan routes across the Arabian Desert, and a centre of commerce which furnished cheap earthenware pottery to half the towns of Egypt. The majority of the older houses retained their enclosed balconies, but, in most cases, the picturesque screens of fretworked *mushrabîyeh* had been replaced by ugly slatted shutters, painted green or blue.

In a busy street, crowded with pedestrians and donkey carts, we found what we sought—a hole-in-the-wall with a signboard written in the square Kufic script and, less legibly, in English lettering which read: "Yakoub Hilmi, Barbar & Headcutter," indicating that the place catered to Europeans.

"This will do," said Smith, and we entered.

We had no shaving tackle with us and our immediate need was to dispose of the stubble on our chins—for self-appointed rulers must set standards which their subjects may readily ignore.

We were the only customers, and the proprietor—a cheerful old villain with a magnificent beard—welcomed us with commercial affability. He spoke English worse than he wrote it, but on finding that we understood Arabic, he became as garrulous as the traditional Barber of *The Arabian Nights*. While I took first turn, and Yakoub wielded brush and blade, he assured me that he shaved every foreigner in Keneh, and went on to add that his business was ruined because the war had interrupted the annual pilgrimage to Mecca.

Smith took my place in the chair, and I sat down on a bench behind them, looking out into the street—a seething panorama of ancient and modern, where vehicles of every age threaded an uneasy way through. Arguments as to whether the rule of the road should be left or right find little support in Egypt, where every driver of anything knows that the natural and obvious route is in the middle.

---

*Not impossible, but to-day an accomplished fact! [Ed.]

Presently, as I watched, an open motor truck with wire-spoked wheels turned in from the direction of the railway station. It looked like one of the Lanchester service trucks supplied to the R.N.A.S., but the driver was an Egyptian, who blared the horn with a viciousness that threatened to run down the battery, and leaned out of the cab to shout curses at those who obstructed his passage. Almost opposite us, he was slowed to a walking pace by a man who strode stolidly in front, dragging a handcart loaded to capacity with flat cakes of bread. Neither horn nor curses proving of avail, the truck driver endeavoured to squeeze past him, and, in doing so, struck a rear corner of the cart, so that half the contents was toppled into the road.

The truck jerked to a standstill. Promptly, and with neat presence of mind, the bread merchant slewed his handcart across the street, to ensure that the truck could not go on. Then, calmly, and taking no part in the pandemonium which ensued, he commenced to pick up his wares, giving each piece a smart slap on his thigh before throwing it back upon the cart. The driver of the truck switched off his engine and climbed down, loudly demanding that the merchant should give way and allow his fallen merchandise to be run over. Others joined in and the scene became animated. But, before it could erupt into violence, a second man stepped down from the truck—a figure so grossly obese that he resembled the rubber man of the Michelin tyre advertisement, garbed in the Turkish costume of baggy pantaloons and waistcoat.

I stared at him and uttered a gasp of astonishment which brought Smith starting upright in the barber's chair.

"Smith!" I cried. "That man out there! That is 'Ali of Istanbul, who nearly strangled me three years ago!"

Smith, bearded with lather, peered across the street.

"Yes," he said evenly. "So it is. Don't let him see you."

He settled himself back, raising his chin and motioning Yakoub to continue, whilst I snatched up a copy of *el-Ahram* from the journals lying on the seat beside me, and hid myself behind it.

"Yakoub," said Smith, "—you who know everything that passes in Keneh—who is the owner of that truck?"

"It belongs to Yildiz Bey," replied the barber unhesitatingly, "who lives in the great house on the hill. Everything in Keneh—may scorpions nest in his beard!—belongs to Yildiz Bey. And the fat one, like a pig, who is neither a man nor a woman, is the master of his *harêm*, who beats his wives and his female slaves."

"Slaves? Under British law, there is no slavery in Egypt!"

"Tell that to his slaves!" Yakoub ground his teeth, producing a most unpleasant sound. "Wealth is the law, *effendîm!* Why, in the name of Allah, the Compassionate, do you not hang him?"

Peeping over the newspaper, I perceived that my old adversary had taken control. Resentful but obedient, the truck driver assisted his victim to gather up his goods and fling them upon the handcart. Then the cart was drawn to one side and the truck edged past. I saw that it was loaded with what appeared to be domestic supplies— baskets, boxes, and three rolls of carpet.

"Fu Manchu is using the place as a storehouse and a centre of communications," remarked Smith, as we left the shop, "while 'Ali of Istanbul earns his keep by looking after the *harêm.*"

We turned the corner into the street which gave access to the station. I did not ask whither we were bound, but assumed that it would now be swiftly back to Luxor. To my surprise, however, my companion directed me through an archway into a *kahweh,* occupied on three sides by a brickwork divan covered with coarse matting.

"It's too late for breakfast," he said, "but you can make do with some coffee till I get back."

"Get back?" I echoed. "Why? Where are you going?"

"Around the town, to listen to all the gossip and find out as much as I can about Yildiz Bey." Smith looked at me with the glitter of steel once more in his eyes. "Perhaps you don't quite appreciate where we stand. Barring accidents, my work for Army Intelligence is ended. General Fernshawe may or may not say 'thank you'—and then I shall be given my marching orders. But I want Fu Manchu! I want him for the crimes which he has committed in the past and for those which he will commit in the future, if we do not prevent him! I have been carrying a warrant for his arrest in my pocket for more than three years, and I won't rest till I serve it!"

"I understand," I said quietly. "But do you think it wise to remain here longer—on the enemy's doorstep?"

"Very wise," he answered with a grim smile, "since it's the last place where they will look for us. While I'm gone, keep a watch on the station, in case some other member of the gang turns up. . . ."

Retreating to a corner from which I could see out without easily being seen, I sat sipping numerous cups of thick black coffee and awaited his return, keeping a weather eye on the station entrance. Trains were few and infrequent, but the forecourt was lively with the hoarse cries of the sellers of sour limes, toasted melon pips, and sweet *halweh,* and alien with the innocent, yet oddly sinister-looking, utensils of the tradesmen. The seller of *fûl mudammes* crouched over a great brass vessel with two bell-mouthed spouts, which looked like something borrowed from an alchemist's workshop, while beside him stood a barrow with countless rings of cummin-flavoured bread speared on tall spikes, and an *'erksoosi,* bearing a huge earthenware jar attached to his left hip by a bandolier, clashed two china cups together, to advertise an infusion of liquorice.

Half an hour after Smith's departure, a black limousine pulled up in front of the station. It was a *harêm* car, the rear windows covered by lace curtains. I thought it might well belong to Yildiz Bey, but no one descended from it and I guessed that it had come to meet someone.

Twenty minutes passed, during which I saw one of the street merchants go up to sell something to the driver. Then, at length, a train pulled in—one of the grimy local horrors from Luxor, which stopped at all stations. Five or six passengers emerged and my vigilance was rewarded as, among them, I recognized Fah Lo Suee, wearing the same beige travelling costume which she had worn at the Savoy.

I drew back hastily, repeating my trick at the barber's, and retreating behind a newspaper. But Fah Lo Suee looked neither to right nor to left. The chauffeur got out to open the door for her, and I saw that it was Salîm, her Nubian bodyguard. Then the door closed and the car drove off. I had neither the means nor the inclination to follow her. In the past, I had twice attempted to shadow an agent of the Si Fan and, on both occasions, come to grief.

Nayland Smith reappeared soon afterwards, listened to my report, and nodded.

"Much as I had anticipated," he commented. "Since we failed to turn up in Luxor, Fah Lo Suee has returned to her base to hold a council of war and organise the search for us. Let's go and have lunch—we have eaten nothing since the snack we had last night at the priest's house. . . ." He frowned, and shook his head. "God! I wonder what happened to the old man after we fled? Those fiends must have left Nagadeh in ruins. . . ."

The thriving town of Keneh—visited only upon occasion by tourists for the nearby antiquities of Denderah—boasted no such amenities as French restaurants, and we settled for a simple eating place where the cuisinier avoided the problems of heat and kitchen

smells by doing the cooking outside, driving off the smoke and the
flies with a palm leaf fan. Seated at a more or less filthy table, we
ate from tin plates, without benefit of knives or forks, with flapjacks
of bread thrown down beside them—the same, perhaps, which I had
earlier seen flung into the road.

"Yildiz Bey lives outside the town," explained Smith, "in a sort
of Moorish palace—the former Governor's residence, built by his
grandfather. The whole place is surrounded by a high wall topped
with broken glass, and patrolled by armed guards—deserters from
the Turkish army, who have a short way with thieves. Inside it, he
does as he pleases, and rarely comes out, other than to go up to
Cairo and enjoy himself in European society, where he is accepted
on account of his money—"

"Which his family obtained by usury and extortion," I said angrily, "and to which the Si Fan now contributes!"

Smith shrugged and, tearing off a piece of bread with his fingers,
dipped it into a repulsive concoction of *molokheya*, somewhat resembling mint sauce.

"No doubt!" he agreed. "But what can we do? Rumour has it that
he buys women, and has disposed of at least four by means of the
bowstring . . . but we have no proof."

We finished our indifferent meal with a dish of *kunáfeh*, sweetened
with honey. Then, at a few minutes before two, Smith stood up to
go to the post office and make contact with Greba, as arranged, at
the Semiramis Hotel.

"I can do it from here more safely than from Luxor," he said,
"where every call that goes out to Cairo will undoubtedly be over-
heard."

In his absence, I re-lighted my pipe and drank glasses of cinna-
mon-flavoured tea, thankful that our official mission had been accomplished, yet disappointed by the feeling that our current campaign against Fu Manchu was destined to fizzle out miserably.

Outside, the noisy life of the town had slowed to a halt. Past
midday, the streets of Keneh were like an oven, with the hot, sandy
winds gusting in from the Arabian Desert. Even the beggar squatting in a doorway opposite rested from his labours and ceased to
importune the occasional passer-by with his eternal whine for
bakhshîsh.

Knowing that it would take time to put through a long-distance
call, I was not surprised when thirty minutes had gone by with no
further sign of Nayland Smith. But, as the afternoon wore on, I

commenced to feel uneasy, and, recalling what had sometimes happened when we had ventured out alone into the deceptively peaceful streets of London, I wished that I had accompanied him. This was not London, but a stronghold of the Si Fan, where British law was openly flouted by Yildiz Bey. . . .

Again I ordered tea, the owner of the place looking at me a little curiously because I was a foreigner, but seeing nothing strange in it that I chose to pass the heat of the day in the shadowy interior of his evil-smelling premises. Others had come in to do likewise, and the room was fairly full.

But still Smith did not come. I looked at my watch, saw that it was now past four o'clock, and had just made up my mind that I would give him another half hour, then go in search of him, when at last I saw him striding across the street. The grim set of his jaw and his whole bearing spelt trouble. Walking with quick, nervous steps, he entered the café, came up to the table, and stood looking down at me.

"Basil Sorensen is in hospital with a cracked skull," he said flatly, "and Greba is missing. She never reached Cairo. . . ."

28

A DESPERATE VENTURE

"God in Heaven!" I cried, aghast.

I started to my feet, upsetting my half-finished glass of tea. It rolled off the table and shattered loudly on the floor.

"Sit down, man!" snapped Smith, thrusting me back into my chair. "You'll do no good to anyone by making a scene!"

Conversation had ceased and we were the focus of curious glances from every corner. The proprietor came up, grumbling and scowling at the broken glassware, but his scowls changed to smiles at the sight of a silver *Nuss Riyâl*.

"My friend has a touch of the sun," said Smith. "Clear up this mess, and bring us more tea."

Sitting opposite me, he charged and lighted his pipe with exaggerated care. Our companions, disappointed in their hopes of a fight, lost interest.

"Tell me what has happened," I urged.

"I made three attempts to call Greba," he replied. "Then I risked it and called your driver, Achmed Da'ud—only to find that he had heard nothing of her. So I went to the railway station, and got my information there. As I expected, Fu Manchu learned that we were on the train, but, instead of trying to get an agent aboard, he decided to take us off. The express was halted at Sohag by an anonymous telephone call, stating that a bomb had been placed on it. All the passengers had to descend and wait while the train was run half a mile up the line and soldiers of the Royal Engineers were brought from the nearest army camp to search it. Altogether, it took three hours, and, in the meantime, Greba had disappeared."

He paused, giving me a chance to say something, but I could only nod dumbly, and he continued:

"We can hardly blame Sorensen. It must have been confusion almighty, with his passengers milling around him, angry and horribly uncomfortable. The station platform was scarcely long enough to contain them all and no cafés or hotels were open. He couldn't keep a watch on Greba all the time—but, evidently, he did his best, since he was knocked on the head. When at last the train had been thoroughly searched—and no bomb found—it was allowed to proceed, and it was then realised that the Cook's man was missing. He was discovered, unconscious, under the tail end of the platform. He had, apparently, been sandbagged, and robbery was assumed to be the motive."

"But what about Greba?"

Smith shrugged. "With Sorensen out of the running, who was there to notice? The guard saw us together, but no doubt supposed that she had got off the train with us at Keneh." He snapped his fingers irritably. "Damn it! This is just what I feared when she came to Luxor. Now Fu Manchu has her, and the price for her release will be the contents of Brooker's damnable suitcase, which we dare not give him—unless we can find some other means of rescuing her."

"We must!" I said desperately. "But what can we do? We have no idea where she is."

"On the contrary, I have an excellent idea! She is here—in the house of Yildiz Bey!"

"But you say that she was kidnapped in Sohag!"

"She was shipped back to Keneh on the down train from Cairo. If the Si Fan's local base of operations is here, where else would they have taken her? She travelled as Cleopatra is said once to have been secretly conveyed to Julius Caesar—rolled up in a carpet! Remembering what we saw this morning, I made inquiries and ascertained that the household goods which 'Ali went to collect from the station were loaded on the train at Sohag." Smith paused, and the corners of his lips twitched in a saturnine smile. "Doubtless you noticed that the truck contained *three* rolls of carpet? They expected to find us too, but, finding only Greba, took her alone."

"Then why are we sitting here?" I burst out impatiently. "We must go to the police—"

Nayland Smith shook his head gravely. "The police? No. They can do nothing against Yildiz Bey."

"But," I protested angrily, "he can't hold a British girl captive. . . ."

"Who says that he *is* holding her? Though I feel certain I'm right, it's no more than a guess, and the *mudîr* would never consent to issue a warrant. No, Petrie, it will be the old story—the two of us against the Si Fan, operating like thieves under cover of darkness. Sunset is not until six, and we cannot possibly attempt it before seven-thirty at the earliest."

I groaned, recognizing that there was no alternative. Smith reached across the table and grasped my arm.

"Be patient," he advised. "I know what you're feeling, but Greba may come to no immediate harm."

"Not if Fu Manchu is there," I retorted, "but God help her if Fah Lo Suee is in charge!"

Smith nodded but said nothing. What, indeed, could he have said? How the next hour passed, or what I thought while I sat and sipped at my fresh glass of tea, which seemed to have lost all flavour, I have no idea. Gradually, as the sun declined by infinitesimal degrees and presently vanished behind the houses on the opposite side of the street, the place became dim. Then, at last, my friend knocked out his pipe against his heel and stood up.

"Time to begin our preparations," he announced. "First, we go back to the hotel. If the suitcase which we left there has been stolen, we shall know that the Si Fan have traced us here."

But it seemed that they had not. At the Hotel Denderah, the manager—who was also the desk clerk—handed us the item without comment. We had already paid our bill and given up our room. Now, however, we asked for another and were quickly shown up to it—a cheerless apartment, similar in all respects to that which we had previously occupied, stone-floored and bleakly furnished.

"Sit here," directed Smith, conducting me to a rickety table by the window. "I am going out shopping. Meanwhile, I have a job for you."

I sat down as instructed and he placed before me a few sheets of plain white paper, obtained from the desk.

"Cover these with figures and scientific symbols. Any old nonsense will do. We might get a chance to negotiate. We've never seen the stuff which Brooker stole, but it must be formulae of some sort."

"I see what you mean," I said doubtfully, "but it will not deceive Dr. Fu Manchu. . . ."

"Of course not! But, if it is his daughter with whom we have to deal, it will deceive her!"

With that he left me, and I set to work. Finding it oddly difficult to set down figures at random, I filled each line with all the algebraic and geometrical jargon I could call to mind, plus Greek letters and a few personal squiggles of no significance, but avoided the symbols of chemistry, since the Midnight Sun project was not, presumably, chemical. Finally, becoming inventive, I added several impressive diagrams of impossible electrical circuits.

I had only just completed the task when Smith returned, looking grim and businesslike, with a coil of rope bound about his waist, like a mountaineer. In one hand, he carried a short, steel crowbar, identical with a burglar's jemmy.

"Finished?" he demanded.

I handed him the papers which I had written. He glanced at them briefly; then, rolling them tightly, so that they might appear to have been contained in the cylinder which we had found, he tied them with tape and put them into the suitcase.

"We're as ready as we can be," he declared. "You have your medical kit?"

For emergencies, when only my pockets were available, I carried a flat tin box of antiseptics, glass ampoules of various drugs, and a tiny hypodermic syringe.

"Yes," I said, shuddering as I contemplated the purposes to which it might be put.

"We need transport and a driver," he continued. "Regardless of how things go, we must have a quick means of retreat, so I've told the manager to find us a taxi. There's not a soul in Keneh whom we can trust, but the man won't know where we're going till we're on the way, and money will persuade him to do what we want. . . ."

Downstairs, in the narrow space behind the desk which served as both office and lobby, we found our taximan awaiting us, cap in hand—a young man, beaked like a parrot, and dressed in shoddy European clothes, oil-stained and reeking with petrol fumes.

"What is your name?" inquired Smith.

"I am named Hamid," answered the man nervously. "Where am I to take you, *effendîm*?"

"I will direct you. Pick up that, and put it on the seat beside you."

As he spoke, Smith gestured towards a voluminous bundle of thick, quilted material which lay on the floor by the desk. Though I had already noticed it, I had not supposed it to have anything to do with us, and, as Hamid stooped to obey the order:

"What do you propose to do with that?" I asked curiously.

"You'll see when we get there!" said my friend, and, following Hamid, we went out into the street.

The vehicle which stood in front of the hotel was a Renault limousine, with a drop-fronted bonnet and coachwork built on the sweeping lines of a landau. Though only three years old, it had seen better days—for wives, beasts of burden, and motorcars age quickly in Egyptian hands—and passed cheaply through a succession of owners, each of whom had used it more disgracefully than the last. One mudguard was lacking, the glass gone from the rear and side windows, the paintwork chipped and dented.

We climbed into the back, while Hamid cranked up the engine—the primitive compressed-air starter having long since ceased to function. At the third try, it responded, and, to this unpromising start, we moved off, with much shouting and horn-blowing, through streets lit only by the light spilling out from the shops, against which flowing robes and flapping sleeves made a sinister, shadowy pattern, like a dance of devils.

On the outskirts of the town, where the lights ended, Smith bent forward and tapped our driver on the shoulder.

"Stop here!" he demanded, and, taking a card from his pocket, held it before the man's eyes. "Hamid—can you read?"

"No, *effendîm*!"

"Then you will have to take my word for it. I am a police officer—"

Hamid gulped loudly, twisted around, and stared at him in consternation.

"No, *effendîm*, no!" he chattered. "It is false! I did not do it. . . ."

"Be silent and listen!" ordered Smith. "We need your help, and we will pay for it. How much would you ask for a day's hire?"

These simple words had all the effect of a magic spell, and, recovering quickly from his fright, Hamid licked his lips covetously.

"Ten *ginêh, effendîm*?" he said hopefully.

"If I cared to bargain, you would take half. No matter. To-night, you may earn wealth beyond your dreams. Serve me for three hours only, and you shall have ten times that which you ask."

"A hundred *ginêh*? Whom must I kill?"

"No one, I hope!" said Smith, smiling. "Take us to the house of Yildiz Bey, and help us secretly to enter it."

"*Ya selám!*" Hamid gasped and bounded in his seat as if he had been stung. "No, *effendîm*! For a hundred *ginêh*, I will do anything. But think of something else! Do not go in there! He is an evil man—"

"Just so!" said Smith sternly. "And, by what we do this night, we will rid the town of his evil presence."

"I fear, rather, that he will rid the town of yours!" muttered our driver. He hesitated, drumming his fingers on the wheel, while cowardice fought with cupidity, then he sighed deeply. "Yet, if I do not do this thing, you will put me in gaol. Verily, the fate of Man is a sealed book, and only Allah may read what is written. . . ."

He let in the clutch and we moved off again, passing swiftly from the ill-lit streets into a velvet darkness pierced only by the shifting beams of the headlamps. Soon we were out upon a road rising steeply through thickets of sugar cane, wide enough only for a single lane of traffic, but surprisingly well surfaced.

"It is the road which Yildiz Bey had made for his cars," explained Hamid. "He has four. . . ."

"Do not go up to the gate," interrupted Smith. "Take us around to the back."

It was easier said than done, since it seemed that the road went only to the front and there was no other. Hamid accomplished it via a donkey track and, finally, across one corner of a cornfield, mowing down the unreaped grain with the destructive enthusiasm of a schoolboy. Then, at length, the car bumped to a stop.

"I can go no farther," he said. "There is a path, but it is too narrow. At the bottom is a canal and, beside it, a wall. Follow it for twenty *qasab* and you will find a door which they use when they sew up bodies in sacks and float them down to the river."

This I hoped to be only a local rumour.

"Now give me the hundred *ginêh*," he went on, "before you go in—for you will both come out in a sack and sawn into seven pieces."

"And if I pay you now you will run off!" Nayland Smith took out his notecase, counted out ten Egyptian pound notes, and handed them to him. "Switch off the headlamps and wait two hours."

I gathered up the mysterious roll of bedding. On the seat beneath it lay the suitcase containing my forged documents; but Smith shook his head, directing me to leave it.

"If the situation arises," he said, "and we are able to make a deal, we will have Greba brought out to the car and conduct the exchange here."

We had partly descended one side of the cone-shaped hill upon which the former Governor's residence was situated, and had halted at the fringe of a dried-up banana plantation, ghostly with the contorted shapes of dead trees—for the construction of the Aswan

Dam, which ensured a constant water supply for the lowlands, had, here and there, done so at the expense of the land on higher ground.

Smith led and I followed, shouldering my light but cumbersome burden. We continued our descent by an overgrown footpath, treacherous with half-exposed roots. Brambles caught at our clothing and the dust rose in clouds from the dry, powdery soil. To the left, through a screen of stunted trees and thorny bushes, I saw the dark outline of a high wall running roughly parallel to the path.

At the foot of the path, we came out upon an embankment, bordered on one side by the wall—which here turned at a right angle—and, on the opposite side, by the placid surface of a minor canal, where a heron was fishing. A hundred yards beyond, we reached the door of sinister repute, set in an arched opening.

We tried it but, as anticipated, found it to be bolted.

"It will make too much noise to force it," said Smith, in a half whisper. "I'll go over the top."

The wall which enclosed Yildiz Bey's property was little more than ten feet high and the familiar construction of unbaked bricks, plastered over but in poor repair. Smith shone his torch aloft, and the light glittered on spears of broken glass cemented along the ridge. I understood now why we had brought the bedding.

While I set it down upon the path and unfastened it, Smith went to work with the crowbar. Without making a great deal of noise, he attacked the plaster, cutting toe holds in the brickwork, and clambered up—then, using the same tool, he broke off the longer spikes of glass. I handed up the soft material, and he heaped it over the remainder.

"All clear!" he said tersely, hauling himself up. "Don't bother to come after me. I'll open the door for you."

He scrambled over and dropped down on the other side. Less than a minute passed; then the heavy wooden door creaked inwards, and, for the first time in three years, I found myself venturing once more into a stronghold of the Si Fan. . . .

29

THE HOUSE OF
YILDIZ BEY

By starlight and the pale luminance of a freshly risen moon, I gazed
in awe at a hillside landscaped in terraces and cloaked in flowering
trees and shrubs—an Oriental fantasy which reminded me less of
the Nile than of Granada. One who would see the enchanted gardens of Edmond Dulac's illustrations to *The Arabian Nights* must go
to Spain—for the fertile land of Egypt is too little to be wasted.

Nayland Smith closed the door in the wall.

"Our way lies upwards," he said. "Come on!"

Cautiously, and keeping an eye open for guards, we ascended a
flight of steps. The wall which rose along one side was draped by
an overhanging network of creepers and scarlet blossoms. At the
top, we followed a mosaic pathway through a dim jungle of broad
leaves and trailing vines, redolent with a mixed fragrance of roses,
oleanders, and lime trees, and came to more steps, leading to a
maze of separate gardens on successive levels—the realisation of an
Eastern fairy tale, achieved, careless of expense, by *corvées* of forced
labour and the nineteenth-century genius of French contractors.

No sound disturbed the perfumed stillness but the splashing of
artificial cascades and the liquid rustling of a tiny stream, carrying
the residue back to the canal, from which it was presumably drawn
up. We passed along one side of a long, shallow basin, where the
scales of golden carp gleamed silver in the moonlight, and silvery
jets of water met in a sparkling trelliswork above.

"So far, we have seen no one!" observed Smith.

"If we are lucky, we may not," I replied.

"I hope that we do! We need a guide."

At the top of the hill, screened by trees and an inner wall, only

199

the upper floor and mosquelike roof of Yildiz Bey's house were visible. Lights within silhouetted tall Saracenic archways fronting a balcony, and several small windows covered by heavy iron grilles.

Smith stopped suddenly.

"Listen!" he ordered.

Far off to one side, I detected the steady drone of an electric generator and the rhythmic beat of a pumping engine.

"We shall find somebody down there!" he said, speaking in the rapid, staccato fashion which he always adopted in moments of action.

The sound came from below, and, after some searching, we discovered an unpaved path. The way was dark and eccentric, but we dared not use a torch. Groping with our outstretched hands, and stumbling over stones, we came at last to a barren tract of land, formed by a broad step cut into the hillside, and peered out through a curtain of spear-shaped leaves at the square, ugly bulk of an engine house, fifty yards ahead. In the cold radiance of the moonlight, I discerned a bench set in front and a figure seated upon it.

"That's our man!" hissed Smith. "Now it's our turn to take a prisoner!"

"But he may not know where she is."

My companion laughed softly. "No? Show me the house in England or in Egypt where the servants don't know everything that goes on! I doubt that there's anyone inside the shed . . . we'll have to chance it. Give me a minute to work my way around behind him. Then keep your pistol out of sight and walk up to him. He'll never suspect you're a stranger till you're on top of him. . . ."

Dropping to hands and knees, he vanished, snakewise, into the bushes. I put my watch to my ear and counted off the seconds— when Smith said "a minute," that was what he meant—then stepped boldly out of concealment and, with a nonchalance which I did not feel, walked towards the man sitting on the bench.

I saw that he carried a Mannlicher rifle slung over one shoulder and wore parts of an old Turkish army uniform. The hooded felt cap, covering neck and ears, was oddly reminiscent of Central Asia—a lingering trace of his warlike Seljuk ancestors. Hearing my footsteps, he looked up but, deceived by my casual approach, showed no alarm. For all he knew, I might have been a guest from the house; he could not know all who came there.

"*Liltak sa'ïdah!*" I said pleasantly.

The man stared, gulped foolishly, and scrambled to his feet, clutching at his rifle. But ere he was fully upright, I had my pistol at his chest. In the same instant, a shadow rose silently behind him, and Smith's arm was locked about his throat.

"Don't struggle, or I'll break your neck!" he warned, and jammed the muzzle of his automatic hard into the man's spine. "Get his gun, Petrie! Detach the bolt, and throw it away!"

I tore the sling from the guard's shoulder and obeyed, hurling the bolt in one direction and the rifle in another.

"Good! Now cover him!"

Again I obeyed, pressing my pistol to the man's forehead, while Smith dragged his arms behind his back and used the tarnished handcuffs which we had taken from Brooker's suitcase to secure his wrists.

"*Teyyib!*" he ground out. "Now, where is the girl? *Feyn el-Inglisiyya?*"

Our victim made no answer. Rarely have I seen a man so terrified. His eyes bulged and the perspiration coursed down his flat, stupid face in rivulets till it dripped from the points of his hairline moustache. He hesitated so long that I began to fear that he might understand neither English nor Arabic, but, encouraged by a painful jab from Smith's pistol, he proved to know both.

"*Wi-hiyât abouya!*" he stammered. "My—my master will kill me!"

"Tell me, or *I* will kill you!" rapped Smith. "Where is she, you spawn of Satan?"

The man groaned, rolling his eyes heavenwards in a mute appeal to Allah.

"They—they have—" he began, stopped, and ended in a rush of desperation: "I swear in the name of the Prophet, on Whom be peace, I took no part in it! They have her in the old prison. . . ."

"*Warrini es-sikka!*" said Smith curtly. "Show us the way!"

A shove completed the demand, and the man stumbled forward in an abject state of fear so intense that it threatened to choke him without the agency of Smith's fingers twisted in his collar. Clearly, he was no soldier but only some hapless Anatolian peasant bundled into uniform, who had fled from our guns in the Sinai and made his way south, to find refuge in the service of Yildiz Bey.

Led by our reluctant guide, we traversed a series of zigzag tracks descending through arid land where the soil had worn away and the

flaky yellow surface of the exposed rock suggested a volcanic origin.
At the bottom, I could see the outer wall and a glimmer of moonlight on the canal. Farther along, the wall was breached by a wide
archway, bricked up, which once had given access to a group of
buildings long since disused.

As we approached, I saw that the nearer portion of the compound
had been destroyed by fire and the ruins left uncleared, with blackened beams clawing against the sky, like the ribs of a broken fan.
Passing to one side, we came into a courtyard strewn with rubbish
and surrounded by empty stables with apartments above, in the
manner of a *wekkaleh,* or Egyptian inn—evidently, I thought, the
former quarters of the *zaptieh,* who, till the turn of the century, had
served as both army and police. No lights showed, and the place
appeared utterly deserted.

"No tricks!" growled Smith, keeping a tight hold on our prisoner.
"Lead us into a trap, and you die before we do!"

We crossed to a tunnel-like aperture with rusty iron gates which
screeched as we opened them. Through this we entered a smaller
courtyard, octagonal in shape, and bounded by a high stone wall,
with a whipping post in the centre. Opposite, a square, brick-built
watchtower loomed above the wall, and to the base of this our man
conducted us, halting before a dark doorway.

"*Ma fihsh fanous!*" he faltered. "I have no lantern!"

"Go ahead and light the way, Petrie," said Smith.

He handed me his torch, and, by its aid, we descended a spiral
staircase as steep and as narrow as that which goes up to the belfry
of Notre Dame, the walls pressing close against our shoulders. At
the twentieth step, it ended in an underground passage, not much
wider, and spaced at intervals on both sides by the massive wooden
doors of dungeons. Halfway along, one stood open, partially blocking the corridor, and here our prisoner stopped, stuttering incoherently.

"She—she was *here*! I swear it, *effendîm*!"

"But she is not here now," said Smith shortly.

Shining the torch quickly around, I saw that the cell—no more
than eight feet by five—was furnished only with a stone shelf attached to one wall, and unoccupied. Being below ground, it was
windowless, but a grating in the ceiling admitted air and a little light
by means of a vertical shaft. The rays of my pocket lamp picked
out a small heap of white material lying on the floor. I stooped

and snatched it up—Greba's linen dress and her lace-edged chemise. . . .

"God! We are too late!" whispered Smith. His fingers tightened on the captive's collar and he shook him as a cat shakes a mouse. "Where is she? Where have they taken her?"

"They—they have taken her to the place where they—"

"Lead us!"

"I dare not, *effendîm*! I dare not—"

"Lead us!"

A gasp of pain answered him, as Smith jabbed viciously with his pistol, and our guide blundered on, babbling in his native language, and so far gone in terror that I feared he might collapse.

"I knew it!" muttered Smith. "I knew that Fah Lo Suee would never be content just to hold her as a hostage. . . ."

Daring not even to imagine what we should find at the end of our journey, I thought how we seemed to be the playthings of an unjust Fate with an ironic sense of humour, and remembered the night when we had burst into an empty house to save Eltham from the horror of the Wire Jacket. Now we must save his daughter—from the same, or worse.

Past the doors to either side of us, the cell block ended in a short flight of steps descending to a second passage, wider, but sloping downwards like the shaft to an Egyptian tomb—a hundred feet long and roughly hewn from the living rock. Though otherwise in darkness, it was fitfully illuminated at the remote end by a lambent glare of firelight, where it terminated in an iron door standing partly open. A stifling wave of heat drifted up to meet us.

Our prisoner halted, and pointed with a shaking hand.

"They—they are in there!" he panted.

"Thank you," responded Smith. He lifted his pistol, and, without compunction, struck the man neatly on the base of the skull, so that he fell stunned and with no more noise than a falling sack of potatoes. We had no further use for him and no time to waste in tying him. As we hurried on:

"We must take them by storm!" said Smith. "In as fast as we can, and don't hesitate to shoot!"

I nodded and pocketed the electric torch. Ahead of us, I could hear the clear, imperious voice of Fah Lo Suee, speaking in short, crisp sentences, though I could not distinguish the words. Who was there with her, I wondered, and how many?

The door at the end was square and solid, like that of a giant furnace—left ajar, I supposed, to reduce the insufferable temperature of the place within—and opening inwards. We paused for an instant, glancing at each other. Through the narrow gap between door and frame, I could see only a stone wall. Then, putting our shoulders to it, we threw our combined weight upon the door. . . .

30

THE CHAMBER OF HORRORS

As the door swung ponderously open, I took one pace forward and halted in mid-stride—frozen to a statue by a scene so appalling that every detail was graven instantly upon my memory, as if upon a photographic plate.

We stood on the threshold of a lofty-ceilinged cellar, hellishly illuminated by flaring cressets and charcoal blazing in an iron basket on a tall brass tripod, behind which Fah Lo Suee stood with her back to us, clad in black silk trousers and a high-necked blouse. Chains hung from the walls, and the place was hideously furnished in a manner which combined the horrors of mediaeval Nuremberg with the Oriental fiendishness of the Osmanli.

Midway across the room, I saw Greba—stripped down to her undervest and mounted astride a fearful, wedge-shaped contrivance like a monstrous wooden horse, with her long, straight legs spread wide apart and huge iron weights attached to her ankles. Her wrists were bound behind her, and she was held upright by a loop of rope passed under her armpits and joined to a pulley—the other end grasped in the blubbery hands of 'Ali of Istanbul.

For an instant of suspended time, all seemed motionless. Then the spell broke. Fah Lo Suee whirled about, facing us, and crouched from the hips like a leopard prepared to spring.

"*Shîl-ha 'uddam!*" she screamed—and 'Ali, responsive as an automaton, bore down on the rope.

I saw it grow taut and heard it screech through the sheaves.

Both Smith and I acted instinctively and like fools—firing at the same target. Our bullets took him in the chest, and 'Ali sank soundlessly to the floor like a melting bladder of lard, while Greba slumped forward over the horse, with her hair sweeping down, but prevented from slipping off sideways by the weights on her ankles.

Simultaneously, Fah Lo Suee seized the tripod and flung it at us, scattering the live coals in a fiery shower. We leapt back, and, diving through the open doorway, she slammed the door with a resounding clang, followed by the crash of a bar dropped into place.

As I coughed and choked in the poisonous fumes of the glowing embers strewn at our feet, it registered only vaguely on my mind that we were locked in. Built out from the wall behind us was a low stone trough, with an enormous wheel fixed above for the horrible purpose of passing the victim, head downwards, through the water. Smith ran to it, snatched up a leathern bucket, filled it, and dashed the contents about the floor. Though there was not much danger of fire, the burning fragments lying about everywhere hindered our movements. Then, taking the sensible precaution of first ensuring that 'Ali would give us no more trouble, he hurried to the spot where the eunuch had fallen, and turned him over with his foot.

"Too bad!" he said grimly. "He deserved to hang!"

But, for the moment, I felt little satisfaction in settling scores with 'Ali, who had put the bowstring round my throat. On a level with my shoulder, Greba lay sprawled helplessly over the fiendish contraption on which she had been saddled, like a corpse heaped on a donkey, and I wondered how on earth we were to get her down without doing her more damage.

Nayland Smith knew what to do.

"Get the weights off her feet," he said, laying hold upon the rope which 'Ali had held, "while I support her."

Taking up the slack, he drew the rope between his hands as gently as possible, raising her once more to a sitting position. Her eyes were wild and unseeing, and she uttered a gasping sigh. I tried to reassure her, but she seemed neither to understand nor to recognize my voice. As she felt herself lifted, she clenched her teeth and I saw her grow tense for the shock of the anticipated drop.

I stooped quickly to unfasten the broad steel collars locked around her ankles. Each was joined to a stirrup with a stack of heavy iron discs dangling beneath, like Chinese coins threaded on a string. Luckily, the shackles were secured only by a simple clasp, and it required but a moment to undo them. Smith hauled again upon the rope, lifting Greba a few inches higher.

"Grab her round the waist," he instructed, "and pull her towards you till she's clear."

I did so, and he lowered her carefully into my arms, then ran across to help me, since I could not hold her and untie her at the same time. Smith drew his pocket knife and cut through the cords which bound her wrists. The rope by which she had been lifted was attached to them and knotted around the upper part of her body in an unspeakably cruel manner. Since it was too thick to be easily severed, he was forced to unfasten it, which might not be done quickly.

While he worked at the knots, I stared around at the grotesque travesties of furniture and machinery which surrounded us.

"Lay her upon that!" I said, and, between us, we carried the girl to a flat-topped table with a roller at either end. The surface was perforated with holes through which a nest of spikes, like a fakir's bed of nails, could be raised at will. But at least it might serve as a couch.

I bent over her and, having no stethoscope, applied my ear, finding the heartbeat strong. I thought that she had fainted, but her eyelids fluttered; she stared up at me, and, though her eyes were dull with pain, now there was recognition in them.

"I—I didn't tell them anything!" she whispered.

She closed her eyes and relapsed into semi-consciousness. The agony of her strained leg muscles must have been excruciating, apart from more intimate injuries which I could not directly ascertain.

"God in Heaven!" I burst out furiously. "Fah Lo Suee has no respect even for common decency!"

"Neither has a Chinese court," said Smith curtly, "when they deal with women of the upper classes. Fu Manchu—"

He was interrupted by a sudden sound of falling water, and, spinning around, we saw a foaming torrent gushing from an opening in the wall into the stone trough behind us, which was already more than half filled. In a matter of seconds, it overflowed and spread across the floor, washing about our feet and setting small objects afloat.

"Just to make things harder!" commented Smith, with a grim smile. "If Fah Lo Suee hopes to drown us like rats in a cage, she'll be disappointed. We'll be out of here long before it rises high enough. . . ."

"Yes—but how?" I demanded.

"H'm!" he said, and, going to the iron door, inspected it closely. "Well, it won't be this way. It would take dynamite to shift this."

The horrible place in which we were now trapped was not really a cellar but a pit, some twenty feet in depth and roofed over. The walls were faced with neatly jointed slabs of stone, running with moisture and green with lichen, which gave me the idea that, in the distant days of the Mamelukes, it had probably been a cistern.

I turned quickly back to Greba, who was slipping in and out of consciousness, her limbs twitching spasmodically.

"Do what you can for her," went on Smith. "But hurry!"

Under these conditions, there was little enough that I could do. Fumbling with impatient fingers, I opened my tin box of emergency supplies and selected an ampoule, but, before I could fill the syringe, he stopped me.

"Don't put her to sleep! Give her something to keep her awake!"

"She's in pain . . ." I protested.

"I know! But, if she's a dead weight on our hands, we'll never get her out!"

I nodded, and, returning the tiny glass phial to the box, took out another, which contained Adrenalin. Forcing myself to act as calmly as I would have done in a traffic accident, I made the injection professionally, then, while I waited for the drug to take effect, began to pull off my jacket, with the intention of wrapping it around her. But again Smith stayed me.

"No!" he insisted. "This is no time for propriety! Let her remain as she is till we're safely outside." He pointed upwards. "Up there! That's the only way."

High above our heads, through the swirling smoke from the oil flares, I could dimly discern a barred aperture in one wall, close to the ceiling.

"If they're waiting for us," he added, "our chances are poor. But I don't think they will be. Yildiz Bey will expect to have the police here at any moment, and all he'll want to do is to get Fah Lo Suee and her accomplices off his premises before they arrive."

I stared up doubtfully at the long, narrow opening, more like a ventilator than a window, and a good twelve feet beyond our reach.

"How can we get at it?" I muttered.

"The rope!" Smith indicated the block and tackle arrangement by which Greba had been suspended. "You can haul me up, can't you?"

"Yes. But it's too far from the wall. You won't be able to reach—"

"Of course not. But if I leave one end of the line free, you can tie off the other end and then swing me across."

The rope which had been used to torture Greba was now to be the means of our salvation.

From a rack of pincers and tongs, Smith took down a long-handled hammer—intended for what awful use I cared not to think—and thrust it through his belt. Then, winding the rope expertly about himself, so that a surplus of two or three yards trailed upon the floor, he grasped it with one hand and directed me to pull.

Though he was heavier than I was, no great effort was needed. The apparatus was fitted with a double-purchase pulley, provided for just such a purpose. The rope creaked and up he went, inch by inch, till his heels hung well above me and his face was hidden in the smoke-veiled space below the roof.

"That's enough!" he shouted.

Looping my end of the rope round an iron cleat, I hurried to the end dangling from his feet and dragged it across the room, to bring him nearer to the wall. The angle proved barely sufficient, but, leaning perilously out, he seized the nearest of the bars set in the opening, and, clinging to it, knocked out the rest with ringing blows of the hammer. Wriggling through, he vanished from sight; then, a moment later, his head and shoulders reappeared.

"Now send up Greba!" he called back to me, and threw down the rope, weighted with the hammer, so that it would fall when I detached it from the cleat.

Greba was now conscious, but breathing rapidly and shivering from the action of the Adrenalin. Her eyes were feverish, and she clutched at me as I worked to tie the rope around her.

"I think I'm going to die!" she gasped. "Kiss me. . . ."

"You're not going to die," I said firmly. "Be brave a little longer."

But I kissed her anyway, and I think it helped.

I am no alpinist, but I was thankful just then for my youthful interest in Egyptology—for the practical archaeologist must know how to tie knots and handle ropes. By much the same means as before, I got her aloft to the point at which Smith could seize her hands and drag her to safety. The water, rising faster than we had expected, was already halfway up to my knees. I guessed that Yildiz Bey's intention was not merely to drown us but to flood the place to the top and conceal all trace of his subterranean torture chamber before the authorities came to search for us.

It remained, now, only to think about my own escape, and, for this, the same rope was useless. Smith uncoiled the line with which he had thoughtfully provided himself, and cast down one end to me.

I could not have climbed it unaided, but, grasping it in both hands and bracing my feet against the wall, I held on while he hauled me up. The opening close to the ceiling was little more than a foot high. Squeezing through it was like entering the awful sixteen-inch tomb shaft in the pyramid of Meydum, but, with Smith's help, I accomplished it, rolled over, and sat up to find myself on sloping ground thickly overgrown with weeds. Below us, I could see the wall which bordered the canal and, to my relief, saw that the door which Smith had earlier opened stood at no great distance.

Greba lay motionless beside me with her solitary undergarment rucked up to her shoulders, and the moonlight gleamed on her unclothed form as though upon a figure sculpted in marble.

"She can't walk," said Smith, unnecessarily. "We shall have to carry her."

"Leave that to me," I said. "I can manage her. You go ahead and keep guard."

Scrambling to my feet, I stooped over the girl and lifted her. Tall and athletic, she was no light weight, and, had she been unconscious, I should have had a hard job to support her. But, thanks to the drug, she was able to lock her arms around my neck and hang on. Smith leading, we descended the slope, meeting with no opposition. Yildiz Bey had more to do just then than to pursue us.

"Smith!" I said breathlessly. "I don't know how seriously hurt she is. We must get her to a hospital."

"I agree," he replied. "But that means Luxor."

The door in the wall remained unbolted, as we had left it, and, glancing up, I noticed and remembered the heap of bedding which my companion had thrown over the jagged spikes of glass.

"Our taxicab will make a poor substitute for an ambulance," I said. "Get that stuff down, and let's take it with us."

"Good suggestion!"

Smith clambered up and retrieved most of the material, though some of it was badly damaged. Then we hurried on our way, alongside the canal, where the dark surface of the water mirrored the moon and the stars, and the heron fished patiently, as if nothing of any importance had happened. From his point of view, nothing had.

At the spot where the wall turned uphill and at which we had climbed down, we wrapped one of the quilts tightly around Greba, to protect her as much as possible from the thorny bushes and brambles through which we had to force a passage back to the taxi—assuming that it was still there.

"If he's deserted us, we're sunk!" rasped Smith.

Still there was no pursuit, but we could not count on it that there would be none. Fah Lo Suee would not take it for granted that we remained trapped in the underground chamber and, if Yildiz Bey did not dissuade her, would send out her men to search. Smith took the lead, shining his torch to guide us, and tearing with his bare hands at the spiderweb of briers. Almost at his feet, a venomously patterned snake slithered away, gracefully, into the undergrowth. Thanking God for giving me the strength, I staggered up after him, clasping the half-unconscious girl close to me with her face buried in my shoulder, my arms aching, and a cloud of tiny, stinging insects busy about my head.

The way seemed endless and, with a feeling of surprise rather than relief, I saw the lights of the taxi glowing through the panes of ornate sidelamps fashioned like carriage lanterns.

"The blockhead!" exploded Smith. "He hasn't turned it round!"

Hamid sat paralysed at the wheel, dumb with fear and kept at his post only by the lure of the ninety *ginêh* owed to him. Smith snatched open the door, seized him by the arm, and tumbled him out.

"Get the car started!"

Smith taking his place in front, I occupied the back, where my first business was to get out my tin box and give Greba an injection of morphine to counteract the Adrenalin. She had suffered more than enough. Hamid cranked the engine five times without success, and Smith slid over into the driving seat to retard the ignition.

"Try again!" he ordered.

The taximan did so, and this time the engine burst into life. Smith revved up, waking the echoes, and switched on the headlamps. In their cold glare, I saw Hamid withdraw the starting handle, stand up, and come around to the side of the car. But, all at once, he stopped, staring past us and up the hill, goggling like a bullfrog, his mouth wide open. Then, with a shrill scream of terror, he threw down the handle, spun about, and went crashing blindly through the bushes towards the canal.

Something hit the back of the car so violently that, although the brakes were on, it was jerked a yard forward, while Greba and I were thrown to the floor, and Smith was all but pitched head first through the windscreen. But for the now fortunate fact that the windows had no glass in them, we should have been cut to pieces.

"What on earth—" I exclaimed.

Smith neither answered nor paused to inquire. Snatching at the handbrake, he sent the taxi lurching precariously down to the limit of the cleared space, and fought it around like a man handling a steer at a rodeo, de-clutching and reversing recklessly, so that the engine howled and the vehicle swayed madly. I feared that, at any moment, we would be capsized, but, somehow, his ruthless tactics succeeded.

Suddenly, we were facing up the hill and, over the back of the empty passenger seat, I had a clear view of the thing which had struck us, floodlit by the headlights. I had thought that I had had my fill of horrors for that night, but this was a creature from the illustrated pages of a Gothic legend. Less than a hundred feet ahead of us, it stood crouching in our way—the figure of a man, or a manlike figure, with flaring nostrils, flat, Neanderthal features, and a *horn* like that of a rhinoceros curving up from its forehead. It snarled, lowered its head, and charged.

Smith thrust his foot hard down on the accelerator and the Renault bounded forward. Had it been of the English pattern, with a high, square radiator, we might have come off worse, but the low-snouted bonnet took the creature amidships, hurling it backwards, followed by another lurch and a sickening, crunching sound. . . .

"Fah Lo Suee's *ifrît*!" I said, speaking with unnatural calm.

"My God, it looked like one!" snapped Smith. "What in God's name was it, Petrie?"

"Only He knows!" I said. "Some ghastly freak of Nature, I suppose—some miserable African savage with a dreadful deformity of the frontal bone, no doubt enhanced by the diabolical surgery of Dr. Fu Manchu. . . ."

Smith nodded. "She turned it loose to find us by its weird powers of scent, in case we had escaped. I think I killed it. I hope so!"

Hamid, our driver, was nowhere to be seen and we left him to his fate. Compared with our recent experiences, the steep ascent and the progress across the cornfield to the road seemed like easy going.

History had repeated itself with significant differences. After rescuing the Reverend J. D. Eltham, we had had only to summon the police and let them take care of him. But we had still to convey his daughter over some forty miles of rough roads to the nearest point where proper medical treatment was available.

"Drive straight through," I said, as the lights of Keneh came into sight. "Don't stop for anything."

"I can't stop!" flashed back Smith. "If the motor stalls, we're stuck. We've lost the starting handle!"

On later consideration, I suppose it was a foolhardy decision. We were not even sure that the tank contained sufficient petrol to take us to Luxor. But neither of us, just then, was clear-minded enough to think of an alternative.

Wedging myself into a corner, I arranged the padded quilts around Greba, couching her across my knees, with her head pillowed on the crook of my left arm. While I watched her anxiously, we sped through the town and out into the darkness. The road was abominable—nowhere better than an English country lane—but Smith, who had acquired his driving skills in Rangoon, coped with it accordingly. He drove not as I would have done but viciously, careless of springs and paintwork.

Fortunately, there was no traffic to contend with. All the way down to Qift and beyond, we saw not a single vehicle or pedestrian. Outside the towns, when night fell, Egypt slept.

Soon after we reached Kous, Greba stirred in my arms and began to murmur deliriously. Her forehead was hot and dry. What she said made no sense, but her half-finished sentences betrayed a guilty affection which I could not return. Yet, since I could do nothing more to comfort her as a doctor, I did so as a lover, caressing her tenderly, and, if I did wrong, I can only say that it would have been inhuman to do otherwise.

The road which we now followed was the same which we had traversed on the way out from Luxor, barely practicable for motorcars. Smith remained silent, concentrating on his driving. I had no idea where we were till, at last, I saw the dark towers of Karnak looming up above the trees.

Minutes later, we were back in Luxor, and roaring down the long, straight thoroughfare called el-Birket, where people still lingered and a few stalls remained open for business, indicating that it was less late than I had thought. At the corner, by the telegraph office, we swung leftwards into el-Manshiya. The hospital was located at the far end, and here our madcap journey ended. We had done it in less than two hours, which I regarded as something of a record. Smith switched off the engine, opened the door for me, and assisted me to carry Greba into the building.

The stir created by our arrival need hardly be described.

Under my terse directions, the nursing staff did their best to make the girl comfortable, but I had no authority to use the hospital facilities, and, in any event, medical etiquette forbade me to treat her. Dr. Deane came hurrying down from the Winter Palace in a great flutter, and took over from me with commendable efficiency, asking only the minimum of questions and postponing his curiosity.

In the interim, Nayland Smith and I sat by the reception desk, awaiting his verdict—and no two relatives of a patient undergoing surgery ever waited more anxiously. We had little to say to each other, and feared to say anything. After some minutes, Smith left me for a while, to go to the telephone and make reservations for us at the nearby Luxor Hotel. We dared not go back to the Savoy, where we knew that agents of the Si Fan would be looking for us.

"They will find us soon enough," he said grimly, "but, probably, not to-night."

It was an hour before Deane came back, having exchanged his dinner jacket for a white laboratory coat.

"I have given her something, and she will sleep for the next twelve hours," he reported. "There appear to be no internal injuries. She is not gravely hurt—"

"Thank God!" I said fervently.

"I cannot, of course, predict the psychological effects of an experience such as this," resumed Dr. Deane, regarding me narrowly. "She is badly bruised. Prior to the incredible mishandling which you describe, she was savagely flogged with something like a strap—"

"A *kurbagh,* I imagine," murmured Smith impassively, "—an instrument of which our Turkish predecessors made frequent use, until we discouraged them."

The hotel physician looked at him, frowning. Our previous interview had already done sufficient to disturb his peaceful practice, in which murder and assault played no part.

"I think you owe me some sort of explanation," he said stiffly. "How did this unfortunate young lady come to be the victim of this atrocious crime?"

Smith hesitated, but I had had more than enough of official secrets and the appalling results to which they led.

"She was kidnapped," I said, "and tortured to make her reveal the whereabouts of certain documents which your patient Professor Brooker had stolen from his employers—"

"Stolen?" echoed Dr. Deane. "You say that he had stolen Government property?"

"Yes!" I said, ignoring a frown from Smith. "He betrayed us. He was in league with the Germans. . . ."

I stopped, realising that Deane was staring at me not only with astonishment but with distinct unfriendliness.

"Dr. Petrie," he said frigidly, "if I am probing into matters which I am not entitled to know, you may tell me so. There is no need to deceive me."

"Deceive you?" I cried. "Why, what do you mean?"

"I mean that what you have just told me is childishly ridiculous!" answered my colleague, glaring at us both. "You expect me to believe that Professor Brooker was acting on behalf of our enemies? I knew little of him, as I have informed you, but I knew that his hatred of Germany was almost pathological. His wife and his daughter—whom his assistant, Dr. Crawford, was engaged to marry—died in the sinking of the *Lusitania.* . . ."

31

THE DIARY OF A
MADMAN

We came out from the hospital thankful to leave Greba in good
hands, but more sadly bewildered than when we had gone in.

Our taxi stood in front, where it must remain till we could have
it towed into a garage for repairs, and Hamid would at least get it
back in a better state than it had originally been in. Smith jerked
open the rear door, and brought out Brooker's suitcase.

"Do we still need that?" I asked.

"Perhaps," he replied. "When we reach the hotel, we will hand
it in at the desk, and if the Si Fan come looking for it to-night they
can leave us alone and burgle the manager's safe."

Past midnight, el-Manshiya was dark and silent, populated only by
a few lean cats searching for scraps, and, as we walked, I thought
over the curious remarks of Dr. Deane.

"I suppose it hardly matters now," I said slowly, "but it's madden-
ing to think that we may have been on the wrong track from the
beginning. Is it possible that Professor Brooker was *not* working for
the Germans? Did Kurt Lehmann go to the Hotel Iskander to buy
those documents, as we have all along believed, or to steal them?
But, if so, why had Brooker himself stolen them?"

"Or were they ever stolen at all?" Nayland Smith laughed shortly.
"Is this all part of some devious plot, of which we must be kept
in ignorance? My God! If Fernshawe has been playing games with
us . . ."

He left the sentence unfinished, unable to think of any adequate
way to end it.

At the Luxor Hotel we found our luggage sent down from the
Savoy, and Smith, who had left his with me when taking up his rôle

of Mohammed the dragoman, came into my room to collect it.

"I need my army codebook," he explained. "I must send a tele-gram to General Fernshawe to-morrow, as soon as the office opens. It's the only way I have left of getting in touch with him, and Fu Manchu may intercept it. But before he succeeds in breaking the code, I shall have my answer and know what to do."

I nodded abstractedly, unable just then to think of anything but the fearful circumstances in which we had found Greba. However, when I mentioned the subject, it seemed rather to irritate Smith.

"Torture in the Far East," he said curtly, "is not subtle, but as brutal and obscene as it ever was in the dark ages of Europe."

Putting one foot up on the bed upon which I was sitting, he pulled up his trouser leg and pointed to a number of tiny white patches above the sock, where the skin was pitted, as though by acid.

"You remember? It's no more than four years since Dr. Fu Man-chu arranged to have me eaten alive by Cantonese rats, in the fiendish contraption called the Six Gates of Wisdom. The thing to which Greba was submitted bears an equally poetic name, but I will not offend your refined susceptibilities by telling you what it is."

Smith was in a bad mood, and I fell silent as I realised that our expedition to rescue the girl had robbed him of his last chance to come to grips with the Si Fan.

A last-minute attempt to secure Brooker's suitcase was still a possibility, but our night passed peacefully. Smith having got up early to dispatch his telegram, I breakfasted alone, then went to join him outside, where he sat waiting for the reply in the large and pleasant garden commanding a nearby view of the Great Temple.

"Fu Manchu will not be pleased with his daughter," he said, smiling grimly. "He has lost not only his hostage but his base of operations. Yildiz Bey will probably sit tight and try to brazen it out, but he can afford to have no more to do with the Si Fan."

"You think that he can get away with it?" I inquired.

"Why not? A man of means, who can hobnob with the right people in Cairo society . . . ?" Smith shrugged and occupied himself with his pipe. "By now, that damnable cellar will be filled to the brim, and, very likely, he has dynamited the place—hoping we are underneath. Greba does not know where she was taken, and there are none to give evidence against him but ourselves—who entered his premises illegally. . . ."

For the next couple of hours, we went on talking, mainly of old times, till our conversation was terminated by the arrival of a special messenger from the telegraph office. Nayland Smith got out his codebook and set to work with pencil and paper, then leaned back in his chair, scowling at the result.

"H'm!" he said. "Well—it's much what I expected. I am to go back to Keneh and wait for a military unit to join me. No instructions as to how I am to get there."

"Shall I go with you?"

"No!" Smith glanced at me across the table. "Stay here and look after Greba. Likewise, look after yourself! Fu Manchu knows that we either have those documents in our possession, or have hidden them somewhere. The danger is not yet over. . . ."

He left directly after lunch, and I went to the hospital. I found Greba lying face down on her bed, in a clean, cool room, with her head turned sideways on the pillow. Dr. Deane had done his best for her, but she looked very miserable.

"Sorry I was such a nuisance!" she whispered. "I've really messed things up, haven't I?"

"Forget it!" I said. "No harm's been done, excepting to you. How do you feel?"

"Awful!" she groaned. "I'm half doped, and, when I move, something hurts. So I don't move. I hate being helpless, and I'm so lonely. . . . You'll stay and talk to me, won't you?"

"Of course—if you feel up to it."

I placed a chair beside her bed, clasped her fingers in mine, and kissed her lightly on the forehead.

"Thank God you got me out!" she murmured. "I didn't think I could stand much more. . . . But how did you ever find me?"

"Partly luck," I confessed. "But we knew that Dr. Fu Manchu had a base in Keneh."

"Keneh? Is that where I was?"

I nodded. "Yes. But you were kidnapped in Sohag. Do you remember anything about it?"

"It's about all I do remember!" Greba shifted slightly and bit her lip. "Damn! Sohag? Yes—that's where they stopped the train and we all had to get off. Nobody knew quite what was happening. They said there was a bomb on the train. . . ."

She looked up at me and attempted a smile.

"Out on the platform, it was like Charing Cross station in the rush hour. Mr. Sorensen tried to stay close to me, but there were people coming up to him all the time, asking him to do things for them, and we kept getting separated. Suddenly, I felt a sharp pain in my left thigh, and I thought something had bitten me. Then, soon after, I started to feel sick and dizzy. I heard somebody say, 'Are you all right, miss?' and then I blacked out.''

Again she paused, but I made no comment, and, after a moment, she continued in the same flat, matter-of-fact tone, as though she were relating the experiences of a third party.

"The next thing I knew, it was daylight, and I was sitting in a chair, with my hands tied, in some sort of old stone building which seemed to be partly ruined, with holes in the walls and ceiling. There were two men there, dressed like soldiers, and talking in Turkish. My head ached, and I was dreadfully thirsty. I don't know how long I was there—maybe an hour. They'd stolen my watch and my pearl necklace. Finally, the door opened, and Fah Lo Suee came in. She didn't say a word to me. She just glanced at me, and, speaking in English, because I don't think she knows Turkish, she said, 'Yes, that is the girl. Take her downstairs and give her forty lashes!'—and then she went out again."

"Good God!" I muttered.

"The two soldiers—or whatever they were—seized me under the arms and dragged me down some stairs to a cellar, where 'Ali, the fat man, was waiting for me with a sort of thick leather strap fixed to a wooden handle, and I knew what he was going to do to me. . . ."

She hesitated, and I broke in quickly.

"It's all right," I said. "You don't have to tell me."

"I *want* to tell you! I want to tell somebody! If I don't, it's as if it was something I have to be ashamed of." Greba's voice was fierce but tremulous. "They untied my wrists, so that they could get my clothes off, and I didn't fight, because I knew I'd only get hurt. There was another man there, who came down to see the fun. He was very well dressed, in European things, with a pointed beard and a Kaiser Wilhelm moustache, and stinking of scent. . . ."

"Yildiz Bey!" I exclaimed.

She had evidently seen him, though Smith and I had not.

"He was perfectly beastly!" Greba flushed indignantly, her cheek glowing pink against the whiteness of the pillow. "He made me stand in front of him, looking awfully silly and awkward with just my vest and no pants on, while he stared at me and sneered. They told me to kneel on the backs of my hands and put my—my top on a horrid-shaped block of wood. Then the two soldiers got hold of my shoulders and shoved me down hard, and 'Ali started belting me.

I screamed like mad, and I think I took it about thirty times before I fainted. Unfortunately, I don't faint as easily as I used to. . . ."

Distantly, through the open window, I heard the call to prayer, which punctuated our days in Luxor like the bell of a town clock. It was midafternoon.

"Don't talk any more," I advised. "You're tired."

"No—let me finish. There isn't much more to tell." Greba licked her lips dryly. "I woke up in a cell, lying on a stone bench, with my dress thrown on top of me. I didn't try to put it on or get up. For hours, I just lay there and cried. After a while, it got pitch dark, and, when I couldn't cry any more, I think I went to sleep. Then the same two men came back and took me down to the place you know about. When I saw it, I thought I was in Hell! 'Ali was there, and so was Fah Lo Suee, and I was left alone with them. She slapped my face and asked me where you were and what we'd done with the things we'd found. Of course, I wouldn't tell them. So then she told 'Ali to put me on the horse—and he did. . . ."

I stayed with her the rest of the afternoon and on into the evening till Dr. Deane came in to settle her down for the night. Walking back from the hospital, I trembled with rage as I thought of the infamous experience to which Greba had been subjected, and felt guilty because I knew that, try as I might, I could never fully appreciate the degradation she had suffered.

Little did I think that soon the day might come when I might be better able to do so. In my anger, I forgot that I was not immune—forgot Smith's warning, and neglected all precautions. Feeling little appetite for dinner when I reached the hotel, I headed first for the bar. But, as I crossed the lobby, the desk clerk called out to me.

"Dr. Petrie, sir! There is a package for you."

I turned, and he handed to me an official-looking envelope, tightly sealed. My name was upon it and, beneath, a message written in an unfamiliar hand: "Colonel Smith requests you to examine the enclosed." It was signed: "Lewis N. Prendergast, Major."

"Who delivered this?" I demanded.

"A British soldier, sir."

I nodded. "Give me my key," I said, and, changing my mind about going to the bar, went up to my room.

This, though quite unexpected, must be something which Nayland Smith had sent down from Keneh by a dispatch rider. I locked the door and, sitting at the table by the window, tore open the envelope in a fever of impatience. It was made of some tough material and closed so firmly that it appeared to be airtight.

It contained no word from Smith, but only a thick, cloth-bound notebook. Opening it, I found the owner's name boldly written on the flyleaf—Richard Brooker. I sat back, staring at it in amazement.

Where had Smith obtained it? The cover was soiled, the pages limp and damp, and it had a disgusting smell, suggesting that it had shared the insanitary conditions of the professor's sojourn at Der el-Melik. If Smith had picked it up there, why had he not shown it to me before? However, as to why he now wished me to examine it, I had no doubt—for it might at least satisfy our burning curiosity to know what our mission had been all about.

I gave my attention eagerly to the task. The book was printed as a diary for the year 1916, but it had not been used as such, all the pages being covered with figures and symbols closely resembling the nonsense which I had written in Keneh. Save to a man who knew the alien speech of higher mathematics, they were incomprehensible.

Still I persevered, tilting the shade of the reading lamp, and holding the book close to my face, since, in places, the ink had run and the figures were hard to make out. Searching vainly for anything I might understand, I came soon to an alarming discovery. Gradually, the handwriting grew worse and the lines were here and there interspersed with the holy name of God. Later, there came phrases, such as: *"the third part of the sun was smitten, and the third part of the moon, and the day shone not . . ."*

Thereafter, each page included passages and misquotations from the Book of Revelation, for which I have scant respect as scripture— the Hell-inspired visions of an insane prophet. All too clearly, Professor Brooker had lost his mind.

I paused, smiling self-consciously and feeling it a trifle sad that an expressed belief in God should automatically be taken as evidence of madness. Yet here there seemed no doubt of it. Close to the end, a simple equation occupied a page by itself—conspicuous, since the rest were closely written.

$$x^2 \times x^2 \ldots \ldots \infty = \alpha \,\&\, \Omega$$

What it meant, I could not imagine, but I recognized the letters *Alpha* and *Omega*—Brooker's synonym for the Creator.

It was surely obvious that no more was to be learned—yet I persisted. There was an occult lure in those unintelligible signs— fascinating and frightening, like the cabalistic letters of a Tantric spell—and now, as I pored over them, I became aware of a phenom-enon yet more strange. It seemed to me that I no longer *saw* but *heard.* Each symbol was a voice, gibbering in an unknown tongue—a babel of voices, screaming in my ears, till I cried out and tried to throw down the book . . . only to find it stuck to my fingers.

Was I, too, going mad? My grip relaxed, and the notebook drifted down infinitely through space to a tabletop which, all at once, had become as distant as the floor of a canyon. My head fell back, and I stared up at a ceiling so far above me that the light hung like a star in the firmament. This was sheer lunacy, but a dreadful coldness descended upon me as I knew the truth—for I had been through this before.

The diary had come to me from Dr. Fu Manchu, impregnated with the secret preparation of *hashîsh* which he had often used, now subtly administered, vaporizing rapidly on exposure to the air. While I sat peering closely at the damp, musty pages, I had breathed it into my system, till eventually it had overcome me.

Though my senses were distorted, the thinking part of my mind remained clear. I knew what had happened, and what I must do—for this, too, I had done once before. But could I do it again? My medicine chest lay on the top shelf of the wardrobe, on the far side of the room. . . .

Closing my eyes on the world of illusion, I braced my hands on the table, levered myself up, and felt my way around. Then, reeling like a man blind and drunk, I stumbled across a floor which rolled and pitched under my feet like the deck of a ship in a storm, over-turning a chair, and tripping over imaginary obstacles.

I had lost all sense of direction, and, forced to re-open my eyes, found myself in a room where the furnishings changed shape as if in the distorting mirrors of a fairground, while the sounds of the town came through the window in streamers of smoke and flashes of colour. Over against one wall, my bed danced on its iron legs, like the enchanted hut of Baba Yaga.

The wardrobe was behind me. I staggered against it, clawed open the door, and reached up for the small mahogany box on the shelf. My fingers touched it and drew it forward, but it fell, striking me in the face, and flew open, spilling the contents across the carpet.

Concurrent with its fall, the floor hit me on the back as the room turned upside down. I can find no other words to describe it. I was lying face-upwards, staring *down* at the ceiling.

Then the last of my senses left me, and I was floating down through a purple sea of clouds, amid which two Greek symbols shone, like sun and moon—*Alpha* and *Omega,* the Beginning and the End. . . .

32

NIGHTMARE

How I am to write of the events which followed, I really do not know. Some of them I would prefer not to write at all, but I am sworn to my conscience to leave a full and accurate record of all that happened while Nayland Smith and I were involved in the strange and terrible business of the Midnight Sun. Setting aside prejudice, I will write, then, of what I remembered—or what I was told that I remembered, from words shouted in delirium. But how much was truth, and how much fantasy, I shall never know.

It appears that, for some time, no knowledge of my actions was registered even upon my unconscious mind. My next awareness is that the purple clouds rolled back, opening up a clear vista of sight, but swirling, misty and indistinct, about the periphery of my vision, as though I were looking through a lens smeared at the edges.

I was walking down a familiar street. I knew it well—yet could not give a name to it. I saw brightly lighted shops and stalls selling picture postcards, exotic brassware, figured leatherwork, damasc-ened trays, and inlaid coffers; hawkers, avid for trade, brandishing barbaric jewellery and spurious antiques. An *'arabîyeh* clattered by, almost running me down, and the coachman leaned out, shouting at me.

I ignored him and walked on. I say that I walked—yet I seemed to stand still, marking time, while the houses and the figures in native and European dress slipped past me like a moving panorama. At that point, I felt no emotion. Something weighed heavily upon my left hand, but I did not look down to see what it was.

I have no recollection of leaving the street. Abruptly, the scene changed, as if two lengths of cinematograph film had been spliced together. Now I was passing through a long, deserted avenue of ram-headed sphinxes, the way unpaved and rough underfoot. At the end, it was closed by a great stone pylon, black against the night, in the form of two adjacent triangles with the points cut off.

Entering, I came to parallel rows of papyrus columns, the aisles between them carpeted with a barred pattern of moon-cast shadows. Considered in retrospect, I think that—if I was ever truly there—it may have been the Temple of Khonsu.

All about me was now dark, but, in the distance, blue lights flickered. Incuriously, I walked on, ascended a ramp, and saw three steps, leading up to a throne. On either side, the blue flames waxed and waned, leaping up from copper bowls upheld by tall stands, fashioned in the shape of cobras.

A figure sat upon the throne—a living, female figure, nude to the waist, with the awful head of a lioness upon her shoulders: Sekhet the Destroyer. I cast myself down, raised the object I was carrying, reverently, in both hands, and laid it at her feet, like an offering— Brooker's suitcase. Hidden amid the forest of columns, an unseen host chanted a litany in the forgotten tongue of Egypt.

The goddess bent close to me and the great, feline eyes blazed into mine, fierce and compelling. Slowly, the beast-features shifted and changed, to become the face of Fah Lo Suee. For the second time in my life, our lips touched and I felt the arctic breath of the eternal snows.

"Your will is mine . . . you have no will but mine . . ."

The temple faded from my sight, and once more I was falling through purple cloudbanks, followed by a vertiginous, spinning sensation, as if I were being drawn down into a maelstrom. Then the clouds cleared and emotion returned—terror and loathing, as I gazed upon sights beyond the sane imagination: scenes of war, torture, and barbarous modes of execution. Clearly, as in a magician's crystal, I saw a darkened city with searchlights fingering the sky—heard the drone of Zeppelin engines and the crash of bombs. I saw a cold, turbulent sea and a great ship sinking by the stern— men in khaki, wading ankle-deep through a morass of mud, the horizon lit by shellbursts and the intermittent flashes of machine-gun fire.

In this saturnalia of horror, all was confused—past and present, places which I had seen and others which I had not. A man clad in jointed armour, like an armadillo, walked past, carrying a severed head by the hair. . . .

"Look!" whispered a silvery voice in my ear. "This is Mimizuka, where the ears of thirty-seven thousand Chinese soldiers lie buried. . . . This is Peshawar, where your prisoners were blown from the cannons, and the skies rained blood. . . ."

Though I knew nothing of the Far East but what I had learned from Nayland Smith, I found myself translated to a landscape of tip-tilted rooves and hexagonal pagodas—an older China, of strange dresses and pigtails, where shrieking Chinese faces loomed up and as swiftly vanished. Helpless to close my eyes—for, in fact, they were closed already—I watched men and women strangled with loops of wire, burned alive in iron cages, and beheaded with saws.

Among these dreadful visions, induced, as I now believe, by the black arts of Fah Lo Suee, were others which were sharper and more personal.

Presently, I saw the bulbous domes and squat, stovepipe minarets of Persian mosques . . . a town square, where a mob clamoured about a scaffold and a masked executioner. Beside him—the object of their hate and derision—stood Greba and Kâramanèh, chained back to back (both naked, of course) and condemned to death by impalement. Behind them, I could see the pointed wooden stakes set up close together, two for each girl. . . .

The confusion of sight and sound persisted, and the screams of the victims seared across my eyes like incandescent sword blades.

Horror succeeded horror, till it seemed that I could endure no more and the mists closed in. For a time, there was peace . . . a gentle, swaying motion, and music in my ears . . . music which I knew . . . the sad, eerie strains of an unearthly composition by Sibelius: "The Swan of Tuonela." I was couched on the back of the swan, floating down the River of Death, with the white wings raised above me. . . .

All at once, I was awake—resting no longer upon swansdown but upon the hard planks of a boat, staring up at the triangular sail of a felucca. Pressing my elbows to the boards, I struggled half upright.

"Quickly! He is coming out of it! *Eddini es-sanduq!*"

It was the voice of Fah Lo Suee, seated behind me. I felt a man's weight thrown across me, bearing me down, as he handed up a sandalwood box to her. She opened it, took out two thin glass tubes, and, holding my head firmly between her knees, inserted them carefully into my nostrils.

I gasped—felt the drug burn through my lungs as if I had inhaled vitriol, and collapsed into timeless unconsciousness.

There were no more dreams, and I knew no more till I was rudely aroused by a deluge of water splashing upon my face. My eyes opened, and I found myself lying upon stony ground, looking up at the night sky. A fierce-eyed man bent over me, holding a goatskin bag under one arm and squeezing it to project the contents upon me in a stream. I turned my head sideways, and saw others arrayed in tribal fashion, each with the *lissam* of his *kafiyeh* drawn up to the nose, so that I could see only their eyes. Two carried lanterns.

My mind was clear now, but my head ached abominably. I tried to rise and fell back, assailed by a weakness such as one feels after a long bout of seasickness. I tried to speak and failed. My throat was parched and constricted to a degree which made all articulation impossible.

"Is he conscious?"

Suddenly, Fah Lo Suee was there beside me, dressed in a workmanlike riding habit of jodhpurs and a plain white blouse. In one hand, she held a sheaf of papers, and her eyes glittered with a cold rage, like those of Dr. Fu Manchu in the moments of insane fury which, occasionally, had possessed him.

"Son of a dog!" she hissed. "Will you play tricks upon me, even yet?" She threw down the papers, stamped upon them, and spurned me with her foot. "You shall see! I have no time for drugs and mind-reading. . . . For such as you, the oldest and the simplest ways are the best. *Take him!*"

Two men seized me and lifted me to my feet. Supported between them, I saw that we were in the wide forecourt of a ruined temple, with nine columns ranged along the façade. Somewhere in the background, I heard the grunting of camels and, with a strange lucidity, deduced that Fah Lo Suee had crossed the river to a rendezvous with her father. These men were her escort.

Dragging me to the colonnade, my captors placed me with my back to one of the tall, papyrus-capped pillars and bound my arms behind me, so that, although I was unable to stand, the rope stretched between my wrists held me partly upright when they released me. Fah Lo Suee approached, put a hand on my brow, and thrust back my head. I heard the thud of it against the stone, but felt no pain.

"Pitiful fool! Do you think I will hesitate to do as much to you as I did to her?"

She hooked her fingers into the V-neck of my shirt and, displaying an unexpected strength in those slender hands, ripped it wide open. Then, with the dispassionate attention of a nurse in a hospital, she took hold of my belt and drew the end through the buckle.

So deeply implanted are the cultured inhibitions of our society
that, despite my drugged senses, I was shocked to the depth of my
being as I felt her hands dragging at my garments and knew myself
now utterly in the power of a woman to whom all civilised standards
of human dignity were a source of contempt.

"Give me that!" she demanded, and snatched a camel-stick from
the hand of a Senussi tribesman who stood grinning evilly at her
side. "And bring the lanterns closer!"

She stood back, surveying me with a frigid smile.

"So you are a man, after all," she said softly. Her icy fingers
touched me outrageously, and I writhed. "Now answer me, *Englishman*"—the tone in which she spoke it made the word an insult—"or
I will hurt you. Where is Nayland Smith? What have you done with
the cannister?"

I parted my lips to revile her, but no sound came from my throat
save a hoarse croak. Fah Lo Suee shrugged, raised the camel-stick,
and struck me smartly and expertly below the hips. It was a light,
glancing stroke, but the bolt of pain which it engendered was out
of all proportion, invading every fibre of my nervous system, like an
electric shock.

"Speak!" she ordered, and again thrust back my head.

But speak I could not. Again I felt the shameless touch of her
fingers and drew in my breath in a gasp. Fah Lo Suee laughed wildly.

"Why do you shrink from a woman's hands, *Englishman*? Have no
fear. I shall not kill you . . . yet, but this time I am really going to
hurt you."

And hurt me she did—for the blinding agony of that second foul
blow was outside anything in my experience. It felt as if a clawed
instrument such as the Ancient Egyptians used to eviscerate the
dead had been thrust deep inside me, tearing at my vitals. My senses
reeled. Had I been able to speak, I would have spoken—but I had
nothing to tell! By this time, Brooker's stolen documents were safely
in the hands of the military, and I knew now what it meant to be
tortured without even the option of a secret to reveal.

"Speak!" repeated Fah Lo Suee, and looked down at me with
sardonic amusement. "If your wife could see you now, she would
weep for you. . . ."

A third time she lifted the stick and, as she did so, I was dimly
aware of movement behind her—camels brought to their knees and
riders dismounting. In the next instant, the tall figure of Dr. Fu

Manchu stood at her shoulder. He caught her wrist, twisting, so that she cried out, and hurled her to the ground.

"By your crude and futile methods, you disgrace my name!" he said. "I was wrong to entrust you with authority."

Raising herself on one elbow, she stared up at him, and I saw fear in her lustrous eyes.

"He will not speak . . ." she protested.

"He cannot. You have given him the tincture of mandragora, which I warned you not to use. He can speak only to me."

Dr. Fu Manchu came closer, raised my head, and looked into my eyes. As of old, I felt the nightmare thrall of staring through a microscope into the lucent depths of an emerald, of falling, to be swallowed up and trapped to eternity in the heart of the stone. I resisted, striving to turn my head aside, then gave way—grateful, by any means, to escape from my shame and the throbbing agony of my body.

"Has the secret of the Midnight Sun been regained by those who lost it?" he asked sibilantly.

"Yes . . . it . . . has. . . ."

I saw the words pass across my vision in letters of fire, like an advertising sign in lights.

"So, for the moment, you have triumphed—yet, ere long, you may wish that you had failed."

Dr. Fu Manchu spoke quietly and without emotion, placed his fingertips upon my eyelids, and drew them down, as one closes the eyes of a corpse.

"Sleep!" he said—and I slept.

In that dreadful night of sleeping and waking to fresh horrors, my next recollection is of a despairing cry, uttered in a voice high-pitched and vibrant.

"No! You rob me of my birthright!"

It can only have been a part of my fantasies, yet the impression lingers so strongly that I must record it—that, though I understood the words, they were spoken in Chinese!

With returning consciousness, a sense of time returned, and it seemed to me that long minutes passed. I no longer felt much pain—only a great lassitude that disinclined me from any attempt at movement. Once more, I was lying on my back, and the violet sky above told me that dawn was not far off.

Turning my head slowly from side to side—which was all that I could do—I looked upon surroundings so unreal that I wondered if I were still in the land of dreams, or dead and in Amenti, beyond the grave. Left and right, my horizon was terminated by the sloping walls of a ravine, above which I could dimly make out the cone-shaped peak of a mountain. By way of human habitation, nothing was to be seen but two roughly constructed huts, dark and, appar-ently, long since abandoned.

At first, I thought myself alone. Then movement caught my eye and I saw that, far from being unpopulated, this prospect of desola-tion was alive with drifting shadows.

A group detached themselves and approached, led by one taller than the rest. He halted at my feet, towering above me, drew the veil from his face, and again I looked up into the Satanic yellow features of Dr. Fu Manchu. At a word and a gesture, two of the others came forward and raised me to a reclining position. Behind him, I saw four men bearing a plain wooden sarcophagus upon their shoul-ders, and, half dead though I was, felt a thrill of fear in the thought that it was meant for me.

At a further command, they set the narrow end to the ground, holding it upright, and lifted the lid.

"Behold! I have avenged you," he said tonelessly. "I will not be served by one who disobeys me at her pleasure."

Within the dark depths of the open coffin lay Fah Lo Suee, as innocent of clothing as I had first seen her in my surgery—and innocent, indeed, she looked, with her eyes closed and her arms folded on her breast, like a dead pharaoh. She did not seem to be breathing.

"No," said Dr. Fu Manchu, answering my unspoken thought, "it is not *Katalepsis*. She sleeps, and will sleep till I awaken her. This I will do only when I am able to exact her obedience, or when I feel my own end to be near. Otherwise, she will die."

Again he gave a terse command, in response to which his tribes-men re-closed the sarcophagus and bore it away.

"You are ill," he said. "But always we have fought with honour, and I will spare your life. Now sleep once more."

My eyes closed and, obediently, I slept. My subsequent, and final, awakening from that phantasmagoria of horror was of a different nature.

Brilliant morning sunlight was streaming into my eyes. Flat on my back, I was staring, backwards, at the multi-columned façades of an imposing edifice, rising in terraces against a vertical wall of rock. An

Egyptian tourist guide was kneeling beside me, holding my arms and shaking me.

"Wake up! Wake up!" he shouted. "Hatshepsut's temple is no right place to sleep your drunkenness!"

33

THE MAN FROM ALEPPO

When they finally understood that I was a good deal worse off than drunk, I was carried down to Cook's Rest House, where I remained till Nayland Smith and some police officers came across the river to collect me. But, by that time, I was in a high fever and delirious.

For two full days, I was conscious of no more, till I woke in a hotel bedroom, with Smith seated in a chair beside me. Of all that had passed, I then remembered nothing. Smith, seeing that I was awake, bent over me, his steely eyes softened by anxiety.

"Thank God you're alive! How do you feel?"

"Tired," I said feebly, "more tired than I have ever felt in my life. . . . Tell me the truth, Smith! Am I very ill?"

"You have been, but you'll be all right now. For thirty-six hours, you were running a ferocious temperature, and raving. It was touch and go. You were heavily overdosed with two exotic drugs."

Peering up at the ceiling and around at the walls, I saw that this was neither my room at the Savoy nor that which I had occupied at the Luxor Hotel. Smith smiled and nodded.

"We are at the Winter Palace," he said. "Dr. Deane had you brought here. Now rest, and try to sleep again."

"I am almost afraid to sleep," I groaned. "I have dreamed—horribly. First, tell me—is it over? Did you find the cannister where we left it?"

"Yes, it is over. We found it, and the Army has it."

"And Greba? How is she?"

"Well enough, but still in bed. We have told her nothing about you, for fear that it might hinder her recovery. I explained your absence by saying that I had sent you on a mission, and promised her that you would take her home to Cairo when you came back."

A telephone bell rang. Smith reached out to answer.

"Yes?" he said, and his eyes narrowed slightly as he listened. "As well as can be expected, I imagine. . . . Yes, I shall take good care that he does not over-exert himself. . . ." He put down the instrument and turned to me with a smile. "That was the doctor."

"Dr. Deane?" I inquired.

"No," said Smith dryly. "Dr. Fu Manchu!"

Next day, we had a more lengthy conversation and exchanged notes—though I had little to contribute. From the time of going up to my room at the Luxor Hotel I knew only that I had dreamed—but of what, I did not know.

"When I reached Keneh," said Smith, yielding to my curiosity, "the town was in an uproar. Fernshawe had taken my warning more than seriously. He had sent six truckloads of soldiers and an armoured car! We went down to Kous, occupied the landing stage, and stopped all traffic on the river. The cannister was just as we had left it—wrapped up in my old clothes. I gave it to them, glad to be rid of it. It was midnight before I got back to Luxor. At the hotel, they told me that you had gone out and not yet returned. That was sufficient! Your door was locked, but I made them open it. Inside, I found a chair overturned and your medical things thrown all over the floor. The desk clerk, who had gone off duty, was got out of bed and informed me that, when you came back from the hospital, a package had been delivered to you—"

"Brooker's notebook!" I said. "I remember that. It was supposed to be from you, and they said it was handed in by a man in British Army uniform. . . ."

"So it was!" rejoined Smith. "But they neglected to mention that the man was an *Indian* soldier!"

"I could make nothing of it," I muttered. "It was all just figures, and it had an unpleasant smell—the pages were damp and mouldy. But it looked genuine."

"Possibly it was—though Heaven knows where Fu Manchu got it from." Smith thought for a moment and frowned. "But it has vanished, so you must have taken it out with you. We know now that it was used in some way to poison you with the drug which he has several times employed to induce auto-hypnosis. Afterwards, you came down to the desk, asked for the suitcase which we had left there, and signed for it. Then you went out. The doorman recalls noticing that, though it was after dark, you were in your shirt-sleeves."

I shook my head slowly, having no memory of the event.

"The precise means by which the hypnotic commands were im-

posed upon you remain a mystery," went on my friend. "It might
have been done by telephone—the hotel switchboard keeps no record of incoming calls—but, having been overcome, I doubt that
you were able to answer the bell. In that case, we are forced to
conclude that it could be—and was—done by telepathy!"

"What did you do?"

"What *could* we do? I had the Luxor police force out, turning the
town upside down and making a house-to-house search. But I knew
that it would be useless." He laughed harshly, and shrugged. "Well,
General Fernshawe has got what he wanted. But, between us, we've
done enough damage for an army. Yildiz Bey is dead—"

"Dead?" I exclaimed.

"The story is that he set fire to the house and committed suicide.
Needless to say, he was murdered. Once he had ceased to be useful
to them, his unwelcome guests killed him and decamped with everything they could lay their hands on. His servants, or his slaves—
nobody knows which they really were—did likewise. No matter—he
got no worse than he deserved."

I waited, saying nothing, and, after a moment, he added:

"Nagadeh has been half destroyed, though Kyrilos, the *Kasîs,* is
safe. Fu Manchu declared his property inviolate, but gave over the
village to his tribesmen. The shops were looted, and houses burned.
All the men they could find were shot in the stomach, the women
staked out in the street and raped. Our people will do what they can
to help with the re-building, but the Army is too concerned with
other things to send out a punitive expedition."

"My God!" I said, shuddering. "Such a proceeding is unlike Fu
Manchu, and unworthy of him. . . ."

"I know! But what choice had he? These desert devils are his
allies, but not members of the Si Fan. Unless he let them proceed
as they are accustomed to do, they would not follow him." Smith
stood up. "Enough for now. I will leave you to get some rest."

"I'm sorry that I couldn't be more helpful," I said miserably.
"But, really, I remember nothing. . . ."

"You may later. During your less lucid moments, you said a lot,
and I have taken notes. To-morrow, we will go over them and try
to make some sense of it all."

In two days of fever, I had lost an alarming amount of weight, but
I made a quick recovery. Fortunately, I possess something of the
constitution of a camel—which can lose a quarter of its weight and
regain it in ten minutes, by drinking twenty-five gallons of water.

Smith got out his notes and we considered them—with the results which I have already recorded.

"Much of it is nonsense," he declared finally. "However, your later impressions seem more reliable. Apparently, they took you across to Kurna, and the place where you next woke up was the Mortuary Temple of Seti the First. But how, I wonder, did Fah Lo Suee know that the papers in the suitcase were a forgery? She cannot have had the scientific knowledge . . ." He broke off, tugging at his earlobe. "Well, what she did after that is certainly a fact. You have a few bruises which will keep you out of mischief for a while."

I flushed with embarrassment, and he laughed.

"Oh, I make no excuses for her, but she claims to have been similarly mistreated in a Shanghai prison."

"Where did you hear that?"

"From you!" he answered, smiling.

I stared at him and shook my head, having no recollection that I had heard or said any such thing.

During two more days of convalescence, I was out and about, but still I did not go to see Greba, being insufficient of a good liar to pretend that nothing had happened to me, and, if the truth be confessed, prompted by male pride to avoid her sympathy.

It was on Thursday—a week since the night of my abduction—that Smith received a long, coded telegram. He worked on it, chewing at his pencil, then turned to me with a wry smile.

"We have been relegated to guard duties," he announced. "A party of distinguished visitors is coming down to Luxor to-night, and I am to take charge of the security arrangements. General Fernshawe is coming too—what for, I have no idea." His smile broadened to a grin. "The last sentence reads, 'Put on your uniform.' "

"If they are to stay here," I said, "M. Duvivier will probably know more about this. Let us go and see him."

We did so, and found him willing to communicate.

"Yes," he admitted. "These gentlemen are high-ranking representatives of the British and, possibly, the French Government. There are only six of them, but General Fernshawe—who spoke to me on the telephone—has demanded the whole of the top floor for their accommodation. At first, he proposed to take over the entire hotel, but decided against it when I mentioned the cost. . . ."

No more was to be learned, and we were forced to contain ourselves in patience till, at six o'clock, Nayland Smith appeared in my room, impeccably turned out in his colonel's uniform, and we went down together to the street. Arrived at the station, we found it besieged by army vehicles and swarming with such a battalion of soldiers as I had rarely seen in one place. They were everywhere— outside, inside, and out upon the platforms.

Making himself known to an eager young captain of infantry, who knew no more than we did, Smith approved his operations with a brusque nod. Twenty minutes later, the morning train from Cairo pulled in. Passengers alighted—but, until the platform had been completely cleared, one carriage remained closed. Then, at last, a door opened and six civilians descended, followed by the stocky figure of Brigadier-General Fernshawe. They were immediately sur- rounded and hustled out to the cars waiting for their transportation. Fernshawe glanced at us, exchanged salutes with Smith, and walked out after them.

We saw no more of him till we were back at the Winter Palace, where the visitors were served dinner in their rooms. Then Fern- shawe met us in the lobby, uninformative, and, as usual, in a bad temper.

"I have put you in charge of security," he said gruffly, "because to-night's business may still concern your Dr. Fu Manchu. Having failed to get what he wants, we think it more than likely that he will make an attempt upon the life of one or more of our guests."

"Guests?" queried Smith, and he scowled.

"That is all you need to know about them. I rely upon you to protect them."

Had he been content to leave it at that, the interview might have passed smoothly. But it appeared that he had personally known Yildiz Bey and, even now, was inclined to regard him rather as a victim of the Si Fan than as an accomplice.

"Man was a member of my club," he grumbled. "Used to play cards with him. . . ."

"I should not, if I were you, be too ready to acknowledge the acquaintance," retorted Smith. "It seems, General, that you have some peculiar friends." He hesitated, then drew his bow at a ven- ture. "If it comes to that, what were you doing in Geneva last June?"

Fernshawe stared at him, speechless for a moment, his bloodshot eyes displaying both astonishment and guilt. Then:

"Mind your own business!" he roared. "And do your job!"

He strode away in the direction of the bar.

We dined quickly in the restaurant, for the moment leaving military matters to the discretion of the same young captain whom we had met at the station, till he presently approached our table to discuss the deployment of sentries for the night. It appeared that the mysterious visitors had a further journey before them, and were to make an early start. Breakfast had been scheduled for 6 A.M.

"We have a large force," said Nayland Smith, "but that makes it the easier for the enemy to infiltrate a man in disguise. No passwords; every man to be relieved by another whom he knows."

Later, when we came out to make our first inspection, we found men with fixed bayonets posted by the big revolving door at the hotel entrance, others across the street, standing with their backs to the Nile, and men on each landing of the double staircase which flanked the lofty, stained-glass window behind us. On the floor above, two sentries guarded the door of each room occupied by the anonymous "guests."

"Who *are* these people?" I said wonderingly. "What are they doing here?"

Smith shrugged. "In the light of what we already know, I should think that fairly obvious. They are to be taken to Aswan and given a tour of the Midnight Sun project."

We were resigned to a sleepless night. So was M. Duvivier, who gravitated unhappily between his office and the front desk, deprecating the effects which all these warlike activities might have upon his more lucrative patrons. Once our dispositions had been made, Smith and I had only to carry out a round of the sentry posts, inside and out, returning at intervals to drink a cup of coffee in the bar, which remained open all night for our convenience. All of the six rooms for which we had been made responsible were at the back—a circumstance which much dissatisfied my companion.

"Fu Manchu still has two or three of his Burmese dacoits working for him," he said morosely, "who can get over the wall and vanish like ghosts. They may not be able to enter, but they can put a rocket or a fireball through any one of those windows."

"How much danger do you think there is? Will Fu Manchu really attempt anything to-night?"

"I don't know!" he snapped. "But Fernshawe thinks so."

Just because the warning had come from the general—whom we knew to be an alarmist—I believe that we were both inclined to discount it. Yet events were to prove him justified. . . .

Our vigil had begun at ten and continued peacefully till midnight, when we came up to the man on duty beneath the terrace.

"Anything to report?" challenged Smith.

"I—I don't know, sir!" came the curious reply. "I'm thankful you came along, sir! I—I couldn't make up my mind whether to give the alarm or not. . . ."

"Why? What do you mean?"

"Five minutes ago, I thought I saw something—like—like a snake crawling up the wall!" The man pointed. "But I can't see anything now, sir. Can you?"

Smith stared up and shook his head.

"No . . ." he said slowly. "Can you, Petrie?"

I peered upwards, seeing only the windows of the third floor, open, as demanded by the warmth of an Egyptian night, but shuttered.

"No," I said. "Nothing."

Smith hesitated an instant longer, irresolute. Then:

"We can't risk it!" he said. "Even if it means getting a member of the War Cabinet out of his bed to no purpose. Come on!"

Together, we raced up the steps to the terrace and across it to the door. To limit the means of access to the upper floors, Smith had put the lift out of service, which we now regretted. We pelted breathlessly up the grand staircase, brushing rudely past the sentry at each level, till we reached the top. Smith knew precisely which door corresponded with the window indicated.

"Stand aside!" he ordered, and hammered on the panels.

There was no response. Things were now happening with a rapidity beyond my capacity to record. The hotel manager came panting up with the passkey. It turned in the lock, but the door opened only a few inches, the chain having been set in place. Smith put his foot to it, tearing the bolt from the socket, and we burst, side by side, into the darkened room.

No sooner had we entered than my senses registered the taste and odour of bitter almonds. I hurled myself back, thrusting my companion out into the passage, and slammed the door shut.

"It's cyanide!" I gasped. "Not a high concentration—but he's either dead or unconscious. We must go in again and drag him out. Take a deep breath, and hold it. Ready?"

Smith nodded. Watched by the startled sentries, whom I warned to keep back, I re-opened the door cautiously and switched on the light. A man lay in the bed, seemingly asleep. Careful to avoid inhaling the poisoned atmosphere, we crossed swiftly, threw aside the mosquito netting and the coverlets, and lifted him out. He was a thickset individual, and we did not attempt to carry him, but, seizing him by the arms, hauled him unceremoniously across the carpet.

Out in the passage, soldiers who had been stationed at the doors of the other rooms had left their posts and come to join us. With the assistance of two of them, we lugged the pyjama-clad man down to the safety of the lower landing and laid him on his back. While I knelt beside him, Smith looked up at the stairs.

"Shut that door!" he shouted. "Wake up everybody, and clear that floor!"

The man whom we had rescued was breathing stertorously, and I saw that artificial respiration would be unnecessary. Even in unconsciousness, he was of striking appearance, with a strong face deeply lined about the mouth, and deep-set eyes, apparently in his late fifties. The horrible and dramatic symptoms of cyanide poisoning were happily absent.

"Administered in small quantities, it's an easy death," I said. "The fresh air will soon revive him."

Dr. Deane came pounding up the stairs, wearing a dressing gown and carrying a medical bag. Kneeling on the opposite side of the victim, he opened the bag, snatched out a bottle, and the acrid fumes of ammonia brought tears to my eyes. Our patient gasped, drew a long, sobbing breath, and blinked up at us.

"*Um Gottes Willen!*" he whispered. "*Was ist denn los?*"

Nayland Smith's hand descended upon my shoulder.

"Let Deane take care of him!" he said. "They are introducing the gas through the shutters by means of a flexible tube, raised on a telescopic rod from the room below! That is what the sentry saw going up the wall. We must stop it before it spreads all over the building. . . ." He turned quickly to the manager, who stood hovering beside us with a stricken expression of incredulity on his face. "Who occupies that room, M. Duvivier?"

"I—I will find out—"

"Do so! And get the passkey!"

M. Duvivier hastened down to the desk. The top floor had been quickly evacuated. Looking down into the lobby, I saw the distinguished visitors, half dressed, and surrounded by soldiers. Unruffled even by such incidents as these, the staff of the Winter Palace were already moving among them, bringing coffee from the bar.

General Fernshawe, who, as I subsequently learned, had consumed two bottles of port before retiring, slept through it all and did not make an appearance.

"Our man will be gone," remarked Smith, "but he has left his handiwork behind him."

Less than two minutes passed before M. Duvivier was back with us, bringing a key.

"The room is occupied by Mrs. Vanderschuyler," he told us, "a highly respectable lady from Boston, who stays here every year. You surely cannot suspect her?"

"I suspect she has been murdered!" said Smith.

M. Duvivier gulped and led us promptly to a door which he unlocked without the formality of a knock. But Mrs. Vanderschuyler had not been murdered. Crowding in behind him, we saw a middle-aged lady outstretched upon her bed, clad in her nightdress, bound hand and foot, and gagged—her face purple with suffocation and indignation. M. Duvivier ran to her side and commenced, clumsily, to unfasten her.

Neither this room nor the one above possessed a balcony, which had made it possible to run up a tube from one window to the other. The casement was slightly open and a small table, moved from its accustomed place, had been set in front of it. Upon this stood a big, evil-looking contrivance, fully two feet high, like an outsized hour-glass, with a thistle tube at the top. From its sinister aspect, it might well have been an invention of Dr. Fu Manchu, but I recognized it instantly as a standard piece of laboratory equipment.

"It's a Kipp's apparatus!" I said. "A gas generator!"

Smith advanced upon it, with the obvious intention of throwing it from the window, but I caught his arm, holding him back.

"No! Don't smash it, or the chemicals will combine and poison half the town!"

"How do we stop it, then?"

"Like this!" I said, smiling, and, reaching past him, turned off the tap.

Behind us, Mrs. Vanderschuyler gave vent to a shriek like a train whistle, as M. Duvivier succeeded in detaching the gag. She was not hysterical, but incoherent with rage at having been assaulted, tied up, and, worst of all, silenced with an item of her own lingerie stuffed into her mouth. It was some minutes before we could calm her down sufficiently to obtain her story, but it proved to be a simple one and not much different from what we expected.

Soon after retiring, she had been aroused by an urgent knocking and a voice crying, "Telegram!" and hurried to the door—only to find herself confronted by a man with a handkerchief over the lower part of his face and a pistol in his hand. Lying helpless on her bed, she had watched him set up the glassware, and, supposing it to be intended for her destruction, promptly fainted. When she regained her senses, the man had gone, leaving his infernal machine bubbling on the table.

Despite the makeshift disguise of the handkerchief, Mrs. Vanderschuyler was able to identify her assailant as an Armenian visitor who had been occupying a room on the same floor.

"He won't be in it now!" said Smith shortly. "And I'll wager a pound to a penny we don't catch him!" He glanced darkly at the Kipp's apparatus. "How the devil did he get that thing into the hotel without being noticed?"

"Merde alors!" cried M. Duvivier, outraged to the point of Gallicism. *"Quelle audace!* I saw him bring it in. He told me that it was a *narghileh* which he had bought in the bazaar!"

Smith's forecast was, I may say, fulfilled. Regardless of all our precautions, the elusive Armenian slipped through our network of sentries, and, to the best of my knowledge, was never heard of again.

We left M. Duvivier to pacify his angry American guest as best he might, and walked out into the corridor to re-organize our defences. A second attempt by Fu Manchu in the same night seemed unlikely, but we could not be too careful.

"Smith!" I said, as we descended to the lobby. "I am completely bewildered! What is going on here? That man whom we pulled out of bed . . . he spoke in *German*! Who is he?"

Smith halted, with his right foot on one step and his left on the next, looking at me strangely.

"Don't you know?" he asked quietly.

"No!" I said. "Should I?"

"Perhaps not. But you might have seen his photograph. . . ." Smith hesitated, with a faraway look in his grey eyes which I found impossible to read. "He is General Erich von Falkenhayn, commander-in-chief of the German and Turkish forces at Aleppo!"

34

THE MIDNIGHT SUN

Breakfast was served in the restaurant, which Fernshawe had taken over for the occasion, leaving hotel guests who wished to have it at the same early hour to eat in their rooms or in the bar.

Nayland Smith and I sat in isolation at one end, separated from the others by a sea of empty tables. Three, I observed, were occupied by Fernshawe and his officers, two more by the visitors.

"Are they *all* Germans?" I asked.

"Either Germans or Swiss," said Smith shortly, "but I don't know any of them, excepting von Falkenhayn."

What lay behind this extraordinary conclave was past all speculation, and my attempt to ask his opinion elicited a shrug.

"Probably we shall never find out," he said grimly, "and it may be as well. There's devil's work here, Petrie. . . ."

Thereafter, we ate in silence. At a quarter to seven, I saw an orderly come in and speak to Fernshawe, who nodded and stood up. Following his lead, the rest stood up also and began to drift towards the door. Then, suddenly leaving his comrades, General von Falkenhayn came striding down the length of the room, and Smith and I rose hastily.

"I have not yet had a chance, *Herr Oberst*," he said, "to thank you for saving the life of an enemy."

"We have a common enemy in Dr. Fu Manchu," replied Smith.

"I know this." The general smiled gravely. "Once, I was an instructor to the Chinese Army. Once, I fought with you against the Boxers. We have not always been enemies, you and I."

Fernshawe came hurrying towards us, red-faced and clearly disapproving of our conversation.

"If you please," he said curtly, "we are ready to start."

Von Falkenhayn glanced at us and at him, still smiling.

"Let them come with us!" he suggested. "Why not? After to-

242

night, there will be no secret to be kept, *nicht wahr?*" Fernshawe hesitated, and the German added subtly: "Besides, these gentlemen already know too much to be left behind—unless you intend to put them in prison!"

Fernshawe grunted, nibbled at his moustache, and glared at us.

"Come with us, then!" he growled. "The cars are outside. Go and get in one!"

Such was our curiosity that neither Smith nor I paused to consider the ungraciousness of the invitation or to take offence at it. Following in the wake of the official party, we passed quickly through the lobby, out through the revolving door, and down the steps.

The wide forecourt of the Winter Palace had been cleared of all but army vehicles—not those which had brought us from the station, but of a kind which I had never seen before. They were Rolls sand-cars, built for desert warfare, with powerful engines housed under a bonnet almost double the average length and vented on both sides.

Von Falkenhayn and his entourage climbed up into one, two more being taken by the British officers. Smith and I were directed to make places for ourselves in a fourth, which carried spare tyres and assorted supplies. A fifth and a sixth formed a rearguard and a vanguard, and, with a thunder of engines sufficient to wake all who were still asleep, our convoy moved out upon the road.

Now, an hour after sunrise, ancient Thebes regained the ethereal beauty of the New Kingdom. Lightly veiled in mist, the Nile was milky and opalescent, the hard lines of the rugged cliffs surrounding the Valley of the Kings softened and painted in pastel shades of violet, as though by stage lighting. This was the magic hour when the Colossi of Memnon had been said to greet the rising sun with a sound like the strings of a harp. But they did not speak to us.

Neither, for that matter, did our driver—who, mute and ill at ease, had evidently been warned to say nothing.

"It seems clear," said Smith, turning to me, "that we are headed for some sort of conference, to which von Falkenhayn has been invited, under a guarantee of safe-conduct. In addition to being Germany's best general, he is keenly interested in politics, and is supposed to be the only person to whom the Kaiser will listen."

"Indeed, there seems to be no other explanation," I agreed. "But why did Fu Manchu try to kill him?"

"Because, for reasons of his own, he does not wish this conference to succeed." Smith laughed without humour. "If the leader of the German delegation had been murdered in Luxor, we would have been blamed for it, no matter what excuses we made."

Ninety minutes after leaving the Winter Palace, we reached Esneh, turned right, and crossed the barrage to the west bank—which rather surprised me, since Aswan was situated on the east bank. An hour later, we came to Edfu.

We passed swiftly through the town, obtaining only a glimpse of the unique Temple of Horus, and continued on. Two or three miles beyond, the convoy slowed to a halt beside a wire fence enclosing a small group of sheds and army huts.

A barrier was lifted, allowing us to enter what was evidently a fuel dump, where we remained while mechanics bustled about us. The petrol tanks were recharged to capacity, the radiators cooled and refilled. Aswan, now little more than sixty miles away, was not our destination. Since the time of leaving Cairo, we had been wrong—dreadfully wrong—about everything. . . .

Two more Rolls-Royce tenders joined us, each equipped with a heavy machine-gun mounted on a tripod. Then, to hoarsely shouted commands and the shrill voices of whistles, we moved off again towards the frowning mountains of the Western Sahara.

By a long, winding valley and a breathtaking succession of hairpin bends, we gained the summit. On the other side, there was no descent—for the Libyan Desert is a high plateau, extending for two thousand miles to the shores of the Atlantic. Now, on the hard, level ground, the sand-cars were able to show their mettle, forging across at forty miles an hour, sometimes fifty. Here the desert consisted of not the soft, undulating sand dunes which surround the Pyramids of Gizeh and abound in the Grande Mer du Sable, but a grey wilderness of stone; no trace of green appeared above the surface, neither leaf nor cactus.

Where were we going? Where *could* we go? The Oasis of el-Kharga lay far to the north, and we were heading south-west.

At one o'clock, we halted again and consumed packed lunches, made up of army rations. Our attempts to draw our taciturn driver into conversation failed dismally. He told us only that his name was Delaney, and that he was a corporal—which, from the stripes on his sleeve, we already knew. Obviously, the man had been threatened with worse than death if he talked to us, and we desisted.

A whistle shrilled, and again we moved on. Now, in the full heat of the afternoon, the glare of the sun on the rocky surface gave it the appearance of snow—an arctic waste, reflecting the flames of an inferno. Onwards we went and on—mile after mile, hour upon hour, till the sun was low and the light fading. The marvel of sunset is the desert's only time of beauty. As the western sky turned to gold, colours seemed to seep up through the earth—orange and amber, violet and mauve—and the whole desolate expanse looked like an artist's palette.

In the last light of day, we came to a hedge formed of helicoidal coils of barbed wire—the arc of a circle, curving away distantly into invisibility. The sand-cars halted, engines idling, while men descended from the first to cut a gap for us to pass through and stayed behind to close it after us. Soon, sunset gave place to nightfall, and we drove on through a darkness now complete, save for the cold rays of the headlamps, sweeping like scythes, and the glowing red eyes of tail-lights. Then there were other lights ahead, which, as we approached, were revealed as powerful electric lamps mounted on tall standards, like those in a railway marshalling yard.

"I think this is it!" said Smith quietly.

But where, or what, was "it"? In the background, the flat surface of the arid plain was interrupted by conical, steep-sided mounds which looked oddly artificial, like slag heaps. In the foreground, blocking further progress, rose the vertical wall of a low cliff with a long, bow-shaped summit tapering off into the shadows.

Lights glowing from within outlined three cavernous openings, in front of which the cars came finally to rest, parked in a neat, orderly line. The British officers and their German guests got out, entered the nearest tunnel, and we followed. My immediate impression was of a mine working—a passage cut through the rock and illuminated by wire-caged lamps, with cables strung along the walls. The air was cool, and vibrant with a soft hum of hidden machinery.

We came into a room, or cave, curiously resembling the lobby of a hotel, where a uniformed man sat at a table, with papers and a telephone before him. General Fernshawe, whom we had not seen all day, came briskly up to us, accompanied by a man in army fatigues.

"Private Atkins will act as your batman while you are here," he said, and turned to the soldier. "Take them to East Wing Six-B."

A passageway similar to the first, save that it was longer, brought us to the room which we were, it seemed, to occupy. Atkins opened the door and stood aside for us to enter.

"I'll be back in a minute, sir!" he said, and left us.

Our quarters were fitted up like a ship's cabin, with berths recessed into opposite walls, the floor uncarpeted, and the furniture limited to two wooden-framed armchairs and a desk. Sitting on one of the beds, while Smith did likewise, I noticed a shelf of books behind me and glanced at them inquisitively. Most were scientific works of a nature so abstruse that even the titles meant nothing to me, but among them was a Gideon Bible, and, when I took it down, it fell open to the Book of Revelation.

"Good God!" I cried. "This is where Brooker slept!"

"And Crawford slept here!" said Smith sobrely. "It was in this hole that they spent the last two years of their lives. Small wonder that they both went mad!"

Atkins reappeared, carrying a stack of clean sheets and towels, put them down, and took two dressing gowns from a wall closet.

"If you would care to put these on," he said, "and let me have your things, I will get them brushed and pressed for you. A late dinner will be served at ten o'clock in the main dining hall."

I stooped to unlace my boots, and, as the sole of my foot touched the floorboards, felt a faint, tingling resonance, hinting at the tireless operation of some heavy mechanism below.

Our batman departed and the next hour passed almost in silence, while Smith and I rested upon our beds, tacitly refraining from a discussion of possibilities beyond our imagination. Since leaving the road at Edfu, we had covered at least three hundred miles. Where were we? What was this place? Smith, I suspected, had an inkling of the truth, but chose to say nothing.

At a little before ten, Atkins returned, bringing Smith's uniform and my sadly worn travelling clothes, neatly renovated, with our boots polished to perfection. We dressed, and he led us to the dining hall—a huge, echoing room which reminded me of a warehouse, equal in size to the restaurant at the Winter Palace, but functional rather than artistic, with massive iron buttresses and a high ceiling supported on cantilevers.

Obviously, it had been planned to feed a considerable working force, furnished with rows of long wooden tables designed to seat eight, those at one end now tastefully draped with Irish linen and equipped with chairs, while the rest were left uncovered and flanked by wooden benches. The visitors and the British officers were already seated, their number augmented by others, whom I took to be residents.

Placed at the opposite end, as at breakfast time, we could hear nothing of their conversation.

It was a strange meal. Orderlies in mess kit served us with English river trout, imported live and carried across the desert with elaborate precautions to avoid boiling them en route—intended, I supposed, not merely to provide our enemies with generous hospitality but to display our illimitable resources. The main course consisted of a boar's head and a haunch of venison—a subtle reminder of happier days and royal hunting parties in Bavaria.

Our banquet continued for over an hour, but the atmosphere was not convivial. The men at the far tables talked in a low grumble of subdued voices, without laughter. At length, Fernshawe rose and tapped upon a glass with a spoon, like a master of ceremonies calling for attention. He said something which I could not catch, in response to which chairs were pushed back and everyone stood up.

I yawned sleepily. We had been up all night, travelled nearly four hundred miles, and eaten enough to make a starving man drowsy. Now, I imagined, we should all go to bed, and, on the morrow, the conference would be held—from which Smith and I would be excluded, our questions left unanswered. But we had yet to rise from our table when the events of the morning were repeated.

As Fernshawe and his guests made for the exit, I saw General von Falkenhayn coming towards us with a bottle of cognac and a glass in his hand—an impressive figure, but denied the distinction which was his due by his plain, civilian clothes. I could not help wishing that he might have worn his German uniform and spiked helmet.

"I come to say *auf Wiedersehen*," he said, and, leaning across the table, filled our glasses. "But to what shall we drink? I cannot drink to your victory, nor you to mine."

"Let us, then, drink to the defeat of Dr. Fu Manchu!" said Smith, smiling.

"*Jawohl, Herr Oberst.* That we may do."

We drank. The general proffered his hand, and I took it, thinking as I did so that I was a poor sort of patriot—for my instincts prompted me to like von Falkenhayn and to dislike Fernshawe.

"One day, we may meet again and talk of these things," he added. "Now let us go out and join the others. It is time. . . ."

Time for what? I wondered.

Passing through the "lobby" and the tunnel, we came out into the floodlit area in front, to find it somewhat changed. The sand-cars which had brought us there had been moved elsewhere, and in their place stood a crescent-shaped line of folding chairs, twenty or thirty in number, with canvas seats and backs. Most were already occupied. Von Falkenhayn left us, to rejoin his compatriots, seated at one horn of the crescent. Several places at the opposite end remained vacant, and Smith and I sat down, uninvited. General Fernshawe, who had ignored us throughout dinner, no longer seemed to care what we did—whether we were there or not.

Four chairs had been set facing us, and upon them sat four men formally and incongruously dressed in the fashions of Whitehall. They had not come with us, but evidently proceeded by some separate route. After a short interval, during which all talking ceased and an uneasy silence descended, one of them stood up and came forward into the light—a short, bulldog-faced man, at the sight of whom I gasped foolishly. I knew him instantly—but, in view of what was done that night, even now I will not write his name.

All was deathly still—the soft night air tangibly charged with an expectancy of which he made the most, while he stared around truculently. Then, at last, he spoke.

"I address myself to all of you," he said, "to the gentlemen from Switzerland, who are here to act as observers and mediators, and, in particular, to the representatives of Imperial Germany. Our work here is no secret to you—just as we know what Otto Hahn and Lise Meitner have been doing at the Kaiser Wilhelm Institute. But where you have failed, we have succeeded. We have at our command the means to destroy Berlin in a single night."

He paused, but no ripple of amazement passed through the assembly—for, of all those present, only we two had been ignorant of what was to come.

"Is it possible?" I whispered.

"I fear so," answered Smith softly. "Listen!"

"We estimate the consequences as at least a million casualties," continued the speaker. "But the hostilities between us must somehow be brought to a conclusion, or, for the next generation, our respective nations will be peopled only by women, children, and old men. If we must kill one million to save the lives of the untold millions who will hereafter perish on the battlefields, we will do it."

Despite the dramatic nature of his words, he intoned them flatly, almost chanting, like a preacher reading a sermon.

"Right and wrong are concepts which our opponents have repudiated, compelling us, for our survival, to retaliate in kind. It was they who first resorted to submarine warfare, aerial assaults upon civilians, poison gas, and the flame-thrower. Against such weapons, civilised measures are of no avail, and good must yield to evil. Fire may be fought only with fire, and evil with evil."

Again he paused, expecting and receiving no answer.

"But we are not barbarians, and to the destruction of Berlin there is an alternative. Therefore, before taking this extreme step, we have brought you here to-night to witness a demonstration—the first of its kind, and, as I earnestly pray, may it also be the last. An explosive charge rests on a steel tower, one hundred and twenty feet above the ground, and, when it is detonated, we believe that it will form a shallow crater no less than six miles in diameter. To-morrow, you will be taken to inspect the effects upon various types of building material and livestock which we have placed within the area. We will then have a short, preliminary meeting, after which we shall demand the immediate surrender of all German forces and their allies. You will be given ten days."

Now there was movement and a low muttering among the audience. Arms folded, the speaker waited patiently for it to subside.

"All this has been known to you for some time. Our invitation was issued to you three months ago, and you accepted it. But, in the meantime, you rewarded us with treachery and sent out a Zeppelin—which, however, we destroyed. . . ."

I glanced at Smith, and, even in those solemn circumstances, could not repress a smile at this smooth opportunism—for the Zeppelin had been destroyed by Dr. Fu Manchu! Distantly, I heard the voice of General von Falkenhayn interrupting.

"Against a threat so monstrous, we had the right to protect ourselves!"

But his interruption was brushed contemptuously aside.

"We have no Zeppelins, but our Handley Page aircraft can reach Berlin. If, even then, you persist in your resistance, they will reduce to ashes every principal city in Germany. You can do nothing, once they have crossed your shores—for, if you shoot them down, the same destruction will take place wherever they may fall. . . ."

The speech had been timed well, for, at that moment, a clear, bell-like note emanated from a number of wireless loudspeakers, fixed to the same poles as the floodlights.

"It is now precisely eleven fifty-eight," said the man in the Whitehall suit, with as little excitement in his voice as if he had been speaking in the House of Commons. "We are twenty miles from the firing base, and we *think* we are safe. Should we be mistaken about that, no further discussion between us will be practicable." He paused for a polite laugh, but no one obliged, and he concluded:

"In approximately ninety seconds, the Midnight Sun will rise in the west. When it does so, turn your faces aside. Do not look at it directly, or it may harm your eyesight."

Hard upon his words, all the lights were extinguished, that we might better appreciate the spectacle to follow, and, simultaneously, the familiar tones of the Westminster chimes sounded from the loudspeakers, heralding the hour. Breathless with anticipation, we listened, and waited for the false dawn—the dawn of a new era of destruction on a scale unparallelled in the annals of the human race. . . .

35

THE SHADOW OF ARMAGEDDON

As the chimes died away, I wondered whether the explosion would coincide with the first stroke of the hour or the last. Then the deep, melodious voice of Big Ben pealed out across the desert and— nothing happened. One, two, three, four . . . I counted out the strokes, reminding myself that the fuse could not be so exactly set as to correspond with any particular second. But the twelfth stroke came, faded into silence, and still nothing happened.

What followed can only be described as the greatest fiasco of the Great War. No Midnight Sun appeared above the horizon. In the interval while we waited, only von Falkenhayn dared to speak.

"Your clock seems to have stopped, *mein Herr*!"

The man who had addressed us turned away without answering. Still we waited expectantly, but, gradually, the tension gave way to a low murmuring and nervous laughter, as it became clear that something was seriously amiss. After some fifteen minutes, the men from Whitehall stood up and, offering no comment, retreated into the underground premises, followed in twos and threes by the others. I saw von Falkenhayn rise from his chair and come up to Fernshawe.

"You have failed," I heard him say. "Now I must go to Jerusalem, and try conclusions with your General Allenby."*

He walked away into the lighted mouth of the tunnel, and I saw no more of him.

---

*War historians have shown some surprise that, though von Falkenhayn had been in Aleppo since September, he did not go to Jerusalem till November 1st. Now we know why! [Ed.]

The floodlights were switched on once more, so that we could see each other's faces. Fernshawe's was waxen, and I feared that he was liable to a seizure. He turned toward us, as if desperately seeking human companionship.

"It doesn't work!" he groaned. "The damned thing doesn't work!"

"Calm yourself!" said Smith quietly. "It may be no worse than a simple mechanical failure. But," he added, "have you considered the possibility of sabotage? Fu Manchu is out there somewhere with his men, and he is determined that this demonstration shall not take place. How long has the site been left unguarded?"

"All personnel were withdrawn to the outer perimeter at eleven," muttered Fernshawe. "But we have sentry posts around the entire zone. . . ."

"Sentries? Where, and how many? Could they possibly be sufficient?" My friend smiled mirthlessly. "According to what we have just been told, the safe distance from the firing base has been decided at twenty miles. My mathematics are not very good, but I seem to remember that the circumference of a circle is some six times the radius—a hundred and twenty miles!"

"We have five hundred men, posted in pairs, with orders to fire signal flares in the event of an emergency." General Fernshawe took a hold upon his nerves, squared his drooping shoulders, and brushed up his moustache with his index finger. "But you are right, Colonel. I will send out patrols to investigate and report."

He hurried away to give the instructions, and, soon after, I saw two of the sand-cars start out into the night, the beams of their headlamps diverging and ultimately vanishing to east and west. Other explanations of the catastrophe were possible, but, in our hearts, both Smith and I felt convinced that Fu Manchu was responsible—a conclusion supported by his attempt to murder von Falkenhayn.

"But why?" I asked. "Why is he doing this?"

Smith shrugged. "No doubt because he is still not satisfied with the miserable state of affairs in Europe and does not want to see either side gain a decisive advantage till we have fought ourselves to the point of collapse."

"It was a risky business," I said. "After the fuse had been set, he had only an hour, and no transport more rapid than camels. It would take the nerve of the Devil—"

"He *has* the nerve of the Devil!" rejoined Smith. "And, if I could only believe that his interference would finish this lunatic venture, once and for all, I might almost wish him luck! But there's no such chance, Petrie. If we are thwarted now, we shall try again, and then, if we succeed, we must shoulder the responsibility of ruling the world—otherwise, when more than one holds the secret of the Midnight Sun, when cities may be destroyed in a night and populations decimated, we shall live in the shadow of Armageddon, the war to end mankind. No wonder that Brooker took his texts from Revelation! No wonder that he ran away from it all!"

"Ran away?" I said vaguely. "You mean that he wasn't acting for our enemies?"

"Of course he wasn't! He was acting for nobody! He was close to a nervous breakdown, but less mad than we thought. At the outset, his grief and rage at the death of his wife and daughter inspired him to place his special knowledge at the disposal of the Government and seek revenge. At that time, he would willingly have destroyed not only Berlin but every town and village in Germany. But later, as his dreams came closer to achievement, he realised the enormity of what he was doing, and decided to have no further hand in it. However, under wartime conditions, he could no more resign his position than a soldier in the field. So he simply deserted!"

"But why, then, if he did not intend to sell them, did he take the papers with him?"

Nayland Smith laughed harshly. "Because Professor Brooker was, first and last, a scientist. Can you imagine any scientist who would abandon his records? And, since he had done most of the work, he probably regarded them as his rightful property."

When Smith gave vent to his feelings, his passion was expended in the initial outburst. Now, lighting his pipe carefully, he leaned back with his hands clasped behind his neck, gazing up at the stars. Almost all the others had given it up for the night, and the long line of canvas chairs was virtually unoccupied. Halfway along, I saw General Fernshawe sitting alone with his face hidden in his hands, like a disappointed author in an empty theatre after the final curtain of an unsuccessful play.

I glanced at my watch, calculating that at the best speed they could make, it would be three hours before the patrols returned— assuming that they went right around till they met at the midpoint of what Fernshawe called "the outer perimeter." The more direct alternative of going out to the tower to inspect an unexploded bomb—and such a bomb!—was not one which any of us cared to undertake.

In the event, however, little more than an hour had passed when I saw the lights of a returning vehicle bobbing erratically across the desert. Smith, still leaning back in his chair with his pipe pointing skywards, noticed nothing; I believe he had the ability to smoke in his sleep. I reached out and caught at his arm.

"They're coming back!"

The Rolls-Royce tender drew up with screeching tyres and a shower of stones, not far from where we were sitting, and the driver jumped out. Smith was the first officer in uniform whom he saw, and he ran up to us, so agitated that he forgot even to salute.

"Post Twenty-six!" he stammered. "They're lyin' out there dead on the sand—an' their 'eads is off! The wire's bin cut, an' the ground's all tore up like a 'erd of cattle bin drove through it!"

"Report to General Fernshawe!" ordered Smith, pointing. He stood up. "Fu Manchu and his Senussi . . . just as I thought. They crept up on the sentries, decapitated them before they had even the chance to cry out, and went in, in force. . . ."

We walked down the line of empty chairs to rejoin Fernshawe, who, having received the driver's report, looked more ghastly even than before. Whatever his qualifications as a general, now that his plans had gone awry, he seemed only too anxious to let my friend take charge.

"There is no point in going to the sentry post," said Smith crisply. "The question now is how much damage they have done at the firing base."

Fernshawe gulped something inaudible, and hurried away as meekly as an errand boy. Sounds of activity followed, and I heard two of the sand-cars started up, the heavy engines thundering into the stillness. Corporal Delaney, who had chauffeured us from Luxor, appeared beside us, red-eyed with sleep and hastily dressed, with one button of his shirt looped through the wrong buttonhole. He had, apparently, been assigned to us permanently.

"Car's ready, sir!" he announced, and led us swiftly to our vehicle. As we piled in behind him, "Oh, my Gawd, sir!" he faltered. "Are we going out to—to *that* thing?"

"No cause for alarm!" replied Smith. "It's out of action."

His tone was reassuring, but failed to reassure me. What had Fu Manchu done? A whistle sounded, and three cars moved off into the forbidden zone of danger, ours being the last, the first occupied by

General Fernshawe and several of his officers, the second crammed with armed men.

For the next twenty minutes, we travelled in silence, seeing nothing but the boundless expanse of the desert under our headlamps and the jewelled vault of the heavens above. Corporal Delaney shouted back to us.

"We're halfway there, sir! Why can't we see it, sir? The rigging crew was supposed to leave the lights on. . . ."

There were now no lights to be seen, but we did not learn the reason till we had come the whole distance and the leading cars halted. Then, as we drew up with them, we saw and understood.

The tower had ceased to exist. All that remained was a shapeless heap of steel girders. As we learned later, the main supports had been cut through at the base, as though by an oxy-acetylene flame torch, bringing down the whole skeletal structure. It seemed incredible that such a demolition could have been achieved in so short a time, but I remembered then the words of Dr. Fu Manchu, spoken to us weeks earlier in the tomb of Zoser: *"I have flame which will burn invisibly through steel . . ."*

Nayland Smith and I stayed where we were, watching the soldiers swarming over the wreckage like ants, poking about in it, and searching with electric handlamps. This continued for some while, till, at last, we saw General Fernshawe approaching us, ashen-faced. In the past few hours, he looked to have aged ten years.

"It's—it's gone!" he said thickly. "He's taken it! He's disconnected the detonators and taken the explosive charge!"

It was a moment before the full significance registered on me. Then:

"Good God!" I burst out. "Then, if what we heard is true, Fu Manchu now has the power to destroy London!"

Smith tapped Delaney on the shoulder.

"Corporal," he said, "go and join the others. We have private matters to discuss." He turned back to Fernshawe. "Sit in here with us, General, and let us consider this quietly."

Delaney vacated his position at the wheel and Fernshawe climbed up beside us.

"Now," went on Smith, "Fu Manchu has stolen Army property, but, since he is working independently of any country with which we are at war, what he does with it is, unfortunately, my concern rather than yours. You have often told me to think as a soldier, so I will do so. From your standpoint, is the situation really so serious? You have suffered some embarrassment, but, with the resources you have here, can you not persuade your German guests to stay until you can rig up the means to stage a further demonstration?"

"No!" gasped Fernshawe. "That's just the trouble! We can't!"

"Why not?"

"You don't know. . . . Of course you don't! I couldn't tell you—couldn't tell anybody. . . ." The general choked and dabbed at his lips with a handkerchief. "Brooker and his confounded scientists . . . after two years' work . . . after all the money and the effort we'd put into it . . . all they'd done was to make enough of the stuff for a single explosion! That damned Chinaman's got the lot!"

"What?" I exclaimed. "You mean it was all just a hoax?"

Fernshawe hesitated.

"Not quite that," he said slowly. "We could do it—but only once. At the present stage of development, the thing's useless as a weapon. It takes too long to produce, and costs as much as a battleship. What should we do, then? If we'd used it to destroy Berlin, the Germans might have surrendered. But what if they hadn't?"

"So you could use it only as a threat," said Smith curtly. "Hence this devious farce of political trickery disguised as a concern for humanity!" He shrugged. "Well, be that as it may, this fearful abomination has now fallen into the hands of a criminal who may use it to commit a crime unprecedented in history, and it is *my* job to stop him. How I am to do that is far from clear, but it certainly won't be here, in the middle of the Libyan Desert! Therefore, I shall be grateful if you will furnish us with transport and get us back to Luxor as swiftly as possible. . . ."

36

DUEL IN THE SAND

Our journey back from the Midnight Sun project need not be described, since it was but a repetition of the outward journey, in reverse, though even more wearisome. Neither Smith nor I had slept for forty-eight hours. Constantly, as the day wore on, my eyes closed and my head dropped forward with a jerk, waking me as often as I fell asleep. Why we were returning to Luxor—what my companion had in mind—I did not know, but I was frankly too tired to ask or to care.

Long before we reached the Winter Palace, the sun had set once more; arrived there, we collapsed thankfully into our beds and slept the clock round. But, since we had retired early, it was early when we breakfasted and went out to take our coffee on the garden terrace. Behind us, the lobby was bustling with sightseers, setting out on their itinerary of tombs and temples.

Nayland Smith filled and lighted his first pipe of the day and looked at his wristwatch.

"We have still a few hours at our disposal," he said cryptically. "A camel can average ten miles an hour and keep it up for eighteen hours at a stretch. But he cannot possibly be here before this afternoon. . . ."

"Fu Manchu?" I asked, and he nodded. "You think that he is coming here? But why?"

"To hide what he has stolen, in the same place where he has left the treasures of the Si Fan and interred his daughter." Smith laughed shortly. "Oh, there's no immediate danger that he will destroy London! Having failed to kidnap the inventor, or to obtain his papers, he has done all that was left to him—to seize the only example of his work. Now he will study it till he is able to duplicate it and threaten the world. But, to do that, he needs all the facilities of his laboratory in Kiangsu—if it still exists. Meanwhile, he will simply put it into storage."

"Perhaps. But what leads you to suppose that he will store it in this area?"

"You do!" Amused by my startled expression, he laughed again. "You last saw Fah Lo Suee asleep in a sarcophagus. Doesn't that suggest a tomb? As to where it may be, the high ground above Hatshepsut's temple is honeycombed with scores of them, open and empty, and scores more which have yet to be discovered. . . ."

Smith paused to strike a match, used it briefly, and broke it deliberately between his fingers.

"The question is, then," he resumed, "where were you? Only a few hours later, you were brought down to Der el-Bahâri, so it cannot have been very far away. You saw a cone-shaped peak, which can only have been el-Qurn—"

"A steep-sided ravine, and two abandoned huts," I added, and shook my head doubtfully. "I wonder if that's sufficient? The land up there is a maze of dry watercourses, like a picture of the human brain, and more than one may contain the disused huts put up by some earlier excavation team."

"True, but not a great many, and somebody must keep records. Our first move should be to consult them."

I considered for a moment. Then:

"No!" I said. "There may be a quicker way. I may have the very man for you—if he is still alive, and still living in Luxor. His name is Hassan es-Sugra."

For the first time in years, I found myself thinking of the solemn-faced young man who, long ago, had shown me how to distinguish Ptolemaic artifacts from Ramesside, and how to unroll a four-thousand-year-old papyrus without breaking it. Hassan es-Sugra had served as the overseer of almost every major expedition west of the river. There was no part of that ancient graveyard which he did not know as well as I now knew the streets of South London.

"Good!" said Smith, standing up briskly. "Then let us go and see if we can find him."

Our search proved not to be difficult. The bleak years of war had left Hassan es-Sugra almost without employment, and we discovered him at home in a humble, but well-kept, abode near the mosque of Mohasseb, waiting patiently till the world came to its senses—the same grave, soft-spoken man whom I had known since childhood.

"I know the valley of which you speak, *effendîm*," he said quietly, "and it may easily be reached from Kurna in an hour or less. But it has an ill reputation, and men do not like to work there."

"Why?" snapped Smith.

Hassan es-Sugra smiled gently. "Eight years ago, *effendîm*, a Frenchman named Lafleur went there, searching for a certain tomb. It was for him that the two huts were constructed. He cut a shaft, but found nothing. Then, one night, when he was alone in the camp, after all the workmen had gone back to their village, he disappeared. Some say that the tomb which he sought was protected by a curse— others that it had become the home of a powerful *ifrît*. His government made a great fuss, but no trace of him was ever found."

I exchanged glances with Smith. Could this be the tomb which the Si Fan had chosen for their storehouse? Was it Fu Manchu who had brought about the Egyptologist's disappearance?

"We must do this alone," said Smith, "for, if we take a larger party, they'll be sure to bungle it. . . ."

With the help of my old acquaintance, our arrangements were soon made. We crossed at midday to Kurna, to find him waiting for us there with a string of donkeys—two for ourselves, and two loaded with supplies. Hassan es-Sugra trudged silently beside us as we ascended the winding track above Der el-Bahâri. As always, the soul of discretion, he asked no questions, but, for the benefit of the donkey boys and any others who might be curious, we gave it out that we were the advance party of an archaeological survey.

By two o'clock, we had entered the *wâdi* in the neck of which the two huts stood—a steep-sided valley, narrowing into the distance. Behind the smaller hut, a lesser and steeper ravine came in at an angle, leading up to the plateau above.

"Is this it?" demanded Smith.

I stared up at the weird summit of el-Qurn, outlined against the cobalt sky.

"I think so," I replied cautiously.

We installed ourselves in the larger hut, where we intended to stay at least for the night—if necessary, for a week. With us, we had brought two camp beds, blankets, a plentiful store of tinned food-stuffs, and a dozen bottles of mineral water. Having supervised the unloading, Hassan es-Sugra saluted us politely and departed with the donkeys, promising to return in two days' time with a fresh stock of provisions, in case we decided to remain there longer.

Prior to our arrival, our temporary premises had contained only a stout wooden table and a quantity of litter strewn about the floor—empty tins and flasks, and scraps of old clothing, half buried by the sand which had blown in through the open window. All of it appeared to have lain there for a decade, and a *Caporal* cigarette packet with faded lettering hinted that Lafleur had been the last inhabitant. In the adjacent hut—a mere shed—we found some digging tools which seemed to belong to the same period.

While we swept up the sand and made our quarters fit for occupation, Smith searched assiduously, picking up each item and inspecting it closely before throwing it away.

"I may have found something," he remarked presently, and showed me a tiny pearl button which, unlike the rest of the assorted débris, looked clean and new. "I think it was here that Fah Lo Suee was prepared for her long sleep."

It was at least a clue to suggest that we had chosen the right spot. Our task now was to lie in ambush and await the coming of Dr. Fu Manchu. The day passed, and he did not come, but we were not disappointed. Though it had been barely possible, we thought it unlikely that he would travel for two nights and a day without rest.

The things which we had carried up from Kurna included a lantern, but we could not use it. If our enemies came by night, the hut must appear deserted. We retired with the sun and rose with the dawn, again dividing the hours of darkness into watches, during which one of us sat constantly by the small, square hole in the wall which served as a window. We knew the direction from which they would come. There was only one way into the *wâdi*—unless they came over the plateau and down through the gully, which was too steep and stony for camels. But the night passed as the day, and still they did not come.

In the morning, we ventured outside, questing around for anything which looked like the entrance to a tomb. But if the sepulchre in which Fah Lo Suee slept lay close at hand, it had been well concealed. We returned to the hut and lunched out of tins.

Thus far, all had gone without a hitch, but, with the sun at its zenith, a breeze sprang up and commenced to blow in gusts, whirling up the sand and darkening the sky. Soon we could hear it whistling and shrieking across the plain above, as one often hears it from Mena House, when it howls around the Pyramids of Gizeh. This was not *khamsîn,* of which the season was long past, but the *simoom*—a hot, dry wind from the south-east, violent and unpredictable. In the valley we were protected, but, by two o'clock, visibility was down to a hundred yards; the end of the *wâdi* had vanished under a yellow pall as thick and impenetrable as the clammy vapours of a London fog.

"Confound it!" burst out Smith. "Is God on our side, or on his? They may be on top of us before we know it."

For half an hour more, we sat by the window and watched—and then, out of the storm, they came. By the track leading from Kurna, mounted figures loomed up through the sandy mist, unreal and indistinct, so that I thought of Brooker's half-insane quotations from the Book of Revelation, and the Four Horsemen of the Apocalypse. But these were mounted upon camels, and they numbered more than four. As they materialised, one by one, I counted ten or a dozen.

"This is more than I bargained for!" growled Smith. "I thought he would bring only two or three."

I muttered an assent, peering discreetly from a corner of the window. But, for the present, no assault on our position seemed likely. Advancing no closer, and clearly with no suspicion that they were observed, the shadowy riders brought their camels to their knees and dismounted.

A curious ceremony appeared to be taking place. Still half obscured in the shifting curtain of sand, they formed themselves into a semicircle, knelt, and bowed their heads to the ground, as if the hour of prayer had arrived. One alone stood upright, facing them like the statue of a pharaoh hewn out of red syenite—and, beyond all doubt, Dr. Fu Manchu. . . . For some while he seemed to address them, then raised his arms in a gesture of benediction.

"It looks almost as though he were taking leave of them!" I whispered, keeping my voice low, but for no good reason.

"He is!" answered Smith tersely. "Now that they have served his purpose, he has done with them. He will not allow them to see where the treasures of the Si Fan lie buried, since he knows that, as soon as he is gone, they will come back and dig them up!"

Such, indeed, was seemingly the explanation of these strange proceedings. Watching, I saw the tribesmen rise and re-mount, while Fu Manchu continued to stand immobile and statuesque till all of them had disappeared into the hazy, turbulent nothingness from which they had come. Then, at last, he turned and began to walk towards us, accompanied by one who had remained behind—the squat, apelike figure of a man sparsely clothed in a loincloth, his leathery skin impervious to the scorching barrage of wind-driven sand. At his side, he bore a broad, leaf-bladed knife tucked through his scanty apparel, and something suspended from his right shoulder by a strap.

"Another of his faithful dacoits," commented Smith, "and probably the last. He alone will be permitted to share the secret of the tomb's location. Hold your fire, Petrie!"

My finger trembled on the trigger. Reason told me that we now had the advantage, but there was something inhuman and infinitely horrible in the way that Dr. Fu Manchu forced a passage through the storm, indifferent to pain and fatigue—a sense of the invincible. Swathed from head to foot in his black garments of the desert, and pausing between each step, he looked like an Egyptologist's nightmare—a walking mummy.

As he approached—his savage servitor capering behind him, like a Satanic bodyguard—I saw that he carried a large, shapeless bag or sack. It seemed heavy and, since he chose to carry it in person, clearly contained something of value. But I wondered—for I thought it surely too small to contain the hellish apparatus which he had taken from the tower.

Now they were close and still heading towards the hut.

"It's possible that they are coming in here!" I exclaimed.

"I hope they are!" returned Smith. "If they go elsewhere, we shall have the devil of a job to follow them. Shoot the dacoit, the instant that the door opens, and I'll deal with Fu Manchu!"

Drawing back from the window, lest we be discovered, we saw them pass it—go on to the smaller hut, and vanish beyond. Smith leaned out recklessly, staring this way and that.

"Damnation! They are going up to the plateau. . . . The tomb is up there! Quickly, man—or we shall lose them!"

He ran to the door. Outside, the tempest struck me in the face with such force that I gasped and, as I stumbled after Smith, wondered how Fu Manchu and his henchman could make headway against it. But there was no sign of either.

The narrow ravine at the back of the toolshed was a giant's staircase of jumbled boulders, between and around which a rough track snaked steeply upwards, and the enclosing walls made it a wind tunnel. As we toiled up, bent double, the ground moved under our feet; rivulets of sand boiled about our boots like the swift current of a stony stream. We could see no more than a few yards ahead.

"If we get within sight of them," panted my companion, "they will see *us!* Be ready for a shooting match!"

We were far from the Thames and the fogbound alleyways of Limehouse; yet here too, Fu Manchu was master of the elements—a shadow eluding pursuit, slipping unseen and unhindered through ways too dark for any but him to traverse. Close to the top, where the ravine shallowed out upon a steep hillside, the horizon ended in a hard, straight line drawn against the seething yellow background of the storm, like the end of the world.

Scrambling up in haste, we had almost gained the summit when it happened: Like a pantomime demon shot up through a star-trap, the uncouth form of the dacoit sprang up above the ridge, as if out of the earth, and stood looking down at us. He snatched at the strap over his shoulder and lifted to his eyes something which resembled a large camera. A feeble shaft of sunlight, striking through the gloom, glittered on a lens.

Fu Manchu, cautious as always, had left the man to stand guard at the brink, and, in the instant that I saw him, I knew that the thing which he held was the same which had killed Captain Desmond, two miles from the Great Pyramid. Needing both hands for climbing, I had thrust my pistol into my trouser pocket. I tried to withdraw it, and it caught in the cloth.

Two paces behind me, Nayland Smith cried out sharply, missed his footing, and went tumbling down the slope, rolling over and over. Simultaneously, the pistol came loose and I fired. The only warlike attribute which I possess is that I am a good marksman. The dacoit uttered a gurgling scream and fell backwards.

Satisfied that he was out of the fight, I turned and ran down to Smith, who was half up on his knees and striving ineffectually to stand upright. As I reached him, he sank back with a groan.

"It's my ankle!" he gasped. "That damnable thing punctured my leg like a white-hot needle—but that's nothing. It's my ankle—I hit it on a rock. . . ."

I stooped and explored with my fingers, while he lay back, gritting his teeth.

"Oh, God!" I said disconsolately. "It's broken!"

"Then it's up to you now!" he rapped. "Get up there, and go after him!"

"But I can't leave you here like this!"

"You must! If I have to crawl on my hands and knees, I can make it back to the hut. For God's sake, go after him, Petrie—or, if you won't do it for His sake, do it for mine!"

It was the first time in our adventures that either of us had suffered a crippling injury.

"Very well," I said quietly, and stood up. "I will do my best. Get down to the hut, and even if I fail to return, Hassan es-Sugra will be there to-morrow."

37

ALPHA AND OMEGA

I clawed my way back up the slope, my mind in a turmoil. Fu Manchu had none to guard him now—it was man to man. But could I find him? Even if I did, might I be a match for him?

At the top, I came upon the dacoit, sprawled face-upwards, his glazed eyes staring horribly and a pool of blood spreading about his head. My bullet had passed through his throat. Here, on the open ground, the *simoom* had become a tornado. Earth and sky seemed to be in motion—a billowing sea, through which dark towers of dust spiralled up, gyrating madly. If Fu Manchu had been but ten feet away, I could not have seen him.

I paused, baffled. Then, as I glanced down at my victim, my gaze fell upon the weapon lying beside him, and I remembered that it was equipped with some kind of telescopic sight. I caught it up desperately. It was a weird instrument, fitted with eyepieces, a pistol grip, and a concave stock resting against the forehead.

By some abstruse principle of optics, colours were distorted—brown and red transposed to green—and the formless cloud of sand resolved into myriad specks, through which I could clearly make out the silhouette shapes of rocks.

I swept the lenses from side to side, searching vainly, till, all at once, I discovered him advancing with slow, relentless strides into the heart of the storm—how far off, I could not tell. Where my pistol was useless, I might, perhaps, turn his own science against him, but not until I tried it did I appreciate how hard it was to aim the thing. Finally, in fear of losing him altogether, I squeezed the trigger. The only indication that the weapon had loosed its invisible bolt was a high-pitched, squealing sound. I thought I saw him stagger, but he recovered himself immediately and walked on.

Again I pulled the trigger, but this time there was no response, suggesting either that the magazine was empty, or that I did not know how to recharge it. A moment later, Fu Manchu had passed out of range and out of sight.

I threw the contraption down and charged blindly in pursuit, but I had taken less than a dozen paces before I knew that no one but a madman—or one who pursued a madman—would have attempted it. It was almost impossible to see or even to breathe. I tore the handkerchief from my pocket, tied it around my nose and mouth, and closed my eyes half shut, shielding them with one hand.

How long I went on blundering through that hot, dry barrier of wind and sand, half blind and half suffocated, I do not know. At last, however, I came to a halt, almost too weary to take another step, and stood looking helplessly around me. I had not only lost Dr. Fu Manchu but also lost myself.

My situation was now not merely uncomfortable but perilous. Standing with my back to the wind, I paused to get my breath. Then, suddenly, I saw a light shining like a bright star through a cloudy sky—a tiny, silver disc in the inchoate whirlpool of sand and atmosphere, seemingly below the level of my feet. Fortified by a hope renewed, I pressed on and found myself standing on a steeply shelving bank of shattered limestone, with the light glowing mysteriously below. Scrambling down was no great effort, and, once I had descended, there was respite from the wind.

I was at one end of a long, shallow trench—clearly the remains of an old excavation, though much of the sides had fallen in. The light which I had seen from above shone from the gaping mouth of a funnel-shaped opening. I hurried towards it, finding, as I expected, that it gave upon a roughly hewn passage, half filled with drifting sand which had been recently cleared, but which now was flowing back into it in a cascade. The brilliant light, flickering and pulsating, came from an opalescent globe placed just inside—the same which I had seen at Saqqara, or another of the same pattern.

Evidently, I thought, Fu Manchu had left it there to guide him on his return. I hesitated, restraining the impulse to go down after him. It was better to wait outside and catch him unawares.

Withdrawing to one side of the entrance, I flattened myself against the rock and took the pistol from my pocket. Minutes passed. Armed and ready though I was, could I hope to stand against such an adversary? Forcing myself to be calm, I waited, and, at last, my patience was rewarded. The black-robed figure of Dr. Fu Manchu emerged from the tunnel and stepped past me, unsuspecting.

Six paces beyond, he stopped, took a square, boxlike object from the bag which he still carried, and put it on the ground—then, stooping over it, drew out a thin metal rod, by which I knew it to be some kind of wireless device and guessed its purpose. His hand moved towards a switch and I dared delay no longer.

"Stand up!" I shouted, and levelled the pistol. "Move away from that, and raise your hands!"

Fu Manchu straightened himself slowly, turned, and raised his hands. We stood face to face, and I thought of the night when, once before, I had held him thus, after the last meeting of the Seven. He spoke, and his first words proved that he, too, remembered.

"I yield to your will, Dr. Petrie! But, this time, I have no hostage to exchange for my life. Shoot, then!"

Had I heeded my duty and done so, the course of history might have been changed. But I had never killed a man in cold blood, and, even though that man was Dr. Fu Manchu, I could not do it now.

"No!" I said. "When your daughter captured and tortured me, you gave me my life, and I will give you yours."

"Permit me, then, to lower my hands," he answered calmly. "I am close to the end of my strength and unarmed. You have inflicted a painful burn upon my left shoulder, and penetrated the clavicle. But the solar projector is of limited usefulness, since it can be fired only once in ten minutes."

"Very well—you may put down your hands," I conceded. "But, though you set me free, I cannot let you go. Your crimes are too great and too many. You must return with me, as my prisoner."

Dr. Fu Manchu responded with a smile which was almost benign—his manner that of a tired old man pacifying a fractious child.

"Till the storm abates, we can go nowhere. Meanwhile, let us sit here, where we are somewhat sheltered from it, and talk together as men of science."

Without waiting for my agreement, he dropped down easily upon the ground, crossing his legs with the smooth facility of an Oriental, and resting his hands on his knees. I hesitated—then, seeing no other course to adopt, sat down facing him, still keeping the pistol trained upon him, and taking the precaution of placing the boxlike contrivance close by my side, where he could not reach it.

"I do not know exactly what this is," I said, "but I know what you meant to do with it. Your intention was to seal the tomb and bury your stolen secrets until it should be convenient for you to recover them and make yourself emperor of the world!"

"Your first assumption is correct," he replied dispassionately. "The object which you have beside you is a remote control mechanism, adjusted to fire a conventional dynamite charge which I have installed at the end of the tunnel. Your second assumption is inaccurate. I have no ambition to rule your hemisphere, but only to exclude you from ours and to dissuade you from such behaviour as may affect us."

Staring at me with the sightless gaze of a visionary, he continued speaking, as though to a congregation.

"Between East and West there can be no reconciliation. We are set apart by fundamental principles, like the north and south poles of a magnet. All things in Nature must have their opposites, by which the balance of the universe is maintained. These basic truths were understood and expressed in philosophical terms by K'ung Fu-tsu—whom you know better as Confucius—five hundred years before your Christian era of ignorance."

"You may call that science," I retorted, "but I call it superstition."

"Nevertheless," he insisted, but without emotion, "it is so. We, in China, know that the cosmos is but a finely balanced machine. Any attempt to alter that balance—as you might have done, if I had not hindered you—results in disaster." He paused, looking at me as if recalling my existence. "You have, I presume, heard of the calamity which took place in Siberia, in the year 1908?"

I thought for a moment.

"You mean," I said finally, "the Tunguska meteorite?"

Fu Manchu nodded gravely. "So it was called—though it was not a meteorite. The explosion was heard at a distance of four hundred miles. Trees were uprooted twenty-five miles from the centre. Had it not happened in an unpopulated locality, where the only known casualties were a herd of reindeer, the incident would have attracted far greater attention. In the absence of any other explanation, a meteorite was proposed."

"You have some alternative?" I suggested.

"Perhaps—but none which I may offer with authority, since I have had no opportunity to investigate." For a long moment, he regarded me thoughtfully, like a master who instructs a disciple. "There is a certain unstable substance widely distributed throughout the world in infinitesimally small quantity. Should that quantity be anywhere exceeded, a sympathetic interaction takes place, releasing the tremendous forces which bind together the structure of matter, and promoting a progressive disruption of contiguous elements. This is none other than a disturbance of the cosmic balance. This, Dr. Petrie, was the basis of your Midnight Sun."

I listened patiently, only half understanding him.

"It may be that the Siberian disaster resulted from some chance concentration of the destructive material beyond the critical limit. I do not know. However, the fortunate circumstance that it occurred in a region so remote and uninhabited seems suspicious. Possibly, it was the outcome of an injudicious experiment such as you intended to conduct. Dmitri Ivanovich Mendeleyev, who died in the previous year, was a pioneer in this field of inquiry."

Again he ceased speaking, glancing at me with the tolerant contempt of a college lecturer addressing a class of unresponsive students.

"I weary you with a discussion of things beyond your comprehension," he said at length. "Let us, then, turn to other matters, which may interest you more. You have been groping in the dark—knowing neither what you were doing nor to what end. Listen, and I will enlighten you. For two years, great quantities of ore were transported from Central Africa, through the Sudan and over the Road of the Forty, to your secret base in the desert, to be processed and refined. The work was tedious—let me remind you that no more than one quarter of a grain of radium may be extracted from a ton of pitchblende. It was also dangerous. . . ."

"When did you learn of this?" I inquired curiously.

"From the beginning. My agents, though few in number, were well informed. I was aware also that similar researches were being carried out in Berlin. The ultimate fate of England or of Germany was of no concern to me, but I could not allow the West to acquire a weapon of such potency, which would later be turned against the East—unless we, too, possessed the secret."

"Therefore you attempted to kidnap Professor Brooker!"

"And at the same time to save his life. I knew that, without my aid, he had only a few months more to live." Dr. Fu Manchu shook his head and sighed. "But I made no plans to that end. It was he who furnished me with the opportunity. Determined though he was to leave your service, he had no idea how to elude pursuit and escape from Egypt. All the arrangements were made by his assistant, Adrian Crawford—a clever man, but a sycophant who worshipped a false god. Here, it is not difficult for one who seeks them to make contact with the criminal classes. On their next visit to Luxor, Crawford sought out a cunning and notorious smuggler, named

Joseph Malaglou. You know of this man, I believe?"

"I saw him once," I said grimly, "after your horned monster had finished with him."

"An end which he well merited. But that was much later. Malaglou was a man of insatiable greed and totally without integrity. To my regret, circumstances have occasionally compelled me to do business with him. In return for a large sum of money—paid in advance—he agreed to help them and to provide passage for them to a neutral country. Spain was mentioned. He had, of course, neither the means nor the intention to carry out his promise. Having advised his principals to go to Cairo on a certain date and to stay at the Hotel Iskander, he then approached the agents of Germany and sold them the information—knowing that they would pay for the chance to secure the person of Professor Brooker and the documents which they presumed he would be carrying."

"I see!" I said slowly. "So that is how Kurt Lehmann came to be there—the man whose mind you erased. But how did *you* know?"

"From the same source! Realising that I, too, would be interested, Malaglou next had the effrontery to approach me, and tell me what he had done. Despising him for his duplicity, I paid him his reward and took steps—with the results which you know. The operation miscarried and the wrong man was killed. Crawford died, and his master fled—how and whither, I had no way of knowing."

By now it was so dark that we could scarcely see one another. Rather than abating, the sandstorm seemed to be increasing in its fury.

"Continue!" I said. "I am listening."

"Though I had lost Professor Brooker, I obtained the notebook which he had left behind—which, recently, I permitted you also to inspect. Much of it was obscure to me, but, from his calculations, I understood why he had abandoned his work and fled. Yet still I failed to see what he planned to do, and, for a time, assumed—as you did—that he had no plan, that study and anxiety had made him mad. I recognized the truth only after my servant had seen you at the priest's house in Nagadeh and reported to me that the suitcase contained only a metal cylinder. Professor Brooker had taken no papers from his employers. He had taken the explosive material— all that existed, and without which the proposed demonstration could not be staged."

"What!" I exclaimed, and Fu Manchu nodded again, his bloodless lips twisting in a smile.

"Yes, Dr. Petrie, you have held it in your hands—the same which I recovered, and which now lies at the bottom of a well in the tunnel behind you. Had you succeeded in opening the cylinder, you would have died instantly. It encloses two insulated compartments, in each of which a maximal quantity of the material is contained. The outer shell is made of thermite—a metal which burns at a temperature of twenty-four hundred degrees centigrade, by the induction of a magnesium fuse. The consequence would be to mix the two parts and cause them to explode."

"But why did Brooker steal it?" I asked, rather unsteadily. The idea that I had actually handled the thing was somewhat unnerving. "What was his object? Since he knew that it was to be used only as a threat, which could not, in practice, be carried out, why did he wish to interfere?"

Dr. Fu Manchu looked at me gravely, with a flicker of emotion in the tired green eyes, shining, catlike, through the gloom.

"Do you still not know? Clearly, then, you failed to read his notebook. We are not talking of a chemical explosion, but of the conversion of matter to energy—a self-propagating reaction, analogous to a forest fire, where the size of the flame which ignites it is of no significance. It spreads until all the combustible material in its path has been consumed. Once an explosion had been initiated, the magnitude was impossible to predict. Theoretically, then, there was a possibility that it might continue unchecked, till, in the space of a minute or less, our entire planet should be transformed into a second sun. This was the message conveyed in the quaint equation which the professor wrote—the square of a quantity multiplied to infinity, and all shall be as it was in the beginning: *Alpha* and *Omega*."

I stared at him, literally speechless.

"Professor Brooker's colleagues admitted that such a possibility existed," he went on impassively, "but they felt it too remote to be worthy of consideration. His employers were indifferent, regarding a world not subject to England as a world not worthy of survival. Therefore, he was overruled. He continued, nevertheless, to believe that, while *any* degree of risk existed, the experiment should not be made, and this was the motive which drove him to act as he did. But he was not what is termed a practical man. After absconding with the device, he did not know what to do with it. He was afraid to conceal it, fearing that it might be found and opened, while, without the necessary facilities, he could not open it himself and disperse the material."

Fu Manchu paused, allowing me an opportunity to speak, but I had nothing to say. The appalling idea which he presented defied reason, so that I felt helpless even to think.

"I regret that I destroyed the Zeppelin," he added. "In spite of Mr. Nayland Smith's opinion, it does not please me to take men's lives. But I did not then know that all the sensitive matter had been removed from your base in the desert, and I feared that an air attack might provoke the very reaction which Professor Brooker had envisaged. I respect his learning and his judgement. I propose only to implement his wishes. At a touch of the switch which lies under your hand, the property which he abstracted will be buried under a hundred tons of rock, and I shall never attempt to recover it. Meanwhile, the life cycle of the material will be completed in a few years. It will become inert and harmless." Again he paused, and met my eyes. "You have never had reason to doubt my word. Do you believe what I have told you?"

"Yes," I said slowly. "I believe that you have told me the truth, as you believe it."

Dr. Fu Manchu leaned back on his heels, raising his hands and interlacing his fingers. His smile was Satanic, and it was then that he said the most dreadful thing to me which he had ever said—while he was yet my prisoner.

"Then I am satisfied, and since you hold me in your power, the choice must now be yours. If you believe as Professor Brooker did, and as I do—press the switch!"

I stared at him aghast. With the wind howling about us, earth and sky reduced to a maelstrom, it was indeed as if we were gods deciding the fate of mankind. Where did my duty lie—to Nayland Smith, to my country, or to the world? These were questions which I could not answer and, after an interminable interval, I submitted them to my instincts and emotions, ceasing to think at all. My fingers moved as if they did not belong to me, closed upon the switch, and thrust it home.

God be my witness that I did not even know what I had done till a dull, sullen explosion ensued and the earth trembled. I jerked back my head and saw a puff of smoke belched forth from the mouth of the tunnel. When I turned again, Dr. Fu Manchu had risen and stood facing me. He could have struck me down with ease, but he did not.

"I congratulate you upon your wisdom," he said, and walked calmly away, ignoring the pistol in my hand.

"Stop!" I cried. "Stop, or I fire!"

He made no reply, but walked on and, in a moment, was lost to sight. Fruitlessly, I blundered after him. At the first step I took, the wind tore the handkerchief from my face, and my eyes, nose, and mouth were filled with sand, burning my skin like sparks, and clutching at my throat. I searched, but without avail.

Out of chaos he had come, and into chaos he disappeared.

GREETINGS AND FAREWELL

"I am afraid, Petrie," said Nayland Smith, "that we have not come out of this any too well. We have ended by compromising with Dr. Fu Manchu, and all I have to show for it is a broken ankle."

We sat in deck chairs, looking out over the port-side rail of a Cook's cruise steamer at a tranquil vista of green fields and brown, mud-hut villages nestling among date palms. This leisurely form of transport, back from Luxor to Cairo, was slow but was easier on my companion, who had one foot in plaster. In any case, there was no longer any occasion for haste.

Three days had passed since I had seen Fu Manchu vanish into the storm. For hours afterwards, I had lain in the shelter of the old excavation trench, able scarcely to draw breath while the wind howled above me. But, with the coming of nightfall, it died down abruptly, and I walked back easily to the valley, under a clear sky filled with stars, as soon as I had managed to get my bearings.

"Tell me, Smith," I said, for at least the tenth time, "did I do right or wrong?"

Greba, who was accompanying us on our return, was in her cabin, writing some letters, so that we could speak freely. Not even she had been made a party to my guilty secret.

"You know that I can't answer that," he replied. "I can only say that I thank God it was you who had to make the decision, and not I. You have sworn no oath of allegiance to the Crown, as I have done, and had only your own conscience to consult."

"I shall never be sure," I said mournfully, "whether I have saved the world, or condemned millions to death by prolonging this interminable war."

274

Smith shrugged.

"It will all come to the same thing in the end," he answered indifferently. "The war will drag on to its miserable conclusion—a year, two years. Who knows? But the secret of the Midnight Sun has not been lost. For a time, it will be forgotten while the world is at peace—while governments do not find it profitable or needful to expend their resources on means of destruction. But when war breaks out once more—as, of course, it will inevitably do—they will remember it and turn to it again. And then, perhaps, if Fu Manchu is not there to stop us, we shall use it. . . ."

After reaching the city, we had necessarily to present a report to General Fernshawe, who had preceded us by train—Smith pointing out to me that, if I said too much, I should very likely find myself locked up in the Tower of London. We told him only that the fatal cylinder lay buried irretrievably in the sand—where, we had no idea—which was no great distortion of the truth. I had made no attempt to note the location of the tomb shaft—already reduced to the dimensions of a foxhole—and doubted that I could find it again, even if I had wished.*

I added that I believed Dr. Fu Manchu to be dead, which was likewise true. Unprotected and exhausted, how could he have battled his way through the storm and down to Kurna? As to this, however, my friend did not share my opinion.

"How often have we thought so before?" he demanded.

Thereafter, Nayland Smith's first action was to resign his army commission and to apply for reinstatement in his Burmese police post. While waiting for the reply from Whitehall, and for his ankle to mend, he stayed with me in Zamalek. But those last days which we spent together in Cairo were uneasy days—fraught with misgiving, as we read the newspapers and followed the progress of events.

In another year, it would all be over—but, just then, it seemed otherwise. Lawrence and his motley horde were hot on the road to Damascus. The third battle of Gaza had taken place, and Allenby had broken through into Palestine. But, in Europe, our efforts seemed as far from victory as they had ever been. The long-drawn-out agony of Ypres had terminated only with the taking of Passchendaele—a village in ruins—at the cost of half a million lives, British and German.

---

*My feelings may be imagined, eleven years later, when I found Sir Lionel Barton digging in the same spot. But I held my peace and said nothing. [P.]

As regards my more personal concerns, I suppose I should say something about Greba. Now fully recovered from her hideous experiences at the hands of Fah Lo Suee and Yildiz Bey, she tended somewhat to draw away from me. After our return to Cairo, I was relieved to note that she was spending a good deal of time at the hospital and taking what I considered a healthy interest in young Basil Sorensen, the Cook's man, who had suffered a fractured skull in trying to protect her.

A week went by without further event. Then, one morning, I found an envelope in my postbox, unstamped, and delivered by hand. It enclosed a single sheet of parchmentlike paper, endorsed with a brief message, in a hand which suggested that the writer might be more accustomed to a writing brush than a pen.

> *Much that I have done has passed without notice. Much that I have not done has been lain at my door. It will be said that I killed Professor Brooker, though I did nothing to harm him, and would have saved him. Those who work under the invisible rays of the Midnight Sun die of a wasting disease. Greetings and Farewell.*

By way of a signature, the missive was ink-stamped in vermilion with a Chinese seal which we had no trouble in identifying.

It was undated. Had he written it at some time previous, or, despite all probability, had he somehow survived the sandstorm? Time alone might tell. . . .

ACKNOWLEDGEMENTS

This story is offered as a tribute to the genius of Sax Rohmer, to whom I owe so much. Not only was he the creator of Dr. Fu Manchu—whose name has become a household word—but he was among the last great masters of the English language.

I have tried to limit myself to the facts as given in his stories and to keep faith with the characters. My impression of Fah Lo Suee is somewhat different from his, but this, I think, is how we might expect to find her some ten years earlier.

Likewise, though readers may be tempted to feel otherwise, I have endeavoured to avoid anachronisms. The principles of the Midnight Sun were known long before 1914, and it remained only to find means of putting them into practice. As regards the singularly "advanced" attitude of the Bisharîn in respect of their unmarried daughters, see Lane's *Modern Egyptians,* first published in 1836.

My thanks are due, firstly, to Okchon, who patiently endured the trials of a writer's wife and accompanied me on a moderately rough journey from Cairo to Edfu, and across the desert to el-Kharga, in search of information. Equally, they are due to the Egyptian people, who showed us every kindness—over and above all, to our good friend Karam Assem Karam of Assiut, who found ways to go everywhere and went there with us. Among those we met, I have affectionate memories of Captain Abd er-Rahman, who gave us passage down the Nile on his oil-tanker barge, and the stately old Coptic priest of Nagadeh, whose name I never knew.

For advice and encouragement, I remain indebted, as always, to my faithful friends Ciaran Murray and Jack Torrance, here in Japan, to Dr. Sumio Kurata for medical matters, and also to Joan Edwards, who did some of the research for me in London.

> Cay Van Ash,
> Department of Literature
> Waseda University
> Tōkyō